A KINGDOM FOR THE BRAVE

A Kingdom for the Brave

TAMARA MCKINLEY

ISIS

LARGE PRINT

Oxford

First published in Great Britain 2008
by
Hodder & Stoughton
an Hachette Livre UK Company

Published in Large Print 2009 by ISIS Publishing Ltd.,
7 Centremead, Osney Mead, Oxford OX2 0ES
by arrangement with
Hodder & Stoughton
an Hachette Livre UK Company

British Library Cataloguing in Publication Data
McKinley, Tamara
    A kingdom for the brave. – Large print ed.
    1. Australia – History – 1788–1851 – Fiction
    2. Historical fiction
    3. Large type books
    I. Title
    823.9'2 [F]

ISBN 978–0–7531–8306–9 (hb)
ISBN 978–0–7531–8307–6 (pb)

Printed and bound in Great Britain by
T. J. International Ltd., Padstow, Cornwall

Clime of the unforgotten brave!
Whose land from plain to mountain cave,
Was Freedom's home, or Glory's grave.

George Gordon,
Lord Byron, 1788–1824

For Liam, Brandon, Brett and Fiona.
May they never forget the pioneers, adventurers
and convicts who struggled so valiantly to bring
prosperity and freedom to Australia.

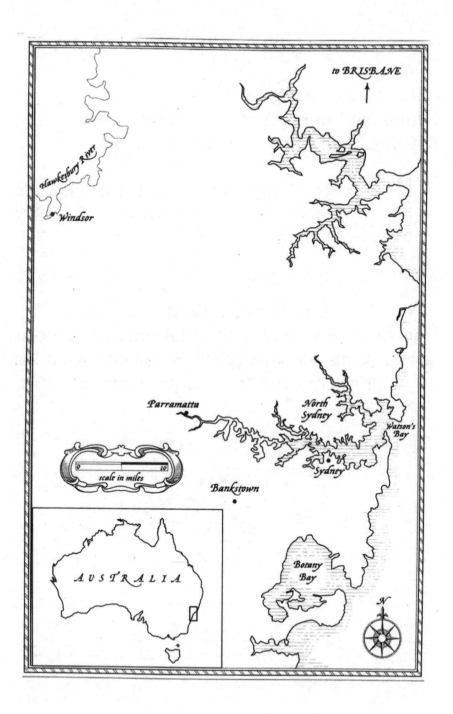

to BRISBANE

Hawkesbury River

Windsor

Parramatta

North Sydney

Watson's Bay

Sydney

scale in miles

Bankstown

Botany Bay

AUSTRALIA

N

PROLOGUE: THE CRY OF THE CURLEW

Brisbane River, 1795

Dawn had yet to lighten the sky, but the group of eight horsemen was already on the move. Edward Cadwallader looked up. The moon remained behind a thick layer of cloud. It was a perfect night for killing.

They made little sound in the stillness of the scrub, for the horses' hoofs and jingling harness had been wrapped in hessian, and the men knew better than to talk or smoke. It was a familiar routine — but Edward felt the excitement he always experienced in the last few moments before an attack. The thought of what was to come enhanced his impatience.

His gaze trawled his surroundings. The escarpment rose on either side, rearing in jagged peaks from the scrub-lands. Dark boulders and stands of trees offered deeper shadows, and the horse beneath him twitched as something skittered through the undergrowth. Edward's hands were firm on the reins, but he was tense for their destination was close. A single sound might give them away.

He glanced behind him at the men who followed him willingly on these night forays, and acknowledged his grizzled sergeant's grin with one of his own. He and Willy Baines had joined the New South Wales Corps at the same time, and had once shared an army prison cell. The older man had stood with him in the dock during their trial for violating a woman and had helped him celebrate their victory — they knew each other's thoughts and understood each other's blood-lust, and although the class divide was great between them, Edward looked upon him as his closest friend.

He peered into the darkness ahead, his night-sight keen after two hours in the saddle. His men could all be trusted to keep their mouths shut when they returned to Sydney. Dispersals were not something to discuss openly, even though they were becoming ever more frequent, and it was common knowledge that the blacks were being forced off the much-needed land. But the less the public knew about the military methods of clearing them out, the better — and, after all, who cared?

The Hawkesbury had already been cleansed, and although the renegade Pemulwuy was still on the loose, Edward was convinced that it would be just a matter of weeks before he and his son were rounded up and shot. Now his task was to clear the last of the Turrbal from the Brisbane River.

These were exciting times, and Edward was at the heart of them. During his years of exile in the wilderness, he had learnt much, and had discovered how thrilling it was to hunt down the black men. His reputation and the high regard in which his men held him had filtered down to the authorities in Sydney

2

Town. Despite his questionable record, he had been promoted to major, responsible for ridding this area of the black vermin with an assurance from the general that his banishment would be shortened by two years. Life was good, and he was looking forward to returning to Sydney so he could make his fortune and build a fine house that would be the envy of every man.

Thoughts of having a white woman once more heightened his excitement. The gins stank, and often fought like cats — but he enjoyed a challenge. Nevertheless, although he had found the black velvet exotic, he preferred the scent of white flesh.

He brought his thoughts back to the job in hand. There would be time enough to think about women after it was done. Now he would need all his wits if they were to avoid an ambush. The blacks might be ignorant savages, but this was their territory and they knew it far better than any soldier, no matter how well trained.

The patrol advanced silently through the scrub, alert for hidden warriors in the shadows. As the sky lightened to a storm-laden grey the tension mounted. This was the most dangerous part of their journey for they were within a mile of the camp.

Edward drew his horse to a halt and swung from the saddle. He waited for the others to join him. "You know what to do?" His voice was barely a whisper.

They nodded. It had been planned in great detail several days before, and they knew they would have free rein with any women they captured.

"Prime your muskets," ordered Edward, "and remember, there are to be no survivors."

"What about the piccaninnies and gins?"

Edward eyed the newest recruit — a thin, bright-eyed young trooper, with a dishonourable service record and a penchant for native women. His expression was grim, his eyes cold as he reinforced his authority. "Gins breed, and piccaninnies grow up to breed. I don't care what you do, or how you do it, but I want nothing left alive after tonight." He glared at the trooper, gratified to see fear spark in his eyes.

The youth's pale face flushed.

Edward turned back to Willy Baines. "We'll do a recce first," he murmured, "just to make sure they're still there."

Willy scratched the stubble on his chin. None of the men had washed or shaved in four days: a native's nose could pick up the scent of soap or pomade a mile off. "They should be," he replied. "They've been coming here for centuries, according to my spies."

"You and your spies, Willy. How do you persuade the myalls to tell you so much?"

Willy shook his head as they moved away from the others. "They may look black to us, and I'm damned if I can tell one from another, but tribal differences linger, and for a flagon of rum or a bit of baccy, the right man will tell all he knows."

Edward put his hand on the other's shoulder. "They're a mystery to me, Willy, and the only good myall is a dead one. Come on. Let's go and see what we've got." They left the others priming their muskets and made their way carefully through the last of the undergrowth to the water's edge. The river was shallow

4

and meandering, the reeds and overhanging trees giving perfect cover on this moonless night. The two men lay on their bellies, their heads just above the long grass as they regarded the sleeping encampment.

The young single men, who made up most of the warriors, lay in a rough, protective phalanx round the women, children and elderly. Most slept on the ground, but there were three or four *gunyahs* — grass and eucalypt shelters — in which the Elders rested. Dogs stirred and scratched, and wisps of smoke rose from cooled campfires as old men hawked phlegm and babies whimpered. Edward smiled as he took in the sight before him. The Turrbal had no idea of what was to come.

Lowitja stirred from sleep and instinctively tightened her hold on her five-year-old grandson. Something had penetrated her dreams, and as she opened her eyes, she heard the mournful cry of a curlew. It was the call of the dead spirits — the sharp, haunting note of souls in torment, a warning of danger.

Mandawuy struggled in her tight embrace and would have cried out if she hadn't put her hand over his mouth. "Quiet," she ordered, with the soft firmness he had learnt to obey instantly. He sat, silent and unafraid, as his grandmother's amber eyes stared beyond the encampment. What could she see? he wondered. Were there spirits in the clearing? Could she hear their voices — and, if so, what were they telling her?

Lowitja listened to the cry of the curlews. There were many more now. It was as if the spirits of the dead were gathering, their voices coming together in a wail of distress that pierced her heart. Then, from out of the grey of a new dawn, she saw ghostly shapes twist among the trees. She knew who they were and why they had come.

They would have to hurry: the camp was stirring. Edward and Willy melted back into the deeper shadows and returned to the waiting men. They found them alert, the hammers of their carbines cocked. The fun was about to begin. "Mount up." Edward caught his horse's reins and swung into the saddle. "Walk."

The line moved forward in practised precision until the men were almost in sight of the camp. Edward nudged his horse in front as they halted once again. The excitement was almost tangible as he raised his sword and the first rays of the sun lit the blade in a blinding flash. He held it there, anticipating the moment, relishing the suspense.

"Charge!"

As one, they kicked their mounts into a gallop. The animals strained, nostrils distended, ears flat to their heads as the men who rode them whooped, yelled and urged them on.

Lowitja was mesmerised by the appearance of the Spirit People. In all her thirty years she had never seen them so clearly, and at first she thought the distant thunder was born of a sudden summer storm. She drew back from the visions, her hands automatically tightening on Mandawuy as she noticed the dogs' hackles rising, and heard the birds cry with sharp alarm as they flew in a storm of beating wings from the trees.

As the thunder grew louder, the rest of the clan were shocked from sleep. Babies and small children cried as their mothers snatched them up. Warriors grabbed spears and clubs, and the elderly froze as the dogs barked with furious intent.

The thunder was nearer now, the air full of it, and the earth trembled beneath her. Lowitja's fear brought her to her feet. Now she understood why the Spirits had come to her, why they had warned her. She had to save Mandawuy. She forced every ounce of strength she possessed into her legs and arms, clasped her grandson to her and ran.

Thorns snatched, branches whipped, roots threatened to trip her as she raced through the bush. The thunder of horses' hoofs and the shattering crack of gunfire ripped through the air behind her, but she didn't look back, didn't stop running.

Mandawuy made no sound as he clung to her, arms and legs twined round her, tears of terror hot on her skin as the screams, shouts and gunfire echoed in the clearing.

Lowitja's heart was pounding, her chest ached, her legs and arms grew leaden as she wove through the bushes with her son's only living child to uncertain safety.

They crashed through the flimsy *gunyahs* and scattered the smouldering fires into a blizzard of scarlet embers. The first volley of lead shot had flung men, women and children into bloody heaps upon the ground where they were trampled by the charging horses. As screams rent the air, and the more agile ran, the sport was on.

The dogs scattered as women clutched children and men scrabbled for spears and *nullas*. The elderly tried to crawl away, or sat with their hands over their heads in a pathetic attempt to ward off the swords. Small children stood in frozen terror as the horses bore down to trample them into the dark red earth. Some of the younger, fitter men tried to defend their fleeing families, but they had no time to throw their spears or wield the heavy wooden *nullas* before they were hacked to pieces.

Edward's blood-lust was up as he wheeled his horse in a tight circle and fired his second shot into an old woman cowering by the remains of the fire. He reloaded swiftly as he watched her collapse into the flames. He would waste no more lead on her — she would be dead soon enough.

He continued to load and reload until the barrel was too hot to touch. When he could fire no more, he used the carbine as a club, wielding it left and right to smash skulls and break necks, to bring down those who couldn't run fast enough, and finish them off with his sword. His horse was lathered, its eyes rolling as *gunyahs* caught fire and smoke filled the clearing. The air was filled with the stench of burning flesh and eucalyptus, the smoke thick and black, making eyes water and throats close.

Two of his men had dismounted and were chasing a couple of women, who had fled into the trees. Willy was making short work of some children and the others were occupied in cutting down three warriors who had raised their spears in defiance.

Edward wheeled his horse in tight circles as he chased two youths and brought them down with a single slash of his sword. The blade was red with their blood, his uniform splattered, the flanks of his horse sticky. But he hadn't finished — his lust was not satisfied — and he sought another victim.

The girl was on the far edge of the clearing. She had almost reached the trees — but her progress was slow for she had already felt the cut of a sabre. He could see the bloody gash on her shoulder, the black flesh gaping like an obscene pink mouth.

He kicked the horse into a gallop and raised his sword. "She's mine, Willy," he yelled, as his friend also spied her.

She glanced over her shoulder, eyes wide with terror.

Edward raced past her and blocked her escape.

The girl froze.

Edward beheaded her with one blow, then raced back to the clearing to discover what the others had left for him.

Lowitja remained hidden in the sheltering branches of the tree, high above the forest floor. She clung to Mandawuy and kept him quiet by suckling him as the carnage raged in the distance. She heard running feet below her, the crack of guns, the terrible screams of the dying — and shed silent tears as she smelt burning flesh. She could only imagine the horror of what was happening to her people, could only pray to the Great Spirit that some would survive this day.

Yet the silence, when it came, was even more terrifying. It weighed heavily on the air, laden with a darkness that, to Lowitja, seemed endless. She waited through the night, her body trembling with the effort of keeping Mandawuy in her arms and her perch secure on the high branch. She dared not fall asleep.

The sun was a thin pale line on the horizon when she clambered down with the precious child on her back. With his little hand clasped in hers, she was poised for flight as she headed back cautiously to the clearing. She feared what she would see, dreaded what she must face. Yet the Ancestor Spirits were calling to her, leading her to the killing fields so she could witness what the white man had done and pass on that knowledge.

She stood on the edge of the clearing, not yet brave enough to enter this place of death. The camp was silent and still — and in that silence she could hear the whispers of long-dead warriors who had come to fetch the people of the Eora and Turrbal and take them to the spirit world. Wreaths of smoke drifted upward in the windless dawn and hung in shifting, ghostlike trails over the scattered cooking pots, mangled bodies and broken spears.

Lowitja stood with her grandson and shivered. No one had been spared — not even the smallest child. She could hear the hum of flies, and see the dark clouds hovering above the shattered bodies that lay trampled into the ground. They already bore the marks of the scavenger crows, and the dingoes that had come in the night to fight over the fresh carrion. Soon the goanna would come, with its sharp teeth and claws, the insects and grubs to make short work of what remained.

Lowitja regarded the killing place and knew that her people were gone. The prophecy of the Spirit Dreams and in the throwing stones had been fulfilled. She would never return to this place, but would move further west towards Uluru. It was a long, dangerous journey for a lone woman — and it would take the rest of her life to complete it — but Uluru was her spiritual home, and she would rather die trying to get there than remain here among the white savages.

She picked up her grandson and kissed him. He was the last of the full-blood Eora — the final link between her, Anabarru and the great ancestor Garnday. He must be guarded well.

PART ONE

Sea-Changes

CHAPTER
ONE

The Atlantica, *July 1797*

George Collinson stood on the plunging starboard deck, telescope to his eye, scanning the heaving swell of the Southern Ocean. It was early morning, but the sun barely pierced the scudding clouds. Gulls shrieked and the wind cut through his coat and sea-boots like a whetted knife as the *Atlantica's* sails took the strain and the rigging protested.

No whales had been sighted for days, and as they already had several barrels of the oil and salted meat in the hold, with whalebone enough for hundreds of corsets, the American captain, Samuel Varney, was debating whether to return to Sydney Cove. They had been at sea for six months and the crew was restless.

The *Atlantica* was a blue-water whaler out of Nantucket, Massachusetts. Not for her the short season of the bay-whaler that worked close to shore, but the wild oceans off Van Diemen's Land and New Zealand, where a ship's company could expect to be away from civilisation for months. She was well appointed, with three masts, a blunt bow, a square stern and seven boats hanging over the bulwark. An ugly brick tryworks stood behind the main mast, the cauldrons above furnaces that would be fired up to boil the blubber from their next catch. The captain and his officers were quartered aft, the specksioneers — the harpooners — assigned bunks in compartments they called steerage. The rest of the crew slept forward and amidship lay the hatch that led down to the vast hold where the cargo, stores and two thousand feet of spare rope were kept.

George grimaced as the sleeting rain and icy spray drenched him, but he kept his eye on the telescope, watching for the tell-tale spume or flash of tail-flukes that would herald the start of the hunt. These southern waters were usually teeming with Right whales at this time of year, and for every catch there was a bonus to his wages.

Almost an hour later the cry went up. "Portside! Whales one league!"

George turned swiftly, and adjusted his telescope. His heart raced and his mouth dried as he homed in on the unmistakable flukes of several black whales. The hunt was afoot — now the excitement could begin.

Captain Varney shouted orders from the afterdeck, his booming voice carrying above the wind as he spun the wheel and turned the blunt bow to port. Sailors scrambled to adjust the sails and rigging, and George joined the stampede to the boats.

They were more than thirty feet long and pointed at both ends so they would ride high in the water at bow and stern. Two hundred fathoms of manila rope lay coiled in each boat, and the twenty notches in the loggerhead marked the number of whales caught in the past six years. Samuel Varney favoured a five-man crew in each boat, so that when the harpooner left his oars the numbers were even on both sides. The sixth thwart at the bow had been hollowed out to take the harpooner's thighs so he was steadied as he threw the barbed weapon.

George clambered into the first boat that was already being lowered into the water. He had been sailing with Samuel Varney for three years and had become a skilled headsman, and as he took his place at the stern and grasped the steering oar, which had a ponderous sweep of at least twenty-five feet from its leather strapping, he felt the familiar thrill. The race was on to see who'd be the first to reach and harpoon a whale.

With the single sail raised to catch the wind, the men pulled on the oars as George encouraged them to greater speed with every oath he knew and steered them towards the nearest of the sleek leviathans. The other steersmen were just as vociferous, their shouts rising above the sound of the sea as they raced for the prize.

George's boat inched ahead. They were close now — close enough for the boat to be cut in half should the great beast thrash its tail. Close enough to see its eye, to feel the turbulence of the water around it. Approaching head on and slightly to its lee, they could feel the pitch and swell of its passage through the water. One flick of those mighty flukes and they would be lost.

"Get ready!" George yelled at the harpooner.

The man drew his oar immediately and stood, wedged at the bow, harpoon poised as he measured his aim.

"Now!"

The barbed iron spear plunged into sleek black flesh.

"Fast fish!" yelled George to the other boats. They would know they had lost the race, and would wait, out of danger, until after the kill.

The whale reared out of the water, to thrash in a boiling turbulence that threatened to capsize them. Rope hissed through iron rings and over the loggerhead as it dived.

George swiftly changed places with the harpooner. He grabbed a lance and waited. It was his task to kill the beast now it had felt the prick of the harpoon.

The whale was fathoms below them, but as it rose again in an explosion of water, it surged forward, hauling the boat behind it. "Peak oars!" shouted George, exhilaration taking him over. "We're in for a Nantucket sleigh ride!"

The oars were peaked, and water was thrown over the harpoon rope, which was whipping so fast over the loggerhead it was at combustion point, hauled in and let out as the creature dived, rose to the surface, and hurtled through the water in an effort to escape the barb.

George bided his time — and after almost an hour the black whale showed signs of tiring. It surfaced slowly for air, the plume from its blowhole not as high or as strong, its speed slackening. George struck — and the lance was buried deep behind its eye.

A spray of blood shot from the blowhole.

"Red flag!" yelled George. "Hold fast."

The whale's death-throes sent it into a final mad dash, hauling the boat behind it. Its great tail thrashed as it rolled and floundered in a frenzy of agony. Blood sprayed them all and turned the broiling sea red. The boat was tossed on the heaving waves, the men inside her hanging on for their lives as the water in the bottom reached almost to their knees. George could do nothing but pray that the harpooner was as skilled as he was with the steering oar, correcting the boat's lie as it followed the crazed convolutions of the mortally wounded beast.

Then slowly, inevitably, the black leviathan lost the battle. With one last spray of blood it rolled over and was still.

"Fin out! Haul her in!" George signalled urgently to the other boats.

They had followed the chase but had stood well off once the whale had been harpooned, for it was the most dangerous part of the enterprise and a man could be swept to his death in a moment of carelessness. Now they would lash it with ropes before it became waterlogged and haul it back to the *Atlantica*, where the blubber would be boiled down to extract the oil, the bones cleaned, the meat salted and packed into barrels. Tomorrow they would head back on the long journey to Sydney.

Sydney Cove, July 1797

George was standing on deck, enjoying the warmth of the sun and drinking in the sights and sounds of

Sydney Town, when he felt a meaty hand on his shoulder. It was Samuel Varney. "Save your money, boy," he boomed, his accent resonant with the drawl of Nantucket. "Whores and rum should be only fleeting acquaintances. Put it in the bank, that's what I say."

George had had the same lecture at every port they'd visited over the past three years, and apart from a couple of incidents ashore when rum and lust had got the better of him, he'd heeded the advice. "My bank balance is doing just fine, Cap'n," he replied, with a grin.

Bright blue eyes flashed in Samuel's wrinkled, weatherbeaten face as he scratched his thick white beard. "I have no doubt of it, son," he growled. "Got a good head on your shoulders for a young 'un."

"Not that young," George protested. "I'm twenty-three."

"Ha! You've a way to go before you're as old as me — but you'll do, boy. You'll do." Samuel had salt water in his veins, and knew more about the sea than most. He was also the ultimate businessman, and his fleet of five whalers and two sealers traded from the southern Arctic to the Spice Islands and across the Atlantic. He had hired George as a raw deckhand, and as he'd gained experience and grown to love the nomadic, but tough life on a whaling ship, Samuel had taken him under his wing. They had recognised in each other an understanding of the sea and commerce, and the joy of the chase. George had blossomed under his guidance.

He stood beside his mentor as they smoked their pipes in companionable silence and watched the last of the whalemeat and oil being offloaded. A consignment of salt beef and pork was already on the wharf, and the barrels of precious rice, tobacco, tea and spices that they'd brought from the Spice Islands and Batavia were already being carried to the government warehouse. It had been a profitable trip, and George had already planned what he would do with his share of the takings.

As if he had read the young man's thoughts, Samuel pointed to a large plot of land at the western end of the quay. "A man could build a fine warehouse there," he rumbled, "should he have the wherewithal and a mind for trade."

"My thoughts exactly," replied George. "In fact, I have a meeting with the port committee this afternoon to discuss purchase of the lease." He looked at the old man, noting the salt-stained cap, knitted tunic, rough canvas trousers and stout sea-boots. No one would have guessed that Samuel Varney was a very rich man. "But it would be profitable to all concerned if a certain whaling captain agreed to deposit his merchandise there so the best price could be gained through my store."

Samuel roared with laughter. "He'd be a fool to turn down such an opportunity." Then his face grew serious. "But can we trust your manager? Running a store single-handedly could bring temptation if the owner is rarely ashore."

"Matthew Lane has a wife and eight children to feed. He'd be foolish to cheat me."

Thoughtfully, Samuel stroked his beard. "If you get the land, you got a deal," he said finally. He took George's large hand in a crushing squeeze.

"Now I'd better get ashore and prepare for the committee meeting," said George, wrinkling his nose. "I need a bath, a shave and a haircut."

"Will you visit your family afterwards?" the older man asked.

George nodded. "It's a fair way out to Hawks Head Farm, but my mother would never forgive me if I didn't make the journey."

Samuel's eyes twinkled. "Has she forgiven you for leaving the land?"

George dug his hands into the deep pockets of his trousers. His departure had caused his parents a great deal of anxiety, but once he'd seen his first whaling ship he'd known where his future lay. Despite his mother's protests, he'd been determined and eventually had persuaded her it was right for him to go. "Not really," he admitted. "But I think she's realised I wasn't meant to be a farmer, and Ernest is quite happy to run the place without me as long as I keep investing in it."

The blue eyes regarded him steadily. "Your tone is light, my boy, but I sense you're still troubled by the events that took your family out to the Hawkesbury River." He paused as George broke eye-contact, then went on, "I've heard the rumours, son."

George stared beyond the cove to the little wooden house on the hill. The memories were as clear as if it had all happened yesterday, the shadow they cast still present after four years. Yet Samuel was right: it was time to confront them.

"It was the worst year of my life. Ernest was engaged to Millicent," he began haltingly. "She'd survived the horrors of the Second Fleet and Mother had taken her in because they came from the same part of Cornwall." The words flowed more easily as he described how Millicent had been seen fleeing after an argument with his sister Florence only to be raped by Edward Cadwallader and his cronies — and how she had found the courage to take them to court.

"My sister ran away rather than admit she had played a part in what happened that night, but I doubt her testimony would have made any difference. The trial was a farce. It destroyed Millicent and rocked the very foundations of our family," he said bitterly.

"Edward's father, Jonathan Cadwallader, the Earl of Kernow, told the court that he and my mother had had a liaison. He used a letter from her to blacken her name and accuse her of revenge for being spurned. Her friendship with Millie, who had been dismissed from his household many years before, merely strengthened his argument. And with the accused standing firm with their false witnesses the case was dismissed."

George clenched his fists. "My father knew of what had happened between Mother and the earl — it was why we came to Australia — but because it had been made public, it meant my poor mother had to tell me and Ernest." Despite the warmth of the day he shivered. "Millicent's suicide and Florence's disappearance led my father to the brink of losing his faith in

God, and my mother to despair. Ernest was intent upon revenge. His rage turned him against everyone who loved him."

"I can understand why your family moved out to the Hawkesbury." Samuel looked towards the little shack on the hill. "The memories here would have been too much for them."

"It was their salvation. Ernest threw himself into working the farm and Father put his energy into founding a mission."

"And for your mother, Susan?"

George's smile was soft. "She's the daughter of a Cornish fisherman, and has a will of iron. She might bend, but will never break."

"Yet she must fret over your sister," muttered Samuel. "Has there been any word from her over the years?"

George shook his head. "Florence has always been a law unto herself, and we've had to accept we'll hear from her when she's ready to return." He took a deep breath and felt the sun's warmth again, the memories dispelled for now.

"I know your visit home will give them solace, and will surely lift their spirits," Samuel told him.

"From the tone of my mother's letters, it seems there is hope for the future. Ernest is courting the eldest daughter of a neighbouring farmer. She's a couple of years older than him, but a nice girl by all accounts. According to Mother, she's plump, homely and as skilled about the house as she is with the stock." He

24

shot a glance at Samuel. "Sounds like a match made in Heaven, if you ask me."

"I suppose it won't be long before some damn female gets her claws into you too, young 'un. Take my word for it, boy. Women ain't nothing but expensive trouble. And I should know — I've had three wives and none of 'em proved worth a damn once the courtin' was over. Couldn't even give me children."

George laughed. "I'm having too much fun to think of marriage," he replied, as he knocked the dottle from his pipe. "A woman would have to run pretty fast to catch me — and as for children . . ." He shuddered. "God forbid."

"We're all caught eventually, son," replied Samuel. "Sooner or later we fall for a pretty face and a well-turned ankle, and our brains desert us."

"Not me," said George, cheerfully. He slapped Samuel on the back, stuck his hands into his pockets and whistled a sea shanty as he strode down the gangway to the quay. Life was perfect just as it was. The last thing he needed was a woman to disrupt it.

Sydney Town, August 1797

Eloise battled to control the sickness that had plagued her throughout the seven months of her first pregnancy, and avoided her reflection in the dressing-table mirror. She knew she was drawn and pale, and that her green eyes had lost their sparkle. "So much for blooming," she said, her voice coloured by the lightest hint of her German ancestry. "I look and feel half dead."

25

Edward Cadwallader's lips fleetingly touched the nape of her neck. "It won't be for much longer," he said, then checked his appearance in the mirror and preened his moustache. "Our son is merely making his presence felt."

Eloise watched him move towards the fireplace. "We do not know it is a son," she reminded him.

"Cadwalladers always have sons," he said impatiently. "And hurry, Eloise, the governor doesn't like to be kept waiting. You're still in your nightshift."

"Go without me," she said. "I'm not well and my condition will explain my absence."

"Self-pity is hardly an excuse," he snapped. "Get dressed."

Eloise faced him. "I have no wish to attend the governor's party," she said. "You will enjoy it far more if I remain here."

"You are my wife and will do as I tell you," he shouted.

Eloise refused to be cowed. Her father, Baron Oskar von Eisner, had shouted at her and her sisters ever since she could remember, and she was used to such hectoring, but he'd never forced his will as unkindly as Edward did. "I am carrying your child," she said calmly. "The pregnancy has not been easy and I do not feel well. The governor will understand the reason for my absence."

He glared at her. "You may speak to the baron in that manner," he said, "but you will find that I cannot allow disobedience."

Eloise maintained her outward calm, but her heart was thudding. His manner told her that he was indeed a very different man from her father. "It's not disobedience, Edward," she said, in a tone she hoped would mollify him, "merely common sense. If I should faint or be ill, there will be a scene, and I'm sure you would wish to avoid that."

Edward eyed her. "I should have known a German *frau* would have an argument for everything." He strode across the room and opened the door. "We will discuss this on my return. I expect you to be dressed and waiting for me in the drawing room, regardless of the hour."

As he slammed the door Eloise flinched.

Then frustration boiled over. She picked up her hairbrush and threw it as hard as she could at the wall. It fell with a thud to the floor, and Eloise sank on to the dressing-stool. Edward was wearing her down, slowly but surely, and she dreaded his return, knowing it would bring a battle of wills that she was fast losing the strength to fight.

She sat in the ensuing silence, listening to the creaking of the house they had rented on the edge of the town. It was small and draughty, the rooms cluttered with bags, trunks and boxes awaiting the day when their house in Watsons Bay was finished. They could have used some of the rooms above her father's hotel on the quay, which Eloise would have preferred, but Edward had refused the offer and they had moved in here after their wedding.

She felt the walls crowd in as the silence lengthened, and when the baby moved inside her, she placed her hands over her belly and fought the tears that would undermine what was left of her confidence. How she longed for her sisters' company, for the good heart of her father, and the comfort of familiar surroundings — for more than her husband's dismissive lack of sympathy.

A log shifted in the grate and sparks flew up the chimney. Eloise watched the wood smoulder as she took stock of her situation. Her father's title meant little here, his building of the successful hotel on the quay distancing him even further from the rigid class-system of this British outpost where tradespeople were frowned on. Her marriage to the heir of the Earl of Kernow had given her a certain cachet in Sydney society, and although she had been well educated in Munich and her English was only slightly accented, she knew she was still regarded with suspicion in some quarters. Eloise had had to harden herself to the artful slights and disingenuous smirks, become expert at ignoring the petty snobbery of some women — but she had few defences against her husband.

They had been married for less than a year, but Edward's constant sniping and dictatorial manner had taken their toll — yet Eloise clung fiercely to the belief that she was not at fault: his true character had emerged within weeks of the wedding ceremony, and he bore little resemblance now to the man he had been when he'd courted her. He was often absent, discouraged visits from her family, sought nothing less than perfection in her bearing, and was increasingly moody and belligerent.

She pulled the silk wrap more closely over her nightshift as she remembered the heady days of his courtship and saw them with the clarity that could only come with hindsight. Her naïvety had been her downfall, for she had never before encountered such sophistication, and had been all too easily impressed with his impeccable manners and winning ways — blind to the man behind the glamorous uniform and the English title he would inherit.

She stared, unseeing, into the flames. She should have followed her initial instincts and refused his suit when he'd first approached her — even then she had sensed darkness behind the dazzling smile. But it had added spice to his courtship and she'd been easy prey to his charm. She'd thought she had fallen in love. Yet love was what she'd witnessed between her parents — it grew deeper, provided solace, security and friendship, a sense of well-being that bound two people and shielded them from the world.

Eloise was forced to accept that what she'd experienced in the heady days of their whirlwind romance was infatuation. She had lived in a fantasy world, believing she had found her prince and that they would live happily ever after — and for a few weeks it had seemed that her dreams would be fulfilled, for their coming child had been conceived during the first month.

Her sigh was deep as she felt an aching sense of failure. Edward's warmth and attentiveness had soon cooled as she'd grown large and debilitated by her pregnancy. Now his drinking concerned her, his temper was unpredictable, and she could feel only relief at his prolonged absences. It had become obvious that he no longer loved her — and she wondered if he, too, regretted their marriage.

She stood up and began to dress. She must learn to live with Edward's fault-finding and disregard of her well-being. The die had been cast: she was tied to him for the rest of her life, and all she could do now was hope that his mood would improve once the child was born. Her fingers fumbled with the strings of her petticoat as she tried not to think of what might happen if it proved to be a girl.

Edward realised he was late for the governor's party, but it was to be an informal gathering so there was little urgency. His black mood and frustration had been soothed by the whore in the room above the tavern. For weeks Eloise hadn't been a proper wife — what else could she expect of him?

As his horse ambled along the dirt road, he breathed in the scents of the night that were so different to those of the north and took stock of all he'd achieved since his return to Sydney. His release from exile had come earlier than he'd expected and he and his men had sailed into the harbour in November 1796. The ship that had carried them north was as battered and unkempt as the men as they'd unloaded the horses and depleted stores, for great changes had come about during his absence. With the right to hold treasury bills now instead of the promissory notes that could only be exchanged for goods at the government stores, he and his fellow officers had increased their wealth accordingly.

He had extended his estates by buying the land grants of emancipated convicts, who had little enthusiasm for farming, and trade was brisk with the sea captains, whose goods he sold to the colonists at vast profit. The rules for the use of convict labour had been relaxed, and now he and the other officers not only had a monopoly on the wholesale trade and ruling positions within the colony but a host of servants, fed and clothed by the government, who cost him nothing.

Edward felt a glow of satisfaction. His exile was over and his fortune grew daily. The house at Watsons Bay was almost finished and he was about to become a father. He had arrived. Nothing and nobody would stand in his way — least of all his father. One day he would regret the part he had played in Edward's expulsion from Sydney after that damned woman had taken him and his colleagues to trial. His mood darkened again. His father had had to get him out of a tight corner, and the humiliation still infuriated him.

As the lights of Government House twinkled in the distance his thoughts returned to Eloise. He had been in Sydney only days when he'd received an invitation to dinner at the German's hotel. It had come as a surprise for he had only met the so-called baron once when he'd gone there for a drink. Although the man was hardly his social equal, Edward had had nothing better to do that night, so he had accepted. The dull evening had been transformed from the moment he'd been introduced to the baron's eldest daughter.

Eloise had the clearest green eyes, fringed with golden lashes, in an exquisite face framed by a tumble of pale curls. She was tall, reaching almost to his shoulder, but her figure was slight in an ice-blue gown, her *décolletage* as flawless as alabaster. There were diamonds at her throat and in her ears, and a perfect white rose held back her hair. The impact she'd made on him had been akin to a blow in the gut, and Edward had found it hard to speak. They had exchanged the usual small-talk and she had moved on, silken skirts rustling, back straight, glorious hair streaming over her shoulders in ripples of spun gold. He had never desired a woman so much, and knew he had to have her.

He had pursued her relentlessly, employing his charm and reining in his impatience as she'd steadfastly refused him even the most chaste kiss. Yet he'd found the pursuit exhilarating, for Eloise was ice and fire, and the challenge she presented irresistible.

Soon Eloise's defences had tumbled and they had married at the end of January, just two months after their first meeting. He'd been right about the fire, for their union had been joyous and he had desired her more than ever when she'd told him shortly afterwards that she carried their child.

Edward's hands tightened on the reins. Love had played no part in his pursuit of Eloise. Possession of her beauty had spurred him into marriage, but now even his desire was sorely tried. The endless nausea had kept her in bed, and when she rose, she wandered about in her nightshift. The stench of sickness and the sight of her bloated body disgusted him, and he was put out when she would not accompany him to social gatherings. He wanted his beautiful, slender Eloise to show off at parties and dances where he could bask in the envy he saw in other men's eyes.

He nudged the horse into a gallop, determined not to dwell on his wife's shortcomings, or his lack of patience with her. When a marriage was at a standstill, a man had to seek comfort somewhere. Eloise should count herself lucky he didn't demand his conjugal rights.

The Cape of Good Hope, September 1797

The *Empress* rolled like a sow as she ploughed through the heavy seas. The storm had hit as they left South Africa and only a few passengers remained well enough to emerge from their cabins.

Alice Hobden could barely stay on her feet as she was tossed about in the tiny cabin. Two years of battling malaria in the heat and dust of Cape Town had taken its toll, and she wondered if she had made a mistake in insisting she was well enough to travel. But the thought of Jack waiting for her in New South Wales had reinforced her determination to be with him. It had been almost another year before she could book passage on a ship going so far east, and now that she was on her way to him she was damned if she'd give in to self-pity and nausea.

She glanced at her companion, a middle-aged woman with a whining disposition and an irritating voice, who was sailing to New South Wales to be with her husband who was in the military. She was asleep, and Alice sighed with relief as she pinned up her thick fair hair. She had spent most of the day tending Morag, and had earned nothing but complaints for her trouble.

Alice shivered as she tried to keep her balance. It was a bitter night and the last thing she wanted was to be out in it, but if she was to get this second flock of merino sheep safely to Jack she had no choice. She checked the money belt that had never left her even during the worst fever attacks. It was hidden beneath her clothes, and although it was much lighter than it had been when she had started out from Sussex, it still jingled satisfyingly on her hip as she adjusted her dress and petticoats. As she pulled on her travelling cloak she squared her narrow shoulders. Her precarious situation might be tough and frightening, but if Jack could survive the hulks and the transport ship, and still look to the future, she had no right to complain about rough seas.

Without warning the ship reared and plunged violently with a shudder that ran through her timbers. Alice was thrown on to the narrow bunk. Her head hit a wooden beam with a thud, and she slumped, dazed, against the pillows. It was as if that blow had knocked all the energy out of her, for suddenly she felt too tired to move. As her stomach churned and her head throbbed, she closed her eyes and turned her thoughts to more pleasant things.

Sussex seemed very far away, and she couldn't help but yearn for it. The farmhouse had been her home for almost fourteen years, and she'd looked around it on that last day knowing she would never see it again but hoping she would carry its memory with her, so that when she was lonely and frightened — as she was now — she could gaze at the thatched roof that drooped low over the tiny windows and be comforted.

She smiled as she remembered the limewashed daub and wattle walls, the stone floor worn by almost two centuries of tramping feet. Her own footsteps had echoed on those flagstones, and the lingering scent of smoking fires had remained in the cold ashes of the vast fireplace and in the oak beams of the ceiling. Sooty smears marked the walls above the candles, and wax hung like icicles from the iron sconces — a reminder of dark winter nights when the wind had howled outside and the early lambs were brought in to be warmed by the fire.

Alice clung to the sides of the bunk, and let her thoughts drift up the narrow, rickety stairs to the bedroom beneath the thatch. The floor dipped towards the front wall and the small window with its iron latch. It was almost as if some part of her remained in Sussex, for as she was tossed about she could see the Sussex Downs folding one upon another as they towered over the ploughed fields and lush pastures. Black-faced sheep grazed beneath a threatening sky, but between the clouds, the sun's rays cast a golden haze over the hedgerows.

Now Alice hardly noticed the roll of the ship for she was lost in the view over the fields to the meander of water that flowed beneath the stony bridge, gurgling over the chalky bed until it rushed past the hamlet of Alfriston to the sea. She could see the ancient church tower and more thatched roofs clustered on the riverbank, and hear the bells calling the parishioners to evensong.

A tear seeped through her lashes as she recalled those last few moments. She'd left the house, not wanting to be there when the new owner arrived, and had hurried down into the yard. The cob had stood patiently by the fence, his nose deep in the lush grass, tail swishing against the worrisome flies that always seemed to come with the summer rain. His brown coat was shaggy, his legs short, back broad — and even though he possessed a devilish temperament, Alice loved him.

"No more eating, Bertie," she'd said, as she fitted the bit and bridle, sorted out the reins and placed a blanket on his back. "You'll be too fat to walk if you're not careful, and we've a fair way to go."

Bertie had shown her his yellow teeth, and she'd given him an affectionate pat on the neck, then led him to the tree stump so she could clamber on to his back. Anything of worth had been sold, and that included her saddle. But Alice had known how to ride from the minute she could sit unaided; the blanket would suffice.

Another tear rolled down her face as she saw her past self lean down to open the gate. She'd left it to swing behind her as she'd dug her heels into Bertie's sides and coaxed him out of the yard. She had looked straight ahead — for her future now lay far beyond the horizon.

Alice smeared away the tears and blew her nose. Poor Bertie was penned with the other horses on deck, and must be wondering what was going on. She clambered out of the bunk, adjusted her clothing and after taking a deep breath in an attempt to quell the mixture of excitement and terror that frequently assailed her, she staggered to the door.

She had embarked on an adventure so daring she could hardly believe it was happening — yet here she was, at thirty-five, on her way to a new life in a new world. As she pushed the door open and was lashed by the rain and spray, she was reminded that her situation was all too real.

The ocean heaved and the decks were awash as they bucked beneath her feet. She had to cling to anything she could find to keep from being swept overboard. Her cloak was soon soaked, dragging heavily on her shoulders as her skirts and petticoats were whipped into a frenzy, then moulded to her legs in sodden folds.

She made slow, unsteady progress along the deck until she reached the smallest of the horse pens, guarded by a young marine who had orders to shoot any horse that threatened to stampede. The eight animals were standing splay-legged, heads drooping, coats darkened with water. She patted Bertie as she met his disgruntled gaze, gave him a handful of oats and left him to it. He was a tough old thing — he'd survive.

Her hair was torn from its pins and strands stuck to her face as she turned sideways on to the wind. It was like trying to resist a battering ram, and she was wondering if she'd ever reach the sheep pens when she was startled by a voice in her ear: "You shouldn't be out in this."

Alice blinked against the rain. "I have to see to the sheep," she yelled back.

He grimaced, took her arm, and they stumbled along the deck until they found dubious shelter in the lee of the captain's cabin doorway. "Thank you," she panted, pushing back her wet hair.

"My pleasure," he replied, with an almost mocking bow. He studied her from head to foot. "Henry Carlton, at your service, ma'am."

She felt a spark of interest as she looked at his handsome face. "Alice Hobden," she replied.

"Delighted to meet you. Where are these blasted sheep?"

"Below deck. It's warmer down there — and drier," she added ruefully, as she plucked at her sodden clothing.

"They must be important for you to risk your life for them," he bellowed, as they were flung against one another.

Alice's face was hot with embarrassment as she tried to disentangle herself and regain some composure. "They are," she replied breathlessly. "They represent every penny I own."

He held her steady, his grey eyes filled with amusement as she reddened. "Are you sure you need to go down there?"

"It's obvious you've never been a farmer," she retorted, as she took in the expensive clothes and bejewelled neck-pin. She remembered him coming aboard at Cape Town with several servants in tow.

"But I *am* a gentleman," he replied. "Please, let me assist you."

"I can manage from here," she told him, "but thank you."

He pulled his cloak collar up to his chin and went back into the storm.

Alice giggled as she watched him go. There was little doubt that he'd been flirting with her — and she was flattered, for he was attractive in looks and manner. Then she berated herself for behaving like a silly girl and made her precarious way down the narrow ladder to the crew quarters.

The stench of vomit, penned animals and cooking hit her and she covered her nose as she stumbled through the swaying hammocks to the pens. It was gloomy down here, with only the glimmer of lanterns and the dancing glow of the fires in the two brick ovens to give light. But at least it was warm, and as they'd become used to her presence, the sailors took little notice of her.

The off-duty men were either asleep or playing cards and drinking. The cook was shovelling pans of food in and out of the ovens as he shouted orders to his assistant, and the young officers were noisily involved in a game of dice. Most didn't look old enough to have left the nursery, she thought, as she watched where she stepped, avoiding a dubious patch on the floor, but that was probably a sign that she was getting older.

The two rams were penned separately, she didn't want them fighting, and the eight ewes were on the other side, packed into a corner next to the officers' sleeping quarters. Their initial skittishness had been tempered by the conditions, and now they stood with their woolly heads jutting through the railings, bleating as they swayed with the motion of the ship.

As she checked them all, she found, thankfully, no injuries, no infections and no letting up of their appetites. She'd had the devil's own task in haggling down their price — she couldn't lose them now. She changed the straw bedding, then replenished the water container and feed troughs. They were a worthy surprise gift for the man who waited for her.

CHAPTER
TWO

Uluru, September 1797

The *corroboree* was almost over, and as Lowitja sat with the men she had grown tired of hearing the same arguments. The white man had decimated the southern tribes and was rapidly spreading north and west, but there was still a reluctance to fight back. Too many of their people had either given in to the white man's ways, or moved out of their territories to avoid conflict, leaving the fight to a handful of warriors who couldn't hope to win against such an onslaught.

"I have seen them," she said, breaking into the discussion. "They kill young and old and use warriors from other tribes to hunt us down."

"We are fighting our traditional enemies," interrupted Mandarg, a young man of the Gandangara tribe. "The Wiradjuric are always trespassing on our land and stealing our women. With the white man's help, we can be rid of them." He glared across the circle to the two Wiradjuric tribesmen, who glared back.

Lowitja eyed Mandarg, remembering him as the boy who had once sat at the same campfire with the Eora when they had united against the marauding

Wiradjuric. "The laws tell us that enmity between us is taboo at the *corroboree*," she reminded him. "If we can meet in peace here, our traditional enemies can become our allies," she went on. "It is the only way to be rid of the white man."

Mandarg snorted, the arrogance of youth clear in his eyes. "I have always respected your wisdom, old woman, but to ally with the Wiradjuric is to break the sacred laws of my tribe."

There was a mutter of agreement from around the circle.

"You will have no tribe if you do not stand with the warriors Pemulwuy and his son Tedbury to fight this enemy."

"Leave war to the warriors," he retorted. "The white man cannot be defeated, so we will use him to vanquish our enemies."

Lowitja rose painfully to her feet. Her joints were aching after sitting cross-legged for so long, and she'd heard enough nonsense for one night. "Mandarg," she said softly, "you are a fool. It is only when the Spirits send the white owl that you will know the truth and accept that I was right. But by then it will be too late."

She heard the soft pad of his feet as he followed her away from the fire. When they had reached the darkness, she turned to him. "I have spoken enough," she said. "Your destiny is already written."

Mandarg's fear was evident in his stance. The arrogance had drained away, and she was reminded of the little boy who had once sat wide-eyed at her feet as she'd told stories of the Evil Ones. "Wise woman, you speak in riddles," he said. "Tell me what you have seen."

"You are young, and the blood of the warrior stirs so hotly within you that you cannot see the truth," she murmured. "But age will bring the wisdom you seek."

He was clearly still puzzled, and Lowitja relented. "You will have a long life, Mandarg," she said, "a life that will see many changes, and take you into the company of men who will try to influence you — but the death of a woman will open your eyes to your destiny." She smiled up at him. "The Spirits will never leave you, even when you do not listen to them, and they will send a sign with the white owl when it is time to return to the true path." She left him, a solitary figure silhouetted in the moonlight.

When she returned to her own campfire, she was just in time to bid farewell to Mandawuy. At seven he was a sturdy child, with an inquisitive mind and a serious demeanour, and tonight he would go with the Elder and the other uninitiated boys to the sacred learning place at the foot of Uluru. His long preparation for manhood had begun, and she felt sad that soon he would no longer need her.

She followed their winding progress through the gathering until they were lost to sight, knowing she must accept the ancient ways of her people and allow others to take over his education. Mandawuy would stay with the Anangu Elder now until the *corroboree* was over, and learn of the sacred stories that surrounded this special place. He'd listen as the wise old man taught him the secrets of the creation of Uluru and Kata Tjuta, then described the progress of the Rainbow Serpent whose winding wake made the rivers spring up — and learn of things forbidden to her by her womanhood.

Lowitja poked a stick into the embers of the fire and watched the flames as they danced in the soft wind that blew across the outback plains. After the massacre, her Great Ancestors had called her to Uluru where she and Mandawuy had been made welcome by the Anangu people. They had given her shelter and taken in her grandson as one of their own — and that had concerned her, for Mandawuy was not of the Anangu.

Her joints complained as she struggled to her feet. It was time to seek advice from the Spirits. Turning from the fire, she walked until the sounds of the camp faded and the soft night enfolded her. The Spirit Stars lit her way as she followed the well-worn tracks through the trees towards Kata Tjuta's soaring mounds. This was a male Dreaming Place and she was forbidden to enter its caves and canyons, worn by time and the Totem Spirits, but her destination was the waterhole that lay to the east.

The silence was profound as she cast the stones on the sacred red earth, and from that silence came the distant drone of a didgeridoo. The vibration of its primal music sang in rhythm with her heart, drawing her back, back to Dreamtime and the Ancient Ones who would guide her on what she'd come to realise would be her final journey.

44

Sydney Town, October 1797

The pains started during the night and Eloise woke to discover she was alone. A terrible fear washed over her, and as she waited for the next wave of agony to subside, she prayed that Edward was in the other room.

She got up, staggered out into the narrow hall and found him in the tiny parlour. "The baby's coming," she gasped. "Go and get help."

Edward's eyes were bloodshot as he lurched to his feet. "I'll send the maid," he slurred, knocking the brass bell off the table. "You'd better go back to bed."

Eloise realised he would be of little help. "Meg," she gasped, as the girl appeared in the doorway, half asleep. "Run and fetch Widow Stott. Tell her it's time." She put out a hand to halt her flight as another pain gripped her. When it had faded she was faint and trembling. "Then go to the hotel and tell my family. Hurry, Meg."

"Let me help you back to bed," said Edward, stumbling as he tried to take her arm. "Can't have you dropping my son on the parlour carpet."

Eloise grimaced at his coarseness and the stink of stale rum that assailed her. Thank heavens for Meg and Widow Stott. She took his arm, leaning on him heavily for support as they went into the bedroom. She sank on to the mattress with a sigh of relief, but there was little respite, for another pain was tightening its grip and her waters broke. "The pains are coming fast, and they're very strong," she panted. "I hope the widow gets here in time."

Edward backed away. "I'll wait in the other room."

45

"Don't go," she begged. "Not yet."

He shook his head as he tried to maintain his precarious balance. "It's woman's work." His bleary gaze drifted over her, taking in the huge mound of her belly and the spreading stain on the tangled sheets. "I need a drink," he mumbled.

Eloise knew this was no place for a man — especially one who had made it plain that he found the business of pregnancy and birth repellent. She closed her eyes and battled to stem the fear of what was to come. She didn't know what to expect, had no idea how long it would take, or how painful it would be — her mother had told her little, only that once the baby was born she would forget the pain. Tears of self-pity threatened and she dashed them away. Her yearning for her long-dead mother would never be fulfilled.

"Eloise, darling," breathed Anastasia, as she flew into the bedroom some minutes later, their sister Irma following close behind.

"I'm so glad you've come," Eloise panted.

"How could we not?" squeaked Anastasia, who had a propensity to become overexcited. "Papa's in the other room, and he's brought champagne to celebrate."

Irma scurried round the bed, tugging at pillows and blankets, trying to bring order to the chaos. "Is it very painful?" she asked fearfully. "You look flushed and uncomfortable."

"Yes," mumbled Eloise, "and you worsen it with pulling at the sheets."

Irma's face crumpled. "Eloise, really! I was only trying —"

"Is widow Stott on her way?" Eloise interrupted.

Before anyone could reply the door was thrown open and the widow bustled into the room, Meg trotting after her. "Go to your father," she ordered the girls, "and try to persuade Major Cadwallader to temper his drinking." She turned to Meg. "Hot water," she snapped, "and plenty of it, then towels and fresh sheets."

Eloise smiled at the rotund little woman with gratitude as order was restored. Her bedding was changed, she was washed and a cold compress placed on her hot forehead. "Thank you," she breathed.

"Bite on this when the pain is bad. It will also help when you need to push."

Eloise shook her head at the proffered strip of leather. "I will breathe through the pain," she insisted. "It is the way in Germany, so my mother told me."

The boot-button eyes studied her thoughtfully. "I don't hold with these new-fangled foreign ideas," she muttered, "but it's your birthing. If you change your mind, the strap's here."

Charles Edward Cadwallader was born at sunset the following day. His feeble wail barely disturbed the silence as Widow Stott bundled him in a towel and placed him in Eloise's arms. "He's a bit scrawny," she said, with a frown, "and that birth-mark is unfortunate, but I dare say it'll fade over time. He'll fatten up when he's had a feed."

Eloise looked at her tiny son and felt a love so powerful it took her breath away. She touched the delicate fingers and toes, counting each one and finding them a miracle. As his tremulous cry touched her heart she took him to her breast.

"I thought I heard a cry," said Edward, as he came into the room. "Is it a boy?"

"Yes," murmured Eloise, still lost in the wonder of what she'd done. "And he's very hungry."

"You shouldn't be doing that," he snapped. "It's not seemly for a woman of your standing. I've engaged a wet-nurse."

"He's my baby and my milk is best," she said, as tiny fingers clasped her thumb.

She could see that Edward was trying to curb his irritation in the presence of the widow. "Has he the mark of the Cadwal-laders?" he demanded.

Eloise drew back the towel to reveal the scarlet teardrop on the baby's skin. "An angel's kiss just below his heart," she replied, almost overwhelmed by his perfection.

Edward regarded his child. "Hmph," he said. "I expected a lusty son, not this puny creature."

Eloise held the baby as tightly as she dared. She noted her husband's disagreeable frown and felt his disapproval. How could she ever have thought she loved him? "He'll grow," she said coldly.

Edward grunted. "I'm expected in the officers' mess," he said, plainly eager to leave. "Your family is still here, so you don't need me."

Eloise heard the front door bang. She didn't care if Edward never returned. This precious baby was all that mattered, and he had to be shielded from his father's disappointment.

Aboard the Empress, *November 1797*

The storm had died and now the *Empress* was wallowing in what the captain called the doldrums, her sails limp on the masts as she floated listlessly on the Indian Ocean. The heat below had become impossible to bear, although the hatches were all open. The mood aboard had changed, the strict lines between the different classes of passenger erased in the camaraderie of making the best of things. Alice and the others from steerage had set up camp on deck alongside the wealthier travellers, sleeping under the stars and sweltering beneath canvas shelters during the day among the pens of chickens and geese. Food was shared, gossip exchanged and the offer of cooler clothing gratefully received by those who had not bargained on such heat.

Alice had stripped off her petticoats, stockings and boots and was sitting on a cushion in the meagre shade of a small sail, her bare toes peeping from beneath the hem of her thin cotton dress. She mopped the sweat from her face and watched some of the male passengers engage a trio of sailors in a game of cards. Children were running about getting in everyone's way, and a gaggle of women chatted over their sewing in the shade of a sail that had been strung over the quarter-deck. Bertie seemed content enough, having been doused with a bucket of sea-water, but she worried about the sheep.

"Good afternoon, Miss Hobden."

The deep, melodious voice interrupted her thoughts and Alice looked up as a shadow fell across her legs. Mr Carlton was older than she'd thought, but the wings of grey at the temple merely enhanced his good looks. His shirt and breeches were immaculate, his hair and moustache smoothly brushed. How could anyone appear so cool and comfortable in this heat? she wondered, as she drew her bare feet swiftly beneath her skirt.

"Do you mind if I sit with you? It seems all the shady spots have been taken."

As she made room for him she was uncomfortably aware of her lack of boots and the thinness of her dress, which was now damp with perspiration and sticking to her like a second skin — but a glance told her he had not noticed; he was looking beyond the ship to the horizon. "I suppose you're still worried about those sheep," he said, after a short silence.

"Of course," she replied. "It's stifling down there and they need watering on the hour — as would you if you were forced to wear a woolly coat in this heat."

A smile lit his face. "Then we must thank God for small mercies," he replied.

"Indeed," she said, clasping her hands on her lap. She was getting pins and needles in her feet, and although she enjoyed his company she didn't know how to respond: she had never been in proper conversation with a gentleman before.

"Do I make you uncomfortable?"

She met his gaze shyly. "A little," she confessed. "But I'm unused to conversing while sitting on the floor."

He laughed. "Perhaps we will set a trend, Miss Hobden."

"It is a little uncomfortable, Mr Carlton. I can't think it will catch on."

"You intrigue me," he said, after a pause. "You travel alone, with sheep and a horse, to a convict colony that is barely civilised — yet you don't seem frightened at the prospect. Most women would be having the vapours by now."

"I'm not most women," she retorted, without thinking, then bit her lip and apologised.

"I can tell you are unlike other women," he responded. "It was evident that night when I saved you from being washed overboard." He regarded her for a moment. "What is your story, Miss Hobden? Who is the lucky man waiting for you in Sydney Harbour?"

Alice wondered fleetingly if he was merely being polite, but he seemed genuinely interested, and she no longer felt so awkward with him. "How do you know someone is waiting for me?" she asked.

"Isn't he?" His grey eyes widened in surprise.

"His name is Jack Quince."

"A good, sturdy sort of name," said Carlton. "In the military, is he?"

"Hardly. He's a farmer, Sussex born and bred, and I fell in love with him when we were still in the schoolroom." She stared out at the glassy ocean whose brightness hurt the eye. "We had such plans back then . . ."

"Tell me," he coaxed.

"When Jack inherited his parents' farm we began to prepare for our wedding, but three weeks before the day Jack was falsely accused of stealing a neighbour's bull. He was dragged off the farm and thrown into one of the hulks on the Thames." Her voice broke. It hurt to speak of those lonely months when Jack's future had lain in the hands of others.

She looked at her silent companion, anger making her more confident. "He'd been after Jack's farm for years and had let the bull in with his cows deliberately. With Jack transported, he planned to buy the farm for pennies." She turned back to the horizon. "Jack was an innocent man, but he was also resourceful, and had a good friend in the squire who helped him sign over the farm to me before he was sentenced."

"His faith in you must have been overwhelming," observed Carlton.

"It was — and I never stopped believing that one day he would be free to come home."

"But you are journeying to New South Wales alone, so I must assume he never did."

Alice stretched out her bare feet. "We'd been ripped apart on the eve of our wedding, but when I'd had no word from him for years, even I began to lose hope. I'd heard terrible stories about the conditions on the Second Fleet — that many of the convicts died — and knew it would be a miracle if he had survived." She smiled. "Then his letters began to arrive, some a year or more out of date, others out of sequence, but all full of hope for our future together."

52

She knew the joy was clear on her face. "He still loved me, Mr Carlton, although he had been beaten, chained and kept in the hold of a convict ship manacled to a dead man for six months. He loved me enough to keep our dream alive even in his darkest hours."

Carlton's eyes had hardened. "The cruelty of man against man never ceases to appal me," he said bitterly. "Punishment should fit the crime, but it rarely does, and those most deserving of retribution often escape it." He dredged up a smile. "But the human spirit is remarkable in its tenacity — and so are you. It must have taken a great deal of courage to leave the farm and travel so far on your own."

Alice noted the steel behind the relaxed demeanour and wondered what injustice he'd borne, and who had crossed him. Whatever it was, she realised Mr Carlton was not a man to let such things go without seeking revenge. "I'd never gone beyond the nearest market town," she admitted, "and if I'd known I'd be stuck in Cape Town for almost three years with malaria, I might not have had the courage to do it." She wriggled her toes. "But here I am, on my way to the other side of the world to a man whose memory has lived on in my heart and through his letters. I suspect he has changed. No man could go through what he has endured without being touched by it, but it is a gamble I am willing to take."

Henry Carlton shook his head. "Miss Hobden, it is rare to be in the company of such an admirable woman, and I would deem it a great honour if you would permit me to become your friend."

"Will that include escorting me to feed and water the sheep, Mr Carlton?" she teased.

"Only if you insist." He laughed. "I have servants in Cape Town who tend my beasts, and know far more than me about animal husbandry — but never let it be said that I am not willing to learn."

Alice gazed at him thoughtfully. "You have listened to my story, Mr Carlton, but what of yours?"

"I am a wealthy man who enjoys travelling," he said lightly. "I thought I would visit New South Wales and see what opportunities there might be."

His expression didn't change, but the hardness returned to his eyes, and Alice knew that Henry Carlton's journey had little to do with wanderlust.

CHAPTER
THREE

Sydney Town, November 1797

Jack Quince had been coming into town regularly in the hope of news from Alice. His partners, Billy and Nell Penhalligan, teased him relentlessly, but after so many years, the joke was wearing thin, and he sensed growing impatience in Billy when he was left in charge of the work on their farm, Moonrakers.

The morning had started like any other, and after a hearty breakfast he'd loaded the wagon. Nell was pregnant again and needed a dozen things for her and the three children, while the convict workforce were muttering about the dwindling supply of rum. Billy had given him a long list of tools and supplies they needed to last the next three months, and these were stacked carefully in the back of the wagon. Now, as he looked at the load, he saw that he'd run out of excuses to linger.

Yet he made no move, choosing instead to remain by the wagon, taking in the sights and sounds of Sydney Town. It had changed almost beyond recognition since the day he'd arrived on the convict ship *Surprise*, and although there was little doubt that it was still a convict colony, there were signs that the rest of the world was taking an interest.

The harbour was busy with American whaling ships and the vast galleons that plied their trade between Sydney, Batavia and the Spice Islands. The scents of tea, tobacco and spices hung sweetly in the morning air, taking the edge off the stench of open sewers and dung. There were shops and warehouses, even a smart hotel on the quayside, and despite the early hour clusters of men and women were strolling along the board-walks or taking the air in their carriages.

He lit a pipe, revelling in the warmth of early morning, and the freedom to do as he pleased. The latter had been hard won, the months chained in the hold of the *Surprise* leaving a permanent legacy in the twisted bones of his hip and knee. Although he'd been emancipated for some years, he never took it for granted. As he leant on the wagon and puffed at his tobacco, he gazed towards the little wooden house on the hill.

Ezra and Susan Collinson had moved out to Hawks Head Farm to be with their elder son, Ernest, and new people had moved in. It still felt odd not to visit them there, for the minister and his wife had accepted him as part of their family once he and Susan's younger brother, Billy Penhalligan, had become partners at Moonrakers Farm. A line of washing flapped in the garden and Jack nodded. It was right for a family to be there again, he acknowledged, for no house should hold on to tragedy.

He watched the bustle as a whaling ship offloaded her haul, and wondered if the Collinson's younger son, George, was in port. It had come as a shock to his parents when he'd gone to sea, but Jack had sensed the boy was too restless to remain tied to the land. Whaling was a young man's game, offering adventure, danger and freedom, and George hadn't been able to resist.

Jack knocked out his pipe and stuffed it into his waistcoat pocket. He'd idled long enough. It was time to return to Moonrakers.

He slung his bedroll into the wagon and was about to clamber into the driving seat when he heard a cry go up and saw a ship round the headland. Leaving the horse and wagon tethered to a hitching post outside the hotel, he hobbled down to the quay where the old sailor still kept his daily vigil.

They had become friends over the years and the grizzled mariner shot him a gap-toothed grin as he approached. "She be the *Empress*," he declared, before he was asked, "out of the Cape, if I'm not mistaken."

"Out of the Cape? You're sure?" Jack squinted into the dazzling horizon.

The old salt nodded. "Fine ship, the *Empress*," he drawled. "Sailed on 'er once when I were younger."

Jack thanked him, then limped back to his horse and the wagon. His hip bothered him, especially when the weather was damp and cold, but now it hampered his agility as he hauled himself into the driving seat. As he slapped the reins and stirred the horse into a trot, he muttered a fervent prayer that this time Alice would be on board. There had been so many false hopes, so many delays — he couldn't bear the prospect of another disappointment.

A crowd had gathered at the newly constructed pier, which reached far out into deeper water. He drove the wagon to the edge and watched as the ship sailed regally up the river, his hopes soaring as he spied the passengers lining the decks. She had to be among them. Had to.

Fresh storms had blown them south and now the sun was shining from a clear sky as the *Empress* slowly approached Port Jackson. It was an auspicious beginning and, like the other passengers, Alice was on deck, impatient to see her new homeland. She was also a little nervous: she didn't know what to expect when she saw Jack again. They would be strangers despite the intimacy of their letters and the memories they shared — changed by circumstance and the years apart.

She made a determined effort to put aside any doubts, and let excitement take over. Bertie had been groomed, the rams and ewes tended, and Alice had taken particular care with her own appearance. She didn't want Jack to be disappointed when he saw her again, and although the tiny mirror she and Morag shared didn't give her a full view of herself, she knew she looked as well as she could. The malaria had left a yellow tint in her skin, despite the tan, and she was far too skinny, but the thin cotton dress was cool, the broad-brimmed hat shaded her face, and her hair was shining from the hundred strokes of the brush she'd given it this morning.

Glad to have escaped her companion's last-minute packing, she mingled with the others, expectation growing as the coast-line became more distinct and Sydney Harbour was revealed. And what a sight it was. In the clear, almost blinding light of this southern land the broad sweep of water glittered in sandy coves and rocky inlets and ran in winding rivers as far as the eye could see. The white sails of many ships gleamed against the turquoise water as they rocked at anchor, while seabirds hovered and dived, their wing-tips burnished gold as if painted by the sun.

The buzz grew louder as everyone pressed forward for a better view. Alice was reminded of the Cape when she saw the sprawl of Sydney Town along the waterfront, the bustle and colour of life as they drew nearer. Beyond the town she could see clusters of houses on the gentle rise of surrounding hills, the spire of a church and the stone walls of the garrison. Away from the port there were tree-lined streets of neat little wooden shacks, and the elegant, sturdier buildings that housed government officials.

As her gaze drifted from one surprise to another she was amazed at how green everything was compared to Cape Town. She had expected an arid landscape, flat and without feature, but the heavily timbered forests came right to the riverbanks and spread over the hills to the horizon like a verdant sea. Lush lawns surrounded some of the houses, gardens were alive with bright flowers, and elegant trees with silver bark or heavy fronds provided welcome shade.

Her musing on the landscape was interrupted by the sailors' shouts as they shinned up the rigging to haul in the sails. A flotilla of small boats was coming to meet them, and as they were piloted slowly towards the stone jetty, she searched the weathered faces of the oarsmen, hoping Jack might be among them.

Then, realising she was being foolish, she returned her attention to the scene before her. Jack probably didn't know she was coming. The mail was unreliable at the best of times, and her last letters might still be on their way — perhaps even on board this very ship. She would have to be patient, wait until they'd docked, then send a messenger to Moonrakers.

As they drew nearer she could make out the broad main street, the smart hotel and some ramshackle shops. She could see the wares piled up outside them, glimpse the flash of uniform scarlet and a line of convicts unloading a ship. She could hear the street cries of fish and pie vendors, the shouts of men repairing boats, and see the red dust raised by a team of oxen as they drew a heavy cart along a track. Horses and cattle cropped grass in the fields and the dart of yellow dresses could be discerned among the rising steam of what appeared to be an outside laundry.

She stared in wonder at the black swans, which glided regally past, and the strange long-legged white birds with hooked bills that tiptoed along the water's edge. Then she gasped as a flock of brightly coloured birds rose in a thunder of beating wings to swirl and swoop overhead.

"I'm reliably informed they're called lorikeets. Pretty, aren't they?"

She recognised the aristocratic English voice of her new friend, and turned to him with a smile. "They're glorious," she exclaimed. "It's all so beautiful."

"The extraordinary light brings everything into sharp focus. Let us hope your enthusiasm is not dimmed on closer inspection, dear lady," he said, lips twitching in amusement. "After all, this *is* a convict colony."

They had spoken every day since that afternoon on deck, and although they came from very different worlds, there was an ease between them that defied convention. She would miss his companionship after they'd left the ship.

Distracted by the rattle of the anchor chain and shouts from the shore, she turned swiftly and was amazed to see that a sizeable crowd had gathered. Without much hope, she searched the faces for any sign of Jack. But there were too many faces, and the throng kept shifting as people waved and shouted.

Then she stilled. Someone — a man — was shoving his horse and wagon recklessly to the front.

"Jack!" she shrieked as he stood up and waved his hat. He was thinner than she remembered, and a strike of grey ran through his dark hair, but his wide grin was unmistakable. "Jack!" She waved frantically and almost went over the side in her excitement. "I'm here!"

Henry Carlton's hands were firm as he pulled her to safety. "It has become my habit to rescue you, Miss Hobden, and it would be a shame for you to drown before he has had time to put that wedding ring on your finger," he said.

Alice laughed. "Indeed it would!" she spluttered. "Thank you for saving me again." She faltered as she saw he was no longer listening to her. There was an alertness about him that was at odds with his cheerfulness of only moments before, and his gaze had hardened, held by something or someone on the shore.

She followed his gaze, curious to find the reason for this change, but it was impossible to tell what he was seeing. Then the colour drained from his handsome face. "Whatever's wrong?" she asked. "You look as if you've seen a ghost."

"Perhaps I have, dear lady," he said quietly.

"You look well this morning, my dear."

Eloise gave her husband a brief smile as she fussed over the baby. "Take good care of him," she said to Meg, who was as entranced as she by the fair-haired infant. "We shouldn't be long."

Edward noted her customary coolness towards him and tamped down his exasperation as she continued to issue orders to Meg. The mewling brat was always the centre of her attention, which annoyed him, but he couldn't help admiring his wife's loveliness. Since Charles's birth she had blossomed again, and it was easy to remember why he'd wanted her.

Her figure was slender, her face glowed, and her eyes sparkled like emeralds. The broad-brimmed straw hat was decorated with pale blue ribbons, which matched the thin muslin of her dress. Her parasol was white, the ruffles fluttering in the warm breeze. In the heat of the late morning, Eloise was as cool, composed and beautiful as ever — and Edward felt the rush of desire.

"Your carriage awaits, and I have brought a picnic to refresh us. Come, Eloise, we've wasted enough time."

"We must wait for Papa," she said, glancing over her shoulder into the gloom of the hotel lobby.

Edward swallowed a sharp riposte. The baron had only been invited because it was good form. He hadn't expected the blasted man to accept. Now, it seemed, his plans to make love to Eloise must be shelved. It was infuriating.

He stood at her side, impatient to be off. He'd left Eloise with the maid at the hotel some time ago and, because he couldn't stand the cooing and crowing over the baby, had taken himself to the quay for peace and quiet. He'd spent at least an hour there, forced to amuse himself by watching the *Empress* sail round the headland and into port. Time had dragged, and his temper was stretched to the limit.

"I hear from Irma that your father is in town at last," she said, as they waited on the boardwalk.

Edward's expression was deliberately non-committal.

"Why have you not introduced us?" Eloise frowned. "We have been married almost a year, Edward."

Edward felt the familiar prickle of loathing. His father had indeed returned to Sydney. In fact, he'd seen him a few minutes ago, wandering by the quayside, but had turned away before his father could speak. He forced a smile. "My father has only just returned from his expedition north. There has been no time to introduce you."

"Perhaps today would be the ideal occasion," she replied, with some asperity. "He could join our picnic."

"My father doesn't enjoy picnics," he replied. "And I believe he wishes to rest before joining the social round."

"What a pity," Eloise returned. "I felt sure he would wish to meet your wife and his grandson, and I know my father is keen to discuss the expedition." Her gaze was questioning. "One could almost imagine he was avoiding us."

To Edward's relief the baron appeared in the doorway, which put an end to the conversation.

Eloise's father was resplendent in a beautifully tailored cutaway jacket, snow-white breeches and silk stockings, his hat tucked beneath his arm. "A fine morning," he boomed. "Yes, indeed. A very fine morning, and another ship is in port." He rubbed his hands and beamed with satisfaction. "New customers are always welcome."

"Oh, Papa," laughed Eloise, "trust you to have an eye on business."

Edward gritted his teeth as the old fool kissed his daughter's cheek, then clambered into the open carriage. The springs complained beneath his weight as he collapsed on to the seat. Climbing up beside them Edward nodded to the driver, and they bowled down the street.

Jack couldn't wait any longer. As the ramps were lowered he raced on to the deck. Pushing through the mêlée, he searched wildly for Alice. Then, as he thought he must have missed her — there she was.

With passengers and crew milling around them, they stood looking at one another. Jack recognised the sweet smile and warm brown eyes that had captured his heart so many years ago, and although she was a little too thin, the beloved face and tumbling hair made his heart leap. Hardly daring to believe she was not a figment of his imagination, he was rooted to the spot.

Alice took a hesitant step towards him. And then another.

He opened his arms, tears almost blinding him as she ran to him. Then he held her tightly — afraid that if he let her go, she would disappear. His kisses rained on to her face as his fingers delved into her glorious hair. How good it was to hold her again — to breathe her scent, taste the sweetness of her lips — and to know she was warm and real and finally in his arms where she belonged.

"I can't breathe." She giggled as she squirmed away. "You've lost none of your strength, Jack Quince," she teased. "Still handle a woman like a sheep in a shearing shed." She touched his face and studied him closely.

What did she see? Could she still love the crippled man who stood before her when her memories must be of a younger, stronger, fitter Jack? His pulse hammered as he prayed for a miracle.

"I've missed you." She blushed. She tipped back her head and looked up at him. "I've been waiting for this moment for so long that I can hardly believe I'm not dreaming." Hesitantly she touched his face again, her eyes shining with unshed tears. "I love you, Jack Quince," she whispered.

He was lost for words, so he dipped his head, kissed her softly and held her to his heart.

Eloise watched the passengers pour down the gangplanks and mingle with those who had gathered by the dock. The *Empress* was a pretty sight, and it was always exciting to see the new arrivals and to wonder what they'd brought to trade.

As her father talked on, her attention was caught by a solitary man whose stillness marked him out from the bustle on the quayside. She had an impression of a sturdy individual of late middle age, whose noble bearing was enhanced by the cut of his coat. He was watching the bustle on the quay, leaning nonchalantly on an ivory-handled cane, his tanned face unprotected by a hat, dark hair winged with silver. He seemed somehow familiar, but for the life of her she couldn't think why. She had no recollection of being introduced to him, and he wasn't a regular guest at the hotel.

He was soon forgotten as the high-stepping horses took them past the chain-gangs, the brick factory and the laundry, then finally towards Watsons Bay. It was a beautiful day, the sun shining from a clear blue sky, the breeze of their passage bringing pleasant relief from the heat that was building as noon approached. How good it was to be free again after her long confinement — if only Edward had permitted her to bring the baby her happiness would have been complete.

Eloise took no part in the conversation he was having with her father. She adjusted her parasol to keep the sun off her face and leant back against the comfortable leather cushioning. They were following the coastline through partially cleared bush, and the scent of eucalyptus and pine was heady. Flocks of parakeets and rosellas were darting back and forth, and above the jingle of harness and the thud of the horses' hoofs she could hear the laughter of kookaburras. She was surprised by how much she was enjoying the little expedition.

A glance at Edward told her he was sober for a change and had taken care with his attire. The red jacket was freshly pressed, the brass buttons and epaulettes winking in the sun. His breeches and stockings were as white as the Bavarian snow and his buckled shoes were polished. He was so handsome that few would suspect the ugliness within him. His dismissal of their son and his behaviour during her pregnancy still rankled.

They reached the top of a low hill. The sun sparkled on the ocean, drenching the pale grass with gold, and casting deep shadows beneath the trees. She spotted the unfinished house through a stand of eucalyptus, and although she hadn't expected to be impressed, she saw it was perfectly placed to catch the ocean breeze.

"What do you think?" asked Edward, and ordered the driver to halt the carriage.

She maintained the coolness that had become habitual over the past months when she addressed him. "Most attractive."

He seemed satisfied with that, and they moved on again. The carriage jolted over the rough ground and finally came to a halt beside the house. There was no sign of any work being done and Edward explained he'd given the men the day off.

Eloise took his proffered hand, climbed down from the carriage and turned at once to her father whose cheeks glowed red. "You appear a little heated," she said. "Perhaps it would be wiser to wear your hat rather than carry it?"

"Daughters!" he spluttered, in mock exasperation, to Edward. "They never cease their nagging." He rammed on his hat and stalked off through the long grass towards the house. "Come, my boy. Show me what all this fuss has been about."

Eloise saw her husband wince and couldn't help but smile. Her father had never been one for convention, and Edward's social standing didn't faze him. She trailed after them, and as her father began to ask questions, she examined the beautiful house with mixed emotions.

A stand of trees sheltered it from the winds, and several stables and barns had been erected on the far side of the broad paddock that lay at the back. The lines of the house were elegant despite the wooden scaffolding, the half-finished roof and chimneystack. Built squarely on the low rise, long windows on both floors gave access to deep verandas, decorated with wrought-iron lacework. The whole had been painted white, the shutters blue, and the front door was a slab of pale wood that had been carved with Edward's family crest. A gravel path ran through the untamed front garden to the beach where the sea rolled like molten glass and broke in a froth of white.

Eloise acknowledged the perfection, but felt little excitement. They would move in soon — and in every line and timber she could trace Edward's hand — but their marriage would have to change if she was ever to call the place home.

Edward answered the baron's numerous questions, but his attention was on his wife. She made a delightful picture, standing among the flowers, admiring his house. At last, he thought crossly, I've impressed her. Perhaps now she would thaw, and begin to appreciate what their marriage would afford her in the way of comfort and status in society.

He wanted to take her arm and lead her round the house, sharing his excitement as he showed her the marvellous views from the windows, the care he'd lavished on the staircase and fireplaces, the crystal chandeliers he'd imported from Italy — for this was the house he'd dreamt of building during the long years of exile. But he knew better than to try. Eloise had made it plain over the past weeks that she wanted little to do with him. He would have to mend his ways, be patient and let the house work its magic. Once she'd tired of the nursery she would seek his company again. Then perhaps they could return to the warmth they had shared briefly during the first two months of their marriage.

Niall Logan was eight years old and the shackles round his ankles hampered every step as he struggled to carry the heavy rock. He had come to New South Wales less than three weeks ago on the convict ship *Minerva*, and had quickly learnt that punishment was meted out regardless of age or crime.

He gritted his teeth as he clutched the rock to his chest and staggered over the rough ground. With the ache in his back and every tear in his flesh, his rage grew against his English captors. It had begun when he was barely weaned, for his family were staunch Catholics and railed against the unfairness of the British rule that kept the Irish enslaved without a voice.

"Hurry up, Mick bastard," shouted the overseer, as he loomed over him, "or you'll feel the lick of the cat."

Niall carried the rock to the pile and let it drop. His fingers were numb, the nails torn, and his stomach felt as if it was sticking to his backbone, he was so hungry, but he knew from past experience that to falter would earn him a lashing. His thoughts churned as he stumbled back to fetch another rock that the men were digging out to prepare the new road. The shock of his arrival in Sydney was as raw as ever, and as he bent to his task, he let the bitterness of those memories spur him to greater strength.

He had been taken with the other surviving boys from the *Minerva* to the stone penitentiary where they were assembled in a courtyard and ordered to strip off their lice-infested rags. Icy water had been thrown over them, and as they'd crouched, shivering and terrified, their heads had been roughly shaved. Starving and bewildered, Niall and the others had been given loose canvas trousers, shirts and ill-fitting boots.

The same overseer who watched him today had strutted into the yard, his bulk and ugly face an instant deterrent. Niall cringed as he remembered how the man had stridden along the lines of shivering boys and told them what punishments lay ahead if they broke the rules. The treadmill, the road gang and fifty lashes were dire enough, but the menace of the leatherhood still made his stomach clench. It was a diabolical instrument of torture, with buckles that fitted round the neck and back of the head, with only the smallest holes to breathe and see through. Those who were forced to wear it for the term of their punishment usually went mad.

Niall was from a poor family with too many mouths to feed and a house that leaked in winter, but his real education in survival had begun on that day. He'd learnt to remain silent and avoid a flogging, for to escape the hood and the lash was to believe in a future. To suffer a thousand cuts or be thrown into solitary confinement in the hood meant surrendering to despair and suicide. Yet each insult had become another spur in his determination not to be cowed and, like the other boys, he strove for the freedom to return home to Ireland.

His lack of concentration made him stumble, the weight of the chains dragging at his ankles and getting entangled with his feet. He fell to his knees on the sharp stones as the whip touched his shoulder, and his inborn hatred of the English burnt like a furnace. One day, he vowed, he would have his revenge.

Sydney Town, an hour later

"Let us complete the formalities and go home to Moonrakers." Jack looked down at her. "You do still want to marry me, don't you?" he asked, almost fearfully.

Alice nodded shyly and linked her arm in his. They left the ship and began to walk along the quay into the town. It felt strange to be beside him again, their pace hampered by his injured hip — she could remember how she'd had to run to keep up with him in Sussex. And yet this quiet shy man touched her heart in a way no other ever had, and she did not doubt the wisdom of coming so far to be with him.

Her initial pleasure in Sydney Town was lessened by the sight of male convicts breaking rocks for a new road, and she was forcibly reminded of Mr Carlton's warning. The men were a pathetic sight in their ragged clothes and heavy legirons, with the hard-faced overseers swishing whips and barking orders. The convict women appeared to be slightly better off, but how awful to have to wear that yellow as a mark of their status and work all day in this heat over the laundry cauldrons.

She tried not to react to the sight of boys hauling heavy rocks and struggling to push the overloaded barrows down the roughly laid road, but it was

72

impossible. "They're so young." She gripped Jack's arm. "Look at that little one. He can't be more than eight or nine, and he can hardly move with that chain round his ankles."

Jack's expression was grim, his thoughts perhaps on his own time in the death ship of the Second Fleet. "The British government takes no account of age," he replied. "They're sent here as we all were, and only the strongest survive." He gave a great sigh. "They're new here — the chains are only a temporary measure for the youngsters. But no child should be treated so. No man, either."

They flinched as the fat overseer flicked his whip over the bony back of a boy who'd paused for a breath. "Men like that should get a taste of their own medicine," he muttered, fists clenched.

Alice froze as the boy's head turned and their eyes met. In that moment she saw how young he was, how thin and pale, yet she was chilled by the hatred that shone from his eyes as the overseer threatened to strike him again. "We must do something to help," she said, and tugged at Jack's arm.

"We'd be breaking the law," he muttered, "and I have no wish to return to the chains. Come, Alice."

She was about to protest when she saw his expression and realised this was an everyday scene to Jack — but it was one she would never forget. She let him lead her away, but as she glanced back she caught the child's eye again and tried silently to offer solace. "Surely no child could have committed such a crime to be punished like this?"

"I suspect those boys were rounded up in Ireland as politicals," he replied. "At least they will be taught to read and write, and most will be apprenticed to the artisans among the other convicts. When they are freed, they'll be the carpenters, cobblers and bricklayers of the future."

"If they don't die first. Life on a Sussex farm might be hard for our youngsters, but it's never cruel."

"If you try to compare life in Sussex with what happens here you will never settle," he told her. His hand sought hers. "And there are good things here too," he said quietly.

She looked afresh at the town as they walked along the road to the government office where they would collect their special marriage licence and her land grant. First appearances had indeed been deceptive, for although there were several imposing buildings, most shelters were made of bark slabs with canvas roofs. There was little beauty to be seen away from the majesty of the countryside, just the harsh reality of a convict colony where colour and grandeur had been dimmed by cruelty.

Behind the facade of the graceful government building she noted the mean little shacks that passed for shops, the shanty dwellings and narrow alleys of the town's poorer inhabitants. She glimpsed drunken soldiers and sailors, whores, beggars and ragged children, saw shambling black men fighting over a bottle of rum, their women as violent as they screeched and clawed for the leftovers, and heard the accents of every county in the British Isles.

74

She lifted the hem of her skirts and put a handkerchief to her nose, for the stench was appalling: human and animal waste lay on the streets and in the gutters. This was no paradise, and she shuddered at the noise, the smell and the unbridled rawness. "Even Cape Town isn't as bad as this," she said. "The Dutch would never allow such — such . . . chaos."

"It isn't like this in the bush," said Jack, as they reached the registration office. "Please don't judge it until you've seen our place."

She saw the lines of worry in his face, and tried to hide her misgivings with a smile. She had waited so long to be with him — how could she falter now? She might dread what lay beyond these rough streets, but she'd come so far, had willingly left everything she'd ever known for the dearest of men. It was too late to change her mind, and with Jack by her side, she would do her best to make a good life here.

The magistrate's office was musty and, despite her good intentions, Alice discovered she was nervous as she stood beside Jack and waited for the brief ceremony to begin. She was about to marry the man she adored, but whom she barely knew any more — and their awkwardness with one another after so long apart made the prospect of intimacy daunting.

Jack seemed to sense her uncertainty and gripped her fingers. "Are you sure about this? We could always wait a few months."

"Are you having second thoughts?" she whispered back.

"Never," he breathed. "Just frightened you don't want me any more."

She returned the pressure of his fingers. "Now you're being silly. Of course I do."

The magistrate arrived with two clerks. "Your papers," he intoned.

Jack handed over his emancipation documents and Alice's birth certificate, and she saw his hand tremble. While the magistrate pored over the papers, she slipped her fingers back into his to give and take courage.

Yet she couldn't help but compare this day with the wedding they had planned so many years ago, for this was no village church resounding to the voices of a choir and a congregation of friends and family. There were no flowers, not even a bridal bouquet, and what lay beyond this dour government building was as alien as the moon.

"Do you, Jack Quince, take this woman to be your lawful wife?" asked the magistrate, who had yet to look at either of them.

Jack slipped his arm round Alice. "I do," he murmured.

"And do you, Alice Lily Hobden, take this man as your lawful husband?"

Alice leant into Jack's embrace. "I do."

"Then I pronounce you man and wife. The clerks will show you where to make your mark, and you will need to register in the other office for the lady's land grant."

Alice and Jack barely noticed him leave for they were preoccupied with each other. "I'm sorry this wasn't the wedding we'd hoped for, but you won't regret it," he whispered, "I promise."

Alice blushed at his intensity, and lowered her head shyly when she realised the clerks were watching them. "Let's get out of here," she said softly. "I have a gift for you on the ship."

"A gift?" His brow wrinkled. "But I have nothing for you." He ran his hands through his hair.

"You have given me my dreams," she replied. "Now, let's sign the papers and register for the three hundred acres that I'm entitled to."

It was swiftly done and they were soon making their way through the parklands that fronted Government House to the docks and the *Empress*.

Alice could barely contain her excitement as she led Jack into the hold.

"Alice!" he exclaimed. "You clever girl! But however did you afford them?"

She was grinning like an urchin. "It's cheap to live in Cape Town, and I thought we could do with a few more animals to boost the flock." She gazed at him in the dim light of the open hatch. "How are our sheep, anyway? I hope you've been looking after them?"

He gathered her into his arms. "Oh, Alice," he said, after he'd kissed her. "They're eating their heads off and dropping healthy lambs every season. I can't wait to show them to you."

She hugged him back. "And I can't wait to see them."

They unloaded Bertie and the merinos, then packed Alice's few belongings with the stores at the back of

Jack's wagon. The sun was already disappearing below the horizon as they set off for Moonrakers.

Her first day in her new homeland was almost over, and as the wagon took them further from Sydney, Alice became aware of a contentment she had never felt before. The clip-clop of the horses' hoofs and the jingle of harness were familiar, and when Jack's muscled arm brushed against her she shivered with pleasure.

Yet as they moved deeper into the forested landscape, so different from any she'd seen before, she felt awkward to be truly alone with him. Silence had fallen, and when she peeped at him, she saw the tension in his jaw. It seemed they had nothing to say to one another.

Jack cleared his throat and tipped the brim of his hat even lower over his brow. "It's only fifteen or twenty miles as the crow flies to Parramatta," he said, his gaze fixed on the woolly backs of the sheep plodding in front of them, "but we have to travel through the bush, which will mean spending the night out here."

Alice saw his cheeks redden and felt heat rise in her own. "What's Parramatta?" she asked, her voice unsteady. "You told me the farm was called Moonrakers."

He cleared his throat again and fiddled with the reins. "It's the settlement nearby. The name means 'the place where the eels lie down'. It comes from the natives."

"Are there many natives in Parramatta?"

"We have a small clan on Moonrakers, and others come and go. They don't usually stay for long in one place."

Alice recalled the drunken black men and women she'd seen in Sydney. "Are they friendly?" Her voice sounded small.

He smiled. "To the point of being a nuisance at times. Their women filch our stores and hang about the homestead, and the men are always disappearing on what they call 'walkabout in never-never' when there's any work to be done."

Alice was intrigued and forgot her shyness. "Tell me about them," she begged. "And tell me everything about Moonrakers."

"The blacks were already on the land when Billy, Nell and me arrived. We decided there was enough acreage to go round, and as long as they didn't kill the sheep or cause trouble they'd be treated with respect." He grinned. "Nell wasn't too impressed, but she and three of the women have become quite friendly over the years, and they help with the children."

Alice digested this news and welcomed it: surely Nell wouldn't leave her family in the care of drunken savages. "Tell me about our land, Jack," she coaxed, "and our house, the sheep, and the convicts you employ — and all about Nell, Billy and the children."

He looked down at her fondly. "You'll soon see for yourself, and to tell you everything would take longer than this journey." He laughed as she poked him in the ribs. "The land stretches for miles and there's a river running right through it that's alive with eels, so we'll never go hungry."

He must have seen her grimace, for he laughed. "I know you've never liked them, but when you're hungry you'll eat anything." He paused, then went on, "The house is small and a bit rough, but it'll do for now, and the convicts prefer being with us than risk the lash in town, so they're a good bunch and willing workers. As for the sheep, they're flourishing."

"Is Nell easy to get on with?" Alice had read Jack's letters carefully, and although Nell was an emancipated convict, her background — in prostitution — made Alice wary.

"She might be flamboyant, and inclined to lose her temper when she doesn't get her own way, but she's a good mother, and one of the friendliest people I know." He concentrated on steering the wagon over a deep rut. "She and Billy met on the hulks, and came over on the First Fleet, so they're true pioneers."

Alice thought it all wildly romantic. "It's exciting, isn't it? Who would have thought we'd end up on the other side of the world with more land than we ever dreamt of?"

His warm brown hand covered hers as he leant over to plant a kiss on her cheek. "You haven't changed since you were a little girl, Alice." His tone was teasing. "You always had an interest in adventure. I reckon I've got what my old dad used to call a 'good woman'."

She nudged him and giggled. "Behave, Jack Quince."

He shot her a glance filled with mischief. "What kind of order is that on our wedding day?"

80

Alice blushed furiously and pretended to be absorbed in the trees, but she heard Jack's chuckle and couldn't quite hide her own smile, for their old teasing way with one another had returned.

As they travelled deeper into the bush Jack brought the horse to a halt so he could kiss her again. Alice melted into his embrace as his warm lips sent a tingle through her. When they finally drew apart they caught one another's eye and broke into laughter. "If we keep on like this we'll never get home," he said.

Alice no longer cared how much time they spent alone, but after another kiss, Jack took up the reins again. "I need to make camp before nightfall," he reminded her, "and pen these sheep so the dingoes can't take them."

Alice was a practical woman and she accepted this wisdom happily. Soon she was asking Jack the names of the different trees, giant ferns and flowers that grew so abundantly in the forest.

Jack had to keep stilling the horse as he pointed out the paper barks, the ghost gums and black she-oaks, and laughed with her as they watched a family of possums at play in the branches of a she-oak. Alice marvelled at the white parrots with bright yellow crests that squabbled and jostled in the branches, and clapped with delight as tiny blue and green budgerigars darted and swooped round them. The contrast between their freedom and the plight of caged birds in England saddened her, and she was reminded, too, of the shackled children in Sydney Town.

"I know what you're thinking, but it'll do no good, Alice. Just be happy that we're free and have found one another again."

She tucked her arm through his and rested her head on his shoulder. It was as if they had spent no time apart — as if they were riding back from a day's harvesting, their dreams of their future keeping them warm and close.

Jack set up the night's camp in a glade. He fixed a makeshift pen with strips of calico to stop the sheep wandering, and hobbled the horses. Alice noticed that Bertie didn't seem to mind the strangeness of his surroundings and was quite happy to rip at the tough grass with his yellowing teeth. She watched as Jack spread blankets on the ground, checked his rifle, and dug a pit for a fire as they were serenaded by a laughing bird. "Whatever's that?"

"The natives call it a kookaburra, and the white men the laughing jackass."

Alice perched on a fallen tree to watch him set a billycan over the flames, and place dough in the hot ashes. She saw how he wrapped the fish they'd bought at the quay in the broad flat leaves of a nearby bush and set them on the hot stones. It was obvious he'd become familiar with the ways of this untamed country, and although she'd lived all her life on a farm, she knew she had a lot to learn. Today had been filled with different emotions and conflicting impressions of this rather frightening country. What hidden terrors lurked in the darkness beyond the glade — and what awaited her at Moonrakers? Then she saw the contentment in his face, the love in his eyes, as he brought over their supper, and knew that whatever lay ahead they would face it with the inbred strength of character that had seen them through the loneliness and hardships of the past.

As the sun sank slowly behind the trees, the sky was set alight with streaks of gold, orange and red. Birds returned to their roosts and numberless insects began their night chatter. Alice lay in his arms on the blanket and watched the celestial display. Even the stars in Africa couldn't compete with this.

As night descended and Jack drew her close beneath the blanket, she experienced a wave of such love that the rest of the world faded into insignificance. The waiting was over. She had come home.

CHAPTER
FOUR

On the track to Parramatta, the next day

Alice became more apprehensive as they drew nearer to Moonrakers and, despite her determination to remain confident, she couldn't help but seek Jack's reassurance.

"We're a long way from anywhere," she began, as they trundled along at almost walking pace. "Is our farm the only one out here?"

Jack put his arm round her. "Elizabeth Farm is only a few miles away, and there's a couple of smaller holdings just to the west of us."

"Are they nice people on Elizabeth Farm?" She didn't like the wistful note that had crept into her voice, but she couldn't hide her longing for a sense of community.

"Mrs Macarthur's a pleasant lady by all accounts," he began, "but we don't see much of either of them."

She heard the wariness in his voice. "Why?"

He shrugged. "The Macarthurs are the biggest landowners in our area, and already way ahead of everyone else with their sheep and crops." He hesitated, as if he were seeking the right words to explain their neighbours. "John Macarthur might only have started out as an officer in the New South Wales Corps, but now he's a very rich, powerful man. He and his wife are not the sort to socialise with the likes of us."

Alice remained silent as he struggled to explain. "In their eyes Billy, Nell and I are still convicts, Alice, and regardless of our pardons and the work we've put into our land, we will always remain so."

"That's ridiculous."

Jack's smile was wan. "Yes. But the strict rules of the British class system are even more firmly entrenched here. We are the 'stain' on the colony, and will remain so for the rest of our lives, never mind what we achieve."

"But our children will be free citizens," she said firmly. "The so-called 'stain' won't touch them." She saw doubt in his face. "Surely?"

"Who's to say?"

Alice fell silent, her gaze on the shifting, dusty backs of the sheep before them. Life here would be similar to that in England. There was little hope of change or advancement — why had she been so naïve as to expect anything different?

It was as if he could read her thoughts. "We have advantages here we would never have in England," he said quietly. "For every hundred acres we clear we receive a hundred more — and the government guarantees to buy our crops and give us free labour, with supplies, until we become self-sufficient."

Alice smiled, but her heart was heavy. Free land was all very well — but would Jack and the following generations ever be free of their convict status?

"We're almost there," he murmured, some time later. He drew the wagon to a halt and took her hands. "I can't promise you an easy life, Alice," he said gently, "and, like me, you'll have to learn to put aside many of your old prejudices."

She was about interrupt when he stilled her with a light kiss. "Billy might have been a banker for smugglers, and Nell might once have been a whore — but they're good, hard-working people who have turned from their old ways and want only to make the best of what they have. If we work together, and forget the past, we'll have one of the best farms in New South Wales."

She kissed him, love pushing aside doubt. This was a new country, promising a new life, and although the system was unfair, and her partners in this enterprise were convicted criminals, she had to forget that and get on with living.

With a slap of the reins the horse was once more coaxed into pulling the wagon, and a few well-aimed flicks of the whip kept the sheep on the move. As they crested the final hill and emerged from the trees, Alice had her first glimpse of her new home.

The sun was on the wane, the sky ablaze with orange streaks. The sweeping corn fields and soft undulations of the earth were gilded, as were the myriad streams and rivers that meandered through the valley. Stands of trees seemed to swim in the heat of the dying sun's furnace, their leaves wilting, silver bark ablaze. And there, sprawling on the crest of a low rise and overlooking the streams, was a single-storey house.

There was no thatch, no limewash or flint walls, just a solid wooden house with a tiled roof and a deep, shady veranda.

"It's lovely." She hardly dared to believe that such beauty, such vastness, could be found after the dark terrors of the bush, and the darker deeds of Sydney Town. The narrow lanes, huddled villages and wild hedgerows of Sussex were indeed a world away from the sweep of empty country before her.

"Our place is over there," he said, pointing upstream. "It's a bit small, but should do us for a while until . . ." He stirred the horse into a fast walk.

The second house was sheltered by a stand of trees. It was roughly built of wood, with a tiled roof and a stout stone chimney, and was certainly not as grand as the other dwelling — but there was a broad veranda to provide shade, and the whole was surrounded by a clearing of rich black earth. The grazing was lush, the water plentiful and, by the look of things, the sheep were thriving. Moonrakers held far greater promise than she'd expected, and for the first time in many hours her excitement began to return.

The track was rough and pitted, and she was tossed about like a sack of potatoes. Alice thought of their unborn children as she clung to the side of the wagon. If they were blessed, her life would be complete.

They reached the riverbank, and Alice was puzzling as to how they would cross when Jack gave a piercing whistle. A number of figures appeared on the far bank, some white, but mostly black. Alice stared at the natives, in awe of them and the way they pointed at her, but she sensed they were simply curious.

The convicts gathered some distance away and began to pull on sturdy ropes that had been tied to thick posts set in the riverbank. She gathered up her skirts, climbed down and brought the wandering sheep back into order as she watched a raft emerge from the rushes and float towards them.

Jack tied it firmly and turned back to her. "I'll cross with the sheep, then send the raft for you and the wagon."

She had serious misgivings about getting recalcitrant sheep on to a flimsy raft, and she hadn't come this far to see them drown during the last half-mile. She quickly gathered up some fresh grass. Two of the sheep followed the trail she was laying, and as she stepped on to the raft, the others followed.

She grinned up at Jack as he took off his hat and wiped away the sweat. "Now it's up to you to get them across without drowning their silly selves," she said.

"Right," he replied, flashing her a smile. "But you're in charge of the wagon and horses. Are you sure you can manage?"

"I've managed well enough on my own for years," she retorted. "I'm not completely helpless."

He reddened, and Alice grinned to take the sting out of her reprimand.

She saw that it would be easier to steer the horses and wagon on to the raft if she remained on foot, so she unhitched Bertie, and stood between them, firmly grasping their harness. She tensed as she watched the slow progress of the raft. The sheep were unsettled and crotchety after the long sea journey, then the trek through the bush, and jostled one another, bleating. The rams, thankfully, were too nervous to lock horns, but stood still as the water rushed past them.

As the raft reached the other side the animals sprang into action, leaping to safety, hurdling ropes and rushes, then bouncing off into the long grass. Alice had visions of her precious merinos disappearing for ever but Jack gave another piercing whistle and a collie appeared from an outbuilding to round them up.

As she waited for the raft, she watched the dog herd the mob into a pen and Jack shut the gate. With a sigh of relief, she led the horses down the slope to the raft.

Bertie tossed his head and tried to back away, his great feet threatening to crush her toes, but Jack's horse was clearly used to this strange mode of transport and stepped decorously on to the raft with an air of disdain for his companion.

Alice engaged the brake on the wagon wheels to ensure it didn't roll over the side and coaxed Bertie into behaving. She was determined not to look foolish, for she was well aware of the male audience on the other side of the river, and could hear the natives' excited babble.

Bertie would have none of it. He stamped and snorted, shook his head and showed his teeth. Alice grabbed his mane. "Move your backside, you useless lump," she muttered, showing him the whip. "Or else . . ."

Bertie's great head drooped dolefully, his lip curled in petulance. The sight of the whip was just another burden — and he'd suffered considerably . . . With a great sigh, he reluctantly put one heavy hoof on the raft, then another.

Before he could think, or panic at his precarious situation, Alice shoved him up beside the other horse, and unhitched the ropes. Now they were moving slowly across the water. "Good boy," she murmured, offering him the apple she'd hidden in her pocket. He took it from her palm and proceeded to crunch.

As the raft bumped the other side and willing hands reached out to help with the wagon, Alice guided Bertie on to firm ground and patted his neck. He might have the temperament of a spoilt child, but she loved him.

"Blimey! Never thought you'd get the old bugger across — you done well, there, girl."

Alice jumped at the sound of a woman's voice, and her smile faltered as she took in, first, the red hair, then the revealing scarlet dress with its green ribbons and gold tassels that did nothing to hide Nell's advanced pregnancy. Jack had used the word "flamboyant" to describe her, which now seemed inadequate. "Thank you," she said.

Nell's blue eyes sparkled as she tossed back her curls and tucked her hand round Alice's waist. "Nice to meet yer at last," she said. "I feel I already know you — Jack's been goin' on about you for years. It's lonely out 'ere without another woman to talk to, though, and I've been lookin' forward so to you gettin' 'ere."

Alice was smothered in a tight embrace and almost overcome by the cheap scent Nell had applied liberally.

Finally Nell released her and stepped back, her smile wavering. "Sorry. Billy always says I'm too eager — but you've no idea how much the sight of another woman means to me."

Alice heard the longing in Nell's voice, saw the delight in her eyes, and knew she was being unfair. "It's good to be here at last," she said, with a smile.

Nell beamed. "I put me best frock on specially," she said, twirling to display an almost naked back and the tops of her drawers. "It's a bit tight, and I couldn't do up all the lacin' 'cos of the sprog, but d'ya like it?"

Alice could only nod. The dress was fit only for a barmaid in the worst kind of tavern. However, Nell seemed content, and tucked her hand into the crook of her arm, pulling her towards the house. "Come in, meet the children, and we can 'ave a talk before tea."

Alice glanced towards Jack, but he was with the other men, his back turned as the stores were stacked away. The wagon had been unhitched and the horses were already cropping the grass in a nearby paddock while the natives leant on the fence or squatted beside it. The sheep were milling in the pen, the dog sitting by the gate, tongue lolling. It seemed she had been forgotten.

"Don't be mindin' them," said Nell. "They'll be out there talkin' about sheep long after dark. Come and rest yer bones. You must be done in after that journey."

Alice felt a prickle of unease as she followed Nell up the steps. She had been raised by strict, God-fearing parents who would have been appalled by Nell's clothing.

The large single room was clearly the hub of the house, and as she stepped through the door she was pleasantly surprised. It was sparsely furnished, but as neat as a pin, without the garish frills and flounces she'd expected. Nell was a good housekeeper despite her blowsy appearance and rough tongue.

"This is Amy," said Nell, with pride, as a little girl looked up from her wooden toys. "She's six, and these two rascals are me twins, Walter and Sarah." She shrugged. "His name's William, really, but it were awkward 'avin' two in the 'ouse. Come as a shock to me and Billy, I can tell you, them arrivin' as they did — but the more the merrier's what I say." She grinned and patted her belly.

Alice smiled at the little girl, then looked across at the chubby babies who had fallen asleep on the day-bed, entwined like a couple of kittens. She felt a tug of longing, and hoped that one day she, too, would have one of her own. "They're so pretty," she said, as she took the proffered chair at the table. "You are lucky, Nell. But how did you find a midwife out here?"

Nell laughed. "No midwife worth 'er salt ever comes this far," she said cheerfully. "It's a case of gettin' on with it yerself." She must have seen the concern in Alice's face, for she patted her hand and smiled. "But when your time comes I'll be 'ere, and 'avin' 'ad three of me own, I reckons I know a thing or two about birthin'."

Alice tried to smile, but her face wouldn't work properly, so she reached for Amy who was standing at her knee and pulled her on to her lap. She hadn't given a thought to such things, had merely assumed there would be a midwife in this colonial outpost, just as there had been in Cape Town — but it appeared she was mistaken. She tried to concentrate on the cat's cradle Amy was making with a length of wool, but her mind refused to be still. There was a lot to learn, and the shock of discovering she was ill-prepared for life here was sobering.

Nell crashed and clattered at the kitchen end of the room as she kept up a stream of chatter, producing tea and home-made biscuits on thick china. She plucked one of the waking twins from its nest of blankets, plumped herself into a chair, and proceeded to nurse him. "I know 'e's a bit old for this, but it keeps 'im quiet," she confided. "Walter's a greedy little beggar and no mistake. Just like 'is dad."

Alice drank her tea. Her face reddened as Jack entered the room. "This is Billy," he said, and nodded towards the man who followed him. "He might behave like a gentleman, but be warned, Alice, he's a scallywag." He winked.

Alice gazed at the handsome, dark-haired man with laughing eyes. He certainly had the look of a rogue about him, with that grin and the lick of hair that curled over his brow, but as he took her hand and kissed the air above her fingers she understood why Nell had fallen in love with him. "Pleased to meet you at last, Alice," he said, his Cornish accent still apparent.

"It's been a long wait, and Jack's been makin' a right freck." He grinned at his friend and slapped his back. "He came to have the look of a winnard at times, but now he's back to his usual cheerful self, so maybe I'll be getting some work out of him at last."

"Billy!" Jack remonstrated.

"Ha-ha!" roared Billy, his hair flopping over his eyes. "You're goin' redder than a girl."

Jack gave him a shove.

Alice could see the affection in which they held one another, and although she only understood part of what Billy was saying, she realised the two men were as close as brothers. As she watched them joke together she tried to ignore Nell, who was laughing and chattering as she carried on feeding her baby as if it was natural to do so in mixed company. Had the woman no shame? And what of Jack? Didn't he feel awkward at such a sight? But it appeared Jack was used to it, and paid Nell little heed as he and Billy got down to discussing sheep.

Alice needed to get away — from Nell and the suckling child, from the noise and clatter. "I think I'll go and tend my sheep," she said, her words cutting through the chatter. "I want to make sure they're settled." She looked at Jack. "Then we can move them on to our place with the others. Have you got pens down there?"

"They'll be penned where they are," said Jack, as he let Amy swing from his arm. "Then, once they've been drenched, we can let them loose in the paddock with the rest."

Alice frowned. "Surely it'd be better to move them just the once? If we take them to our paddock now, they'll settle sooner."

Nell sat her sated child on the floor, gave him a biscuit and covered her breast. "There ain't no *your* paddock or *our* paddock," she said. "This place belongs to all of us."

"But the sheep are mine," replied Alice. "Mine and Jack's. And I want them near our place so I can keep an eye on them."

"Alice." Jack's voice held a note of warning. "Nell's right. We have equal shares in everything. I thought you understood that?"

Alice rose from the chair and faced him. "The land share I understand, but you never said anything about the merinos."

"I thought you knew," he said quietly, his gaze darting from one face to another.

"Yeah," broke in Nell, hands on her hips, fiery hair glowing in the lamplight. "Share and share alike — cows, 'orses, crops, convict labour and sheep."

"We all need to calm down," drawled Billy, as he stretched out his legs and lit a pipe. "It's dinner time and me belly thinks me throat's been cut."

Alice glared at him. She was exhausted after the long journey, while the terrors and uncertainties of this new land had brought her to the end of her patience. She turned back to Nell. "I sold everything I had to buy those sheep," she said. "I've travelled alone across dangerous seas to be here — lived with the knowledge I could be murdered for the purse of gold I carried —

and battled to get the merinos at a fair price. The sheep are mine."

"No, they're not," snapped Nell. "Jack and me and Billy 'ave worked our arses off to get this place goin'. We've earned them sheep just as much as you."

"My money paid for them," retorted Alice, "and unless you want to buy them from me, they remain mine."

"If Jack 'adn't give you 'is farm, you wouldn't 'ave had no money to buy 'em in the first place. And in the second place, who the bloody 'ell do you think you are, comin' 'ere layin' down the bloody law?" Billy shot Nell a warning look, but it was ignored. "You think you've 'ad it rough? Try a convict transport ship, lady — then you'll learn what rough is."

Alice was furious. "Some of us lead decent, honest lives," she hissed. "If you'd managed to keep your drawers on, you wouldn't have had to see the inside of a transport ship."

"I'll 'ave yer eyes for that, bitch!" Nell's fingers were clawed as she lunged at Alice.

Unused to being attacked, Alice was rooted to the spot.

Billy grabbed Nell round her thickened waist and struggled to keep her under control as she fought to get at Alice. "For God's sake, Jack," he shouted. "Get your wife out of here."

Jack took her arm. His face was pale. "You're tired and that sort of talk will get none of us anywhere. Why don't we go to our house and discuss it quietly?"

She threw off his restraining hand. "Don't patronise me, Jack Quince. You've got a lot of explaining to do —

96

and I want to know why that *trollop* has a share in my sheep." With that she left the house, the door slamming behind her.

Nell kicked and squirmed until Billy gauged it was safe to let her go. "Hardly the best start," he murmured, a smile tweaking his lips.

"Get off back to bloody Sussex," shouted Nell towards the shut door.

In the ensuing silence she eyed Billy as she eased her bulk on to a hard chair. The children had remained unfazed throughout, but they were used to her temper. "I knew it the minute I saw 'em! Them bloody sheep'll be more trouble than they're worth. The sooner 'er and 'er flamin' animals are off the place the better. Can do without 'er sort 'ere — and that's a fact."

Billy's eyes were twinkling and his mouth twitched with a smile he could no longer contain. "Seems like you've met your match, Nell, and no mistake."

The temper tantrum died as swiftly as it had been born. She threw back her head and roared with laughter. "Trollop!" she spluttered. "She called me a trollop!"

Billy chortled. "I reckon you and she'll end up the best of friends."

Nell was still smiling as she packed a clay pipe with tobacco. "Don't count on it just yet, mate. That one's got a lot of learnin' to do first."

Alice strode away from the house, her anger taking her ahead of Jack, who was hobbling behind, calling for her to stop. She was determined their argument would not be held in the open for all to witness — and there would be an argument because she would not stay at Moonrakers with that harpy a minute longer.

Her breath was ragged as she stormed over the rough clearing and took the shallow steps up to the porch. The front door was open, and she could see the interior. It was half the size of the other house — and shabby in comparison — which was another bone of contention.

She let the door slam behind her and stood in the middle of the main room, arms folded, chest heaving, as she waited for Jack.

Eventually he appeared, out of breath and in distress.

"You're letting in the mosquitoes," she snapped, determined not to yield at the sight of his ashen pallor and pronounced limp.

"Alice," he begged, "please don't be like this." He closed the door, plunging them into darkness until he'd lit a lamp. Night had fallen abruptly. "I know you're tired," he continued, as he stood before her, "but you had no right to say that to Nell."

"No right to tell her the sheep are ours? Or no right to call her a trollop?" Her voice was dangerously low, scarcely containing the anger she knew might explode at any moment.

"No right to say either."

"So you take her part?"

He ran his fingers through his hair, making the shock of white stand on end. He looked far older than forty-one, and appeared haggard in the lamplight as he leant against the rough wooden table to ease his crippled hip. "There are no parts." He sighed. "Like it or not, Alice, the farm, the stock, the sheep and everything you see belongs to all of us."

Alice was unmoved by his distress and pain. "Jack, she's a whore and he's a thief, and if you think I'm about to hand over my sheep and live alongside them, you're mistaken."

He took a step towards her, thought better of it and sank into a chair. "Nell's no whore," he said, as he eased his hip and rubbed his knee. "She might flare up now and again, but she's a good wife, housekeeper and mother. She rarely complains, and works as hard as any of us." His dark eyes were troubled. "As for Billy, he's the best friend a man could have and I'll not let you blacken his reputation."

"If I didn't know better, I'd have thought you were discussing pillars of the community, not convicted criminals." Alice could hear the sarcasm in her voice, disliked it, but was beyond caring.

"You forget, Alice," he said flatly, "I'm also a convicted criminal. Are you refusing to live and work beside me?"

"That's not what I meant," she blustered. "You're innocent of any crime."

"Not in the eyes of the law."

"Maybe not. But you're a decent man. That woman would have had my eyes out, given half a chance. She's got no shame, with her clothes hanging off her, nursing her baby in front of you and anyone else who might walk through the door."

"That's *enough*." Jack slammed his hand on the table with such ferocity that Alice flinched. He stood up and moved with a speed surprising in one so lame. He grasped her wrist. "Sit down, Alice," he said, "and hold your tongue."

She obeyed, her anger pierced now by fear. This was not the gentle, quiet-spoken Jack Quince she'd known for most of her life.

"Nell was an orphan of the workhouse," he growled. "She was barely seven when the man in charge began to pass her round his friends. She was ten when she ran away. She wasn't protected by a close-knit country community where there was always someone to care for her — she didn't have a family and an education like you and me."

Alice saw the anger in his eyes, but it was no longer aimed at her, and for that she was grateful. But she was beginning to understand what had made Nell the woman she was, and a shaft of pity doused her fury.

"Nell came here on a convict ship, just as I did, but she was violated by the guards and sailors, starved and chained in the holds with violent men. She kept her spark and survived. She's served a much longer sentence than Billy and me, and it's because of her fighting spirit that we have this flourishing farm."

Alice was chastened. "I'm sorry," she murmured.

"You'll say that to Nell, not me," he retorted. "She's the one who deserves it."

She was aghast. The thought of Nell gloating over her climb-down was too awful to contemplate. "I can't," she whispered.

100

His gaze was steady, his expression set. "You will," he said quietly, "or I'll take you back to Sydney and put you on the first ship home."

Nell's disappointment slowed her footsteps as she moved round the house, tending Billy and the children. She'd foolishly assumed that she and Alice would be instant friends. How wrong she'd been, she thought, as she settled the twins and prepared to sing them a lullaby. Alice had notions far above her station, and she couldn't understand why Jack loved her.

She gazed down at her twins, their eyelids fluttering with the onset of sleep, and knew she was blessed. With Amy asleep in the other cot and Billy smoking his pipe on the veranda, her life had turned out very differently from how she'd expected — and if Alice thought she could come here and disrupt everything . . .

"Flamin' 'eck," she groaned, as a sudden band of pain girdled her swollen belly and squeezed. This pregnancy had been difficult compared with the others. She'd suffered with sickness, headaches and dragging pains all the way through — but on her only visit to the infirmary in Sydney Town, she'd been assured all was well. Now she was about to go into labour.

She leant against the wall, biting back a whimper — she mustn't wake the children. Cursing softly, she waited until it had ebbed, then tottered out of the house in search of Billy.

He was sitting in a chair on the veranda, at peace with his pipe and the great silence of the outback night.

"Look at the stars, Nell," he said. "They're so clear, it's almost as if you could reach out and touch them."

"To 'ell with the stars." She gasped, as another band encircled her. "The baby's on its way and it's in a bloody 'urry."

Billy shot to his feet and guided her back into the house. "How long have you known?"

"A while," she panted. The pains had started shortly after Alice and Jack had left, but she'd been too fired up to pay them much heed. She told Billy to prepare water and a sharp knife, then help her strip the bed. The pains were relentless now, coming swiftly in a crescendo of agony. Her waters broke and she pulled off her sodden clothes and tried to find a comfortable position on the bed.

"Should I fetch Alice?" Billy was hovering at the foot of the bed.

"No," Nell ground out. "I managed before, and I'll do it again without 'er." She arched her back and grasped the iron bedstead as she felt the urge to push. "Go and find something to do, Bill," she snapped. "You're makin' me nervous."

She didn't hear him leave, was unaware of him pacing the floor outside, or the piping voices of the waking children: her attention was focused on the ruthless, tearing determination of her child to be born.

The sweat drenched her as she strained and pushed. Wave upon wave of nausea and fear mingled with the agony as she struggled to give it life — but it seemed determined to remain inside her.

102

Finally she fell exhausted against the pillows, in tears of frustration and anguish. Something was very wrong — she knew it as surely as night followed day.

The colour had bleached from Alice's face. "You can't mean that?"

"Alice, I've loved you since I was a boy, and it was my dream to make you my wife, but circumstances have changed us. We aren't the children we once were."

She saw he was serious and was about to reply when he held up his hand to silence her. "I admire your strength and independence, but I can't allow them to destroy everything we've built here. Billy, Nell and I have paid the price of our freedom, and we will defend it regardless of any sacrifice."

"You would sacrifice our marriage?" Her voice was small.

"Even that," he replied, his eyes sad. "You see, Alice, England abandoned us to perish or survive. There's no going back, no ties to bind us to her any more, so we're determined to make the best of what we have here. One day, Alice, England will realise what can be achieved by men and women once thought worthless — our children and their children's children will know we weren't cowed."

The tears were hot on Alice's face. She had never heard him speak so passionately or with such conviction. "You were never worthless to me," she sobbed, "and I'm sorry I lost my temper." She took his hands, so rough from his labours but so dear to her. "Please don't send me back."

"You'll say sorry to Nell?"

"Must I?"

"If you love me you will."

"That's blackmail, Jack." She released his hands.

"If that's what it takes to put things right, then so be it," he said stubbornly.

Alice bit her lip. Jack had always been mulish, and in this he hadn't changed. She was about to continue the argument, but thought better of it. If they were to have any kind of life together she would have to do as he asked — but the quarrel with Nell still rankled, and she was damned if she would let the woman have it all her way. She rose from the table. "I'll do it," she said softly, "but only because I love you."

"The lamps are still burning over there," he said, gesturing towards the window. "No time like the present."

He was testing her, and she didn't know how she felt about that. She had been independent for so long and it was hard to follow orders. Yet she would do it for him — for them both.

As she reached for the latch he stopped her. "Thank you," he breathed, as he kissed away her tears. "I never wanted you to cry, but I had to make you see how things are."

Alice forgave him and leant into his embrace, vowing that from now on she would keep her opinions to herself and her temper in check. Jack and the others had experienced horrors she could barely imagine, and her arrogance had come close to destroying her marriage.

They smiled at one another as they left the house, and she tucked her hand into his elbow as they walked through the moonlight. The stars were magnificent, the moon like a gold coin reflected in the meandering river. Everything would be all right.

"Thank God you're here!" Billy raced down the steps to meet them. He grabbed Alice and dragged her towards the door where the children stood in their nightclothes. "Quick!" he rasped. "Nell's in trouble!"

"What's happened?"

Billy ran his hand distractedly through his tousled hair. "The baby's stuck and won't be born — we've tried everything."

Alice gathered up her skirt and flew past the children into the house. She didn't need to be shown the way for she could hear Nell's groans. She ran across the main room to the bedroom doorway.

Nell was contorted on bloodied sheets as she struggled to reach down and drag out the baby.

"No!" Alice darted across the room. "Let me help you — let me see what's wrong."

"Gerroff!" Nell twisted in pain, her face scarlet.

Alice grasped her knees. "Stop pushing," she said. "You're making it worse."

Nell panted and groaned as Alice examined her. "It's breech," she said. "I'll have to turn it."

"Whad'ya know about birthin'?" yelled Nell. "Don't you flamin' touch me, or I'll 'ave yer eyes."

Alice spied the basin of water on the nightstand. She went across to it, then soaped her arms and hands.

"I've birthed more sheep than you can count," she snapped, "so stop pushing, and let me get on."

Nell slumped back on the pillows. "I s'pose I ain't got no choice."

"This'll hurt," warned Alice. "Take that, and bite down on it."

Nell took the belt and clenched it between her teeth. "You'd better know what you're doin'," she growled.

Alice picked up the knife.

As Nell screeched the belt fell out of her mouth. "You ain't cuttin' me with that!" She lashed out and caught Alice a glancing blow to the side of the face.

Alice hit her back and held the knife to her throat. "If I don't cut you, the baby will die and so will you."

Nell replaced the belt between her teeth and screwed her eyes shut. "Get on with it, then," she mumbled.

Alice was sweating as she sent up a swift prayer to the Almighty for help. She was fully aware of the danger to mother and baby, but the labour was so far advanced she had no other option but to widen the birth passage so that she could ease the baby into a better line.

Nell screamed as Alice pushed aside the baby's bottom and grabbed its legs. She screamed again as the shoulders appeared.

"Don't move!" snapped Alice. "The cord's round his neck."

Nell froze, her pain forgotten. "I 'ope to Gawd you know what yer doin'," she moaned.

Alice put a finger beneath the cord, cut it with the knife and tied both ends. She eased out the head — and her heart sank.

"Is it all right? Why ain't it cryin'?" shrieked Nell.

The baby's skin was marbled with death. Alice slapped the tiny behind, hoping to startle him into life.

He didn't move.

"He's dead, isn't he?" Nell was sobbing.

Alice was too busy to answer. She breathed into his mouth and gently massaged the little chest, desperate for some sign of life.

He still didn't move.

With a sob of despair she raced with him into the kitchen. "Cold water," she shouted, to the startled men and children who'd gathered there.

She followed their pointing fingers and plunged the baby into the bucket. "Now get me hot water," she ordered. "Come on, little one, breathe! For the love of God, please breathe!"

She plunged him into the hot water, then back into the cold. "Please, please, God, don't let him be dead," she sobbed, as she repeated the dousing over and over again and tried to blow life into the little mouth.

"He's gone, Alice. There's nothing any of us can do."

Alice glanced up into Billy's tear-streaked face, then returned to her desperate task. "There is," she wailed, through her sobs. "He mustn't be dead. I won't let him."

Nell stayed her by reaching for her baby and cradling him in her arms. "Leave 'im be," she said, as tears fell down her cheeks. "You done all you could. It weren't meant for 'im to live."

"I'm so sorry," sobbed Alice, into her hands, as she slumped to the floor. "So very sorry for everything, and

I wish . . ." But Nell and Billy had taken their children into the bedroom and closed the door firmly behind them.

"She knows, Alice," murmured Jack. He helped her up and put his arm round her as he led her to a chair. "I'm so proud of you. Nell would have died with her baby if it hadn't been for you."

Alice attempted to dry her tears, but they wouldn't be stemmed. "She needs to be stitched. And I was so nasty to her, shouting at her, bullying her . . ."

Jack held her tightly. "You did what you had to do," he said softly. "The stitching can wait till morning."

She sniffed and looked at him through swollen eyelids. "There's the risk of infection, you know that."

"Ewes aren't as clean as Nell. It won't hurt to wait."

She straightened, determined to gain control of herself, but her voice trembled and more tears threatened. "If I hadn't been here, she would have gone through that alone. She would have died."

Jack drew her head on to his shoulder as she cried for the lost child, the bewilderment of her first day at Moonrakers, and the isolation of her new home where life hung on an edge and no one seemed to care.

"We deal with birth and death, fire, flood and sickness as they come out here," he whispered as her sobs calmed. "We rarely have visitors, and the only doctor for miles is based at the Parramatta garrison, and he refuses to treat people like us unless we can pay him in coin." He sighed. "You've had a harsh lesson tonight, Alice, and I wish things could have been different. But I hope it's shown you that we must work together in trust and friendship — we only have each other to rely on."

Her eyes were still brimming. "I'm frightened," she murmured.

"We all are," he replied tenderly, "but we won't admit it most of the time and just get on with living."

Alice nestled against his chest. She had never imagined life could be so harsh — had never experienced such a sense of abandonment — yet as she heard the steady drumming of his heart she knew that if she was to survive in this awful place she must find the same strength as the fearless Nell.

Nell had persuaded Billy eventually to take the children to their beds. Now she lay beside him as he snored, staring out of the window at a star-studded sky, waiting for dawn. The night seemed endless, the exhaustion and sorrow so overwhelming that she wondered if she would ever recover the energy that had got her this far.

She turned her head on the pillow and could just distinguish the tiny, still form in the cradle by the bed. He would never know her voice, never suckle at her breast, and the pain of losing him was raw and all-encompassing. A fresh onslaught of tears welled, and although she wanted to scream out her anguish, to writhe, howl and curse, she steeled herself against such a selfish outpouring. Billy had been so comforting, so understanding and gentle — as heartbroken as she — and the new day would be bad for all of them. It was better to let him sleep while he could. She closed her eyes and battled silently with the pain that was tearing her apart.

The sky was pearl grey when she woke. The cradle was gone, and Billy was standing by the bed in the same crumpled clothes he'd slept in. "Where is he?" she asked.

Billy's usually ruddy, cheerful face was haggard. "In the other room with Amy and the twins," he said gruffly. "I made him snug with a scrap of blanket, and used the finest pine for his . . ."

Nell took his hand and squeezed it hard as he fought to contain his tears. She had no words to ease his pain, just the conviction that if they stayed strong, they would come through this ordeal.

"I brought you tea," he said, once he'd got himself under control. "There's a dollop of rum in it."

Nell attempted to smile as she took the rough, earthenware cup. She sipped and pulled a face. "Bill!" she gasped. "There's enough grog in this to knock out a horse."

The bed dipped as he sat and took her hand. "You'll need it," he said softly. "Alice is here to stitch you up."

Nell drained the cup and thrust it at him. "Pearl and Gladys will see me right."

"This isn't the time to rely on native gins. They're filthy, and don't know the first thing about real nursing." He took her hands again. "Alice saved your life last night. Why can't you trust her?"

Nell glared at him, torn between the knowledge that he was right and the deep-seated suspicion that Alice

110

had brought bad luck to Moonrakers. "All right," she said reluctantly, "but fetch Gladys and Pearl anyway. I'll want their berries and herbs if I'm to get through today."

"I'll fetch more rum too," he said quietly.

Nell winced as she moved on the bed. There was no doubt she needed attention, she was already light-headed and hot, which had nothing to do with the rum. It was likely she was going down with fever.

Alice scooped the needle and a thick length of cotton out of the boiling water and placed them on a clean strip of linen. Her night's sleep had been uneasy and her hands shook as she lifted the pan from the range and set it to one side.

"Wait there until the missus is ready for you," said Billy, from the doorway.

A mutter was followed by an incomprehensible gabble.

Two women were peering at her in wide-eyed curiosity through the open door, Alice saw. They bore little resemblance to the African natives for they were shorter and smaller-boned, with wild, unkempt hair, amber eyes and stick-thin limbs. Dressed in what looked like Nell's ragged cast-offs, they stank to high heaven. "What are they doing here?" she asked.

"Nell needs their medicine," said Billy, shortly.

"You shouldn't let them anywhere near her," she said.

Billy shrugged. "Nell believes in their hocus-pocus, and I reckon a few leaves and berries won't do much

111

harm. The native women use them all the time in birthing."

Alice tamped down the urge to argue. It was none of her business, and if Nell believed in such rubbish, then no doubt she would find comfort from it. She finished her preparations and Jack began to read from the Bible. Turning, arms laden, she regarded the sad little tableau.

Billy had moved to the table and was sitting with a twin on each knee, Amy leant against his hip her thumb in her mouth. The tiny coffin lay on the table in front of them — an awful reminder of the night's tragedy, a stark precursor to the day ahead.

Jack looked up from the tattered pages and gave her a smile of encouragement. She took a deep breath and tapped on Nell's door.

Nell's blue eyes regarded her with animosity and, uncharacteristically careless, Alice spilled some water as she placed the bowl on the chest beside the bed. "Yer 'and better be steadier than that with a needle in it," Nell snarled.

"It'll be steady enough as long as you don't fight me," Alice replied, with a calm she didn't feel. She heard Nell's snort of derision, but didn't rise to the bait. The time had come for reconciliation.

Satisfied that she was ready, she returned Nell's glare with a steady gaze. She saw a woman who would not be bowed, no matter how sorely she was tried, a woman in pain from her injuries and her loss, but determined not to show it. Alice felt a rush of admiration, and wondered if she would be as stalwart in the face of such adversity. She prayed fervently she would never be put to the test.

As she looked into those defiant eyes she saw that Nell had not forgiven her, despite what they had endured. Yet she understood and accepted the reason for the other woman's animosity. Nell had ruled Moonrakers, was mistress of her house, an undoubted matriarch — and she'd seen Alice and their subsequent conflict as a threat.

The silence grew as they regarded one another, and Alice realised that this moment would determine their future relationship — and that it must be she who made the first move. "I wish with all my heart I could take back what I said to you yesterday," she said, and reached out a hand, but withdrew it without touching Nell's arm. She knew that the gesture would be spurned. "And I wish I could have saved the baby."

"You did what yer could," Nell muttered, "but it ain't easy to be grateful when there's a baby to bury."

Alice watched her pick up and drain the cup, and realised that this was Nell's way of acknowledging her help. But her forgiveness would be hard won. It would take more than a few words to bridge the void that had opened between them.

Moonrakers' cemetery was a half-acre corner of home pasture, well away from the river, marked with a picket fence and a line of paper-bark trees. A single cross stood in the long grass: a crude memorial to a convict workman who'd died after a snake bite.

The heat was already dancing on the horizon as they gathered at the graveside. It washed over the land in great ripples that flooded the trunks of the delicate eucalyptus trees and made their silver leaves droop. The sky was colourless as the sun blazed down, and above the ever-present hum of flies, Nell heard the mournful caw of the crows echoing in the stifling silence.

Nell leant heavily against Billy as Jack read from the Bible and their baby was laid to rest in the dark earth. The words meant little to her: she had never understood how God was loving and all-seeing yet allowed babies to die and innocent children to be harmed. But as she struggled to concentrate through the haze of a raging fever, she was bitterly aware that her baby would lie in unhallowed ground without the rituals and prayers of a minister to send him on his way to whatever lay beyond the grave.

She glanced to the line of trees where the natives watched with blatant curiosity. They had their own rituals and beliefs and she wondered, fleetingly, if those primitive people had a better way of understanding death: it came to them in the cry of the curlews, and on a song that could not be denied. The body was cremated or left in the open so the spirit could return to the dust that had given it life. But their mourning rituals were also a celebration: they believed that the dead had begun their final journey into the sky where they would meet their ancestors and become as one with the stars.

Nell struggled to follow the prayers, but the heat buzzed in her ears, and black clouds of oblivion gathered in her head. She swayed and would have fallen if she hadn't been clinging to Billy's arm. The fever was taking a strong hold, despite the berries Gladys had given her, but she was damned if she'd give in to it yet.

Her sight was blurred as she looked across at Alice, and her thoughts clamoured. They'd been all right until she'd arrived. Moonrakers had been a haven — a home isolated from the ugliness of the city — a refuge from the past. She blinked and tried to clear her vision, for Alice appeared to be hovering in the waves of heat, her figure shifting in and out of focus like a wraith. "Bad luck," she muttered. "She's got the evil eye."

She glanced up at Billy, but he'd not heard her. How could he not see that Alice would bring them down?

As Jack closed the Bible, two of the convicts began to shovel earth over the coffin. When it was done, a rough wooden cross was hammered into the ground. The epitaph was crudely carved, giving only the meanest of description: "A son. Born dead November 1797." The soft mound was stark among the silvery grass, but as they covered it with the dark red boulders that lay strewn about, it took on the appearance of belonging.

Nell decided she would deal with Alice later and forced herself to concentrate. She leant heavily on Billy's sturdy arm as they walked close to the grave. Then she fell to her knees, crammed a posy of wild flowers into a jar and set it at the head. Her baby was gone, lost to her for ever. "Goodbye, little one," she sobbed. "Sleep well."

Alice was finding it hard to hold back her tears. Jack's reading from the Bible and the subsequent prayers had reminded her of home, although the leafy village churchyard, with its ancient headstones and sheltering yews, where she'd left her parents was a world away from this primitive corner of Australia.

She glanced at the black men and women, like dark shadows among the trees, and watched as the convict men doffed their hats when Nell placed her posy on the tiny, stone-covered mound. A shiver of apprehension ran through her as she acknowledged that she had chosen to live on the very edge of civilisation. Had she made a terrible mistake?

"Let's leave them to it." Jack offered her his arm, and Alice took it, but as they were about to turn away they were stilled by a scream.

Nell had struggled to her feet, and her face was a mask of hatred as she pointed at Alice. "It's your fault," she yelled. "If you 'adn't come 'ere, none of this would 'ave 'appened."

"Nell!" Billy grabbed her as she swayed. "Nell, please — don't do this."

"She's a witch," spat Nell, eyes blazing with fever and rage. "She killed my baby."

Alice stared back at her in horror. "I did — I did no such thing," she stammered.

116

"Of course you didn't." Billy tried to restrain his distraught wife. "Nell's sick. She doesn't know what she's saying."

Nell fought with almost demonic strength to escape his grasp. "I ain't lyin', Billy," she yelled, "and I ain't sick. She's gunna bring us all down."

Alice knew that only a sharp slap would shock Nell out of her hysteria — but she wasn't about to try it: Nell hated her enough already.

"Take the children indoors, Alice," ordered Billy. "They shouldn't see this."

"Touch them and you die!" Nell struggled furiously.

Jack gathered up the sobbing twins, and Alice perched Amy on her hip. The little girl was stiff in her arms, so frightened by her mother's behaviour that she couldn't even cry.

"She's brought a curse to Moonrakers," yelled Nell, at their departing figures. "She's bad luck, Billy — you see if I ain't right."

Some time later Billy came through the door, with a silent, limp Nell in his arms. "She fainted, thank God," he said grimly, as he laid her on the couch and covered her with a blanket. "She was beyond all reason."

Alice dampened a cloth and pressed it to Nell's hot forehead, as Jack tried to distract the children with a story. Poor little mites, she thought. They'll have nightmares for weeks after this. Then she noticed Nell's colour. "She's burning up," she told Billy.

Billy had remained stalwart throughout, but now his grief and weariness were apparent as he gazed down at his wife. "I can't lose her too," he whispered. His troubled gaze settled on Alice. "I've got one of the convicts to prepare the horse and wagon. I'll take her to the garrison infirmary in Sydney."

"How can I help?"

Billy looked at his children. "I can't take them with me . . ."

"We'll look after them," she replied.

"I might be gone for a while — I can't leave Nell on her own — not when she's so ill."

Alice put a hand on his arm. "Take all the time you need," she said softly. "Jack and I will see to the animals and make sure the children come to no harm."

Billy glanced at his friend, who nodded, then hurried into the bedroom to pack. Alice sent Jack and the children outside while she sponged Nell with cold water and replaced her dress with a thin cotton nightshift. No sooner had she finished than Billy returned. He kissed the children, shook Jack's hand, scooped his wife into his arms and carried her out to the waiting wagon.

Alice tried to soothe Amy, Walter and Sarah, who were crying now, as they watched Billy lead the horse to the raft, then disappear among the trees as he set off down the track for Sydney. She had no fears that she could cope with the children — she'd looked after her younger sisters until they'd married — but Nell's accusations would not be silenced.

"What if she was right?" she said to Jack. "What if I have brought bad luck to Moonrakers?"

"Superstitious nonsense." Jack took the twins and went back into the house.

Alice stood in the glare of noon, watching the dust sift along the ground in the hot breeze that had sprung up. She hadn't missed the shadow of doubt that had flickered in his eyes.

CHAPTER
FIVE

Waymbuurr (Cooktown), 24 December 1797

Lowitja heard the singing of the Spirit Ancestors as she walked, and knew she was dying. They had told her to leave Uluru, and the trek to the north-eastern shores of the Ngandyandi people had taken many, many moons. Now the weariness had settled deep into her bones, her resilience and strength finally defeated. She longed to lie down, succumb to those siren songs and drift up to the Great White Way to be reunited with her family — but she had come too far to give in now. Death would have to wait.

She glanced down at the seven-year-old boy beside her. Mandawuy had grown tall, and now reached almost to her shoulder. He was slightly built, his hair framing his face in a dark haze of curls, but his amber eyes held knowledge far beyond his youth for the visions of what had happened at the Place of the Honey Bee Dreaming remained with him.

It was the reason for the great journey that had brought her to the end of her fearsome courage — the Spirit Ancestors had spoken to her in the stones and led her through the arid wastelands, over mountains and swamps to these northern shores so that he would be protected from the white man's influences.

"Is it far to go, Grandmother?" he asked.

Lowitja sniffed the salty air. "We are close. Waymbuurr lies just beyond that line of hills."

Mandawuy's gaze reached far into the shimmering horizon. "It will be good to be with our people again. Then you can rest and grow strong."

Lowitja felt the soft bump of the last water-filled emu egg against her bony hip. The others had long been discarded, and her frailty meant that even that light weight was wearing her down. She pointed to the dunes. "Find us food, Mandawuy. It is almost time to eat."

He raced up the shifting sand, his youth and excitement unimpeded by heat or weariness. At the top he stood for a moment to look in awe at the great glittering sea, then darted out of sight, plunging in a hectic run down to the shore to search for the shellfish his grandmother had described during their trek.

Lowitja trudged on, each step defying death, every heart-beat bringing her closer to Anabarru and sanctuary. She admired his youth and strength of character, for he had never faltered, never questioned the wisdom of such a journey. Mandawuy would make a fine warrior and guardian of the land.

She knew the story of their travels across the hostile plains would be painted on the walls of a sacred cave and told round campfires so that this precious earth would be guarded and nurtured by the generations to come. She and her grandson were the last of her people, the final southern link between the great Ancestors Djanay and Garnday who had once led the vast tribes of the Ngandyandi and Kunwinjku. The journey they had begun so many moons ago was almost at an end, and once she had fulfilled her promise to the Ancestor Spirits and put Mandawuy into the care of her cousin, Anabarru, and the Ngandyandi people, she could sleep until it was time to be reborn.

They stopped to rest in the shade of giant ferns as the sun reached its zenith and heat blurred the horizon. Mandawuy dug a pit in the sand and cooked the black shellfish and tiny crabs he'd found in the rock pools. It was as if he understood that his grandmother needed only the sounds of nature to soothe her weariness.

Lowitja ate a little of the delicious meat, but her appetite was gone. Sharing the last of the water from the emu egg, she slumped against the scratchy white bark of a gum tree, revelling in the cool shadows and soft chortle of drowsy birds. The sigh of the salty wind was welcome after the burning heat. Her limbs felt heavy, and although she had barely the strength to move, she could hear the persistent songs — closer now and more commanding. She didn't dare sleep or yield to the demands of her body, for she had defied the Spirits long enough. Time was running out.

The sun was moving towards the west as they left the trees and walked along the soft white sand. The haunting, mournful call of the curlews filled the air, but for once she was not afraid. They had not come to warn her of danger, but to welcome her as she approached the end of her final journey.

122

"Grandmother."

She heard the fear in his voice and saw how he clutched his stabbing tool. Grasping her spear, she followed his pointing finger. Her heart thudded as she saw the man's warlike stance. She no longer had the strength to defend the boy. They were at his mercy.

Then she recognised him as her cousin Anabarru's husband, Watpipa — the Elder of the tribe. She called his name, and introduced herself, then turned back to the boy. "We are home," she said. Then darkness veiled the sun, and she was only vaguely aware of Mandawuy's cries as she crumpled to the ground.

When she opened her eyes she was confused. Instead of being surrounded by her Spirit Ancestors, she was in a leafy shelter being tended by her ageing cousin Anabarru and her daughters. "But I heard the singing," she protested.

Anabarru pressed her back on to the soft bed of grass and aromatic leaves. "The song is not yet finished," she murmured. "Rest, Lowitja."

"Mandawuy?"

"He is with my husband in the circle of Elders, telling them of your great journey. Our grandson is safe now. You have fulfilled the promises you spoke of in your sleep."

Lowitja rested, content now that she knew their precious boy would be well guarded. The water was cooling to her parched throat, the berries sweet on her tongue, and after a while she gathered her strength and

123

told Anabarru of the terrible thing that had happened at Meeaan-jin.

There was a long silence as Anabarru digested the news. "What of the Jagera, the Quanda Mooka, Eora, Cadigal and Gubbi people?"

"Nearly all dead."

"And our uncles?" Her wrinkled face was drawn with fear.

"Bennelong has found the white man's ways to his liking," Lowitja sneered. "He lives with them and struts about in their clothes, telling us to learn from them and forget hostilities. He even sailed with them to meet their great leader king who lives far across the sea."

She paused in an effort to retain her strength, but her heart was fluttering, making every breath a struggle. "Colebee was captured, but escaped and, with Pemulwuy and his son Tedbury, continues the fight."

"Then the white man will leave," said Anabarru, "for how can they win against such strong warriors as our uncles?"

Lowitja battled with despair. "There are so few willing to join them," she said. "The war is already lost. The white men increase in number every season, and our spears and *nullas* are no match for their weapons. They have stolen the land surrounding the Deerubbun and call it the Hawkesbury. The lands of Wallumetta and Parramatta have been renamed Prospect Hill, Kissing Point and the Field of Mars." She grimaced as she recited the white man's names for the once sacred Dreaming Places; their spirituality was lost to her people for ever.

"Those of us who do not wish to live with them are forced from our hunting grounds into the empty lands beyond the mountains where we must cross sacred, forbidden song lines and live with tribes who have always been our enemies." She fought to breathe. "We are strangers, and not welcome. The hunting is poor. For many it is easier to put down their spears, join the white men and forget the ancient ways."

Anabarru bit her lip in distress, and Lowitja noticed how her cousin had aged. Her hair was laced with white, her face wrinkled, her once slender, taut body grown thin, the flesh loose on her bones. She took her hand, knowing the same changes had been even more deeply wrought within herself. Neither of them would live as long as the white women did, for it was unknown among their people to survive to the fortieth year.

"You and Mandawuy will be safe here," she soothed. "It is too far for the white man to come and there is nothing here they could want."

Anabarru shook her head. "The white man has already walked upon our land and eaten at our campfires." She wiped the tears from her cheeks and sniffed. "But he was good," she said, "a friend to all of us."

"You speak of the white fella who came many, many seasons ago?"

Anabarru nodded. "He returned. Jon came with the summer rains and spoke with my husband and the other Elders." She grasped her cousin's hand. "But he came to warn us, Lowitja. His knowledge of our language is poor, but he could tell us of the changes in the south, and how we must prepare to defend ourselves."

Lowitja wondered what manner of white man he could be for, if Anabarru was to be believed, he bore little resemblance to the devils who'd slaughtered her people in Meeaan-jin. "How can you be sure he is to be trusted?" she persisted. "Was he alone?"

"There were others, but he made them camp on the beach, and they were not allowed to approach us or go into the bush." She paused and ate a few berries. "Watpipa hunted with him every day and is a good judge of men. He admired Jon."

Lowitja nodded, but her thoughts were jumbled. Anabarru's husband was a respected Elder, and his opinion was highly regarded — yet this man, Jon, was a danger to them all now that he had found his way so far north. "I respect his wisdom," she began, "but the white man has two faces. How can you trust him not to lead others here?"

"We were out one day when Jon saw something that excited him. Watpipa and I were puzzled, for it was only a cave we'd found many moons ago, and of no use to anyone."

Lowitja frowned. Anabarru wasn't making sense. "Why should a cave interest a white man?"

Anabarru shrugged. "It wasn't the cave," she explained, "but the shiny rock he found lying within the walls." She pulled a face. "He called it 'gold'."

"Gold," muttered Lowitja, the word strange on her tongue. "What is this gold?"

126

"He told us we must never show it to anyone else — not even the other Elders — and he vowed on a sacred totem he called a bible that he would never tell another white man about it."

Lowitja saw that her cousin trusted Jon's promise. "This gold must be important for him to take such an oath," she said

Anabarru swept back her greying hair. "Jon said the white man seeks this gold and looks upon it as a great god." She pulled a face. "They are strange people, Lowitja, for what possible use can it be? It cannot be used as a weapon, eaten or even worn against the cold of night."

Lowitja was as puzzled as her cousin, but she was too weary to give it any more thought. The songs were louder now, the spirits drawing nearer, warming her with their breath and easing the pain. She closed her eyes.

Anabarru's voice melted away as the Great Canoe drifted down towards her. She saw that it was beautiful, made of stars and clouds that shimmered in the darkness, guided only by the breath of the Great Spirit Creator. She climbed in, unafraid and eager to see what lay beyond that night sky.

The Canoe rocked as it rose from the earth. Then it took flight, soaring high among the stars and along the Great White Way. She felt the love and warmth of the Great Spirit Creator's embrace as she left all earthly cares far behind her, and as they reached the distant, star-laden shore her joy was overwhelming. For there,

127

waiting to welcome her, were her ancestors Garnday and Djanay. Her journey was over.

Sydney Town, 24 December 1797

The *Atlantica* had returned to Sydney the day before and wasn't due to sail again for a month and, as he didn't have to leave for his promised visit to Hawks Head Farm for another day, George decided to attend the governor's ball. There was nothing like a party to set him up for the long months at sea, and besides, he reasoned, he might get a chance to discuss some business.

He had dressed carefully for the occasion and knew he cut a fine figure in the newly tailored coat and white breeches, even if the powdered wig was far too hot for such a sticky summer night. He strode up the gravel path, humming to the music that was pouring through the open doors of the ramshackle old building. Candlelight blazed through the windows and from the lanterns that had been strung on the trees around the garden, the darkness lending the scene a mysterious, magical air.

He handed his tricorn hat to the convict maid, accepted a glass of rum punch from another and ambled through the colourful throng.

"George! What the devil are you doing here?"

"Thomas Morely!" He grinned at the young lieutenant and wrung his hand. They had become acquainted some years ago and were close friends. "You shouldn't need to ask," he went on. "Where else would

I be when there is wine and food — and pretty girls to dance with?"

"Quite so," replied Thomas, and cast an appreciative eye over a pair of young women walking past.

"On your own, Thomas?" asked George. "That's not like you."

Thomas took his arm and steered him towards the ballroom. "You must meet Anastasia," he said, his voice rising to compete with the music and the sound of stamping feet. "She's quite the most exquisite creature."

"Oh dear." George sighed. "Don't tell me you've been snared as well. It seems an epidemic of romance has swept Sydney since I last came back."

Thomas eyed him solemnly. "It's about time you stopped racketing about on that ship, George, and settled down."

"God forbid."

"I mean it, George. You've made your money and now it's time to find a wife."

"Plenty of time for that," said George, above the hubbub. "I'll marry when I'm ready."

"There she is. Isn't she the most beautiful creature you've ever seen?"

George dutifully admired a rather plump fair girl, being hauled about the dance-floor by a rotund colonel. "Certainly she is," he said, as he noted fleshy shoulders and flushed cheeks. "And the colonel's enjoying the dance," he added wryly, as Anastasia winced when he trod heavily on her foot. "Pity one can't say the same for the lady."

Thomas frowned. "Poor sweet, she'll be glad when her duty's done. I'll introduce you later."

They left the ballroom in search of food and, managing to avoid the circling matrons, found a quiet alcove in which they could talk.

"How's army life?" George asked.

"Good," Thomas replied. "I've made a tidy sum through rum sales and bought a nice parcel of land near Rose Hill."

George was astounded. His friend was the second son of a schoolmaster and had escaped poverty by joining the army, where he'd gained a reputation for honourable conduct and as an expert swordsman. "I thought you were set upon a military career."

"Macarthur has proved there's a fortune to be made here," Thomas confided, "and I mean to have my share." His gaze drifted towards the ballroom. "Anastasia and I could do well, if her father approves."

George raised his brows. "You're not about to ask for her hand?"

Thomas blushed to the roots of his dark hair. "Why not? I love her."

George groaned. "Another good man bites the dust." He finished his food and drank some punch. "The lady can have little taste if she's in love with you, you rogue, but you're plainly smitten, so you must tell me more about her."

"First, she is so beautiful," he began. "Blue eyes, fair hair, skin like cream and —"

"I saw that for myself," George interrupted. Thomas had a habit of rambling. "Who is she?"

"She's the second daughter of Baron von Eisner."
Seeing this meant little to George, he explained about
the hotel and the three daughters. "They've caused
quite a stir," he continued, "and although the eldest girl
is hailed as the beauty, Anastasia outshines her, for her
character is sweet and gentle, and she has a naughty
sense of fun that I find most appealing."

George laughed. "The baron won't have difficulty in
finding them husbands here. We men far outnumber
the ladies."

Thomas regarded him thoughtfully. "The eldest is
already married, but I should introduce you to Irma,"
he said. "She may not be as beautiful as my Anastasia,
but she has a twinkle in her eye that you will find
irresistible."

"Oh, no," laughed George. "I'll find my own
lady-friends, thank you."

"I may have done her a disservice," Thomas said.
"She's certainly striking, with brown eyes and golden
hair, but she's too tall and slim for my liking." He
nudged George's arm and winked. "I prefer a plump
armful."

But George was no longer listening. His eyes were on
the man standing in the doorway and he felt the old
anger rise. "So Cadwallader's back from exile."

Thomas nodded. "He's a major and already on his
way to a fortune. Unfortunately he's married to
Anastasia's eldest sister."

Bitterness rose in George's throat. Edward Cadwallader
was still cocky and arrogant. What wouldn't he give for
the chance to punch his supercilious nose? "If you plan

131

to marry Anastasia, I don't envy you him as a brother-in-law." His fists were clenched. "After what he did to Millicent . . . How did he manage to snare Anastasia's sister? She must have had the pick of beaux."

"He used his considerable charm to court her," Thomas told him, "and made it plain in the officers' quarters that she was his and his alone."

"You should have enlightened her as to his true character," said George. His eyes narrowed as Edward retreated from the doorway. "He's a dangerous man."

Thomas signalled for more punch. "I had no opportunities," he said. "It was a whirlwind romance, and as Anastasia thought him wildly romantic and dashing, I dared not blacken his name thereby spoiling my own chances." He sighed. "One can only hope that marriage has changed him, even if he's still a blackguard in the mess. But they seem content enough and their first son was born two months ago — perhaps she has tamed him."

"Once a devil always a devil," said George. "I wouldn't trust him." Then he made himself smile, determined not to let Cadwallader ruin the evening. "Come, Thomas, we're gossiping like two old spinsters. Let's join the dancing."

Edward's jealousy meant that Eloise had gaps in her dance card, so she sipped lemonade and watched as her sisters joined in the lively quadrille. The governor's ball was in full swing, and the room was ablaze with candlelight as the convict musicians played lively tunes.

132

Edward was dancing with the wife of his commanding officer, and Eloise coolly acknowledged his smile as he glanced her way. He'd been solicitous all evening, and was on his best behaviour, for he was still sober. He was trying hard, but she found even their most intimate moments an ordeal.

She adjusted one of the camellias in her hair, and decided she was in need of fresh air. Edward would be occupied with his duty dances for a while so now was the perfect time to slip away.

She pulled the light wrap over her arm and stepped into the garden. The night was warm, the stars twinkling in a clear sky, the moon flooding the lawns with its silvery light. Eloise breathed in the scent of freshly watered grass and clipped hedges, and strolled towards the arbour at the far end of the garden. The vast team of convict gardeners had worked wonders. The sounds of the party faded as she moved away from the house, lifting the hem of her ballgown to keep it dry. Her dancing slippers were already soaked so, with a swift glance to make sure she was alone, she took them off and ran on barefoot.

What joy it was to be away from the stifling pomposity of the social round, to be out here with only the moon and stars for company. She was breathless by the time she reached the stone path that led to the arbour, but her delight in this rare moment of freedom was undiminished. She stretched out her arms and began to dance, twirling until her skirts billowed around her.

"Bravo."

Eloise jumped, heart pounding, and stumbled to a halt as a figure detached itself from the dark shadows of the arbour. Her head was spinning. "Who's there?"

He took a step forward, but his features remained invisible. "Forgive me for startling you," he said, his deep voice modulated by the rounded tones of England, "but you looked so pretty, dancing in the moonlight, that I couldn't help but applaud."

Eloise felt the heat rise in her face and knew it had little to do with her exertions. "I believed myself alone," she replied, uncertain as to how she should deal with the situation.

"I won't tell anyone," he said, as he moved out of the shadows and smiled down at her.

Her eyes widened as she saw the wings of grey in his hair, the fine moustache and startling blue eyes. "It's you," she gasped, without thinking.

"It certainly is," he replied. "But you have the advantage, ma'am, for I don't recall us having been introduced."

Eloise blushed again. She squared her shoulders and tried to appear calm and in control. "I saw you on the quayside when the *Empress* docked," she said.

"That was some weeks ago." He frowned briefly. Then his handsome face lit up in another smile. "I'm flattered you remember me. But our paths must have crossed only fleetingly, for I am certain we haven't met before."

She chuckled and relaxed. He was easy to talk to — and to look at, even though he must be about the same age as her father. She threw caution to the winds.

134

"Indeed we haven't," she said. She looked up into his sun-weathered face. "The rules of etiquette have already been broken, so I shall take the opportunity to introduce myself. Eloise Cadwallader." She curtsied.

He bowed, took her hand and kissed the air above her gloved fingers as his eyes twinkled. "Jonathan Cadwallader at your service, ma'am."

George had accompanied Thomas and been introduced to Anastasia, her sister Irma and the baron. It was a jolly gathering, but as the girls were taken on to the floor for the next dance, George had made his excuses and wandered off.

Now he stood entranced on the terrace as the ethereal figure danced into the darkness and was lost. She was the most captivating girl he'd ever seen, and although he'd only glimpsed her as she'd left the ballroom, he was in danger of losing his senses.

He left the terrace and followed her, amused and intrigued by the way she had danced alone in the garden. There had been a freedom of spirit in that private performance — a joy in life that touched him profoundly. He had to find her.

George slowed as he heard the voices. Had she come out here to meet a beau? He hoped not, but he had to accept that one so beautiful must be greatly admired. That he was spying on her troubled him, but curiosity won and he moved silently among the surrounding trees so that he could watch her.

She was too far away for him to catch what she was saying, her light voice interposed with the deeper tones of a man who remained out of sight. He had no real interest in eavesdropping, though, for he was too taken by her. She wore shimmering white silk, which clung to her slender figure, and her hair, dressed with camellias, shone gold in the moonlight. She was the loveliest of women, with a mellow voice that held the merest hint of an accent he couldn't place but found mesmerising. George stood in the shadows, and found it hard to believe that he was behaving like a lovesick fool.

Edward scoured the ballroom for his wife. He'd endured his duty dances with the simpering matrons, and now he wanted her in his arms again. The ball had been his first chance to show her off since the child was born, and he wanted to hold her, to draw her close and feel her lithe, supple body against his. He'd seen the sparkle in her eyes and the flush on her cheek as they had danced earlier, and had sensed that tonight he might once again ignite the fire in their marriage bed that had been dormant for so long.

His gaze travelled round the room. Her father and sisters were still here so she hadn't returned to the hotel, where they would be spending the night, and there was no sign of her on the dance-floor or in the dining room. "Where the devil has she gone?" he muttered crossly.

"Are you looking for Eloise?" asked Thomas Morely.

"It's Lady Cadwallader to you," growled Edward. "Have you seen her?"

The lieutenant's expression hardened. "Maybe she has no wish to be found."

Edward eyed him coldly. They were of similar age and height, but Edward outranked the other. "I'll be the judge of that," he snarled. "Do you know where she is?"

The other man returned his glare. "Perhaps she should be permitted to come and go as she pleases," he responded.

Edward was all too aware of the other people around him, and although he would have liked to knock the man to his knees, he knew better than to cause a scene. He moved closer so that his words wouldn't carry. "Any man who dares challenge me will find his liver at the end of my sword."

The other maintained his rigid bearing. "You don't frighten me, sir. I have no personal interest in the lady, merely concern for her well-being."

"Her well-being is none of your damned business!"

Thomas Morely didn't flinch. "I wonder if she knows yet what degree of man she has married?"

Edward leant towards him until they were almost nose to nose. "And I wonder if you are quite aware of how close you are to feeling my sword in your gut?"

"Do you demand a duel?" The eyes were steady.

Edward swallowed. Thomas Morely had a fearsome reputation as a duellist and he would not risk life and limb. "Not at all," he drawled. "And I would advise you to keep your sword sheathed if you wish to continue your pursuit of Anastasia. As her brother-in-law I have her father's ear. I bid you goodnight." He strode off, his thoughts full of revenge for the insolent cur who'd dared to stand up to him.

After another sortie through the mêlée, Edward's temper was further fuelled by the suspicion that Eloise must be in the garden. But with whom?

He stood on the terrace and waited for his eyes to adjust to the darkness surrounding the moon-drenched lawns. Several couples were taking the air, but he saw no glimmer of his wife's white silk dress. He stepped on to the grass, and made for a shadowy corner. As the sound of the ball grew fainter, he became aware of the murmur of voices. He drew nearer, and froze. "Eloise? Is that you?" he barked.

"Edward?" Her voice was filled with laughter as she emerged from the arbour. "Do hurry — there's someone here whom I know you'll want to talk to."

Edward's fists were clenched at his sides as he hurried across to her. He could hear a man's voice and jealousy tore through him. Whoever he was, Edward would have his gizzard.

Eloise waited for him in a pool of moonlight. "Look," she said, as he drew nearer.

Edward saw her high colour and the sparkle in her eyes and felt a wave of fury that another man could bring her so alive. He peered over her shoulder to the arbour as someone came towards him.

"Edward."

"Father," he managed, the word sticking in his throat.

"We've had such a lovely talk, Edward. I wish you had introduced us sooner."

Edward's bearing remained stiff and formal.

"Yes, Edward," said Jonathan, into the awkward silence. "Your wife is charming, and I understand my grandson is the most engaging child."

Edward had to draw on all his resources to be pleasant. "If I had known my father was ready to see us, then of course I would have introduced you," he told Eloise. His cold gaze met Jonathan's amused eyes.

"He's been telling me about his recent journey up the coast," said Eloise. "It sounds so exciting — so brave of him to go all that way."

"He enjoys adventure," said Edward, with a hint of the sourness he couldn't quash. "In fact," he added, "he prefers it to his paternal duties. He was away so often when I was a boy that I hardly recognised him as my father."

"Oh." Eloise looked at them both hesitantly. "Then surely it is time to put that right." Her hand touched Edward's arm in entreaty. "Your father has expressed his regret to me for the years you spent apart, and he wishes to make amends," she added. "Now that we have a son of our own, you will understand that."

He knew she was trying to defuse the situation, and that any show of open hostility on his part would lessen him further in her eyes. Yet the knowledge that his father had shared such intimacy with her infuriated him. How much had he told her? "New South Wales is a big land, Eloise," he said. "There is much to explore, and I'm sure he's impatient to be off again."

"Not at all," declared Jonathan. "I'm finding Sydney Town most agreeable, and I must meet my grandson."

"Then you shall call upon us tomorrow," said Eloise, with a radiant smile. "I will invite my father to join us. He does so enjoy good company, and would love to hear about your travels."

"I would be honoured," he replied, with a little bow.

Edward felt sick with impotent fury. "You must be cold, my dear," he said, as Eloise shivered in the cool breeze that had sprung up. "Come, I will escort you back to the party."

"There's no need," she replied. "I shall leave for the hotel once I've found my sisters. Charles will be fretting for me, and you may enjoy a quiet moment with your father."

Edward was trapped. He watched her bestow a dazzling smile on Jonathan, then hurry back towards the house.

George had seen Edward cross the lawn to the arbour, and although he hadn't been able to catch what they were saying, he could hear tension in the voices. Was Cadwallader with his father? The voice sounded aristocratic enough. And, if so, was the girl Edward's wife or Jonathan's mistress?

He melted into the shadows as she passed him, with a rustle of silk, and caught a tantalising hint of her perfume. He longed to follow her, halt her progress and speak to her — but in doing so he would reveal his shameful spying and leave himself open to difficult questions.

He remained where he was, stomach churning, as he waited for her to go inside. Then he hastened back to the ball. His search of the dance-floor yielded no sight of her, so he returned to the terrace, frustrated, and stared across the lawn to the arbour. Cadwallader was still there — the glint of his epaulettes betrayed his presence.

Something on the lawn arrested his attention and he wondered what it was. He went to pick it up. It was a camellia blossom — it must have fallen from her hair. He lifted it to his nose, surprised that such beauty held no scent, then carefully put it into his pocket. It would remain in his possession until he had the chance to return it.

"She is very charming," said Jonathan, as he lit a cheroot, "and quite beautiful."

"She's mine," snapped Edward. "So keep away from her."

Jonathan eyed him through the smoke as he propped himself against a wooden post. "I can admire beauty without needing to possess it," he said mildly.

"Hmph."

"You may have a low opinion of me, Edward, but I am not as black as you wish to paint me."

"You are singularly lacking in moral fibre," he retorted, "and I don't trust you."

Jonathan raised an eyebrow. "For one so lacking in it himself, you take a high-handed stance."

The desire to hit his father was almost overwhelming, but Edward was aware their conversation might be overheard by others in the garden. This was neither the time nor the place to vent his spleen.

"Is it not time to bring an end to the hostility between us?"

"Why? We dislike each other — as we always have."

"That is not true." Jonathan stood away from the post and ran his fingers through the grey hair at his temples. "At least, not on my part. You're my son, my only son, and now that you have a child, I'm surprised you cannot understand the love that binds a man to his offspring — no matter how sorely it is tried."

"It's a pity you could never practise what you preach," Edward rasped. "What price a father's love when he is noticeable only by his absence? What depth of affection forced me into exile?"

"You were guilty of violating a woman," Jonathan reminded him. "I saved you from prison — perhaps even from the hangman's noose. I had hoped you would learn from that, and return from exile a better man. But I hear you have not changed. Remember the boy you tortured at school? You escaped prison then, too. In hindsight, I wonder if it might not have done you good."

Silence fell, but Jonathan's contempt lingered between them.

Edward wanted to walk away, but his father's penetrating gaze held him where he stood. He could find no words to defend himself and, for the first time, he regretted the lost years, the lack of a father's guiding hand. Shocked by these disturbing thoughts, he dismissed them.

Jonathan watched him through the smoke curling from his cheroot. "As for my absence, I regret not being available to you as you grew up — but we are both aware that your mother did her best to keep us apart."

At this point Edward found his voice. "How fortunate for you that she's no longer alive to defend her reputation from your slander."

Jonathan crushed the cheroot stub beneath his heel. "Edward, Edward," he sighed, "why are you so determined to hate me?"

"I don't care for you enough to hate you, but I'd prefer never to set eyes on you again."

Jonathan put his fingers into his waistcoat pocket and pulled out his watch. Its silver casing gleamed in the moonlight as the musical chimes struck the half-hour. "That is not possible now that I know I have a grandson."

"It's a little late for you to play patriarch, is it not?"

Jonathan didn't answer the bitter question. "Your Eloise is a sweet girl," he said, as the chimes faded. "She will make a fine countess, when the time comes, if you treat her with the love and respect she deserves." He closed the watch. "Remember, Edward, that letter is still lodged with the judge-advocate. One wrong move from you and I will see that she learns the truth about your past."

"That's blackmail."

"An ugly word for an ugly situation," replied Jonathan. His steady gaze didn't falter. "Your marriage is still young, yet as time goes on it will bring you, perhaps, the maturity and wisdom you lack. Eloise is a clever young woman, and I look forward to meeting her father, the baron."

Edward had little interest in his father's opinions. In any case, his mind was elsewhere. "I don't remember that watch," he said.

Jonathan seemed taken aback by the sudden change of subject. "I bought it in London before I sailed here."

"Where is Grandfather's pocket watch?"

Jonathan frowned. "How could you know about that?"

"Grandmother mentioned it. She said it was made of gold, with a large diamond in the casing, and that eventually it would be mine."

"I gave it away some years before you were born." Jonathan slipped the watch back into his waistcoat pocket. "My mother should not have made that promise."

"You had no right to give it away," snapped Edward.

"It was my watch to do with as I pleased," Jonathan said. "The girl who has it appreciated the sentiment in which it was given."

"And how many other heirlooms have you presented to your paramours?" sneered Edward.

"None." Jonathan smoothed his moustache. "I was young and far from home in Tahiti. The watch was the only thing of value I could give to Lianni. She was dear to me, and as it happened years before I married your mother, it should not concern you."

Edward snorted. "So, you saw fit to give what should have been part of my inheritance to a foreign doxy. I wonder why that comes as no surprise?"

Jonathan shrugged. "What's done is done," he said, "and your inheritance is more than substantial without the watch." He picked up his ivory-handled cane. "As our conversation seems to have run its course, I will be on my way. Goodnight, Edward."

Edward watched his father stride away, and saw that the cane was a mere ornament. The old bastard was as fit as ever, despite his forty-six years. Yet in spite of his rage, a part of Edward yearned for things to be different between them. But the dice had been cast many years ago and he had to accept that the gulf was too wide. Now he was going to get very drunk.

CHAPTER
SIX

Hawks Head Farm, Christmas Day 1797

The heat shimmered over the pastures, so Susan and Bess had laid the table on the veranda to make the most of the breeze from the river. The six convicts who worked at Hawks Head would eat their dinner in the clearing by their bunk-house, and the small clan of Aborigines who had set up camp further down the river had received a leg of pork as a treat, although Ezra had yet to convince them of the importance of Christmas.

Sated, George pushed away his plate and leant back in his chair as Samuel Varney regaled them with one of his stories. He was a consummate story-teller and it had become a tradition to listen to one of his tales during Christmas dinner.

As everyone laughed and raised their glasses in a toast to Samuel, George felt content to be with his family. Ernest and the plump, bustling Bess seemed very happy now they were married, and even Nell had some colour in her cheeks. She was much restored by her stay at Hawks Head after her ordeal at the hands of a surgeon in the Sydney infirmary.

He watched his mother serve the plum pudding and realised that, despite the lines on her face and the silver in her golden hair, Susan had retained the beauty of her youth in her startling blue eyes. Yet she glanced frequently at his father, those lovely eyes shadowed with concern, for Ezra had aged considerably in the past few months.

George studied his father surreptitiously as he ate his pudding, noting the wan face and hooded eyes, the way Ezra's hand shook as he lifted his spoon to his mouth. Florence's absence was a sadness that lived on in his parents, and days like this made it more profound.

"Must you leave at the end of the week, George?" Susan's voice drew him from his thoughts. "We see so little of you."

"I have business to attend to in Sydney, Mother," he replied, deliberately vague, as he passed his empty bowl to Bess.

Susan's affectionate gaze held more than a little exasperation. "I suppose I'm not permitted to know what it is?"

"Knowing you, brother, some female has you on the hop," said Ernest, laughing.

"There's always a woman involved somewhere," interjected Nell. "I wouldn't mind bettin' 'e's got a wife in every port."

George flushed even though he was used to Nell's teasing. "No wives! But I can't help it if I'm irresistible to the fair sex," he protested. He grinned at Ernest's guffaw. "It's only polite to spread myself around so they all receive a fair share."

"How noble," laughed Ernest.

"George, *really*," remonstrated his mother. "You sound like Billy did when he was younger."

"Your brother's a fine, upstandin' citizen, Susan," said Nell, defensively. "But if I caught 'im out 'e wouldn't last long!"

"Quite rightly," said Susan. "Thankfully, Billy is older and wiser now. It's a great pity the same can't be said for George," she added thoughtfully. "But I have the feeling my younger son is smitten this time. He's been far too quiet these past few days."

"It ain't put 'im off 'is dinner, though," said Nell, with a wink. "Love must 'ave given 'im an appetite."

George caught Samuel's questioning gaze and looked away. This conversation was making him hot under the collar and he knew that, sooner or later, his mother or Nell would winkle out of him the true reason for his return to Sydney. He pushed back his chair. "Time for presents," he announced and went to fetch the parcels he'd hidden in his room. He had spent the nights following the ball dreaming of the girl with camellias in her hair, and although he suspected his mother was right, and that he was as lovesick as his friend Thomas, he wasn't ready yet to share this with his family.

There were gifts for everyone, and his mother's face lit up at the sight of the South Sea pearls he'd bought for her from a sailor. Nell squealed in delight over the ruby earrings he'd found in Batavia, and Bess was thrilled with the embroidery silks from a Sydney shop. For Samuel there was a new telescope to replace the one he'd dropped overboard one night when they'd both had too much to drink, for Ernest a long oilskin coat, and for his father a new Bible. He handed over the last bulky parcels to Nell. "The coats are for Billy and Jack, the saddle is for Walter, and the dolls are for Amy and Sarah. I didn't know what Alice would like as I haven't met her yet, so . . ."

Nell eyed the white ribbons on the simple straw bonnet. "It's perfect," she said, and swung her fiery earrings.

George tried not to smile. He'd heard about Nell and Alice's quarrel from his mother, and had been warned against probing what was probably still a sore spot with Nell. Alice was still caring for her children. "I can always find one like it for you," he teased.

Nell favoured him with a withering stare and struggled out of her chair. "I need to lie down," she said. "I'm not used to eating so much."

As Susan and Bess made her comfortable on the day-bed that had been set up on the veranda, George took the last of the dishes to the kitchen. The washing-up on Christmas Day was always done, with varying degrees of skill, by the Collinson men, but today, they had decided, it could wait until it was cooler.

George perched on the veranda railings to light his pipe as the others took their ease in the chairs and Samuel went for a stroll by the river. The mood was quiet and contented as Susan and Bess sorted through the new embroidery silks. "This breeze is pleasant," he said, to no one in particular.

"It's why we put Nell's bed out here when Billy brought her from the Sydney infirmary," said Ezra, putting aside his new Bible. "Cool, fresh air will help her recuperate, and Billy will soon have her home again."

George grinned as Nell winked at him from her pillows. "Oh, the lovely Mrs Penhalligan is well on her way to good health," he said, with a chuckle.

"Indeed she is," said Ezra, his thin face transformed by a smile. "Her body may have ailed, but her spirit has kept us on our toes."

Nell giggled as Bess and Susan went indoors to find a suitable item of clothing to embroider.

George puffed a cloud of smoke into the air. "Some things never change," he observed.

Ezra's lined face sagged. "But some do, and it is not within our power to prevent it. I wish Florence were here," he said sadly. "This is the fourth Christmas we have spent without her, and it doesn't feel right." He looked up at George. "Your mother never says anything, but I hear her crying sometimes and it breaks my heart. Why doesn't your sister come home, George? Were we such bad parents?"

George saw the anguish in his eyes, which reflected the pain he'd witnessed in his mother's. Surely Florence must understand that they needed to see her again, to know she was safe? Yet she seemed determined to keep her distance, no matter the cost to their well-being. George itched to slap her for her thoughtlessness. "You are wonderful parents," he said. He wished he could say more to ease his father's

150

misery. "She'll come home eventually, Papa," he added softly. "She knows how much you love her."

"I wish Billy and the children were 'ere too," interrupted Nell, moving restlessly on the day-bed.

Ezra smiled, but George could see what the effort cost him. "So do I," he said quietly. "Children always make Christmas special. I'm sorry you couldn't go home to Moonrakers, Nell, but you aren't strong enough to travel yet and the army surgeon forbade it."

"'E could've brung 'em 'ere."

"Now, Nell," said Ezra, with indefatigable patience, "you know that isn't possible. The journey's too long for such young children — especially in this heat."

George saw her face fall into weary lines of acceptance, and as the women emerged from the house, he felt the day's mood change. He was about to suggest they joined Samuel in his stroll when Ernest rose from his chair and startled Bess by grabbing her round her plump waist.

"I . . . We . . . have an announcement to make," he said, his face suddenly scarlet. "Bess and I are to be parents."

George clapped him on the back and congratulated him, then stood back as Nell and his parents bombarded the pair with kisses and questions. As he watched the joyous scene he felt a swell of pride for Ernest. His brother had overcome so much to reach this happy day, and Bess was the perfect match for him.

Yet that pride was tempered with a traitorous envy alien to George, and as he struggled to understand it, he could only surmise that it stemmed from his uncertainty over his own future. No matter how hard he fought the need to find the girl with the camellias, he knew he wouldn't rest until he did.

Sydney Town, 28 December 1797

"Come, Willy, show your hand!" Edward lounged back in the chair. He had no fear of losing the pile of treasury bills on the table for he was holding four aces.

"Got you this time," Willy Baines said, triumphant, as he slowly revealed his cards. "Full house."

"Not enough, old chap," replied Edward, fanning his aces. "My pot, I think." He scooped up the bills. "Another hand?"

The others threw their cards on to the table and left.

"Too rich for them, and for me," Willy muttered. "I've already lost a month's wages and haven't settled my mess bills yet."

Edward tossed a few notes back across the table. "Keep them," he said, with the carelessness of one who could afford to be generous.

"I'm obliged to you." Willy gathered them up and took a long draught of rum. He showed no embarrassment at Edward's gesture for it was familiar to him.

"No doubt I'll win it back," rejoined Edward. "You have yet to learn the art of bluff and card counting. You're an easy target."

Willy stuffed the money into his pocket. "I'll get even one day," he said, without rancour, then headed for the bar.

152

They both knew Edward cheated at cards, but Willy would never say anything while his senior officer paid off his debts. It was an arrangement that suited them both, for despite Edward's low opinion of Willy's skill at cards, Willy was astute, and they had often shared the pot after a night of bamboozling their colleagues.

Edward shouted for another bottle of rum and lit a cheroot as he stretched out his long legs. The room was dimly lit with oil lamps that added to the smoky atmosphere, and furnished with the bare minimum of rough tables and chairs. The chambers upstairs could be rented by the half-hour, and the back door opened into a dark alley that guaranteed anonymity. It was a favourite haunt of the military and marines, those who liked women and gambling: although the governing officers knew of its existence, they turned a blind eye to it. Men had to let off steam — and as long as there was no trouble, they were happy to let it continue.

The owner of the ramshackle boarding-house was a ticket-of-leave convict — a scruffy individual who was a stranger to soap and water — but he knew how to make money, keep his mouth shut and his customers happy. His whores were rough, but passably clean, there was always rum and other spirits, and the beer was stored in a brick-lined ice-house he'd sunk into the ground behind his premises.

Edward glanced at the bar and the woman who seemed never to move from behind it. She was as black as night and as filthy as her man, their brood of mulatto children no better. The thought of coupling with her made his stomach heave.

He turned his attention to those who had left the table and were making a great deal of noise on the far side of the room. They were his men, who followed him into the bush on the cleansing routs that had to remain secret from their commanding officer. He could trust them with his life, and to keep him informed. "Isn't anyone man enough to take this from me?" he shouted, above the din.

"I am. But only if you're prepared to lose it all." The voice was deep and unmistakably English.

Edward took the stranger's measure. He was a tall man of middle age, with an aristocratic, handsome face. Edward noted the heavy gold ring on his finger, the diamond pin in his neck-cloth, and the expensive cut of his attire. "I never play cards with a man who will not give me his name," he said, with a coolness that veiled his excitement. Here was a pigeon ripe for plucking.

"Neither do I," the stranger replied. "Henry Carlton."

They shook hands. "Edward Cadwallader. I don't remember seeing you before," he said. "New chum?"

The older man raised an eyebrow at the flash term used to describe recent migrants to Australia. "I came on the *Empress* from Cape Town two months ago."

Edward maintained a nonchalance he didn't feel. "The Cape, eh? I hear they've found gold there," he said casually.

"A little," Henry replied. "But I had other business."

Edward waved him to an empty seat at the table, and poured rum into a clean glass. The man intrigued him, and he would have liked to ask more questions — but there would be time enough for that when he'd seen the size of his purse. "Well, sir," he said, "if you have the money, I have the cards."

Henry Carlton placed a leather drawstring bag on the table. His eyes were grey and steady and he took his time to light a clay pipe. "What's the limit?" he asked.

"None between gentlemen," replied Edward.

Henry tugged the purse-strings and spilled gold coins on to the table. "Enough?"

Edward couldn't help but lick his lips. More than a hundred guineas lay before him. "Yes, indeed," he said, his voice tight in his throat. "I'll cut the cards, and you may deal the first hand."

Henry Carlton's expression was bland as his long, supple fingers shuffled the pack. But Edward felt a twinge of unease as he saw the steel that had crept into the grey eyes.

Sydney Town, 2 January 1798

George had returned from the Hawkesbury the night before and, eschewing Samuel's offer of a bed, had booked into a boarding-house by the quay. He'd borne the usual lecture from his mentor about women and the importance of avoiding marriage, but had spent the evening trying to find someone who could tell him about the girl who had worn the camellias in her hair.

He'd climbed into bed in the early hours, still none the wiser and somewhat puzzled by the lack of helpfulness among his army acquaintances. Yet despite his weariness and the comfort of the soft mattress, he had given up on sleep and sent a message to the barracks, pleading with Thomas to meet him at the hotel on the waterfront.

As he washed and dressed he berated himself for being carried away so easily. "If you weren't such a realist, George Collinson," he muttered, to his reflection, "I'd begin to wonder if you hadn't lost your mind and dreamt the whole damned thing."

Yet the knowledge that she was real, and that she might be only a few streets away, gnawed at him, and as he paced the room after breakfast, he felt as though the walls were closing in. He screwed up the short reply he had received from Thomas, snatched up his hat and cane, then ran down the stairs and into the street.

His thoughts were jumbled as he strode along in the mild morning air. His shore leave had already been curtailed by his visit to Hawks Head, and there were piles of dockets and bills to go through at the warehouse and store before he sailed at the end of the month. He pulled out his pocket-watch and sighed. Thomas was engaged in military duties and couldn't meet him until a quarter past one, which was still three hours away. He had better find something to do.

After he had checked the warehouse bills of lading and stock sheets he went into the store and spent the rest of the morning on the ledgers with Matthew Lane. When next he consulted his watch, he discovered it was noon and stepped out into the furnace heat of the street.

156

Eloise had waited until Edward had left for the barracks before she ordered the carriage to take her, Meg and the baby to her family's hotel. She had arrived just after nine and would remain for the rest of the day as she preferred the company of her father and her sisters to the loneliness of the rambling house on the shore. They had moved in two weeks before Christmas, and her initial doubts had been confirmed: it had to be kept as clean and impersonal as the hotel's public rooms.

She looked at the tiny gold watch pinned to her dress. It was just past noon. Edward had an appointment at one with her father, and she would avoid him by going into the garden after the light luncheon that had been laid out on the table. Charles was asleep in the old wooden cradle her father had brought from Bavaria, so she told Meg to find something for herself to eat in the kitchen, then wandered round the family's private sitting room, feeling at peace.

She had dressed carefully, as always, and the mirror confirmed that the pale green dress and emerald velvet choker enhanced the colour of her eyes. Her hair had been pinned into a waterfall of curls that tumbled artfully over one shoulder, and she knew that, despite her disastrous marriage, she had never looked better.

Turning from her reflection, she gazed out of the window and down, over the hotel sign and bright awning, to the bustling street. There were sailors mending canvas and convicts unloading ships, and she could see familiar faces among the women shopping and the men who rode by. A group of Aborigines were lounging beneath a shady tree, their naked children playing in the dust, heedless of passing wagons and horses. Beyond the town the blue haze of the surrounding hills shimmered in the heat.

Sydney Town had changed in the four years they had lived there, and although the chain-gangs, whipping-posts and gallows were still stark reminders of the brutal penal system, there was a growing sense of excitement and adventure among the arriving migrants. It was a raw country, far removed from orderly, rather staid Munich, and the pristine splendour of the Bavarian countryside, but it appealed to Eloise in a way she had not expected. How wise Papa had been to build his hotel here, and how brave to forge a new life for his daughters away from the memories that had sung in every corner of their old house in Munich after their mother had died.

If only I hadn't fallen for the first handsome man I met, she thought. If only I could turn back the clock and begin again. Then, angry with herself for allowing regret to spoil the day, she surveyed the room that was the heart of her old home. All of Papa's money had gone into building and furnishing the hotel to his exacting standards, and the evidence of his depleted funds lay in the worn carpet, cheap tables and chairs that stood about her. It was a far cry from the baronial quarters they had once occupied, but Papa was convinced he would soon make his fortune.

And it seemed that his unerring eye for a business opportunity had remained true, for the hotel had quickly become a focal point in the town for landowners and government officials, as well as military officers. Her father had known they would appreciate the quiet luxury of the public rooms where they were shielded from the rougher elements outside, and that they would pay handsomely for the good food and wine he served. He was already on his way to recouping his investment.

Her reverie was broken by the arrival of her sisters. "You look lovely," Anastasia said breathlessly.

"Just like Mama," agreed Irma.

"I miss her even more now I've become a mother," Eloise told them. "She was so wise." She crossed the room to little Charles, asleep in his cradle. His fair hair was damp despite the breeze coming in through the window, and his little face was flushed.

"Motherhood suits you, Eloise," said Irma, as she peeped at her nephew. "No doubt your dashing husband is also the cause of your glow," she added coquettishly.

Eloise had no reply for her. How could she tell her of the dreaded nights when Edward forced himself upon her, of the silent, lonely days and the absence of even the slightest affection between them? How could she speak of Edward's lack of interest in his son, and the long evenings she spent in her room while he and his friends drank themselves into a stupor downstairs? "Let us eat," she said instead. "Where's Papa?"

"He's busy with the accounts. I shan't disturb him — he's rather prickly today."

"I hope it has nothing to do with his meeting with Edward," said Eloise, as they sat at the table. The cold chicken pie and new potatoes looked delicious, but the heat was such that no one had much appetite.

"Papa wasn't in the best of moods when he came home from your dinner-party the other night," said Irma. Her dark eyes studied Eloise thoughtfully. "They didn't exchange sharp words, did they?"

Eloise recalled the stilted conversation between Edward and his own father; Edward's barely concealed rudeness had ruined the evening. "Papa was in good form," she replied carefully. "He and Jonathan get on well." She could see that Irma wasn't satisfied with this, and explained Edward's resentment over his father's absence during his childhood. "Edward and Jonathan are trying to retrieve the lost years, but it makes for awkwardness between them," she ended.

"Poor Edward," murmured Irma, as they returned to the more comfortable chairs by the window. "How strange it must have been for him not to know his father."

Eloise had only heard Edward's side of the story so she did not comment. She arranged her skirts and tried not to look as nervous as she felt. "I wonder what's keeping him," she said. "It's almost one and Father was most insistent that he should not be late."

"It's most mysterious," said Anastasia, cheeks pink with intrigue. "Papa's face was like a thundercloud when he sent the message to the barracks yesterday."

Whatever it was, Eloise hoped it wouldn't plunge Edward into a fury for, unlike her father's short-lived blasts of rage, which hurt no one but himself, Edward's were all-consuming and lasted for days.

"He's here," squeaked Anastasia, who'd been watching for him.

Eloise peered through the window and saw Edward leap from his horse.

"He's so handsome," sighed Irma. "You are lucky, Eloise."

"He's not as handsome as Lieutenant Morely," declared Anastasia, who was passionately in love and had recently became engaged.

Eloise recognised her husband's sour expression as he disappeared from view, and her heart was pounding as she heard his footsteps on the stairs and the baron's gruff voice as he replied to Edward's knock on the study door. The signs in both men suggested that an argument was about to ensue.

"I can't bear the suspense," exclaimed Anastasia. "What do you think Papa wants of Edward? He sounded angry."

Eloise put on her hat, tied the ribbons, then gathered up her parasol and a slim volume of poetry. "I don't know," she replied. "Please look after Charles for me until Meg gets back. I'm going into the garden."

Edward had had no idea why the baron had demanded to see him but, judging by his expression, he was furious. His mind was in a whirl as he tried to think of a misdemeanour that might have stirred the old German to such rage. He stood to attention, knowing it would force the baron to do the same, but the room was stifling, despite the open window, and sweat trickled down his back.

"My daughter is unhappy," said Eloise's father, as he stood before the empty fireplace, hands clasped behind his back. "What have you to say for yourself?"

"Has she told you she's unhappy, Baron?"

"She has no need to. I know my daughter, and she is not content with the way you treat her." His voice had risen and his face was puce.

"I have provided the best house in New South Wales, the finest clothes and jewellery, and servants to attend her every need," retorted Edward, his voice rising to match the baron's. "What else do you expect me to do?"

"Be a proper husband," barked Oskar. "Remain at home and look after her."

Edward could feel a pulse jumping in his cheek, and knew he had to contain his anger. "My military duties keep me away," he said. "Eloise knew they would before we married. She can hardly complain now."

"My daughter does not complain! She is too loyal to you to do so. But I hear the rumours. I know your duties are not what keep you from her side. And I will *not* have my daughter humiliated by your loutish behaviour."

Edward flinched at the insult. "My behaviour is *never* loutish," he growled. "And even if it were, it is no business of yours."

"It damned well is when I see the hurt in my daughter's eyes," the baron thundered. "And what of your son? I heard what you said on the day he was born

162

and have watched how you ignore him. It is breaking my daughter's heart."

"Charles is far too young to be of interest," Edward snapped. "I doubt you spent much time in the nursery when your daughters were small."

"You will mend your ways, sir."

Edward felt a bead of moisture run down his cheek. "I will live my life in the way I see fit," he said softly, but with menace. "Eloise is my wife, and Charles is my son. You have no jurisdiction over either, and you would be wise to keep your nose out of my business."

"Is that a threat?" Oskar von Eisner's eyes bulged with fury and disbelief.

"Only if you wish it to be," replied Edward. He relaxed, and dug his hands into his pockets. The old fool knew nothing of any significance. "If you have no more to say I will collect my wife and son and return home."

"I haven't finished," rapped the baron.

Edward sighed and sat down. "Will this take long?" he asked, with studied indifference.

"It will take as long as I wish," rumbled Eloise's father, plumping into his chair so hard that the springs complained. "I have deep concerns over matters other than my daughter."

Edward kept his expression bland. "Concerns? What concerns?"

The baron stared at a point beyond Edward's shoulder. "Not of your heritage, certainly," he said. "Your father is a fine man, and would be shocked, I am sure, to hear of your recent behaviour."

Another bead meandered down Edward's cheek, but he made no move to brush it away. He swallowed and attempted to maintain his outward show of calm, but he was in turmoil now. His father and the German had become close friends. Had the baron heard of his son-in-law's secret forays into the bush to wipe out the blacks — or was his cheating at cards at issue? "My father has his own failings," he replied. "You must remind me to tell you about them when you are more composed."

"Don't play games with me, boy," Oskar shouted as he rose from his chair and towered over Edward. "Your father is an honourable man — which is more than I can say for you. He pays his gambling debts."

Edward almost laughed with relief. "Mine will be settled at the end of the month, as always," he said. "My creditors know that."

The baron sank back into the chair, but his gaze was steady on Edward's face. "I hope they will," he said, more quietly. "But don't expect my help if they grow too large."

"My finances are in order," barked Edward. "And now I will take my leave."

The baron held up his hand to silence him. "My other concern is your lack of kinship with your father. I have had the pleasure of spending many hours with him, and find him most delightful company. It is a pity you do not share my view." The beetling brows knitted.

"My father and I are virtual strangers," Edward said. "His travels meant he was rarely at home during my formative years, and once I'd joined the army, there

164

were even fewer occasions for us to make better acquaintance."

"You have the opportunity now," replied the baron, "and yet on the rare occasions he is invited to your home your manner borders on insolence. Don't trouble to deny it, sir. I witnessed it the other night. Eloise has said nothing, but I know she wishes to entertain him without fear of an uncomfortable atmosphere." He puffed out his chest. "My daughter is not used to a divided family. It is only right that your father becomes part of her life now that she is your wife."

Edward detected his father's hand in this, and the German was clever. He'd cornered him with reasonable argument and, although the baron couldn't possibly know it, the threat of his father's statement to the judge-advocate still lingered in the shadows. That statement would ruin him for it proved Jonathan had lied under oath to save Edward's neck. It also contained proof that Edward and his men had procured false witnesses, and were indeed guilty of violating Millicent Parker.

"My father will always be welcome in our home," he lied, "and he will be honoured to know that Eloise thinks so highly of him. He has told me he admires her very much."

Oskar remained silent, and Edward realised he must go further into the realms of fantasy to satisfy him. He took a deep breath. "The gulf that exists between my father and me is my deepest regret," he said, "but my service duties have kept me out of Sydney for long periods, and he has been away on exploration." The words slid from his lips as if he had rehearsed them. "We share the desire to make amends. What son could bear to be at odds with the one man to whom he has always looked up, and what father could shun his own flesh and blood, his heir?" He forced himself to smile. "Your advice is wise," he said, "but may I point out that I already had every intention of forging a closer relationship between us, and I regret you should think so badly of me."

The baron grunted. "You have a glib tongue, but the proof of your intent will be shown in your actions."

Eloise had been tempted to listen at the study door, but she had continued down the stairs. With her parasol to shield her face from the sun, she had set off on a stroll in the garden, and although her nerves were in shreds and her thoughts ran haywire, she could still appreciate its beauty.

The ticket-of-leave man they'd hired to bring this plot to life had worked wonders. With the help of several convict boys, he'd turned the arid patch of scrub into a smooth lawn, with circular beds of colourful flowers and a sturdy fence along the boundaries to keep out the kangaroos. The trees and shrubs had been left to give shade, and in the far corner a vegetable patch supplied the hotel with fresh produce.

The baron was a keen collector of exotic plants, and had spent time and money importing them. She inspected the bright red blossom of the native waratah, the delicate white frangipani stars, and then plucked a perfect hibiscus bloom. She paused to marvel at the delicate, jewel-like display of the camellias, then walked on to the arbour, furnished with cane chairs and brightly covered cushions. Roses and honeysuckle clambered up the sides, their scents wafting in the stillness as bees hummed back and forth.

As she sank into the cushions, she couldn't help but glance at the upstairs window of the hotel. She could hear them shouting, but little of what was said. With a tremulous sigh, she tried to block out the angry voices and concentrate on her book.

George felt proud of his achievements as he left the store and the warehouse that had his name over the door. Samuel Varney was an ideal business partner, who never interfered but was always on hand with advice when needed. They were doing a roaring wholesale trade, and George smiled to himself with satisfaction as he walked towards the hotel. Not bad for a scruffy boy from Cornwall who used to keep frogs in his pockets.

He ignored the heat and the buzzing flies as he stepped round horse dung. New South Wales had a way of taking the pomposity and egotism from a man — why, even the governor's house was hardly worth a second glance. Set squarely in parkland, facing the bay, it appeared quite substantial, with its shady veranda and deep windows, but he knew that on closer inspection the white paint would be blistered, the wooden shutters rotten and the tiled roof as leaky as a sieve. Yet it looked respectable in the sunlight, the blue shutters giving it an air of faded grandeur.

167

George had heard that plans were afoot to tear it down and rebuild the governor's country retreat at Parramatta. If the rumours were true, he would miss it. It was there that he had seen the girl with the camellias — and it was also a tacit reminder of the colony's first months when it had been the only proper building among a sea of tents and bark hovels.

A ship's bell rang as he stepped inside the hotel, and he heard a buzz of male voices emanating from the taproom. He entered, and as his eyes grew accustomed to the gloom he was gratified to see several familiar faces — but no sign of Thomas. Forcing himself to concentrate on something other than the matters of his heart, he joined the group.

He had little fear that his youth would be a stumbling block in such company: he was already earning a reputation in business circles for sniffing out undiscovered markets — but he wasn't joining them to give away his secrets, more to listen and learn. He ordered a drink and joined in the boisterous conversation.

When the others wandered back to their offices and there was still no sign of his friend, George became impatient. Thomas was usually so reliable — something must have delayed him. He threw himself into a comfortable chair by the window with a pint of porter and relaxed a little in the light breeze that drifted in from the garden. Soon he was pondering the opportunities open to a man of vision in this colony. He had long ago realised he had both the vision and the ability to see an enterprise fulfilled, and what he'd heard today had piqued his interest. Ideas flowed and took shape — interrupted only when the clock struck.

Thomas was now very late and George wondered what to do. He grimaced as his stiff collar chafed his neck. Used to the soft, loose clothes and informality of life aboard ship, or on horseback, his formal attire was restricting, and he felt ill-at-ease now that his friend had let him down.

Battling disappointment, he gathered up his hat and cane and inadvertently he glanced out of the window. What he saw made him abandon all thought of leaving.

Edward stared at a point above the baron's shoulder as the older man catalogued his faults and berated him again for his neglect of wife and son. When the tirade was over, silence hung between them as the clock on the wall ticked towards two.

The baron was first to speak. "You have said you wish to form closer ties with your father, so it will please you to know that he will be joining us for tea at four."

"I have made other plans."

"Break them," demanded the baron. His gaze bored into Edward. "You will attend."

Edward rose from his chair and slammed the door behind him. His rage was such that he could barely breathe. His father's influence on the baron was clear, and he resented being told what to do. As for Eloise, how dare she whisper in her father's ear?

George's legs gave way and he collapsed on to the window-seat, riveted by the vision before him. She was

169

the most exquisite girl and as she sat in the arbour, surrounded by flowers, he wondered if she had any idea of what a glorious picture she made. His pulse raced as his dreams took on wondrous reality. Her shoulders were pale, her waist narrow, and her golden hair tumbled from beneath the fetching hat to caress her skin. Her elegant hands held a slim, leatherbound volume, whose pages had been held down with a hibiscus blossom. She was perfect, and George knew in that moment he could never love another. There was little sign in her now of the hoyden who had danced across the lawn in the moonlight, but this quieter side of her intrigued him: he saw self-assurance, which told him she was comfortable in her solitude.

She seemed unaware of his scrutiny, seemingly captured by her book. She was quite tall, he realised, and elegant in that pale green tea-gown. Her *décolletage* was flawless, and the green ribbon round her neck emphasised its slender arch.

He made a concerted effort to pull himself together and find someone to introduce them, when she lifted her head and met his gaze. He was frozen to the spot. Her eyes were like emeralds in the heart-shaped face, and her amusement at having caught him staring made him blush. A flash of dimple appeared in her cheek and she returned to her book.

George rose from the window-seat and discovered he was alone in the room but for an elderly gentleman sleeping off his lunch. Another glance through the window told him she was still there, but the frustration of knowing she could be gone at any minute, that he might miss his opportunity, was almost too great to bear. If only Thomas were here! He was torn between the desire to do the right thing, and wait for an introduction, and the heady temptation to disregard convention and approach her anyway.

Eloise closed her book. Shakespeare's sonnets usually calmed her, but today her nerves jangled and she was easily distracted. She glanced up at the study window again and frowned. Edward and her father had been in there for a long time, but at least they had stopped shouting.

The garden had grown chilly now, so she picked up her parasol and the book, then walked away from the arbour to a more isolated spot in the garden that still caught the sun. The young man she'd seen through the taproom window wouldn't be able to spy on her here. She settled on a stone bench. His blush had made her smile, and she'd had the impression that she'd seen those handsome features and the dark hair before.

She opened her book again, but the words danced before her. Again she tried to concentrate, but the words remained a blur. How could she feel so when she was married and a mother?

She snapped the book shut, determined not to allow her wits to desert her. The argument between Edward and her father had unnerved her, that was all, and she'd let her imagination run wild. She had seen merely a face at a window — an anonymous face that meant nothing to her.

She looked towards the study and bit her lip. It was time to go in and discover what had happened. She stood up and made for the door that led up to the family's apartment.

Edward loomed out of the gloom of the stairwell and grasped her arm. "In there," he said. He pushed her into a storeroom and slammed the door.

Eloise was not cowed by his rough handling. This was her father's hotel and Edward wouldn't dare to hurt her under its roof. "Whatever you and Papa were arguing about is none of my business, Edward," she said. "Open the door and let me out."

"Not until I'm ready to do so." He pinned her against the wooden wall among the sacks of flour and potatoes. "If you complain to your father again, or run to him with tales of how poorly I treat you, you will be punished. Do you understand?"

"Lay one finger on me and I'll scream," she said.

Edward appeared unmoved. "If I hear you have spoken ill of me to him I will beat you black and blue." His voice was low. "No one will hear your screams."

Eloise knew he meant every word and tried to still the trembling that had overtaken her. "I do not discuss you with my father," she managed. "Your accusations are insulting and misplaced. Besides," she added, surprised to hear how calm she sounded, "my bruises will speak for me."

"Your bruises won't show," he replied, "unless you take off your clothes."

"I knew you felt little for me," she said softly, "but I hadn't realised you hated me so."

172

"I don't hate you," he rasped. "If you become the wife you should be, you need have no fear that I shall touch you. Disobey, and you will find me unforgiving."

Eloise was too frightened to speak.

Edward released her and straightened his jacket. "Now you may go upstairs while I return to the barracks. My dear father has arrived, and I'm assured by the baron that you enjoy his company so you must not keep him waiting."

"George, forgive my tardiness."

"Where have you been?" George took his friend's hand. "But never mind, it doesn't matter now. Come, she's in the garden."

"Wait, George. There's something I must tell you."

He saw the dullness in his friend's eyes and experienced a pang of fear. "Whatever is it, Tom?"

"You'd better sit down."

"But the girl I told you about is out there and might be gone at any minute. We must hurry."

Thomas clasped his arm and steered him towards a seat. He signalled to the barman and ordered them both a hefty glass of rum. "She has already gone," he said quietly.

"Nonsense," spluttered George. "I saw her just moments ago."

Thomas shook his head. "Her name is Eloise Cadwallader."

George slumped in his chair, his hopes washed away in a tide of despair. "How can you be so certain?"

"From the description you gave, but I knew whom she must be when I saw her in the garden."

"You were here earlier?" George's voice was sharp with pain.

"No more than ten minutes."

George knew from the pity in his friend's eyes that his agony was clear. "Why didn't you come to find me?"

Thomas reddened. "I was late because I had to attend a court-martial that endured longer than expected. Anastasia caught me as I was about to come in here." He jutted out his chin. "That was when I saw Eloise in the garden. Your own words confirmed the identity of your girl. I'm sorry."

George swallowed the lump in his throat. His hand shook as he lifted his glass to his lips.

"I wish it wasn't so," Thomas said, "but perhaps it's for the best."

George groaned. "What am I to do?"

"Forget her. There are other beautiful women in Sydney Town, who are free and only too keen to find a husband."

"None as beautiful as Eloise," he murmured.

"By Gad, you've been bitten hard," said Thomas. "And this is the man who swore only weeks ago he'd never succumb. You must pull yourself together, George. She's a married woman with a young child, and that's an end to it."

"I cannot forget her."

"You must."

The rum burnt his gut and the room closed in on him. George dragged himself out of the chair and ran his finger inside the tight collar. "I need air," he muttered.

"I'll come with you." Thomas made to rise.

"Not now, Tom. I need time to myself."

Without waiting for a reply, George stepped through the double doors into the garden.

PART TWO

Entangled Alliances

CHAPTER
SEVEN

Hawks Head Farm, 9 January 1798

It was early morning, but the sky remained leaden as the heat rose and thunder rumbled in the distance. A dog was barking, and the cattle in the nearby pasture were milling about, on edge with the threat of a storm. Horses and men moved around the clearing as they prepared for another day, and the heavy air rang with jingling harness and the strike of hammer on anvil.

Susan and Nell emerged from the stifling homestead on to the veranda in the hope of a breeze from the Hawkesbury River. But today there was none.

"I don't like the look of the weather," said Susan. "Not a good day for travelling."

Nell knew her sister-in-law was reluctant to let her go. They had become closer than ever during the past two months, and she hoped it had gone some way to filling the gap Florence had left when she'd gone into self-imposed exile. "A drop of rain won't 'urt," she said, with a lightness that masked her thoughts.

Susan mopped her brow with a handkerchief. "Are you sure you're well enough to travel?"

Nell nodded as she flapped at a swarm of flies. "I've already missed Christmas with the children. I don't want to miss the twins' birthday too," she replied. "I've been away so long they'll 'ave forgotten me."

"I doubt that, but it's certainly been a slow recovery," said Susan. "There were times when Billy and I thought you'd never find the strength to fight back."

Nell's memory of those first weeks was a blur, consisting mainly of burning heat, icy chills and terrifying visions accompanied by pain. "Most of the time I didn't know what day it were." She grinned. "I reckon that were a blessin' in disguise an' all. Gawd knows, I'm bad enough when I'm well."

"That's what I love about you." Susan's face creased into a smile. "You never give in."

Nell gave her a hug. In fact, she'd come close to giving in many times — especially when the army surgeon had told her there would be no more children. But the love and warmth of the family had pulled her through, and there was no adequate way to thank them. "I couldn't 'ave done it without you," she said.

They drew back from the embrace. "I wish I could have put some more flesh on your bones. Your children won't recognise their new, skinny mother."

Nell looked down at her depleted cleavage, which barely showed above the tightly laced bodice. "I ain't never seen 'em so small." Then she tossed her curls and stuck out her chin. "They'll come back once I'm in me own 'ome and in charge again. You'll see."

Susan chewed her lip.

Nell knew what she was thinking and, not wanting to discuss Alice, forestalled her. "I'll say goodbye to the others," she said. "Tell Billy I'll be ready in about 'alf an hour."

It was almost an hour later when Nell climbed into the wagon beside Billy. She had said her goodbyes and was ready for home, but as she looked at each of the upturned faces, she couldn't help wishing she could take them with her.

Ezra had become a father to her over the past months. He was fifty-five, but seemed a decade older in that rusty black coat and broad-brimmed hat. His hair was white, his face long, pale and lined, his shoulders stooped. He'd never recovered from Millicent's suicide and Florence's departure, while the burden of running the Hawkesbury mission was eroding the last of his strength. Yet his kindness had shone through during her convalescence: he'd spent many hours reading to her and helping her to learn her letters.

Ernest had his father's height and reserved nature, but there the resemblance ended. His robust health was plain to see in the tanned face. The resilience of youth had seen him through the loss of Millicent, his first love, and now he looked forward to a bright future with his wife and the baby she was expecting.

Nell grinned down at Bess, a down-to-earth girl who worked hard and had a cheerful way with her that Nell could only envy. Plump and bustling, she'd swiftly become a favourite with them all. Nell blinked away tears as she blew a final kiss to Susan. "Let's go, Billy," she murmured. "Another minute and I'll be howling."

Moonrakers, 9 January 1798

Alice left the laundry basket on the ground and eased her back. She was exhausted, but elated by the endless round of work she and Jack had achieved over the past few months. The farm was prospering, the children were happy, and the only real difficulty she'd encountered was the Aborigines. The native children were a delight, but as mischievous as mice and constantly underfoot. The men were rarely seen, coming only to the homestead when they wanted to beg baccy or a tot of rum — they scorned the idea of working for such perquisites.

Now three women had wandered across the yard to lean against the fence beside her. Gladys, Pearl and Daisy were as idle as any three women could be. They refused to help in the house, stole food from the pantry and generally got in the way — but she'd come to accept their malodorous presence and appreciated their help with the children when she was busy with the animals. The little ones loved the freedom of the native camp, where they could strip off, get dirty and eat questionable food that had been cooked in the ashes of the campfire. Still, she thought, as the line of washing flapped in the breeze, a peck of dirt didn't hurt anyone, and the children thrived on it — even if it did mean more laundry every day.

"Reckon you missus now," said Gladys, breaking into her thoughts. "Two boss alonga you." She nudged Alice and the three Aborigines broke into raucous laughter.

Alice looked at them askance. "Certainly not," she said. "Two boss, two missus. Nell will be back soon."

"Missus Nell away alonga time," said Gladys, sagely. "Boss get lonely."

Alice was glad that no one was about to hear this exchange. She was mortified that anyone should think *she* was such a woman. "Jack my boss, not Billy," she said firmly. "And I'll thank you not to repeat such slander."

Gladys's eyes sparkled with good humour as she gabbled something to the others.

Alice didn't understand a word of it, but the meaning was clear in the gestures they were making. Gladys was shaking her head and the others were cackling as they ambled off, and she sighed with exasperation. If Nell heard such gossip there would be no end of trouble. For now she would ignore it and hope it went away.

She left the laundry basket where it was and entered the new shearing shed, with its welcoming scent of freshly cut timber. Jack and the convicts had finished it this afternoon, and there had been rum for everyone as they celebrated this next step in the taming of Moonrakers.

She enjoyed the silence as a few dusty sunbeams forced their way through the high, raftered roof to cast pools of gold on the floor that would eventually be bleached by the sweat of the shearers. Now the stalls were empty, the heavy table clear, but one day thick fleeces would be sorted there, and the wooden ramps would ring with the trampling of hoofs. She could almost hear the shouts — "Wool away! Tar! Sheep!" — and smell the lanolin, sweat and tar in the cathedral silence.

Her boot heels echoed as she walked round the little grindstones with their cranky handles and broad, rough surfaces, and up to the far end where the great wool-press waited for the first bale of a new season. The windows of each stall were shuttered now, but when the men came in April, they would be pushed wide open.

She hugged herself with delight. It had all been possible because of the success of the late shearing. The wool yield had surpassed all expectations, which had meant they had been able to build this magnificent shed and had bought more merinos from their wealthy neighbour, John Macarthur. Now their flock had been increased three-fold by the spring and summer lambs.

"Mama," came a piping voice from the doorway.

Alice's heart twisted as she walked back down the shed and took Sarah into her arms. She'd fallen in love with Nell's children, especially Sarah, and as she kissed the soft curls and held her close, she wished she had one of her own.

"Mama, what are you doing?" Sarah asked.

"She's not our mama," said Amy, crossly, as she came towards them. "Mama's at Aunt Susan's." Red curls ablaze, she glared at her sister as she crossed her arms and tapped a tiny foot.

184

Alice had to bite back the laughter. Amy was so like her mother, and although she was not quite seven, she already had Nell's manner. She smiled at the little girl. "You're right," she said softly. "I'm not your mama and, Sarah, you must remember to call me Aunt Alice."

"Don't want to," pouted Sarah.

Alice took their hands and led them outside before a full-blown tantrum erupted. "Papa will be home tomorrow," she said. "Why don't we make a special banner to welcome him back?"

"Is Mama coming home with him this time?" Amy's gaze was unwavering as she waited for an answer.

Billy had visited Nell as often as he could over the past months, and Amy, especially, was always disappointed when he returned alone. "Perhaps," Alice hedged. "If she's well enough to travel such a distance."

"I don't want my other mama," sobbed Sarah. "I want you." She flung herself against Alice's legs and clung to her. Alice picked her up and balanced her on her hip. "I'm not going anywhere," she soothed. "But your mama will be here soon, and she can't wait to see you. She loves you so much, and must have been very lonely without you all while she was at Aunt Susan's."

Sarah sniffed and Alice wiped her nose. "Come, Amy, you can help me with the banner, and if we say a really good prayer tonight, perhaps your mother will come home too."

Amy seemed happy with the idea and skipped along at her side as they headed for the homestead. Alice's heart was heavy, though, for if Nell did come back tomorrow she would not be allowed to continue her

185

close, loving relationship with the children, and she didn't know how she would bear it.

She set them to work on the flour-sack banner as she prepared their evening meal. Her day had begun before dawn, and would continue until long after the children were asleep, yet the weariness wasn't a burden for she felt fulfilled and happy.

She smiled as the girls chattered and drew pictures, and hoped this peaceful state could continue. She had instigated a routine that helped the days run smoothly: care of the house and the children had to be interspersed with care of the stock. The children ate at the table, went to bed at the same time each night and bathed regularly. They had simple lessons for an hour every morning, and said their prayers at night. Billy had been happy for her to take charge, and had expressed his relief at how orderly life had become. He had added that Nell would be pleased with what she'd achieved.

Alice, however, suspected that Nell would see the organisation of her family as unwarranted interference.

On the track to Moonrakers, the next day

"I can't wait to see the children," said Nell, as the horse splashed along the muddy track. "They must have grown so much. I 'ope they'll know me."

Billy was concentrating on steering through the lesser puddles and potholes. The earlier cloudburst had been violent but, thankfully, short-lived. "Of course they will," he muttered, "but there's been changes at Moonrakers."

186

"What changes? You never said before."

He tugged at his hat. Water was still dripping down his neck even though the sun was high. "Alice suggested we build a shearing shed now we have more stock. It was almost finished when I left to collect you."

Nell knew him so well that she could tell he was uneasy with this conversation, but she remained silent, waiting for him to reveal what else had changed in her absence.

"Alice teaches the children every morning. They've learnt their letters and can count to ten now," he said proudly. "Walter comes out with me sometimes on his pony, and is quite the little man. And the girls . . ." He paused. "Alice has taught them to do the lighter work in the house. They hardly ever throw tantrums now because they get regular meals and go to bed at the right time. She's been a marvel, Nell."

His praise for Alice was the culmination of her worst fears. "I'm sure she has," she said bitterly.

Billy drew the wagon to a halt and shook the last of the water from his hat, then squashed it back on his head. He took her hand. "Nell," he began, "you're the loveliest, kindest, most precious thing in the world, but sometimes you drive me to the edge of reason."

"And why's that?"

"Without Alice, me and Jack couldn't have managed the farm and the children. Without Alice, none of us would have had a decent meal for months and the children would be running wild. Why can't you be grateful to her?"

"I *am* grateful," she retorted.

"No, you're not. You're jealous."

"Damn right I am. How would you feel if I got another man in to look after me and the children while you were away? How would you feel if when you got back I told you he was better at running the place than you?" She folded her arms. "You'd be jealous, that's what."

Billy stared moodily into the distance. "You're right," he said finally.

"You'd be ready to flatten him, not kiss his cheek and thank him."

His eyes were troubled beneath the brim of his hat. "You've changed, Nell," he said. "I fell in love with a soft, warm, loving woman who would have been grateful for another's help, made friends with her and counted her blessings. What happened at Hawks Head to change that?"

"Those months with Susan and her family made me see 'ow precious you and the children are to me," she said softly. "I love your sister and 'er 'usband, and am grateful for what they done — but I hated being so far from Moonrakers, knowing Alice had taken my place."

Billy covered her fingers with his work-roughened hand. "Alice could never take your place. She's not my wife, not the mother of my children, just a good, kind soul who stepped in when she was needed."

Nell felt the prickle of tears and blinked. "I'm frightened, Billy," she admitted. "What if the little 'uns don't love me no more? I couldn't bear to lose 'em."

Billy drew her into an embrace. "They talk about you every day — I made sure of that, and so did Jack and

188

Alice. They haven't forgotten who you are." He smoothed back a damp tendril of hair from her forehead and kissed her brow. "The fever made you confused. Nothing important has changed."

She pulled away from him and blew her nose, determined to put on a show of strength and prepare for whatever she might find at Moonrakers. "Then why are we sittin' 'ere? Let's get 'ome."

Moonrakers, the next day

The children were sitting on the veranda in their best clothes, their hair brushed until it gleamed. They were supposed to be looking at the picture books Billy had brought from the government school in Sydney, but they were too excited to sit still and were soon running up and down the wooden floor.

The banner had been nailed to the veranda roof and flapped in the warm breeze as the sun began to dry the yard. The downpour had been heavy, but had done little to alleviate the heat.

"I told them not to get dirty," said Alice, as she stood beside Jack at the yard fence and watched Walter jump into the puddles.

"They're excited," he replied, his gaze fixed on a point at the other side of the river. "The thought that their mother might be on her way is more important to them than clean clothes."

Alice's spirits plummeted when she saw distant movement in the trees.

"I know you love them like your own," said Jack, "but they belong to Nell." He put his arm round her waist. "You've loved them well, Alice. Now it's time to give them back, and concentrate on starting our own family."

Her smile was wan. It was early days yet, but there was still no sign of the longed-for child. Perhaps she wasn't meant to be a mother. Perhaps she'd left it too late.

A piercing whistle tore her back to the present. The horse and wagon were waiting for the raft, and there, sitting beside Billy, was Nell. The children rushed off, shrieking, to the river. The pain in Alice's heart was almost overwhelming. "I've moved our things," she said. "I'll leave you with the children to welcome them home and get started on the drenching."

"It can wait," he said, his arm still round her waist.

"No, it can't." She wrenched herself away from him and knew she must look a sight with the tears running down her face. "I need to be alone," she sobbed. "Just for a while." Without waiting for his reply, she ran towards the new shearing shed, and was soon out of sight of the joyful reunion.

The long day was almost over, the sun dipping towards the horizon, the sky livid with purple and orange. It was cooler now, and the swarms of flies were gone, replaced by mosquitoes. Roosting parrots and kookaburras called sleepily from the surrounding trees while kangaroos and wallabies emerged from the bush to feed on the grass.

Alice was exhausted, not only from hours of back-breaking work with the sheep but from the heartache she'd suffered all day. She sat alone on the rough wooden bench by the pond, watching the sunset as she searched for the energy to go back to the house and face the first night without the children.

A rustle made her turn.

"Jack said you might be 'ere," puffed Nell, as she waded through the sea of long, silver grass. "I thought we should 'ave a quiet word away from the men. Clear the air."

Alice made room for her on the bench. She wasn't ready for a confrontation — and certainly not prepared for the slender, pale Nell who sat next to her.

Nell chuckled. "You needn't look so frosty," she said. "I ain't gunna bite yer." She nudged Alice's arm. "Though I could certainly do with fattenin' up — Billy's already callin' me 'is vanishin' woman."

Alice smiled hesitantly. "You look lovely," she said truthfully.

"So do you, though the sheep dip in yer 'air don't do you no favours."

Alice saw the gleam in her eyes and couldn't help but giggle. "It does wonders for the wool so I thought I might try it," she said.

Nell smiled, then turned to the horizon where the sun had left a trail of scarlet. "I ain't been fair to you, Alice," she began. "The surgeon put me straight about everything, and I know you weren't to blame for what 'appened."

"You weren't well." The memory of those two days was still sharp to Alice.

"Yeah, I know, but that ain't no excuse, 'cos I was angry with you before that." As the last of the colour faded from the sky, her eyes reflected her regret. "We've both 'ad to learn the 'ard way, Alice, and although it ain't been easy, I think we understand each other better now." She paused. "You done well with the little 'uns by the way."

"They're beautiful," Alice said, unable to mask the wistfulness in her voice as she thought of bathtime and the sweet-smelling sleepy heads on the pillows last thing at night.

Nell nodded. "You'll make a good mother when it's your turn," she replied. "But I think it might be best if you leave 'em to me for a while. They need to get to know me again."

Alice swallowed, but the lump in her throat refused to go away and she could only nod. Nell's message was clear, and she could understand the sense in it — but, dear God, it hurt.

Nell stood and brushed the grass seeds from her cotton dress. "I don't know if we can ever be close friends," she said, after a moment's silence. "We're too different. But we're stuck out 'ere with only each other for female company. Billy and Jack don't like trouble, and neither do I, so for their sake and ours, I reckon we should put our differences aside and make the best of it. What d'ya say?"

Alice stood and faced her. "That's a very good idea," she replied. "But my place here is as important as yours."

"As long as you remember what that place is and don't overstep the mark with my children," Nell replied.

"Oh, I think you'll remind me if I do," said Alice.

CHAPTER
EIGHT

Sydney Town, March 1798

George had been at sea for almost two months and, on his return, had made a short visit to Hawks Head. He had come back to Sydney the night before, but the visit home had been a sharp reminder of how little he saw his family, and anxiety for his parents still niggled. His father was becoming frail, and although his mother kept up a bright smile and an efficient bustle at the homestead, George could see that she'd aged.

"If only Florence could be found and persuaded to come home," he muttered, as he dressed for Governor Hunter's garden-party. "Surely she's punished them enough."

His sister had disappeared on the night before the trial. There had been little news of her, other than that she was travelling with a couple of missionaries, who seemed intent on trying to reach the most inaccessible parts of Australia so they could preach to the natives. George snorted. Florence was the last person he'd expected to do such a thing. She'd always been an unpleasant girl, often clipping him round the ear when he was younger, and had shown little sign then of religious fervour.

He picked up his hat and left the boarding-house, striding along the street towards the governor's residence, determined not to let his worries spoil the party, or his thoughts to wander to the possibility that Eloise might be there. Despite his weeks at sea, the blow that had been inflicted when Thomas revealed her identity still pained him — and he knew he must brace himself for when he saw her again and act appropriately.

The garden-party was in full swing as the sun beat down on the swirling colours of the women's gowns and hats, and the scarlet uniforms. The chatter and laughter were threaded together by the melodious harmony of violin and piano, and the less melodious yapping of dogs. A pleasant breeze alleviated the heat, and awnings had been set up to provide shade from the sun. As George sauntered across the lawn, stopping now and again to greet a friend or business acquaintance, he found it impossible not to look for her.

He was in conversation with Elizabeth Macarthur and Richard Atkins, the judge-advocate, when he saw her. He murmured an excuse as John Macarthur joined the group, and left the two old adversaries to their well-worn arguments. He found a shady spot close by, then stood and watched her.

She was with Thomas Morely and her sisters, saying something that was making them laugh. Her dress was the colour of a tropical sea, changing from green to the deepest turquoise as she moved. Her hat was tilted to shade her eyes, her glorious hair glittering like gold on her left shoulder. But it was her face that captured him, and as she met his gaze his heart began to thud.

She smiled, the dimple flashing, then turned back to Thomas and they all looked at him.

George had been caught wide-eyed again, but he couldn't walk away for Thomas was coming towards him.

"Cadwallader might be out of town, but others look after his interests when he's away," Thomas muttered.

George could no more turn down the opportunity to speak to her than fly to the moon. He adopted his usual grin and shook his friend's hand. "Hang it all, Thomas," he said. "I only wish for an introduction."

"Very well," he said. "But I know you of old, and can see only disaster ahead."

"Lead on, Thomas. The ladies are waiting."

Thomas's hand stopped him before he could move. "Cadwallader is a dangerous man to cross. Remember that, George."

George knew too well what kind of man Cadwallader was, but Eloise was waiting for him, and even the thought of her husband's wrath couldn't deter him. He touched the slim volume he'd tucked into his pocket. The camellia blossom was pressed between its pages. "I hear your warning, Thomas," he said cheerfully. "Now for goodness' sake, introduce me before she tires of waiting."

For all his bonhomie, George was nervous as he followed his friend across the lawn. His mind whirled. What could he say to her without looking a fool?

196

"Anastasia, my dear, do you remember my friend George Collinson?"

George bowed over the plump hand.

Then Thomas introduced Irma, and as George kissed the air above her fingers, he couldn't help but notice the blatant flirtation in the pale blue eyes that he'd seen at the governor's ball before Christmas. She was the plainest of the sisters, and rather too forward.

Thomas cleared his throat. "Lady Cadwallader, may I introduce George Collinson?"

George hadn't missed the deliberate way in which Thomas had introduced her, and knew it was a reminder of who and what she was. But as he took her hand it was as if he'd been struck by lightning. All reason fled. "A pleasure," he said.

"I do believe we have crossed paths once before, Mr Collinson." She retrieved her hand and her eyes twinkled. "Was it not you at the taproom window some weeks ago?"

She remembered him. His heart sang. "It was indeed," he replied, unable to keep the joy from his voice. "Forgive me, if I disturbed your privacy."

Her throaty chuckle sent a thrill through him. "When one lives in a hotel one becomes used to being spied upon." She tilted her head, her eyes alight with humour.

"I was not spying," he said quickly. "I merely happened to . . ."

Her hand touched his arm. "I know," she said softly. "I was teasing."

George melted.

★   ★   ★

197

Eloise had felt the shock when their hands met, and found she was entranced by his deep brown eyes with the golden flecks. On the awful day when Edward had shown his true colours, she had noticed only George's dark hair and eyes, but on closer inspection his hair and moustache gleamed with copper lights, and his strong, handsome face showed an innocent pleasure in life, and an openness she found most appealing.

"Would you ladies like some tea?"

She was startled by Thomas's interruption and dragged her gaze from the young man to find that everyone was watching them. "That would be lovely," she said, unusually flustered. "Perhaps we could find a table out of the sun."

The two men went off in search of tea, and she saw that Mr Collinson walked with the sway of a man used to being aboard ship.

"Eloise? Eloise, *really!*"

She jumped, startled.

"What has got into you?" asked Irma.

"Nothing," Eloise replied, a little too sharply. She tempered her tone. "Come, let us find that table in the shade before they are all taken."

"He's very handsome," chirped Irma, as they moved through the crowd towards the awnings that had been set up at the far end of the garden. "I remember meeting him for a moment at the governor's ball, but I had no time to discover more than his name."

"Thomas told me he owns a farm, a warehouse and a shop, but is often away on the whaling ships," said Anastasia. "He has a certain piratical swagger that is

198

most attractive," she added, with grin at her eldest sister. "Had you forgotten you already have a handsome husband?"

"Of course not," Eloise replied, as she sat down. The mention of Edward had brought her firmly to her senses. She was foolish to allow Mr Collinson to turn her head so wantonly . . .

"As I seem to be the only one without an admirer, it's only fair that I should be permitted to get to know Mr Collinson," said Irma, as she arranged her skirts decorously. "He's young, handsome and rich. It might be fun to be courted by a buccaneer."

Eloise laughed with her sisters, but somehow she didn't find Irma's remark amusing. Irma was perhaps a little too desperate to find a husband, and Mr Collinson appeared far too sensible to be taken in by her outrageous flirting. She snapped open her fan and tried to restore calm. Really, she thought, it was too bad of Mr Collinson to cause such a stir.

George balanced a cup and saucer on his knee and nibbled at a piece of cake. Irma was blatant in her coquettishness, her eyes wide and shining above her fan as she fluttered her lashes and giggled at everything he said.

"Is whaling as dangerous as they say?" she asked.

"It is," he replied. "The seas are rough, the whale doesn't want to be caught and it's a gory death."

"Ooh!" squealed Irma, with too much feminine horror. "You must be very brave, Mr Collinson."

"No braver than any man who rides the sea for a living."

"So modest too. Why, I should have thought you would love to tell us of your exploits," said Eloise.

George saw she was teasing him again. "They aren't suitable for ladies to hear," he said. "Life on a whaling ship can be gruesome."

"Then I admire your candour, Mr Collinson, and thank you for your sensibility in not sharing them with us." She smiled, and he melted again. "More tea?"

He was about to accept, even though he'd had enough to sink a ship, when a meaty hand fell on his shoulder. "There you are, young fella. Been looking for you everywhere."

George introduced Samuel Varney who clearly had something other than tea on his mind. "I need a word, son. It's important."

George rose to take his leave. "Forgive me, ladies," he said. He threw a longing glance at Eloise, then turned away. The triumph of having met her was tainted with the knowledge that he might never talk with her alone — and that after today he'd never be able to forget her.

Eloise busied herself with the teacups but her thoughts ran amok. It was a shame George had been called away — she was sure they could find many things to talk about — and she had enjoyed his company. But there were many social functions in Sydney Town, and they were bound to meet again. She adjusted her hat as a blush crept into her face. She felt ridiculously pleased at the idea.

As she looked down she caught sight of a slim volume lying in the grass beneath George's empty chair. It must have dropped from his pocket, and she was curious as to what manner of reading interested such a likeable man. Thomas was occupying her sisters with an entertaining story, so she placed her foot upon it and drew it gently towards her until it was under the hem of her skirt.

"I've had enough tea," said Anastasia, some time later.

"So have I. Shall we stroll round the gardens?" Thomas rose from his chair and she took his arm.

"I hear the new convict gardener has done wonders with the roses." Irma looked at Eloise. "Will you join us?"

Eloise settled more firmly in her chair. "I will sit in the shade for a while," she said. "You go."

Eloise waited until they were out of sight, then bent to pick up the book. She opened it to the first page and read: "To George on his tenth birthday from Mother and Father."

She smiled inwardly, for she could picture Mr Collinson as a boy, and suspected that the gift had been a disappointment. He would have been far more delighted with a hoop or a ball. So why had he carried this book in his pocket?

Eloise saw that it was Shakespeare's *Othello* and the smile lingered. It was an exciting tale, so perhaps it wasn't so surprising. She flicked through the gold-edged pages, noting the thumbed corners and that something was pressed between them. She stared at the camellia and wondered why it was there. A memento, perhaps, of a tryst, or a girl he'd once met? Then she remembered the camellia that had fallen from her hair when she'd danced in the garden.

She looked across the lawn to the two men, deep in conversation. Had George been at the governor's ball that night? Had he watched her dancing in the dark, and found the camellia? Or was her imagination running away with her? Eloise's diamond ring glinted as she clasped the worn leather. There was little doubt that George Collinson was enamoured of her: it was in his eyes and his voice — and she was drawn to him.

Eloise placed the book in her reticule. She was a married woman and shouldn't be having these thoughts — but her heart was beating like a drum and she couldn't resist another furtive glance at the man on the other side of the lawn.

"I must get back to Nantucket," said Samuel. "The Sowerbury brothers have shown their hand by burning down the ware-house and try-works. They've been my rivals for years, but I never thought they'd go so far."

"I'm sorry you're so distressed, Samuel," said George, "but what can you hope to achieve by racing back there?"

Samuel waved the letter in his face. "This is already weeks old, and those renegades need to know I'm not easily beaten," he rasped. "Besides, I must see that my men and their families are safe." He clasped his hands behind his back and glared into the distance.

George knew there was little he could say to console his friend. "When do you plan to leave?"

"Tonight," he replied. "Can I expect your company, or are you otherwise occupied?"

George shifted from one foot to the other as he weighed up his conflicting emotions. Samuel was his friend and mentor and he knew he shouldn't have thought twice about going with him. But there was Eloise too. Cadwallader was out of town, and there was just a chance he might see her again. The contest was unfair. "You won't need me if it's not a whaling trip," he hedged.

Samuel's expression softened and he gave a great sigh. "I suppose you're right," he said.

"But if you need me, of course I'll come," George said hastily, ashamed of his lapse in loyalty.

"She's very beautiful," Samuel said. "I can see why you're smitten."

"How did you know?"

"Ha! Your face says it all." He scratched his white beard. "Women! They get us all in the end." He studied the object of their conversation. "You're heading for trouble, young 'un," he said quietly. "There's already a ring on her finger and it ain't yours."

"I know," he admitted. "But my heart won't listen."

"Hmph. It's your head that needs seeing to," he said gruffly. Then his woeful expression cleared and he smiled. "Youth is a joyful time, when all things seem possible and the heart and head are in constant battle.

You'll be hurt, son — but that's part of growing to maturity." He leant towards George, his voice low and confidential. "But if you love her as you say, you'll leave her alone. Any liaison between you will bring only heartache to all concerned."

"I don't know that I'm strong enough to walk away, Sam," he admitted. "And I'm sorry I won't be coming with you. I feel I've let you down."

"Never," he retorted. "You've been like a son to me, George, and I'm proud of everything you've achieved. This is my dilemma and I'll resolve it." He threw his arms round George and gave him a hug. "Good hunting, my boy. Keep an eye on the business for me, and I'll see you before the year's out."

George watched him stride away, torn between the desire to follow him and the yearning to seek out Eloise.

"Mr Collinson?"

He whirled round, and coherent thought fled. "Lady Eloise," he breathed.

"You have mislaid something."

"Only my wits." He gazed into her eyes. "It seems my usual manner has deserted me this afternoon."

The dimple flashed as she reached into her reticule. "I was alluding to your book, Mr Collinson. As to your wit, I suspect it never truly deserts you."

George took the book, aware of how close to him she was. "It must have dropped from my pocket. Thank you."

"*Othello* is an interesting choice for a boy of ten," she said. "I wonder that one so young could grasp

204

Shakespeare's understanding of the darkness that lies in the human soul."

She had read the inscription — but had she discovered the camellia blossom between the pages? And, if so, could she know what it represented? "I'd wanted a sling-shot, and was bitterly disappointed."

"So, as I'd thought, you were not a boy to sit still for long."

"I was an urchin with torn jackets and frogs in my pocket. My poor mother despaired."

Her eyes were very green. "*Othello* is certainly preferable to frogs, Mr Collinson. What a stir they would have caused if it had been they that had slipped from your pocket during tea."

Her laughter vibrated through him and he found he couldn't look away from her. "*Othello* is my companion when I'm at sea," he said softly. "There are long hours of idleness; and I find the story compelling, no matter how many times I read it."

"I agree," she replied. "Yet it is a tale of treachery, madness and jealousy."

"But at its heart there is a man in love."

The silence stretched between them and the sounds of the party faded. "Othello's love was his downfall," she reminded him.

There was no mistaking the message in her words, and his spirits tumbled. "Only because his traitorous friend, Iago, made it so," he returned.

"Iago manipulated Othello until it became an obsession." Eloise held his gaze. "And obsession is dangerous when stoked by jealousy — therein lay Othello's madness."

He admired Eloise's intellect. She already suspected Othello's possessive jealousy in Edward Cadwallader, and was warning George that they were playing a dangerous game. "Othello was a fool," he said.

"Yes," she sighed, "he was."

"To love deeply and honestly is a joy. To blacken it with jealousy and possessiveness can destroy the truest heart."

"Indeed it can," she murmured.

George heard the sadness in her voice, but managed to resist tipping her chin so that he could look into her eyes. "It seems we think alike," he said.

Her confusion was written in her face. "Are you familiar with the tale of Abelard and Eloise?" she asked, after a long pause.

"I have heard of it," he said, "but my education is lacking, for I have no intimate knowledge of it."

"They fell in love," she said. "It was a powerful love that neither could deny, but ultimately it destroyed them." She smiled into his eyes. "A book in my father's library tells the story. Perhaps you may wish to borrow it?"

"I would like that very much," he said, his breath tight in his chest.

She opened her parasol and hooked her reticule round her wrist, as if preparing to end their conversation. "My mother was a romantic, and it was her favourite story, which is why I bear the heroine's name." The blush on her cheek was most becoming. "Will you be ashore for long?"

"Until the end of the year." He explained Samuel's dilemma, desperate to keep her with him for a little longer.

The dimple flashed again. "No doubt you will be attending the Macarthurs' party at the end of the week. I will bring the book, and when you have read it, perhaps we shall discuss it." She bobbed a curtsy. "Good afternoon, Mr Collinson."

George watched her walk away, unable to contain his joy. She wanted to see him again, had made an excuse to seek him out. The miracle had happened. Now all he had to do was wheedle an invitation to the party.

Eloise's heart was light as she returned to the house on the shore and ran up the steps. Edward was away and not expected back for a couple of months. For once the house had lost its malevolent air and she had never felt so free, so girlish and full of joy. She flung open the doors to the drawing room and gazed at her reflection in the mirror above the mantelpiece.

George Collinson had wrought a great change in her, and although she knew it was wrong, even dangerous, to feel this way, a certain recklessness in her would not be denied. She would see him again — how could she bear not to after today? To an outsider their conversation might have appeared quite ordinary, but the code in their words, the meaningful silences and the frisson of excitement were far from bland.

"Will you tend Charles, your ladyship? Only 'e's been frettin'."

She whirled round, shocked to be so caught up in her thoughts of George Collinson that she had neglected to visit her beloved baby. "Of course," she said, rather too sharply.

"Are you all right, your ladyship? You're a little flushed."

Eloise took the baby and held him close to avoid Meg's penetrating stare. "I'm well, thank you," she said. "Very well indeed."

CHAPTER
NINE

Georges River Mission, March 1798

The tiny settlement of Banks Town consisted of three tin huts and a native encampment, and lay between two branches of the Georges River. It had only recently been surveyed by Bass and Flinders and named in honour of Sir Joseph Banks, the botanist who had accompanied Cook on his travels. The first land grants had been snapped up, and soon the swamps and encroaching bush would be cleared for farmers and settlers.

Florence Collinson closed the Bible and shooed the native children back to their grass shelters. She watched them splash through the mud unperturbed by the downpour, joyous in their freedom after the long time spent indoors. The rain had come late, and now the thundering on the roof drowned all other sound, making it impossible for her to finish the nightly reading.

"You're very good with the children," shouted the missionary, Cedric Farnsworth, above the noise. "They love to hear you read."

Florence ran her hands down her much-mended skirt. As usual, Cedric was standing too close to her; his fat, sweating face and pungent body made her feel nauseous. "I doubt they understand much," she replied, raising her voice, "but I find myself drawn to them despite their nakedness and heathen ways."

She returned to the shadows inside the bark hut that was their makeshift church. It was a poor place, barely worthy of the name, with its rough benches, dirt floor and slab of blackwood that served as an altar. The stench of unwashed bodies, damp and mould permeated the stifling shack, and the only beauty was in the silver cross that Cedric and his sister had brought from England, which glimmered now in the lamplight.

"Will you join me in a little supper?" Cedric followed her as she collected the Bibles and tidied up the few roughly hewn toys he'd made. "I find the evenings lonely without my dear sister."

Florence closed the trunk on the precious books to keep them from mouldering. "I have already eaten," she replied. Celia Farnsworth had died a month ago, since when she had had barely a moment to herself. Cedric's company underlined the fact that they were marooned until the rains passed.

"Just a tot of rum with some honey," he coaxed. "You're too thin, Florence. You don't eat enough."

"Rum doesn't agree with me." Thin she might be, but her appetite had always been small, and the thought of having to share a meal with Cedric made her shudder. His table manners were repellent. She batted away moths the size of her palm and blew out the lamp. "It's late," she said. "I bid you goodnight."

Cedric's hand clamped on her arm. "Don't go yet, Florence. I must talk to you."

Florence eyed him coolly until he released her. "What can be so urgent that it will not wait until morning?" She took in the rotund figure, the mottled face with its piggy eyes and heavy jowls. He was well over forty, she guessed, and his girth never ceased to amaze her for food was in short supply — but, then, he had a liking for rum and honey, and the fatty meat of the water-fowl the natives caught.

"It is wrong that we live as we do now that Celia is no longer with us," he began.

She maintained a stern expression but her thoughts were legion. "We can hardly do anything about it during the rainy season. And I doubt the natives care."

"But I care, Florence. I care deeply."

She read his intention and, with horror, forestalled him. "Then I will ensure I keep my distance. When the rains are over, I will return to Sydney."

"There's no need for that," he said, reaching for her again.

"I believe it would be best," she said, taking a step back.

"You have expressed no wish to return before today," he said. "Indeed, you have always insisted on staying away from the town, even when there are supplies to be bought. Why this sudden change of heart, Florence?"

Florence took another step back. "As you say, Cedric, it isn't fitting for me to remain now that we are alone."

He moved swiftly and had grabbed her hands before she could escape. "Then marry me, Florence," he shouted, above the rain. "Be my wife, and together we will do the Lord's bidding, just as my dearest sister wished."

Florence wrested her hands from his grip. Despite the dread she'd felt ever since Celia had died of fever, she was appalled that his proposal had come so soon. "No! I could never marry you," she said.

"Why not?" he barked. "You have forsaken your family, your home and your friends. You are alone in the world, Florence, as am I. We are free to do as we please."

His words chilled her. She had indeed abandoned her family and the comforts of home for this primitive outpost — but to face the reality of what she had lost and to hear the truth shouted above the drumming rain was shocking. "I do not love you, sir," she retorted, "and never could."

He made no move to touch her again, perhaps realising that if he did she would flee into the night, but he said, "Please, Florence. Consider my proposal — for what other alternative is there for either of us? You are no beauty. Surely you have no wish to be an old maid. You are still young enough to have our children."

Florence had heard enough. She ran out of the church and through the teeming rain to her hut. Soaked to the skin, she slammed the door behind her, wedged the wooden latch with the back of a chair, then collapsed to the dirt floor in a storm of tears. His words had been cruel but viciously accurate, and the hurt they had inflicted was unbearable.

Edward reined in his horse. He was in a foul temper, his uniform soaked and heavy, making him sweat after the long, torturous ride through the bush. If the black trackers had led him on a wild-goose chase he would see to it that they were flogged to within an inch of their lives before he slit their throats.

He peered into the half-light, but it was impossible to see anything through the rain. "Where are they?" he snapped.

"Gone ahead," replied Willy Baines, mopping his red face. "They won't be long. The camp isn't far."

Edward grimaced as water dripped from his hat-brim and down his neck. "Can we trust them?"

Willy nodded. "They're Gandangara — sworn enemies of the Wiradjuric."

"They're black, Willy, and sometimes that's all it takes to turn them against us." Edward tightened his hold on the reins as his horse stamped and snorted. His impatience was growing and the pounding of the rain on his hat was making his head ache. What he wouldn't give now for the comfort of his house on the shore and the company of his wife.

His arousal was immediate as he thought of Eloise. It was doused just as swiftly by the knowledge that her body was far from desirable when she lay there unmoving and silent, her loathing tangible as he covered her. Temper rising, he lashed the horse's flank as it refused to be still. Eloise and this animal had much in common. Both needed to know who was in charge. "And, by Gad, I'll have her begging for it when I get back," he muttered. "I've had enough of her coldness."

"What's that?"

He shook his head, thankful Willy hadn't overheard, but there was no time to explain now: he'd seen the two trackers moving towards them.

"Camp alonga big rivva, boss," said the elder of the two. "Plenty Wiradjuric."

"White man and missus there," said the other. "Live alonga strange *gunyahs*. Make trouble, boss."

Edward waved them away and turned to Willy. "That must be the missionaries we heard about. I thought they'd moved on."

"Should we abandon the attack?"

"No," he snapped. "A couple of Bible-thumpers are easily dealt with." He chewed his lip. "No gunshot, tonight, Willy, sabres only, but we continue as planned."

Florence shifted on the lumpy mattress, trying to find a cool spot. She was hot and miserable beneath the thin muslin curtain that had been strung over the bed to protect her from mosquitoes, perspiration soaking into the pillow. But her physical discomfort was nothing compared to the clamour in her head.

She had blithely said she would return to Sydney, unwittingly voicing the longing that had haunted her over the past five years. The loss of her family was keenly felt — but had she the courage to face her father, to witness his disgust at the part she'd played in Millicent's ordeal, and her subsequent cowardly departure? Her pride was still strong, had been the driving force of her actions ever since — but marriage to bloated, middle-aged Cedric, or life alone in the wilderness at the mercy of the natives, was unthinkable. It seemed there was no alternative but to swallow her pride and risk humiliation.

Florence pulled at the high neck of her nightgown. The material was thin and worn, but it was too much in the awful humidity, and clung to her like a second skin. She rolled on to her side and stared into the gloom, her ears filled with the hammering of the rain, which couldn't shut out the memories that continued to trouble her.

The convict, Millicent, had wormed her way into the family because of her link to Jonathan Cadwallader. She had dared to believe that Ezra and Susan had taken her in out of compassion, that they loved her as a daughter, thereby supplanting Florence. Florence's jealousy had grown too strong for her to contain, and when Millicent had arrived that fateful evening, something in her had snapped. She had relished telling Millicent that Susan had had an affair with Jonathan — and that Susan had taken her in only because of her own guilt.

Florence groaned. "How was I to know the stupid girl would run off like that? It wasn't my fault she was violated." The bitterness remained, the memories as clear as if it had happened yesterday. She thumped the pillow and turned on to her back, staring at the roof.

She had crumpled the note Millicent had brought from Susan and watched as Millicent ran down the path, her elation heightened by the knowledge that she had set a dark cat among the pigeons in revealing that she'd always known of her mother's liaison. Millicent had been suitably shocked, which served her right for presuming she could steal Florence's family so easily, and it would be a salutary lesson to her mother that her secrets and lies were in the open. She wished she could have been a fly on the wall when Millicent faced Susan on her return.

Yet a worm of doubt had gnawed at her as she'd closed the door on Millicent's fleeing figure. Had her revelation served only to distance her from her father? He had forgiven Mother, had taken her back, despite her unfaithfulness, and Florence had had to admit he'd seemed happier and more settled after he'd done so.

Florence closed her eyes as she remembered how furious her father had been on that last day. She could hear his anger and feel his unwillingness to be bowed even when she'd clung to his rigid torso and resorted to the tears that had always worked before. On that day he'd been impervious to them. He had stood, grey-faced and cold, refusing to be swayed. His innate ability to forgive had deserted him in the light of the assault on Millicent, and his belief that his daughter's spiteful tongue had set off the chain of events had made it impossible to argue. He had pushed her away, and as he'd left the house he'd forbidden her to approach him until he could forgive her.

Florence dashed away the tears and sat up. "You forgave Mother," she muttered. "Why not me?" She sniffed and ran her hands distractedly through her damp hair. Millicent's ordeal was too awful to contemplate, but the fact that it had brought her even closer to Ezra and Susan still made her burn with jealousy. She supposed Millicent had married Ernest now, which meant she would be even more firmly entrenched. But why hadn't her father come to find her?

She sat in the gloom as the heat rose, the rain pounded and the whining insects batted against the muslin. After that morning there had been little point in remaining in Sydney, so she had packed her few belongings and gone to the quay to join the missionaries who were about to sail up-river. Cedric and his sister had often visited her father's church, and Florence had entertained them after the services, listening as they spoke of their plans. She hadn't wanted to be a missionary — had never felt their fervour to spread the gospel — but they offered a means of escape and she'd taken it with little thought of the consequences.

Their destination was to have been further north, and she had sent a message to her parents accordingly, in the hope that someone would search for her and bring her home. But when they had encountered nothing but impenetrable forest and swamp, they had abandoned the idea and headed south-west along the Georges.

She sat in the darkness, tears mingling with sweat. She hated her life, hated the bush, the natives and the piety she'd been forced to adopt. If only someone had cared enough to rescue her from this self-imposed hell she would be free of Cedric and this primitive existence.

She hugged her knees. It had been hard to accept they didn't love her, and after two years of silence, she had forbidden Cedric and his sister to contact her family or give her news of them, should they hear it when they went into Sydney Town. She had seen this as the only way in which she could retaliate. Now she knew she had only been punishing herself. As fresh tears threatened, she put her hands over her ears to shut out the battering rain and the voices from the past.

"How many guards?"

Mandarg held up five fingers, then ran them across his throat and grinned. "No worry, boss."

"Good," barked Edward. "When we enter the camp, I want you to find the white people and keep guard on them until we've finished the rout. They'll be in the shacks. If they give you trouble, slit their throats."

Mandarg frowned, and Edward grunted with annoyance at the man's inability to understand the simplest order. "Explain to him, Willy. I don't want those blasted missionaries to escape by boat."

"Looky missus and boss alonga *gunyahs*," said Willy. "Take 'im and keep until boss say so." He drew his finger across his neck. "Kill 'im if trouble."

Mandarg swiftly translated the order to his fellow tribesman.

Edward signalled to his men. They advanced through the scrub, the trackers leading the way through the curtain of rain. When he saw them pause and melt into the long grass, he knew they were near.

He dismounted and squatted beside Mandarg. The camp was like any other but for the three bark shacks, one of which had a crude cross above the door. As he suspected, there were dugout canoes on the riverbank. He would send Willy to sink them when the rout began.

"Find missus and boss here or here," he murmured, indicating the two closest shacks. He put his finger to his lips. "Wait until I tell you."

Satisfied that they understood, he returned to the others. "Stay mounted until we've struck. The rain will muffle the sound of hoofs, but the ground is slippery." He gave them an encouraging smile and was gratified to see they were still keen for this rout, even though they were soaked to the skin. "Willy, see to the boats once we've started." He could feel the others' excitement now. "Form a line and wait for my signal."

Edward led his men through the bush and towards the clearing. The tension was high, thrumming through him like the scorch of a bullet. As the first of the bark shacks loomed out of the shroud of rain, he nodded to the trackers.

The black men moved stealthily in the darkness and positioned themselves beneath the windows, knives between their teeth.

Edward raised his sword and kicked his horse into a gallop. The rout was on.

Florence had stripped off her nightgown and was trying to cool herself by washing when she heard a terrible scream from outside. She dropped the cloth into the cracked bowl, snatched up her nightgown and pulled back the sacking from the window.

A black face, with a knife between the teeth, looked back at her.

Florence screamed and clutched her nightgown to her as she backed away.

The Aborigine slid through the window and dropped silently to the floor. He advanced on her, knife raised.

"Go away!" Her frantic fingers tore at the nightgown as she tried to cover her nakedness. "You can't come in here," she shrieked. "Cedric! Cedric, help me!"

The man kept advancing, eyes riveted to her body, knife steady. "Boss no come," he said. "Missus alonga me."

Florence found she was backed into a corner. "Cedric! Help me, for God's sake."

"Boss no come." He drew his finger across his throat.

She was on her own. She began to tremble as she smelt the animal fat smeared on his body, and saw the tribal markings on his chest. He wasn't a Wiradjuric so he must be on a raid — and she was his prize.

"Dear God," she breathed. Her legs buckled and she slid down the wall to cower at his feet. "Don't hurt me," she sobbed.

Strong hands yanked her up. The knife was at her throat, the blade cold on her skin as he sniffed her shoulder. His fingers ran through her hair, and he lifted it to his pierced nose. With an exclamation of disgust he let it drop.

Florence could barely stand, and her teeth were chattering with such fear she couldn't speak. A keening rose in her throat as he stared into her eyes with undisguised curiosity and traced his fingers over her naked breasts and down her belly. She stood transfixed for what seemed an eternity as the screams from outside competed with the drumbeat of her heart.

Then he was dragging her across the room.

Florence clawed at his eyes and beat his chest, spat in his face and kicked his legs. But she was no match against his wiry strength.

The chair was thrown to one side, the door crashed open and she was dragged outside. Naked and terrified, she realised that this was only the beginning, for she had been thrust into a scene from hell.

The rain had ceased, and the dying fires had been stoked by the burning *gunyahs*. The smoke and flames cast eerie shadows on the carnage as the black night was rent by screams, and black flesh was slashed with steel. Swords flashed, red with blood and the dancing flames. Horses whinnied, ears flat, nostrils distended, manes flying, as their hoofs trampled the children and those too weak to run. Women and old men were slaughtered as they huddled in the mud and the warriors lay dead or dying, their spears useless beside them. And, through the firelight, she could see the silhouettes of the men who had brought this apocalypse.

This was not a native raiding party but a punitive strike by armed soldiers. Florence couldn't believe what she was seeing, and although she wanted nothing more than to look away, she was too paralysed by shock to do anything but watch.

A rider was bearing down on Kulkarawa, a young woman Florence had befriended. He blocked her escape, speared the new-born child she was carrying with his sabre and held it aloft in triumph. At the mother's screams he tossed the little body into the bush and, with one, brutal blow, decapitated her. As he spurred his horse back into the fray, the flames lit his face.

Florence moaned and would have fallen if the native hadn't held her up. Her head hung low, her hair forming a blessed veil over the scene as the massacre continued. She had recognised Edward Cadwallader, and knew he wouldn't stop until they were all dead.

She withdrew into herself, trying to bury the sounds, sights and scents of this awful night. Time lost meaning but, no matter how hard she tried to block them out, the endless thunder of hoofs, the screams of terror and excited shouts of the soldiers battered her. She could only pray that her end would be swift and merciful — her white skin wouldn't save her now that she'd witnessed the butchery.

Edward stood in the clearing, chest heaving, sweat trickling down his face. The air was thick with the smells of burning eucalyptus and blood. Smoke lay in a choking cloud that hid the rising sun and twisted through the surrounding trees. But this dawn was different from any other: there was no birdsong.

222

He shivered as he glanced into the trees, skin crawling with some undefined fear. He shook himself, then dismissed the feeling that someone or something was watching him, and cleaned the blade of his sword with a handful of grass.

"A good night's work," said Willy.

"Are they all dead?"

"All but the missionary woman. Mandarg's got her."

"Give her to him," replied Edward, still troubled by the evil that drifted to him with the smoke. "After he's finished with her she won't have the wit to tell anyone what happened." He trembled with exhaustion as he took a long draught of rum. Sleep was all he wanted, but first they had to get as far from here as they could before the sun rose any higher.

"Should we bury the missionary?"

Willy seemed determined to pester him with questions. He eyed the body slumped against the door of the makeshift church. "Leave him," he said sharply. "We used only swords tonight, and should anyone happen to come this way it will look as if it was a black raiding-party. Bury him, and you'll give the game away." He swung wearily into the saddle. "Let's get out of here."

Florence peered through her hair at Edward Cadwallader. She wanted to beg to go with them — to plead with him not to leave her with this savage. But a small, sane part of her mind kept her silent, and she lowered her chin as he approached. This was the man who had violated Millicent — the man who had escaped justice and wouldn't think twice about inflicting the same horror on her.

The men rode by, mud splashing on her. She could hear the ribald remarks, could feel their hot eyes, and knew that one word from Edward would mark her fate.

"Mandarg alonga missus," said the man, who rode behind Edward. "Keep 'im."

"No want white missus," Mandarg retorted.

"Then slit her bloody throat. I don't care."

Florence moaned and slid to the ground as the native released her and the men rode away. She hugged her knees and began to rock as the silence closed in.

"That man is a devil," muttered Mandarg. "He kills women and babies for pleasure. Now I am left with you."

His voice seemed to come from far away, the words unintelligible, yet she could feel his touch on her arms. She flinched and buried her face in her hands as she continued to rock. "Father," she sobbed. "I want my papa."

"Lowitja spoke of a white woman," said Mandarg. "But you will not die — not by my hand. Take this and put it on. Your white skin offends me and I do not like your smell."

Florence didn't understand the babble of words, but she felt the softness of her nightgown and hugged it as she rocked. The rhythm must be maintained — like a clock, tick, tock, tick, tock ... She began to sing, unaware that the words made no sense.

"The Spirit is with you, white woman. Have no fear, I will not touch you." Mandarg fetched a blanket from the bark hut and put it over her shoulders. "Should I take you with me?" He shook his head. "There would be too many questions. I will leave you food and the Spirits will decide your fate." He walked away and joined his fellow tribesman, who was gathering up spears and sacks of food.

Florence rocked forward and back as something shifted in her mind. She felt nothing, heard nothing, knew only that she must finish the song.

A bush camp, two weeks later

The dark, shifting shadows took shape and advanced through the trees. The night was filled with shrieks and the smell of blood, and Edward knew the demons were searching for him. He stood, stock still, as they multiplied, whispering his name, their spears rattling against war-shields like loose teeth in an empty skull.

He tried to run — but he was fettered by the clutching hands of the dead that reached through the mud. He opened his mouth to scream, but it filled with the oily smo ke of burning eucalyptus and seared flesh. And still the army of the night drew nearer, their malevolence reaching out to him with accusing fingers.

"No! Go away! Leave me alone!" Edward reared from the camp-bed, clawing the air to fend them off. As he opened his eyes and was met by the familiar surroundings of his campaign tent, he almost wept with relief.

Collapsing back, he felt the dampness of his sweat on the sheets as he tried to calm his racing heart. The nightmare had been with him ever since that rout on the hinterland river three years ago, but it had become more frequent since they had cleared the Banks Town mission. The lack of restful sleep was taking its toll. His temper was shorter than ever, his men were muttering about his odd behaviour, and he was finding it increasingly difficult to concentrate.

He threw off the bedclothes and staggered into the clearing. Willy Baines kept a supply of brandy in his saddlebag. As he fumbled with the buckles he looked around fearfully. It was still night, the dream had lost none of its power, and he thought he could see his tormentors in the dancing shadows. "Pull yourself together, man," he mumbled, as he found the bottle. "There's no such thing as ghosts."

He drank deeply as he stumbled back to his tent and sank on to the camp-bed. Thunder rolled in the distance, and although he could hear faint snores from the other tents, he felt unnervingly vulnerable. There were shadows everywhere. It seemed even his waking hours were haunted.

He set about lighting a lamp, then went outside to stoke the fire. When the flames were high enough, he sat close to it for warmth. Soothed, he put the bottle on the ground and began to relax.

It was hardly surprising he was suffering, for he was under immense pressure. He thought of Henry Carlton and the mounting debts. If Carlton called them in, and his commanding officer heard of it, he would be in danger of ruin. He picked up the brandy, swigged, and let it trickle down his throat. Carlton had the luck of

226

the devil — or was cheating — but Edward, astute as he was, couldn't see how he did it.

He stared into the fire, his thoughts fogged by drink, the remnants of his nightmare lingering. There were other concerns apart from his gambling debts, and although the situation wasn't serious, it would become so should it continue. Several business deals he'd thought were his had been lost, and two parcels of land he'd been after had mysteriously been bought hours before he was to sign the deeds. Edward drank the last of the brandy and was forced to admit that the sleepless nights, and the amount he had to drink to blot out the dreams, had dulled his wits.

He returned to his tent and took a cigar from the box that stood next to his open pocket-watch by his camp-bed. Rolling it between his fingers, he breathed in its rich scent, then lit it. His gaze drifted to the miniature watercolour portrait of Eloise set in the watch's silver casing. It was a reasonable likeness, painted by Irma and presented to him after the wedding. "How can a man cope with his worries when his wife lies in the marriage bed like a cold fish?" he said aloud.

Eloise had pushed him too far — and when he returned to Sydney, he would teach her a lesson she would never forget. He rose to his feet, the need to be occupied by something other than his nightmares and troubled marriage driving him back into the clearing. "Wake up!" he shouted. "There's work to be done. Get out and fall in."

"It's three in the morning," grumbled Willy, bleary-eyed with sleep. "For heaven's sake, what's got into you?"

"There are blacks out there in the way of progress," he bellowed. "Our job is to clear them out. Move yourself, Willy. I want everyone ready to leave in five minutes."

Willy Baines remained where he was. "The men are exhausted," he said. "There's no use in disturbing them. The blacks will still be there in the morning."

Edward clenched his fists. "Are you disobeying the order of a senior officer?"

Willy's lined face was haggard in the dancing firelight.

"Good. Because if I thought you were, I'd have you court-martialled."

"If I go down, so will you."

"Do you threaten me?"

"The men will remain in their tents until morning," Willy stated, then walked back to his tent.

Edward swayed, and caught sight of astonished faces peering out of the tents. "Get back to bed," he roared, "and if any man repeats a word of this, I'll shoot him."

Silence fell, seeming to mock him. Darkness closed in, and the rustle of the trees sounded like the whispers of the dead. Edward went in search of more brandy.

The track to Parramatta, two days later

Florence clutched the silver crucifix as she stumbled over the dead branches and through the thick scrub.

228

The words of a nursery rhyme kept slipping away, the tune melting into a droning hum. She stopped at a shaft of light piercing the canopy of trees. It was pretty and warm and, if she hadn't been in such a hurry to meet Papa, she might have sat down for a while.

"Tick, tock, tick, tock," she muttered, as she wove through the trees and followed a path that only she could see. "Hickory dickory dock, clock, tick, tick, tick."

A sound stilled her and she cocked her head. As the riders emerged from the trees she clutched the crucifix and sank to the forest floor.

"What have we here?" said the man, who led three troopers. He drew his horse to a halt and leant forward in his saddle.

Florence flinched as she peeped at him through her matted hair. There was something about men on horses that she should remember. Something frightening and dangerous. She sang faster: "Tick, tock, tick, tock, hickory dickory dock."

"She's white, I think, but it's hard to tell under all the filth. She must have been out here for some time."

"Lost her mind, that's plain. What should we do with her, Minister?"

The word "minister" sounded familiar. "Papa?" she whimpered.

"We can't leave her here."

Warily, Florence watched him climb off his horse. She shook her head to be rid of the annoying buzz in her ears. He was playing a trick, tick, tick, tick — this wasn't Papa. She skittered away and peered at him from behind the slender trunk of a ghost gum.

"I'm not going to hurt you," he said, as he squatted down. "My name is John Pritchard," he said, "and I'm a minister at the Parramatta garrison. Is your father a minister?"

The buzzing was louder now, like angry bees.

His gaze fell on the crucifix. "That is a beautiful cross," he said. "Will you show it to me?"

Florence could see only his outstretched hand and instinctively shied from it.

"We're wasting time, John, and they're waiting for us at the garrison."

The minister straightened and put his hands on his hips. "She's lost and troubled, and will die if we leave her. She's very thin, and I can hear the breath rattling in her chest." He gave a great sigh. "What on earth can she be doing out here in her nightdress, carrying what looks like a church crucifix?"

"I don't know and I don't care," said the other man, gruffly. "Hurry up or we'll be in trouble with the commanding officer."

Florence didn't like the look of them. They wore uniform, rode horses and carried swords — somewhere, behind the buzzing in her head, there was a memory of terror and danger.

Strong arms lifted her and she stiffened.

"It's all right," he said, as he carried her to his horse. "I'm going to take you home."

She stared at him as he settled her in front of him and took up the reins. The buzzing was louder now and

230

the rhythm of the clock had become a drum in her chest.

As the horse began to move, and the arms tightened round her, the drum beat faster until it was thundering. It filled her head and body, and squeezed the breath out of her.

A flash of agony was followed by blessed silence, and a momentary glimpse of reason. Her father had come for her at last. Then darkness enveloped her.

CHAPTER
TEN

Balmain, April 1798

It was unseasonably warm for autumn, the sky clear and the water dazzling with pinpoints of light. George had spread a blanket on the sand at the edge of the trees and they sat, propped by cushions, in the dappled shade. The remains of the picnic lay scattered nearby, and as he poured the last of the wine, he felt content.

He and Eloise had met nearly every day since he had wangled an invitation to the Macarthurs' party, and although they were both aware of how dangerous it was, neither was willing to end it. With each meeting had come deeper understanding, and a yearning to be together that demanded to be fulfilled. By tacit agreement, Edward was never mentioned, but his ominous presence hung in the background. Now they were taking greater risks than ever, for Edward was due back soon and urgency had gripped them.

Eloise was so very beautiful, and at that moment George knew he couldn't love her more. "Do you realise it's been a month since we met? And since then we have discussed Shakespeare's plays and sonnets, the Arthurian legends, politics, whaling, and the vagaries of living in this colonial outpost. You're the most surprising woman, Eloise."

"Our meetings have brought me such happiness. You have allowed me to be myself, and that is a precious gift. Thank you, George."

"I wish it could always be like this. Our snatched moments only make me long for more — yet I know that is out of the question." He kissed her fingers. Her nearness was torture: he had never kissed those lips, never held her close or dared to whisper what was in his heart. "Sweet Eloise, you have turned my life upside-down."

Eloise let her hand rest in his. "I have been reborn, thanks to you," she replied. "This is the only place I feel completely at ease. The only place I know we can be truly alone. I'm so glad you found it."

George took in the deserted beach, the sheltering trees and the glittering water. The only sounds were the soft lap of waves, the chortle of a bird and the jingle of harness as their horses cropped the grass. "Thomas brought me here to look at a plot of land he was thinking of buying," he said.

"He knows about us?" She withdrew her hand, eyes wide with fright.

He hastened to reassure her. "No, my love. It is our secret, and will remain so for as long as you wish." His heart ached with the knowledge that it would always be like this. With every meeting they tempted fate, and Eloise was constantly on edge. "I've been selfish and unfair to you," he said.

She took his hand again. "Oh, George, how wrong you are." Her fingers entwined with his and she leant towards him. "If you are selfish, then so am I. If you are unfair, then I am guilty of the same crime. Let's not spoil this perfect day with such talk."

"Has it been perfect?" He was mesmerised by her eyes, the way her lips parted as if for a kiss.

"Very nearly. But I know what would make it so."

George put his arm round her waist and drew her close. Her breath mingled with his and he could see the wanting in her eyes as she tipped back her head. He ran his fingers up the slender column of her neck and buried them in her hair as he kissed her for the first time.

His fingers brushed the swell of her breast above her bodice and her back arched. Now his lips were tracing up her neck to the tender spot where it met her shoulder.

She reached for his shirt buttons, but he pulled away.

"We mustn't do this." His voice was hoarse with passion.

"It's too late," she murmured, and undid a button.

"Are you sure, my darling? If we continue, then . . ."

She put a finger to his lips. "I know exactly what I'm doing," she said. "You have shown me how real love can be, and my heart is full. Now I wish to give you something in return."

"Eloise . . ."

Her hand rested over his heart. "We might not have known each other long, but I love you, George, more deeply than I can say."

George crushed her to him. "My love, my most precious love." He showered her face with kisses.

Sydney Barracks, May 1798

They had returned from bush duty the day before, and Edward had concluded that browbeating Eloise would get him nowhere. He would court her again for, despite all that had happened, he still desired her. Yet he had known he couldn't go straight to her: his clothes were filthy, he hadn't washed or shaved in a month, and he stank, so he had stayed at the barracks. After a long soak in a hot bath he had had, for once, a good night's sleep.

He scrutinised his reflection in the fly-spotted pier-glass as his manservant flicked an invisible speck from his immaculate red jacket. The dress uniform had been laundered so the gold buttons and epaulettes shone in the frail beam of sunlight that struggled through the window of his apartment. His chin was clean-shaven, his moustache trimmed and he thought himself very handsome. "What do you think, Willy?"

"She'll be impressed," drawled the other, as he lounged in a chair and sipped from his glass.

"Good," Edward said, and waved away the servant. He fidgeted with the silk cord that held his scabbard and sword against his hip.

"Have a drink to calm your nerves," said Willy, and poured a generous tot. "You're sweating like a rutting stallion."

235

The coarse observation jarred and, not for the first time, Edward decided that Willy Baines had overstepped the mark, with his vulgar over-familiarity. Nevertheless, he ignored it, took the drink and downed it in one. Willy knew too much, and therein lay the need to keep him sweet. "Is everything set for tomorrow's game?"

Willy sank further into the chair and hooked a leg over the arm, mindless of the delicate silk. "Carlton's ready, and I've rented a private room so you won't be disturbed."

Edward winced at the damage to the chair. It seemed that everything this afternoon was designed to irritate him. "If you can't sit properly, then stand," he growled. "That chair wasn't made for lounging."

Willy's eyes were bloodshot. "No need to take out your ill-humour on me," he snarled.

Edward lifted his chin and eased the neckcloth. He felt as if he was being strangled. "I'm merely distracted by the thought of seeing my wife," he said. He shot the older man a rueful grin in an attempt to defuse the tension. "I don't know why I'm so nervous, but it's worse than waiting on a rout."

"Nothing beats that for excitement," said Willy, barely mollified.

"Oh, I don't know," Edward mused. "Holding four aces against Carlton is hard to beat." He flashed a smile. "Pour us another drink, there's a good fellow."

Willy did as he was told. After they had taken a sip, he began, "This thing with Carlton . . ."

Edward gritted his teeth. "I know what you're going to say, Willy, but everything is under control."

"You lost a fair-sized purse last time, and your debts are mounting."

"I'll clear them tomorrow."

"That's what you said before."

Edward knew all too well that he owed Carlton a huge sum, and he didn't need Willy to keep reminding him of it. "Win some, lose some," he said carelessly. "I took twenty guineas off him just before we left for the bush."

"And lost almost fifty before that."

Willy seemed determined to rile him. "I have to lose now and again, or he'll suspect me of cheating, but I have his measure now. Henry Carlton has met his match."

"If you're sure," murmured Willy, as he fetched his cap and settled it over his greying hair. "I've watched him over the months, and I don't like what I see. You might think he's a gentleman player — a man with too much money and a casual approach to the game — but he's sharp, Edward. The size of your debt proves that."

Willy was only confirming his suspicions, but the need to prove himself against the man was consuming him. "He might be," he said tersely, "but I'm sharper, and the debt will be cleared." He saw doubt in the other man's eyes. "If you're so concerned," he rasped, "then why don't you find out more about him?"

"I've already tried, but no one seems to know anything, which is a mystery in itself. A man of his wealth and education usually leaves a trail."

"Then dig deeper. I need to know who I'm dealing with."

Mystery or not, though, Henry Carlton had outwitted him and the debt had reached frightening proportions. He would soon demand repayment and Edward knew it would mean having to sell some prized investments. "Damn the man," he muttered, as he left for home. "I'll show him I won't be beaten."

Kernow House, Watsons Bay

Eloise giggled as she watched Charles experiment with his single tooth on the dry biscuit. He was making such a mess that his smocked gown would soon have to be changed, but that didn't matter: he was enjoying himself.

They were sitting on a blanket in front of the fire. The autumn winds rattled the windows as pounding surf lashed the beach. The lamps had been lit to dispel the day's dullness and she leant against the couch watching her son, her heart so full it almost brought her to tears. If only George was here, her contentment would be complete. The memory of their lovemaking warmed her, and she returned to the days they'd spent in each other's arms, the rapture of flesh upon flesh, their overwhelming need for one another and the glorious release of passion.

"You've got a visitor, Lady Cadwallader."

She was ripped from her day-dream by the convict servant's rough voice. "Who is it?"

"The Earl of Kernow, madam."

"Then show him in," she said, flustered to be caught unawares.

"Don't get up, Eloise. You make such a charming picture."

She stood anyway and curtsied. "You should have let me know you were calling," she said, with genuine pleasure. "I would have changed Charles's clothes."

Jonathan Cadwallader picked up his grandson, who offered him the now soggy biscuit. "He's fine as he is," he said, as he held the child high. "Becoming sturdy too," he observed, "and is that a tooth I see?"

Eloise retrieved the biscuit before it damaged Jonathan's waistcoat. "There's another on its way," she said proudly.

The baby grabbed his grandfather's watch-chain. "So you wish to see my watch? It might not be as grand as the old one, but come, Charles, let's sit and I will show you something special." He balanced his grandson on his knee, opened the silver casing and pressed the catch. Charles's face lit up as the melody chimed, and he reached a dimpled hand towards it.

"You may have this when you're older," said Jonathan, letting the little boy's fingers curl round it. "For now, I think this might be more appropriate." He put away the watch and Charles's face crumpled. "Here we are," Jonathan said quickly, to stall the onset of tears. "Just the thing for those troublesome teeth." He held up a heavily chased silver teething spoon. Charles grabbed it and put it straight into his mouth.

"What a generous gift," said Eloise.

"Grandsons are for spoiling," said Jonathan, as he set the baby on the floor. "So are their mothers." He drew a scarf from his pocket.

Eloise gasped with delight. It was the palest green and as soft as featherdown. "It's beautiful," she murmured, draping it over her shoulders. "You are too kind."

He acknowledged her thanks and remained silent as the servant brought in tea and Meg carried Charles off to the nursery. "My gifts today are my way of saying goodbye, Eloise," he said, as she handed him a cup.

"I didn't think your expedition over the Blue Mountains began until spring?"

"I have to leave for London tonight. The expedition will go on without me."

"Tonight? Why the urgency?"

Jonathan seemed to gather his strength for what he had to say. "I received a disturbing letter from my agent in London," he said. "The news it bore is already weeks old, and my journey might be a waste of time, but perhaps I can salvage something by getting back as quickly as possible." He frowned into his teacup.

"Tell me what happened."

He took a deep breath. "Suffice it to say my house in Cornwall is crumbling, my estates have been mismanaged in my absence, and my shipping interests in the Mediterranean have been sorely damaged by that upstart Napoleon. But the most urgent reason for my return to Cornwall is the discovery of something I had once thought lost to me for ever." He fell silent, his gaze fixed beyond the room.

"Whatever is it, Jonathan?"

"I am not at liberty to say more until I uncover the truth. But perhaps on my return you will understand

240

my reticence. It is a quest I have followed ever since . . ." He collected himself. "I'm sorry, my dear," he said. "I did not wish to burden you today with my concerns. You and the boy looked so content."

If only he knew the truth. "I'm sorry you are troubled," she replied. "You have become a good friend, and I will miss your company."

"I'm glad we're friends."

Eloise knew he was trying to say something important, but was at odds to find the right words. "What is it?"

"As a friend, I feel I should speak out. But as your father-in-law, I wonder if I am not being disloyal."

Her heart was pounding so hard she was certain he must hear it. "Say what is in your mind, sir. I will not take offence."

"I have seen you blossom in the past weeks, Eloise, and know the signs of a woman in love."

His voice was soft, but the effect the words had on her was shocking. "I am still in the first years of my marriage," she said.

"But is it my son who brings colour to your cheeks and a sparkle to your eye?"

Eloise swallowed. "Of course," she managed.

His gaze was steady, his expression not unkind as he leant forward. "I think not, Eloise."

His words hung between them and she found she was trapped in his gaze.

Jonathan Cadwallader reached for her hand. "There's no need to say anything, Eloise, for I understand your dilemma. I fell in love many years ago, and that love lives on in my heart. But it was a love that almost destroyed us, for it could only be fulfilled by breaking the trust of others. And once that trust is broken there is no going back."

Eloise felt the warmth of his hands, heard the anguish in his voice, and knew that, indeed, he understood. Yet she couldn't tell him about George, didn't have the courage to voice what was in her heart. Tears trembled on her lashes.

"I know this is painful, Eloise, but you must end it. My son guards his possessions with jealous zeal — and he will neither forgive nor release you."

Eloise knew he was right — but the thought that she would never share another intimate moment with George was too much to bear. "How did you know?" she whispered.

"I have eyes, my dear," he said sadly. "You positively glow when you are with Mr Collinson but with Edward you are pale and less sure of yourself."

Eloise was shocked at how easily she had betrayed herself. "I didn't realise," she breathed. "Was it obvious to everyone?"

He shook his head. "I think not. But if it continues it will become so." He patted her hand. "I, too, fell in love with a Penhalligan so I understand how hard it is to break away. Be brave, Eloise. Do what you know is right — if not for yourself, then for Charles. That little boy needs you."

So the rumours of his affair with Susan were true.

"How very cosy."

Edward had entered the room silently. Eloise knew she had paled, that tears were streaking her face, but she didn't have the wit to wipe them away. How long had he been standing there? How much had he heard?

"I might have known you'd be here the minute my back was turned," he snapped, as he strode across the room. "What are you doing with my wife in such an intimate huddle?"

Jonathan stood. "I am here to visit my grandson and to drink tea with my daughter-in-law," he said coldly. "I take exception to your manner, sir."

"It is quite justified." Edward turned to Eloise. "Aren't you going to welcome me home? After all, I have been away for almost two months."

Eloise was about to kiss his cheek when Edward grabbed her and bent her backwards as he bruised her lips. She smelt brandy on his breath, felt the scratch of his moustache, the probe of his tongue, and had to fight the desire to push him away.

Edward released her, face flushed, eyes bright. "I think it's time we were alone, don't you?"

"Your father came to tell me he was leaving for London," said Eloise.

Edward spun round. "London?"

As Jonathan began to speak, Eloise saw that her husband had forgotten her for now. She backed out of the room, closed the door, picked up her skirts and fled to the small parlour. Edward's raised voice didn't bode well, and she dreaded the night ahead.

Balmain, May 1798

George hobbled the horse beside Eloise's bay. It had been two weeks since their last meeting, and he'd begun to worry for he'd heard that Edward Cadwallader was back in Sydney Town.

He retrieved the blanket and a bottle of wine from his saddlebag, then walked through the trees, his boots crunching dead leaves until he reached the glade.

Eloise ran to him. "I thought you'd never come," she sobbed.

He dropped everything and held her. Something terrible must have happened for her to lose control. "What is it, my love?" he asked urgently.

She drew back, held his face and kissed him with such fierceness it took his breath away. "I love you, love you, love you."

Gently he held her away. Her eyes were awash, and the way she clung to him meant that she was in trouble. "What's happened, Eloise?"

"We are discovered. Edward's father knows."

George froze. "Has he told his son? Has Edward beaten you? Are you hurt?"

She shook her head. "My heart is all that is hurt. Edward doesn't know." She was clinging to him even more tightly now. "Oh, George. We must not meet again — we cannot risk anyone else discovering us."

He was reeling. "Eloise, you cannot mean that. Please, my love, calm yourself. How did the earl find out? We have been so careful."

244

He listened as the tale was revealed, each word falling like a drop of icy water, but his love still burnt like a furnace, and he knew he could never let her go. He held her as she cried, felt his own tears well as he tried to order his thoughts.

As her sobs ebbed, he drew her down to the blanket. "Leave him," he said softly. "Bring the child and we will go to America."

She took a tremulous breath. "I wish I could, and I have dreamt of us being together — but it is only a dream, George, for it is impossible."

"No, it isn't," he urged. "We can leave today. A ship is due to sail tonight." He grasped her hands. "I know what a scandal it will cause and I understand how frightened you must be, but we'll be together, Eloise — and together we can rise above anything."

"Edward would come after us." She sniffed. "He's rich and from a powerful family. He would kill you without a moment's thought and drag me back here so he could punish me for the rest of my life."

"We'll find somewhere to hide. Please, Eloise," he begged. "You can't stay with him."

"I have to," she whispered. "Darling George, I love you. I wish things were different. But we began this knowing it was foolish, knowing that no matter how much we loved one another our plans for the future could only be realised in our dreams. We knew it would have to end one day — and that day has come."

"But how can I let you go when my heart beats only for you?"

"Because you love me," she said. "And because we could never be happy with the shadow of Edward hanging over us. He would travel to the ends of the earth to find his heir."

"Then leave Charles behind," he said in desperation.

"I could never do that! And I'm shocked that you even suggest it."

He gathered her back into his embrace. "Forgive me, beloved. I hardly know what I'm saying."

"My heart is breaking too, but there is no way to resolve this."

"There is."

She withdrew from his embrace. "You sound very fierce."

"That's because I will not have you stay with that man a minute longer." He tried to think of the right way to tell her what he knew.

"He is my husband, and it is my duty to remain with him."

He gave her a shake. "He's violated a woman, Eloise."

Eloise pulled away from him. "All charges were dropped. Edward was falsely accused, and the convict girl was a proven liar."

George stared at her in disbelief. "You knew about the trial?"

"From the first," she said. "Edward told me of it after I'd heard the gossip."

"Did he tell you he'd been banished to the northern hinterland for five years after that?"

246

"He wasn't banished," she replied. "His commanding officer needed a small troop up there, and he thought it best that Edward should lead it so the scandal had time to die down."

"And you believed him?"

"Edward might be many things, but I do not believe him capable of such depravity. Otherwise I would not have married him." She drew her knees up as if defending herself from further onslaught. "Edward has his faults, and they are many, but he *is* my husband and my son's father. My marriage vows mean I am not free — will never be free."

He wanted to tell her about Millicent and Ernest — to describe his parents' anguish, and how Jonathan Cadwallader had blackened his mother's reputation — yet as he looked into her determined little face he knew he couldn't. Eloise's belief in her husband's innocence would not be shaken. It would serve little purpose to vent his spleen.

"Please, George," she whispered. "Don't let it end like this. It's too painful."

"I'm sorry, my love. Will you forgive me?"

"Of course."

George drew her down until they lay on the blanket. Their kisses were soft in the stillness of that coastal glade. Their lovemaking that day was the sweetest yet, for it was the last time.

George watched her ride away. Her head was high, but he knew she was crying. He longed for her to look back at him but knew she couldn't.

"Farewell, my sweet," he murmured, as she was lost to sight.

He swung into the saddle, but was reluctant to leave the glade. It was clear that Eloise knew only the barest facts of Edward's trial. Neither did she have any notion of how deeply involved his own family had been. She had made the only decision she could, in the circumstances, and he'd been forced to accept it.

The sun was lower now, casting deeper shadows beneath the trees as the birds took off in their final flight of the day. The air was alive with the chatter of parrots and lorikeets, the soft croon of magpies and the raucous laughter of the kookaburra. Nature's orchestra, discordant but melodic, was playing the finale.

CHAPTER
ELEVEN

Moonrakers, September 1798

"Be careful how you do that, Nell," said Alice. "Cut too much and we lose money."

Nell gritted her teeth and resisted slamming the unwieldy shears on to the sorting table. She was doing her best, damn it, and if Alice stopped poking her nose in she'd get on a lot quicker. She glared at the fleece on the table and felt like throwing it to the floor. It was hot and sweaty in the shearing shed and the noise was giving her a headache. Why did *she* have to cut the dags off the fleece?

"I know it's a dirty task," said Alice, kindly. "Would you like me to take over so you can rest awhile? You've been here all day."

"So have you." Nell was determined to carry on despite her aching back. She wiped the sweat from her face with a sweep of her arm. "Thank you," she said, "but the day's almost over and there's only a few more to do."

"If you need help, call me," said Alice.

Nell watched as she walked to the far end of the shed where Billy was manhandling the heavy wool-press with

Jack. She saw how they bent to listen to her, showing their acceptance of her skill in running the shed. There was no doubt about it, she thought, Alice was an asset to Moonrakers. Not that she would ever tell her so, of course.

They had employed five shearers to help with this late-winter shearing, and they worked with the economy of movement that came from long years of experience. As the sheep were herded by the Aborigine boys up the ramps to the waiting pens, their aunt Daisy opened the gate and let them into the smaller enclosures two by two. A shearer reached in, grabbed a beast, dragged it to his station, flipped it on to its back and made the first long sweep with the shears.

Gladys was padding back and forth with a bucket of water and a tin cup so no one went thirsty, and Pearl was sitting with her husband and his brothers by the fire outside, keeping an eye on the cauldron of pitch. Her youngest son was the tarboy, waiting with his bucket and a thick brush to smear the cuts left by any careless sweep of the shears.

Alice had returned to the sorting table and was expertly spreading the fleeces and checking them before she allocated each to a pile. Billy and Jack were sweating as they worked the press, while Walter and his sisters swept away the dirty wool and sheep dung. Despite the heat, the ever-present flies and the stench of sweat, it was an exciting scene: shearing was the culmination of their year's work.

Nell took a drink from the cup of water the little boy held out to her. He was a cheeky fellow, with a taste for

250

mischief. She wiped her mouth on her sleeve. "I thought your mother was supposed to be doing this, Bindi?"

He grinned up at her. "She sleep. Bindi betta watta," he said.

She watched him run down the shed to a shearer who was yelling for a drink, saw the man ruffle the boy's hair as he returned the cup.

"He's a good kid," said Billy, as he came to stand beside her. "They all are," he added as two others raced to pick up the trimmed fleeces and take them to Alice for grading.

"They certainly seem more eager to work than their parents," she said, through a vast yawn. "Pearl hasn't moved from that fire all day, and the men seem content to sit and do nothing."

"I reckon Bindi's generation will see that our coming here isn't a threat. As long as we respect the differences between us, we'll rub along together." He put his arm round her waist and gave her a quick hug. "How are you bearing up?"

"Nearly finished for the day," she replied. "And you?"

Billy's eyes twinkled as he gave her a roguish grin. "Oh, I'm full of energy," he said, with a wink.

Nell giggled and dug him in the ribs. "Gerron with you, Billy Penhalligan. I got work to do." She felt a glow of happiness as she thought about the coming night. Billy could still weaken her knees, and the promise of making love to him renewed her flagging energy as she returned to her task.

★ ★ ★

Alice kept an eye on Jack as she finished sorting the last few fleeces. They had all been up before first light and he was showing signs of exhaustion. It was in the lines on his face, and in the way his shoulders sagged as he tried to keep his weight off his bad hip and knee. Yet he seemed determined to keep going, and she knew better than to try to persuade him that someone else should take his place.

She moved away from the table as the native boys gathered up the bundles and took them to the press. They loved shearing time: it meant extra food and tea, and tobacco for their parents — and when the last sheep had gone down the ramp into the drenching pool there would be feast to celebrate. She looked forward to that: the Aborigines would play their didgeridoos and clap-sticks, and chant to the starry heavens as they must have done since time began. It was an eerie sound, but now she was used to it she found it touched something inside her that seemed to bring her closer to this ancient land.

With a sigh of satisfaction she looked down the shed. The bustle and noise, the bleating of the sheep and the smell of lanolin, sweat and wool made up for her aching back. Nell's children were sweeping the floor and arguing over the rights to do so. Amy stamped her foot and prodded Walter's arm. Bossy little thing, she thought fondly, and as spirited as her mother.

She left the shed and went out to the drenching pool they'd dug at the bottom of the release ramp. A shearer sent a ewe slithering down it, and the Aboriginal man directed his younger charges in the correct way to immerse the animal in the evil-smelling brew of sheep dip. She couldn't help but smile at the boys' delight as they pushed it with their long, padded sticks to make sure it was fully submerged before they chivvied it out. The ewe shook itself and, in a series of leaps, pranced across the pen to join the others that were standing about, dazed by the experience.

"I bet you never thought we'd have such a large flock," said Jack, as he came to lean on the fence beside her.

Alice looked beyond the holding pens to the broad sweep of grassland dotted with the snowy white of newly shorn sheep. "Only in my dreams," she murmured, as she rested her head against his arm. "But we've done it, Jack. We've made a success of it."

His pale face broke into a smile as he put his arm round her shoulders. "We couldn't have done it without you," he said. "I'm so proud of you, Alice."

Alice blushed as he kissed her cheek and the native boys whistled and exchanged what she suspected were ribald comments. "Jack," she protested weakly.

"There's nothing wrong with kissing my wife," he said, his dark eyes teasing as he pulled her closer.

Alice gave up resisting and kissed him back. Despite the long day, the heat and the weariness, she could always find the energy and time to let Jack know she loved him.

"No regrets?" They had drawn apart, but Jack's arm was round her waist now.

"Only that we have no children," she replied.

253

A shadow seemed to fall over his eyes and he gave her a consoling hug. "We have each other, and that is miracle enough," he said. "When I thought I'd lost you, all those years ago, I never dared dream of such happiness. But you're here, and this is what we have done together." He swept his arm in an arc to encompass the sheep, the pens, the new bridge over the river and the grasslands. "Be proud, Alice, and thank God we were given this second chance."

"I love you, Jack Quince."

"And I love you, Mrs Quince."

Their murmurings were drowned by the bell Bindi was ringing. It was the end of work for the day.

"Come on, you two," said Billy, as he emerged from the shed with Nell. "Billing and cooing at your age isn't seemly, Jack."

Jack laughed and the lines of weariness faded. "Just remember you're two months older than me so you should listen to your own advice."

"Come," said Nell, "we're wasting time and I'm hungry." She looked at Alice and rolled her eyes. "Men!"

"Different breed," Alice replied. "We'll never understand them."

"When you've quite finished demolishing our characters, Alice, I would like to point out that any misbehaviour on our part is the fault of you women."

"How's that, Billy?"

"I'm too much of a gentleman to say."

"Well," said Nell, as she took his arm, "perhaps now you've finished teasing Alice we can have our tea."

"But I like teasing Alice," protested Billy, with feigned innocence. "You don't blush half as well."

"That's 'cos I've 'eard it all before," she said, and tugged at his arm. "Leave poor Alice alone. She's enough to put up with already."

"It's all right, Nell," said Alice, as she linked arms with Jack. "I don't listen to him half the time anyway."

Billy clutched his heart. "I'm hurt to the core, Alice."

"You'll get 'urt somewhere far more painful if I don't 'ave somethin' to eat soon," said Nell darkly.

A government farm, October 1798

Niall's bare feet sank into the soft earth as he and Paddy Galvin tried to drive a straight furrow with the unwieldy plough. It was a warm day, but a breeze was blowing through the trees and Niall was enjoying his freedom from the hated shackles.

"Looking pleased with yourself there," grunted Paddy, as he leant his slight weight on the handle. He was fourteen, and had been on the farm longer than nine-year-old Niall, who had arrived six weeks before. "Though how you can when you're up to the arse in mud and muck is beyond me."

"'Tis a fine day," replied Niall. "I'm free of me shackles, and me feet are enjoyin' the feel of the good earth between me toes. It's almost as if I'm back home."

Paddy grimaced. "This is about as near to Ireland as my arse."

Niall smiled. Paddy liked the word "arse", and used it as often as he could. "It's better than Sydney Town," he replied. "The air's cleaner, I've lost me chains and the trooper's not so handy with the whip."

"Aye, you're right there," puffed Paddy. "Are you sure you're pullin' yer weight, boy? This feckin' thing is the very divil to steer."

"That I am, Paddy Galvin. But me arms are surely bein' ground in their sockets."

"If I push any harder, me arse will explode."

"That'll save on the fertiliser, to be sure." Niall chortled.

There was a loud clang and the plough-share juddered to a halt, sending a shudder up their arms.

Niall hauled on the reins and Paddy went to see what had happened. "Arseholes," muttered the older boy, as he scratched his shaven head. "Another feckin' rock."

"Hurry up, you two. You should have finished this run by now."

Niall and Paddy looked at the English soldier who'd been watching their progress throughout the morning. He was young, inexperienced and prone to sitting in the shade for most of the day. "We'd go a lot faster if the field had been cleared properly before we started ploughin'," muttered Paddy.

"Don't cheek me, boy, or I'll send you to Marsden."

Niall and Paddy knew all about the Flogging Parson and, although this particular trooper was more bark than bite, they kept their mouths shut as they struggled to reverse the plough, then dig out the rock. Even though he was a man of God, Marsden enjoyed flogging prisoners, and was detested by everyone who was forced to work on this farm.

With the rock removed to an edge of the field, they continued ploughing until the shout went up to down tools for their permitted rest at noon. Niall and Paddy found a shady spot beneath the trees, then gobbled the potato soup and thick bread they'd fetched from the field kitchen.

"Not half as good as me mammy's soup," sighed Niall. He wiped the bowl clean with the bread, savouring the taste and chewing slowly to make it last.

Paddy flopped on to his back, hands pillowing his head as he stared up at the sky through the leaves. "Will you look at the colour of it? Hard to imagine it's the same sky we have at home."

Niall swallowed the last crust and put the bowl to one side, then joined his friend on the ground. "'Tis blue enough," he agreed, "but I'd give anything to have the grey skies of home and the smell of a peat fire in me nose instead of these gum trees."

Paddy closed his eyes. "It's what we all want," he said wistfully.

"How long have you been here, Paddy?"

"Too long. Four arsin' years too long. How about you?"

"It'll be a year next month."

"How long you got?"

"Seven more." He felt the tears well and angrily blinked them away.

"That's a fearful long time." Paddy returned to his scrutiny of the sky. "What did you do to the English to earn that?"

Niall closed his eyes as the memories flooded back. "Me brothers fought at Wexford," he began. "I took food to them at the safe-house and, like an eejit, didn't see I was bein' followed by the Redcoats."

"Wexford, eh? I heard about the battle of Vinegar Hill — I wish I could have been part of it." His keen gaze was on Niall now. "What happened?"

"Me two eldest brothers were hanged for sedition, and me and me other brother were put on the *Minerva*. He's on Norfolk Island for life." Niall's hatred of the English burnt in his gut. His family had been ripped apart and loyal Irishmen were imprisoned or dying for fighting against England's tyranny.

"A lot of good men are on that island," said Paddy, gloomily. A thought struck him. "You must have sailed with Joseph Holt and James Harrold if you were on the *Minerva*. Is it true they're great leaders of the United Irishmen?"

"They are." Pride swelled in Niall as he remembered his heroes. "They might be on Norfolk Island, but that won't stop them fightin' our cause," he said stoutly.

Paddy grinned and got to his feet as the shout went up to get back to work. "With God's blessin' and the luck of the Irish, let us hope so, Niall. There are men on the farm who are plottin' to escape, and when I'm older I'll join them. I don't be plannin' to till an Englishman's field for much longer."

Niall put his hand to the plough and squinted into the sun. Paddy was talking sedition, and the very idea was thrilling.

Sydney Town, November 1798

Alice was hurrying along, her thoughts on the list of things she had to buy before she and Jack returned to Moonrakers, when she was almost knocked into the street by someone emerging from a doorway. A firm hand caught her and swept her back on to the pavement. "My sincerest apologies, ma'am."

Alice recognised the voice. "Goodness," she breathed. "It's Mr Carlton."

He doffed his hat. "Miss Hobden. May I apologise again for my carelessness? I wasn't looking where I was going."

"It's Mrs Quince now," she corrected him, "and you have no need to apologise for you rescued me quite expertly."

"It must have been all the practice I had aboard ship," he replied, grey eyes alight with pleasure. "I don't need to ask after your health, Mrs Quince, for you are positively blooming. I take it you're enjoying life in the wilds?"

"It's hard work, but farming's the same wherever you are." She tilted her head as she regarded him. He still had the aura of power that she'd found daunting at first, but on closer acquaintance she had come to accept it as merely an intrinsic part of this fascinating man. "I see you are prospering too," she said. "Australia agrees with you."

"It holds certain charms," he agreed, as he tried to swat an annoying fly, "though one would prefer there to be fewer insects."

Alice smiled. "So, what keeps you here, Mr Carlton?"

"I do wish you'd call me Henry. It isn't as if we're in polite society and have to be formal." He glanced wryly at a group of Aborigines, fighting with a couple of Asian sailors over a bottle of rum.

She hadn't missed the way he'd avoided her question, and concluded it was none of her business. "We have had this conversation before, Mr Carlton, and now I'm a married woman it wouldn't be right."

He roared with laughter, which caused several people to stare as they walked by. "You and your sense of propriety," he spluttered. "I do so admire you, Mrs Quince. May I offer you tea at my lodgings?"

"I couldn't possibly," she stammered. "My husband is waiting for me and I have many things to do before we leave town."

"You would be quite safe," he said, with a conspiratorial wink. "There is a drawing room and my housekeeper will be there to guard your honour."

She felt the blush flood her face. "Mr Carlton," she giggled, "are you flirting with me?"

"Of course," he said. "I like to see you blush. It makes your eyes very bright."

She was reminded of Billy and his teasing, and realised that Henry Carlton was being playful. "Thank you for the compliment, and for the invitation to tea," she said, "but I really do have to go. Jack will be wondering where I am."

"Then go and fetch him and we can have tea together," he coaxed. "It's been so long since we had a chance to talk. I've missed your company."

She read something in his expression that made her feel a tingle of uneasy excitement but chose to ignore it. "We have to go back to Moonrakers," she said. "I'm sorry, Mr Carlton."

"Then perhaps we will meet again the next time you're in town," he said. "I shall be in Australia for a while, and you could send a message to my lodgings." He dug his fingers into his waistcoat pocket. "My card. Please take it."

Alice put it into her reticule. "We don't come into town very often," she told him, "but thank you." She curtsied and went on her way. The meeting had unnerved her, and although she'd been flattered by his attentions, she hadn't known how to handle his flirting. She couldn't wait to get back to Jack.

Yet as she walked down the road she was almost sure she could feel Mr Carlton's gaze, and wondered what he expected of her.

Kernow House, Watsons Bay, December 1798

Edward eyed his wife as she lowered herself into the chair and settled against the cushions. Her bloated belly ruined the line of her dress, and even though her breasts were magnificent he couldn't bring himself to go anywhere near her. He noticed the dark shadows under her eyes, the beads of sweat on her top lip and had to look away. She was about as tempting as a sow.

The door opened and Meg came in with Charles, who had recently celebrated his first birthday. "The drawing room is no place for an infant," he barked.

"I asked Meg to bring him down so you could see him," said Eloise. She struggled to her feet and took the sobbing baby into her arms. "Really, Edward," she said, as the maid left the room, "you made poor Meg jump and Charles cry."

"He's always grizzling about something," he muttered pouring himself a drink.

He heard her coaxing the child out of his tears and turned his back on them to stare out of the window at the magnificent sunset. With the doors open to catch the breeze, he could smell the roses that clambered up the side of the house. It was a pity Eloise was so ungainly. How pleasant it would have been to go for a ride along the beach.

"Oh, Edward, do look. He's trying to walk on his own."

He saw that Charles was clinging to her hands, his skinny legs almost bowed with the effort of keeping himself balanced. The expression on his face showed intense concentration, and for a moment Edward felt a spark of interest in him. "Let go of him," he ordered.

Eloise released her hands and Charles swayed like a drunken sailor.

"Come, boy," Edward commanded. "Walk to your father."

Charles put out one tiny foot. He grinned up at Edward and dribbled with delight at his achievement.

"That's it. And again."

"He's not on the parade-ground, Edward," said Eloise. "You don't need to shout."

Edward ignored her. "Come, Charles," he boomed. "Let's see what you're made of. Walk to Papa."

Charles's face crumpled, his toes caught in the Turkish carpet and he sat down with a bump.

Edward winced as his son wailed. "For God's sake, Eloise, quieten him." She scooped Charles into her arms, regardless of the drool on her neck. "Take him away," he snarled. "That caterwauling makes my head ache."

"He's a baby," she protested. "You can't expect him to be silent all the time."

"He's fourteen months old, Eloise." He took a deep draught of rum and slammed the glass on to the table. "Let us hope the next one isn't as feeble."

"Charles is not feeble," she retorted.

"Look at him," roared Edward above his son's howls. "There's more muscle on a chicken's leg. No wonder he can't walk."

Eloise made for the door.

"I suggest you tell the cook to feed him porridge and potatoes instead of the pap you give him. And if the next one's anything like Charles, you can bring it up on your own."

He raised his eyebrow as she slammed the door. Then he grinned. Eloise still had some fire left in her — but it was a pity it only manifested itself when she thought she had to defend her brat. He poured another drink, downed it in one and went out to the stables. He'd had enough of playing dutiful husband and father. He would ride along the beach, then go into town.

Paramatta Mission, Christmas Day 1798

Mandarg crept closer to the sound of singing and squatted in the doorway of the strange building. He clutched his spear in readiness as he looked at the gathering of black men and women and white soldiers, but they hadn't noticed him.

His gaze trawled along the brightly coloured pictures on the wall and came to a halt on a shiny object that stood on the table at the far end. It reminded him of the thing he'd found at the mission house in Banks Town. As he stared at it, he realised it *was* the thing. How had it got here? He and the other warrior had left it behind.

He turned his attention to the white man who was standing by the table, and talking. He looked strange in the long white robe, but his voice was pleasant to listen to and Mandarg tried to understand what he was saying. After a while he gave up and padded away to a pleasant sunny spot by the big stones that littered the ground. They weren't Dreaming Stones, so it would be all right to lean on them.

The heat made him drowsy, and he settled down to sleep. The remnants of his tribe lived on the other side of the mountains, but something had drawn him back to this place where the eels lay down. It was beyond his tribal boundaries, but with the white man's coming that didn't seem to matter, and there was good hunting here.

As sleep claimed him he thought he heard Lowitja's voice, whispering her warning, taunting him with the things she had seen in the Sacred Stones. He grunted and shook his head to still the voice that had haunted him since the raid on the Wiradjuric. He had not touched the white woman — had taken no part in the slaughter — so why was Lowitja determined to torture him?

"Merry Christmas, brother," said a cheerful voice.

Mandarg was on his feet, the spear held aloft.

"I am not your enemy," continued the man.

"You white man," snarled Mandarg, in his own tongue. "Black feller your enemy."

"My name is John Pritchard," said the man, who didn't seem concerned that Mandarg's spear pointed at his heart. "I am the garrison preacher and run the mission here. What is your name?"

Mandarg's eyes widened and he took a step back. The white man was speaking his language now. "I am Mandarg," he muttered. "How is it that a white man speaks our tongue?"

"It is the will of God that I have the gift of learning many tongues," Pritchard replied.

Mandarg frowned. "Who is this God? Is he a Sacred Dreaming Spirit who gives you this gift?"

John Pritchard smiled. "Not a spirit of your dreaming, friend, but the creator and giver of all life."

Mandarg was confused. How could a white man know of the Great Creator Spirit — and why had he been granted such a powerful gift? "You speak of strange things, white man in a woman's clothing. Leave me to my sleep."

"Are you hungry, Mandarg?"

The man annoyed him, but Mandarg hadn't eaten for many hours.

"It is a special day today," said Pritchard. "We are having a feast to celebrate the birth of our Lord Jesus Christ. Why don't you join us?"

Mandarg could make little sense of what the other man was talking about. Yet the word "feast" had been unmistakable and his belly growled. "You have plenty food?"

Pritchard nodded. "Plenty, and afterwards I will tell you the story of Christmas and how Jesus came into the world to save us."

Mandarg's mind was centred on food, but the promise of a story was just as tempting. He drew himself up and looked down his nose at the other man. "I am Mandarg of the Gandangara. I will look at what you offer, and if it pleases me, I will eat." He followed the white man, Lowitja's voice growing louder in his head with every step.

CHAPTER
TWELVE

Parramatta Garrison, January 1799

The weather was charged with the oncoming storm, and despite the lowering clouds, Nell was uncomfortable in the cloying heat. If only it would rain, she thought. The water-holes were drying up, the earth was parched and cracked and it was increasingly difficult to keep the stock fed and safe from marauding dingoes. She glared up at the sky, defying it to let her down again; it had promised rain before, which had never arrived.

She stood at the horse's head as the soldiers unloaded the wagon and took the mutton into the kitchens. Then she led the animal to the water-trough and hitched him to a post. It was time to eat, but she didn't feel like entering the garrison kitchens — they reminded her too strongly of the London prison where she'd once been held — so she took the basket out of the wagon and strolled towards the chapel.

The grass was still green at the water's edge. Black swans and squabbling water-fowl were taking advantage of the only water for miles. She picked a pleasant spot and ate some cold mutton and bread, her thoughts drifting with the gathering clouds.

Alice was out with the men, and Nell had accepted long ago the other woman's knowledge of farming, and the close bond she'd forged with Billy. She resented neither. Nell's children adored the childless Alice, and although she'd tried not to let her jealousy show as her daughters sought Alice's help with their lessons, and snuggled up to her as she read them stories, it was hard to deny it.

Nell lifted the hair from her nape to cool herself. She was being foolish and selfish: she knew Alice wasn't trying to steal her children, merely filling the gaps left by their mother's lack of education. It didn't mean her children loved her less, or that she was in danger of losing them.

She shook out her hair and brushed the crumbs from her skirt. Alice meant no harm, and she should feel sorry for her. She glowered at the sky. The ominous weather was irritating her, and her skinny backside was still numb after the journey. She would walk off her ill-temper.

Having tramped along the river until she was out of breath, she meandered into the graveyard. She hadn't come here before, and lingered to read the markers. It was still and peaceful, a fitting resting-place for the soldiers and convicts who had succumbed to native attack, sickness and old age. It reminded her of the cemetery at home, the baby buried there, and she decided to leave. She was about to turn away when she saw the words on one particular marker:

This young white woman is known only to God.
May her troubled mind be healed in Heaven.

"I see you've found our mystery girl," said the voice behind her.

She squinted at him through a shaft of sunlight that had pierced the clouds. "Hello, John," she said, to the garrison minister. "I didn't know you were back from Sydney Town."

"A short sojourn for the new year only." He pointed at the marker. "That was the only gift I could give her. The only way to mark her tragic life, whose poignancy still touches my heart."

Nell remained silent.

"She intrigued me, and when a girl so young and troubled dies in your arms, it becomes important to discover who she was."

"And did you?"

He nodded. "After a long search." He went on to tell her how he'd come across the girl in the bush. "She was carrying a crucifix," he said, "which had clearly come from a church or chapel, and that was my starting point."

John Pritchard had come to Parramatta a year ago. To Nell, he seemed a surprising man; unlike any other minister, he preferred the company of natives to his garrison duties, and spent days, even weeks, out in the bush rather than in his pulpit. His work with the local Aborigines had caused alarm among the white settlers, but he paid it no attention, and for that she admired him.

"So you followed the trail?" she prompted.

"Yes. I persuaded my new acquaintance, Mandarg, to accompany me to Banks Town." He paused. "He was most reluctant, but once we'd got there, it seemed he needed to be rid of a great weight of guilt he'd been carrying."

"You've lost me," Nell said.

John Pritchard's smile was wan. "We are all lost in one way or another, but I can only hope that the poor souls who were slaughtered at that mission have found the peace of Heaven. Certainly Mandarg found consolation in having told me of what happened."

Nell listened as he described the massacre that had taken place. His words were carefully chosen, but she had enough imagination to picture the terrible scene, and when he fell silent, she turned once more to the marker. "So she was there," she murmured. "She survived only because of her madness."

"Mandarg's beliefs wouldn't allow him to harm one who has been touched by the Spirits. He has never tracked for the Corps again — he calls the major a 'debil with white skin'."

Nell had heard of the corps, and because of Millicent's violation and the subsequent farce of a trial, knew the character of the man who'd been in charge of this rout. She and Billy had long suspected that the clearing of land involved the slaughter of native people. It was one of the reasons they gave sanctuary to their own little clan. "Will you tell the authorities?"

"I have tried to, but the army is a closed society. They shield their own."

270

"But they killed the missionary and left the girl to fend for herself in the bush. They should be punished."

"One can only pray that it will be so, Nell."

Nell doubted prayer would have much effect. "So, do you know who she was?"

"I do now, for my enquiries in Sydney led me to her family," he said. He hesitated. "Nell, it is fortuitous that we should meet today, here at this particular graveside."

She could see he was hunting for the right words, and although she knew what he was going to say, she needed to hear her suspicion confirmed. "It's Billy's niece, Florence Collinson, isn't it?"

He nodded sorrowfully. "I didn't recognise her, of course, because I hadn't arrived on these shores when she went missing. But I will have to inform her parents, and although I have had the pleasure of meeting Ezra Collinson, and admire his work, it is not a task I relish."

Nell touched his arm in sympathy. "Perhaps it would be better not to," she said. "Ezra and Susan still cling to the 'ope she'll return 'ome. Shatterin' that may destroy them."

"My conscience wouldn't allow me to remain silent," he replied. "They must be told."

She knew he was right, and that she couldn't keep such a thing to herself without feeling guilty every time she visited Hawks Head. "Leave it to me and Billy, then," she said. "We'll tell 'em."

Hawks Head Farm, three days later

The heat was almost unendurable, the air as thick as treacle beneath a threatening sky as Billy told his sister and her husband what had become of Florence. Nell knew he was finding it difficult, for his face had lost its usual ruddy cheerfulness, and his fingers folded and twisted the brim of his hat as he held it between his knees.

Silence fell, and Nell saw Ezra's chin drop to his chest as Susan stared beyond the veranda to the horizon as if she could see that pathetic grave with its sad little marker. There had been no tears — not yet — and Nell suspected that, despite the hope they had borne so valiantly over the past years, they had accepted that their daughter would never come home.

"So many deaths," Susan said at last. "So many young lives taken in this wild, unforgiving place." Her blue eyes were filled with pain. "If only she'd come home to us she might still be alive."

Ezra took her hand. His face was ashen, his eyes dark with grief. "Don't torture yourself, Susan," he begged. "Florence made her choice, and God chose to take her into His care."

Susan pulled her hand from his grip and stood. "It wasn't God who took her, but that damned Edward Cadwallader," she hissed. "And I'll make sure he pays this time for what he's done."

"Susan!" gasped Ezra. "Be mindful of your language."

She whirled round to face him. "Don't, Ezra! Don't *dare* lecture me. Not today."

Ezra hauled himself out of his chair and gathered her into his arms as she gave in to a storm of tears.

272

Nell flashed a glance at Billy and they moved off the veranda. "Well," she said, once they were out of earshot, "I never knew your sister 'ad such a temper."

"Marriage to Ezra made her a lady, but the Cornish fisher-girl has always been in the background." His smile was wan. "I can remember her let fly a string of curses when she got into a fight on the quay with another girl. It was over a gutting-knife, as far as I can remember."

Nell chuckled as she remembered similar fights she'd had in London and on the convict ship. "I always knew she had spirit," she said.

They came to the pens and Billy eased his hat back from his brow as he regarded the horizon. "She'll need all her strength to see them both through this. Ezra's faith won't be enough this time."

"At least they've got Bess and Ernest, and the new grandchild is bound to ease the pain." Nell leant on the railing and tried to remain cheerful. She lived with the memory of her own lost child, and the dread that something might happen to the others.

Billy put his arm round her shoulders. "Our children will be all right," he said quietly. "And so will Susan and Ezra once they've visited the graveyard and put up a proper memorial to Florence." He kissed her. "Thank you for coming with me, Nell. I couldn't have done this without you."

The sound of footsteps made them turn.

"Billy . . . I didn't mean to lose my temper, but when hope is finally gone . . ." Susan's smile was tinged with sadness.

He took her into his arms and held her.

She drew back eventually and smiled up at him. "You would have made our parents very proud, little brother, and I constantly give thanks that we came to Australia at the same time — how could I have managed without you?"

His face was burning as she gave him another swift hug. "I'm too old for all this," he objected.

Susan touched the wings of grey that glinted at his temples. "We're all older, Billy — wiser too — but I'll hug you whenever I choose to, regardless of your blushes." She lifted the hem of her dress out of the dust. "Now I must pack a few things and kiss my grandson before we leave for Parramatta. Ezra wants to hold a service for Florence and arrange for a decent headstone."

"How is he?" asked Nell.

"Well enough, though the news is a terrible blow to us," she replied, "but I will see him through."

Moonrakers, February 1799

Thunder rumbled in the distance and lightning momentarily lit the dark clouds as Alice caught the terrified lamb and slit its throat. The crows had pecked out its eyes and she was close to despair as she laid down the little body. Everything was dying. The ewes had dropped their lambs late and they were prey to starving dingoes or predatory crows. The land was parched, the grass so dry it gleamed silver and held little nourishment. If it didn't rain soon they would lose even more stock.

She took a shuddering breath as she hitched up Jack's old trousers and tightened the length of string that acted as a belt. They were far too big but, like the heavy boots she always wore now, they were practical for life here.

Alice scanned the sky. The clouds were gathering, black and fat with precious rain, but would the storm break this time? She took off her hat and wiped the sweat from her brow and neck as flies buzzed around her head. She rammed it back on, then pulled down the veil she'd sewn to the brim. It protected her from the flies, but it smothered her, too, so she yanked it back again and climbed on to her horse.

The chestnut mare picked her way over the gaping cracks that had opened in the ground, and Alice felt her tremble as the thunder crashed closer and lightning forked in the darkening clouds. "Steady, girl," she murmured, as the mare's ears went back. "We've a long day ahead."

As she rode through the dying pasture in search of her flock, she compared the barrenness of the land to herself. The longed-for child hadn't come, and she'd had to accept that she would never be a mother. It was her greatest sadness: to bear Jack's baby would have been the culmination of her dreams. Yet she'd been blessed with the love of Amy, Sarah and Walter, and she cherished it.

Alice's hands slackened on the reins as they passed the dwindling billabong. The bank had dried into a fractured crust, the reeds were brown and withered and a vast congregation of birds squabbled over the shallow, murky pool that was left. The rotting carcasses of a kangaroo and its joey lay some way off, the ever-present crows fighting over the feast.

A sudden thunderclap shook the earth.

The mare whinnied and reared.

Alice lost her grip as lightning struck the earth with an earsplitting crack.

The birds rose from the water in an explosion of wings and sharp cries as the mare bolted and Alice hit the unforgiving ground with a bone-jarring thud. She lay there, winded and helpless, as the mare galloped away.

"This is getting us nowhere," muttered Billy, as he drew his horse alongside Jack's and squinted to search the dazzling silver grass of the empty landscape. "The sheep have scattered so far we'll never round them up."

"We must," said Jack. The weather was playing devil's advocate with his hip today, and the pain was constant. "They're here somewhere, and you can bet they'll stay close together. Let's try the other waterhole." He grimaced as the thunder drew nearer and his horse began to dance, bringing the agony to an even greater height.

Billy took off his hat, wiped away the sweat and tugged it back on. "If they're not there, I'm for going home," he said. "We've already been out two days, and there's nothing we can do but leave the dead for the dingoes."

Jack's face was grim. "I hope Alice isn't still out on the western pasture. That storm's very close."

"She has plenty of sense, which is more than I can say for you, my friend. But we'll try Snake Creek anyway." He whistled up the dogs and set his horse at a canter.

Jack followed, and as each jolt sent fire through his hip, he became even more determined to ignore it. The sheep had to be found and brought closer to the homestead where they could be fed and watered more easily.

"I should have done this earlier," he said, as he caught up with Billy. "It was stupid to trust to luck and the weather."

"None of us thought the drought would go on for so long," said Billy. "Don't blame yourself."

Jack battled with the pain and the knowledge that he was indeed to blame. The sheep were their livelihood but he had ignored Alice's warning and put them at risk by not bringing them into home pasture months ago. Now they had lost most of the late lambs along with several ewes. Thankfully, Alice had insisted that the rams were brought in, and they were safe in the homestead pens.

They rode in silence as their horses flinched at the lightning and trembled at the thunder. The dogs ran back and forth, noses to the ground, tails wedged firmly between their legs. They didn't like the storm either.

Snake Creek was so named because it meandered through the vast swathe of trees that still covered a third of their land. It trickled over a gravel bed and fed the broad expanse of water that, during the summer, was smothered with pink and white lilies, and was a haven for wildlife.

The two men drew their horses to a halt and stared in despair. The creek was a shallow, muddy trickle, and although the sheep had found it, some had got stuck in the mud and perished, their grotesquely bloated bodies black with flies.

In silent accord they climbed down and rescued three survivors that were trapped and bleating. Having chivvied them to join the others, Jack whistled up the dogs. He watched as they rounded up the sheep — only a fraction of the large flock they'd once had.

A flash of lightning and a crack of thunder brought him sharply alert. "Did you see that, Billy?" he shouted.

"What?" Billy was having trouble with his horse: it was threatening to bolt at any minute.

Another flash, and Jack pointed. "Over there in the scrub. I thought I saw someone watching us."

"Jesus, I hope not," muttered Billy, as he slapped the horse's flank and tried to calm it. "The last thing we need today is an escaped convict." He came alongside Jack and peered into the gloom. "Are you sure it wasn't just shadows? This light's deceiving."

Jack was wondering the same thing when he saw a small figure dart from behind a tree and plunge deeper into the bush. "It's Bindi! What's he doing out here?"

"Bindi!" yelled Billy. "Get your black backside out here now!"

There was no reply.

278

"Bindi, if you don't get out here I'm coming after you and I'll leather you with my belt!"

Jack looked at him in horror and Billy grinned. "I've no intention of strapping him, but he doesn't know that, and we can't wait about for him."

They heard laughter, which was drowned in the grumble of thunder.

"We'll have to go in and find him," said Jack. "It's too dangerous to leave him here." He climbed painfully into the saddle. The dogs were keeping the sheep in a tenuous huddle. "You go with the animals and I'll find Bindi."

"Are you all right?" shouted Billy.

"Right enough," he lied, as he tried to calm his prancing horse. He wove it back and forth to help bring in the strays the dogs had missed, but he could feel the power of the elements as they gathered force. The storm-laden clouds were overhead now, bringing an eerie twilight. An unearthly stillness wrapped itself around them as if the world was holding its breath, waiting for the onslaught.

A crack of thunder made them all jump. For an instant they were transfixed in the white of the lightning strike. Then all hell broke loose.

The sheep scattered, the dogs raced after them. The horses bucked, ears flat, nostrils flaring as Billy and Jack fought for control.

Jack almost bit through his lip as his foot slipped out of the stirrup. He held on — if he fell off he wouldn't stand a chance.

Crash after crash rent the air. Lightning struck with whiplash cracks, and the surrounding trees shook as the ground vibrated.

Then a finger of lightning touched a tree with the explosive force of a bullet. The dry trunk burst into flames, the sparks igniting the eucalyptus-laden air into a ball of fire that shot into the surrounding undergrowth. The parched forest was easy prey. Leaves shrivelled and blackened, trunks became pillars of flame and the forest floor was soon laced with a network of glowing rivers of fire.

"Bindi!" shouted Jack, as he searched wildly for the boy through the smoke. "Where are you?"

"Bindi, come out. Fire, fire!" Billy wheeled his horse in a tight circle. "We gotta find him, Jack," he yelled. "Forget the bloody sheep."

"Boss! Boss!" Bindi's high, frightened voice echoed to them through the trees.

"Stay where you are!" yelled Jack, as he yanked on the reins. "We're coming to get you." He dug his heels into the horse's sides and drove it into the trees towards the boy.

Alice ached all over, but at least she hadn't broken anything. She stumbled to her feet and scanned the horizon for her horse. The empty pasture stretched before her in the strange half-light. The solitary clusters of trees stood silhouetted against the black sky and all was deathly still as the storm gathered its forces.

280

"Damn you," she muttered crossly, as she picked up her hat and knocked off the dust. "Bertie wouldn't have thrown me, let alone left me stranded." She took her bearings. She was at least five hours' ride from the homestead, and if old Bertie had still been alive she could have done it in ten. As it was, she would have to walk.

Alice watched lightning flicker dangerously over the distant trees. One strike and there would be a fire — the fear of every settler for it ravaged hundreds of acres at a time, killing everything in its path, men and beasts, swifter than a swarm of locusts. She prayed Jack and Billy had avoided the bush, and were already on their way back to Moonrakers.

As the thunder rolled and the eerie darkness closed in, Alice realised how vulnerable she was. The bolting horse had left her without water-bag or rifle, and if she should encounter marauding dingoes, which hunted in packs now the drought had taken hold, she would be easy prey.

She regarded the lonely land that stretched to every horizon. It was beautiful, even now, majestic in its solitude and grandeur, touching a primal part of her soul, which sang with recognition for this ancient, isolated place. Yet it was dangerous to be out here alone and unarmed . . .

She made a forceful effort to pull herself together. "It's no good thinking like that," she muttered. "Jack and Billy are bound to be going in the same direction. You won't be alone for long."

She waded through the mud of the waterhole and took a long drink. It would be the last she'd get and, although it tasted foul, it was better than dying of thirst. With a final scan of the horizon she hitched up the trousers, turned her back on the distant storm and set off for home.

Nell left the wagon in the yard, rubbed down the horse and set him free in the pen. The storm was still some way off, but she could feel the tension in the air and knew they were in for another bad one. She went towards the house, so safe and solid now that Billy had added three more rooms.

"Big storm come, missus," said Gladys, from her favourite chair on the veranda, "but no bluddy rain in dem clouds."

"That's what I thought," replied Nell, with a shudder. She hated dry storms. Their intensity shook the earth, terrifying children and animals alike. She looked at Gladys, who was chewing tobacco. "Where are the children?"

"Alonga rivva," she replied. "Dem bluddy hot."

Nell ran, yelling at the children to get out. "There's a storm coming." She grabbed Walter and Sarah and hauled them up the bank. "You don't go bloody swimming when there's a storm."

"You shouldn't use that word, Mama," said Amy who was eight and considered herself to be very grown-up. "Aunt Alice says it's rude."

Nell was in no mood to hear Alice's opinions on anything. "I'll use any bloody word I want," she snapped. "Get in the house."

282

"It's no good you getting cross. We had nothing else to do," grumbled Amy, as she wrung water from her nightshift, "and Gladys said we could."

"You know better than to play in the river," Nell snapped. "There might be a lightning strike."

Amy flicked her wet hair over her shoulders. "The storm's still way off."

Nell was at the end of her patience. She grabbed her elder daughter, dragged her towards the house with the twins, and thrust them inside. "Gladys, that's the last time you look after my children."

Gladys opened a sleepy eye. "Yeah, missus," she mumbled. "But Bindi no like."

"Where is he?"

Gladys shrugged and looked as if she was going to fall asleep again, so Nell prodded her shoulder. "There's a dry storm coming, Gladys. Go and find him and the rest of your children. Make sure they're safe."

Gladys grumbled incoherently as she pulled herself reluctantly out of the chair and ambled away.

Nell stood, hands on hips, and watched until she was out of sight. "Gawd 'elp us." She sighed, exasperated.

"Why can't I go and find Papa?" piped Walter some time later, his fiery hair shining in the light from the lamps Nell had lit to dispel the gloom.

"Because you're too young." Nell was still unnerved by the storm and beginning to fret over Billy's whereabouts. "Your father has work to do and he can't be with you all the time."

Walter threw himself into a chair with the wilfulness of a seven-year-old used to getting his own way. "He likes me to help him. He said so."

Nell ignored him and went on preparing the evening meal. There was little point in arguing with her son — he was as stubborn as his father. She served the food, but soon found she had no appetite and pushed away her plate.

With the children finally settled in their rooms, she raised the wick on the lamp and sat in the shadows. The storm was closer now, the lightning so bright it lit up the yard. As the heat rose and the storm closed in, she got up and began to pace.

Billy and Jack had left the house two days before, and Alice had gone before sunrise this morning. They should have been home by now. They could be anywhere on the vast acreage, perhaps lost in the brutality of the elements, injured even.

A mighty thunderclap made her jump. She stood in the breathless silence that followed, nerves taut, waiting for the next. When it came it was as if the heavens had fallen on the roof for the house shuddered.

"Mama!" Sarah flew into the kitchen and flung herself into Nell's arms.

"It's all right," soothed Nell, as she stroked her hair. Then she saw Amy in the doorway, her face pale. "It's not like you to be afraid of a storm," she said.

"Walter's not in his room," said Amy.

Nell stared at her. "Of course he is. He's probably under the bed."

Amy shook her head. "He's not."

Nell tore into the smallest bedroom. "William Walter Penhalligan come out this instant," she yelled.

A sizzling crack of lightning was the only reply.

The flames had devoured the trees and spread like a river in flood across the debris of the forest floor. Jack was choking in the smoke as he clung to his terrified horse and tried to find a way through. "Bindi, where are you?"

There was no reply and Jack realised that even if there had been he probably wouldn't have heard it above the roar of the blaze. He suddenly saw Billy through the smoke. "It's hopeless." He shouted, then coughed. "We'll never find him in this."

"Boss, boss." A small figure raced through the swirling smoke and hurtled towards Billy.

Billy grabbed his shirt, and hauled him across the saddle. "The waterhole's this way," he yelled to Jack. "Follow me."

A tree crashed to the ground in a shower of sparks that ignited another close by. Jack could no longer see his friend and, as his horse danced in ever-tighter circles, he lost all sense of direction. The fire was closing in. If he didn't find a way through it he would die.

The horse skittered, eyes wide, ears flat, and reared to paw the air as another tree fell and the inferno crept nearer.

Jack slipped on its back, and clutched at its mane.

The horse reared and screamed in terror.

Jack's crippled hip gave little strength to his thighs and he lost his grip, fingers clutching wildly for the flying mane as his feet slid out of the stirrups — but the horse seemed determined to lose him. With one great thrust the animal bucked and twisted like a tightly coiled spring. Jack flew off and landed with a ferocious snap of bone.

Free at last the horse tried frantically to find a path through the smoke and flames, its hoofs flashing close to Jack's head as it dashed back and forth in increasing desperation.

Jack watched helplessly as it was swallowed behind the wall of roiling smoke. He heard its frantic whinnies, but felt disoriented and distanced from reality. Billy and the boy would have made it to the waterhole, and he felt neither pain nor fear.

He looked up at the swirling smoke, the crackling flames, heard the leviathan roar of the ravening beast that now surrounded him and felt at peace. To die a free man on his own land was all he'd ever wanted — but he wished it hadn't come so soon, that he could see Alice once more and tell her he loved her . . .

"Stay here," Nell ordered the girls, as she grabbed a rifle and searched for ammunition.

"It would be quicker if we all went to look for him," argued Amy.

"Do as you're told," yelled Nell, at the end of her tether. "Stay in the house and look after your sister."

She ran out of the door and across the yard. The lightning was flashing repeatedly as the earth was shaken by the thunder, and she could hear the rams bellowing. She raced past their pens to the stables. If Walter had planned to look for his father he would have come here first. But how long had he been away?

"Walter!" she screamed. She stood in the sweet-smelling barn and peered into the darkness.

His pony was gone.

Almost collapsing with fear she fumbled to tack up her horse. "I'll kill him when I find him," she sobbed.

The air was ominously heavy, without a breath of wind to alleviate the ever-rising heat. Lightning rent the black sky as she headed for the native encampment. "Walter's taken his pony and gone looking for his father," she shouted, as she rode into the centre of the startled gathering. "I need your best trackers to help me find him."

"Bindi gone too," said Gladys, face streaked with tears. "Tracker out find 'im."

"Then we'll need more than one to look for both of them," Nell yelled to the circle of men surrounding her.

They rose swiftly and melted into the darkness as she set off for the convict shacks, urging her horse into a gallop. "They could be anywhere," she told the sleepy men. "Get out there and look for them. Fire a shot if you find either of them — they might not be together."

Without waiting for a reply, she turned the horse towards the home paddock and used the light from the storm to search the empty landscape. "Where are you, Walter?" she howled.

★　★　★

Alice tramped on across the baked ground, watching one foot follow the other as the storm raged overhead and the grass whispered against her legs. There were no stars to guide her, only the innate sense of direction that had never yet failed her, and the familiarity of a well-trodden pasture. She was tired, and there were blisters on her heels where the old boots had begun to rub — but she didn't slow her pace: each step was one nearer to home.

She peered into the darkness, blinded momentarily by the lightning strike that ripped through the sky and touched the earth with a whiplash crack. The heat was rising and a hot wind sifted the dust under her feet. She plodded on, gaze fixed on the horizon that still hid the homesteads and barns of Moonrakers. One more rise and she would see them — just a few more miles and she would be there.

She had no idea of how long she'd been walking when she heard a noise behind her. She felt the hairs rise on her neck as she recognised the soft pad of paws and panting breath. A glance over her shoulder confirmed her worst fear. The dingo was matching her pace as it loped behind her. Its eyes were feral and steady, its intention all too clear.

Nell had seen the fire on the far horizon and knew that time was running out. Walter and Bindi were in grave danger. Her heart was pounding and her mouth dry as she slowed the horse to a walk and forced herself to remain calm as she searched for some sign that Walter was safe and the men were on their way home.

Then she heard a familiar sound. She reined in and stood in her stirrups.

Walter's pony charged out of the darkness, stirrups flying, saddle at half-mast. Wild-eyed, it passed Nell and continued its mad dash for home.

"Walter!" Nell screamed. "Where are you?"

"Mama!"

It was a faint, piteous wail but it pierced Nell's heart and she kicked the horse into a gallop. "I'm coming," she cried. "Keep shouting, Walter, so I can follow your voice."

"I'm over here," came the piping voice during a lull in the thunder. "Come and get me."

Nell could see him now, a tiny figure silhouetted by the red of the distant fire. As her horse skidded to a halt she flew from the saddle and gave him a hefty clip round the ear, then gathered him fiercely into her arms. "Don't you *ever* do that again," she scolded, through her tears. "You could have been killed and I were almost out of me mind with worry."

"I was trying to find Papa," he sobbed, "but Flash got frightened and threw me off, and I didn't know how to get home."

Nell held him at arm's length. She felt such love for him, such tenderness . . . Then she remembered: "Where's Bindi?" she asked.

"I don't know," gulped Walter. "I haven't seen him since this morning."

Nell felt sick with fear as she searched the empty landscape. Bindi might have the inbuilt knowledge of his people, but he was only seven. "Did'e tell you where 'e was goin'?" she asked.

He shook his head. "He just said he was going to look for fish." He looked up at his mother. "He'll be all right, won't he, Mama?"

Nell held him tightly. "He's probably back at the camp eating his catch."

Walter wiped his nose on his sleeve and looked towards the blaze on the horizon. "Papa, Uncle Jack and Bindi didn't go over there, did they?"

Nell climbed into the saddle behind her son and picked up the reins. The fire was glowing in the sky, and although it was many miles away she could make out tongues of flame reaching into the darkness as the wind picked up. She shivered with dread. "Of course not," she said, and turned the horse's head for home.

"What's that?" Walter stiffened and pointed.

Nell peered into the darkness. A flash of lightning illuminated a distant figure that was walking purposefully towards them. Her heart missed a beat as she realised that, whoever it was, they were not alone — and the dingo was closing the gap between them.

"Hold on tight, Walter." Nell pulled the rifle from the saddlebag, and kicked the horse into a gallop.

The panting was closer now and Alice could smell the dingo's breath as it quickened its pace. She glanced over her shoulder and her mouth dried. The yellow eyes were still fixed on her, the lips had curled back to reveal sharp teeth, and the ears had flattened. It would strike at any minute.

290

Her every fibre told her to run — but the dingo was already tensed for its attack and to run was to spur it into action. She strode on, searching for a rock or something else she could use as a weapon.

A shot rang out, echoing in waves across the empty land.

The dingo died before it knew it had been hit.

Alice almost fainted with relief, and her legs trembled so badly she found she couldn't move.

Nell galloped up and came to a skidding halt that covered them all with a cloud of swirling dust. She swung from the saddle. "That were a bit too close for my likin'," she gasped.

Alice stared at the dead dog lying within inches of her heels. "If you hadn't been such a good shot I dread to think what might have happened." She took Nell's hand. "You saved my life," she said, close to tears.

Nell squeezed her fingers. "You got Walter to thank. It was 'im wot saw you." She must have seen the question in Alice's eyes, for she grimaced. "Don't ask what 'e's doin' 'ere. It's a long story, and we've yet to find Bindi."

Alice smiled up at the boy, noting the tracks of his tears, the weariness and fear in his eyes, and felt a pang of love so deep she had to battle against the need to hold him. "Bindi?" she asked instead. "What about the others? Are they back yet?"

Nell shook her head. "There ain't been sight nor sound of 'em. I just hope to Gawd they aren't over there."

The two women stood in mutual dread as they watched the inferno that now stretched along the skyline. Its glow reddened the dark clouds as flickering flames leapt in the growing wind. They could only pray their men had survived.

The storm raged through the night and into the next morning. The fire on the horizon drew ever nearer as the wind shifted direction. Alice stood next to Nell and the children as they prayed for their men to come home. No one had slept and no one spoke; to voice their fear would give it substance.

The convicts gathered in the lee of the barn, the natives spilling from their camp to join them. There had been no sign of Bindi, and Gladys was inconsolable.

As the storm finally rumbled into the distance the air cleared and the temperature plummeted. The heavens opened and the rain fell in a deluge.

It hammered on the roof and on the parched, compacted earth of the yard, collecting in pools that spilled into streams and raced for the river. All eyes turned to the distant hills where the flames died beneath the onslaught.

"We must get a search-party out before it's dark," said Alice.

Nell's hope was in her eyes. "I'll leave the children with Pearl and Daisy and come with you. We'll need everyone out there in this."

Alice hurried to the barn. The men were saddling up, and the natives, having spent hours searching for Bindi, had gathered their spears in readiness — they would lope across the miles, their eyes far keener than those of any white man.

She approached the oldest, most reliable convict first. "Go to Elizabeth Farm and get help. Explain what's happened," she said. Then she turned to the others. "Stay in pairs," she said. "Spread out across the paddocks and head towards the seat of the fire." To the natives she nodded. She didn't need to tell them what to do.

She checked that each group had a different route, and possessed either a gun or a whip they could crack. "One shot if you find them alive." She swallowed and held on to her own fragile hope. "Two if not."

The rain was an almost impenetrable curtain as they set off, the sound of it muffling everything so it seemed they were riding in a void. Alice and Nell rode side by side, their husbands' long, oilskin coats becoming waterlogged and heavy, the hat-brims acting like conduits for the streams that rolled down their necks. They had elected to take a section of the southern boundary between them and the vast paddocks of Elizabeth Farm.

The horses splashed through the paddles, their hoofs churning up the loose top layer of dust into mud as the two women rode in silence, keeping their thoughts and fears to themselves.

As the day progressed the rain softened. Now it fell like a smothering blanket, veiling the landscape, deadening all sound. Trees, blackened by smoke, loomed out of the mist, their leaves shrivelled and dropping, while the carcasses of animals trapped on the edges of the fire lay stiff and charred like obscene sculptures.

The fire had spread across a great swathe of Moonrakers' land, and as Alice and Nell halted to look at the tar-black earth, the burnt trees and wisps of smoke that still lingered, their hopes faltered.

"They might not have come this way," said Alice. "And even if they did, they could have outrun it and got out on the other side."

"There's a waterhole about three miles on. They would have gone there." She gathered up the reins, determination setting her mouth in a thin line. "That's where they'll be."

Alice wished she could feel the same confidence, but followed Nell into the blackened, dripping remains of the forest. The horses churned up the mud, shying as flames crackled into life, then hissed out again. Each sound in that dead forest made the women flinch — and they averted their eyes from the black lumps that had once been sheep or dogs. The stench of roasted pig was almost overpowering as they passed the seared corpse of a wild boar.

A gunshot pierced the silence, echoing through the charred, dripping forest and into their hearts.

Alice and Nell reined in their horses, hearts hammering as hope soared that there wouldn't be another.

The second shot was the death-knell they had dreaded.

In silent accord they moved towards it, each clutching the frail hope that the body of an escaped

294

convict or a tramp had been found — to think anything else was to yield to their worst fear.

Four men and two natives were waiting for them as they approached the waterhole. The convict grasped their reins as they came to a halt. "Stay out of there," he said, face blackened with soot, eyes red-rimmed.

Alice and Nell climbed down and stood in the mud. "We have to know for certain," said Alice, her voice cracking.

"It's certain enough," said the man, his expression grim. "Trackers found 'em."

"It could be anyone," cried Nell, on a note of hysteria. "How do you know it's them?"

He shook his head. "Sorry, missus," he said.

Alice's head swam. She leant against the horse while she regained her composure. "I have to see for myself," she muttered. "I have to know."

"It ain't pretty," said the convict, his gruff voice soft. He took the tarpaulins from the saddlebags. "I've sent for the wagon. We'll see 'em right." He began to make his way back through the clinging black mud.

Hand in hand Alice and Nell followed him.

The figure was a grotesque parody of a man. Blackened beyond recognition, the leathered flesh hung loose to reveal the gleam of bone. He was arched towards the sky like a taut bow, hands reaching in supplication, head thrown back, mouth open in a silent, endless scream. A horse lay a few feet from him.

"Which one?" breathed Alice.

"It's Jack," said the convict.

"How can you be so certain?" she whispered.

"I'm sorry, missus. We found this next to him."

Alice looked at the pocket watch she'd given Jack for Christmas. It was dented and scorched, the dial cracked from the heat. Her hand closed round it as she stared at the blackened figure. She couldn't believe it had once been the man she loved — couldn't take in the sheer horror.

"I did warn you," said the convict. "I'm sorry, missus," he said to Nell. "Billy's over there."

"No!" It was a cry from the very depths of her soul, and Nell would have fallen to the ground if he hadn't held her. "Not my Billy — please not my Bill."

Alice went to her and held her, her face white with anguish. "We have to stay strong for each other. Or we'll both be lost."

Billy had died within feet of Jack, his poignant remains, fused to the once-heavy branch of a ruined tree that had pinned him to the ground. Both men had been within yards of the waterhole that might have saved them.

"Bindi?" breathed Alice.

"He was in the waterhole, missus," said the convict. "He was a bit singed and scared, but he told us Billy'd thrown him in seconds before the tree fell. His father's taken him back to the camp."

Jack and Billy were wrapped in the tarpaulin and transported back to Moonrakers in the back of the wagon. Alice and Nell rode beside it in silence, their grief harnessed for now as the convicts rode behind them and the natives loped alongside. Both women knew the tears would come soon enough, the loss would descend like a great weight and the emptiness of the vast wilderness would close in. They also knew they had to share their grief, to put aside any lesser cares and hold on to each other: it was their only hope of surviving this terrible ordeal.

The funeral would be held the next morning, but the mourners appeared through the night for news travelled fast. George was at sea, but Ernest travelled at breakneck speed through the night with his wife and parents, and they arrived just, after daybreak.

Susan was clearly battling with her own grief, but she sat with Nell and Alice to share her memories of her brother and the man who had become his closest friend as Ezra sought comfort in his Bible.

As the sun rose and the women prepared for the second longest day of their lives, the little cemetery was packed with people who had come to pay their respects to two men who had fought hard to make a new life for themselves and their families. They came on horseback, in wagons and on foot, bringing bedrolls, food and words of comfort.

The Moonrakers natives stood beside the convicts as Ezra's voice rang out in the stillness of a clear, sunny day. Their faces had been smeared with the clay of mourning, and after the white man had finished the ceremony they would hold their own to call on the Great Creator Spirit to send the canoe so that Boss Billy and Boss Jack could be taken to the stars. They had given their lives for the child Bindi, and their story would be painted on the walls of the underground caves in their honour.

When it was done and the house was silent, Alice and Nell took the children back to the deserted graveyard. They could hear the clap of sticks, the deep, rhythmic drone of the didgeridoo and the chant of the natives, and it comforted them to know that their men had been loved by the original keepers of this land.

The two women stood in the twilight by the single mound. Their men had borne the chains and lash as convicts and had survived the terrors of transportation. They had lived as brothers, gained their freedom and been rarely apart from the day they had met. It was right that they should lie together in the land they had cleared, tilled and finally called home — right that their women should at last find solace and strength in one another.

PART THREE

Rebellion

CHAPTER
THIRTEEN

A government farm, September 1800

Niall Logan sat at the back of the tent and listened to his fellow convicts discuss the planned uprising. He was eleven now, and apprenticed to the convict smith who ran the forge with almost ruthless efficiency. As he listened, he felt the fire of rebellion rise to a furnace. He wanted to go home to Ireland, and be free of the British laws and injustices that had no right to bind him yet refused him the Catholic Mass.

"We have been lashed, imprisoned, and our leaders exiled to Norfolk Island," said Thomas Brannon, quietly. Soldiers were patrolling outside and it was imperative that they weren't discovered. "Our children are brought here in chains and our faith is reviled. We, the veterans of the Wexford battles and proud members of the United Irishmen, have learnt how to fight oppression. We are stronger now and more determined than ever to be free of the British yoke."

Niall saw that Paddy was as excited as himself at the rousing speech.

"We have learnt the lessons of Wexford, my boys, and if we are to succeed, we must have weapons. Marsden didn't find the pikes Furey made for our August uprising. We will assemble here on Sunday morning when those in charge of us will be in church. We will pike the soldiers and march on Sydney Town."

"There are not enough of us, Thomas."

"I know a man who will help to change that," Brannon replied. "He will go from farm to farm and encourage others to join in. Rebellion has been in the air since the revolutions in France and the Americas. Many have heard the call for freedom and will march with us." He smiled. "It will be a joyous sight, me boys, marching into Sydney Town."

"I say we get rid of Marsden before we march," said Fitzgerald, who was Brannon's second in command.

A murmur of agreement rippled through the tent. "That goes without saying," said Brannon.

Niall remembered the day a month ago when Samuel Marsden, magistrate and Anglican minister, lover of the cat-o'-nine-tails, had sent their Catholic preacher, James Harrold, to Norfolk Island, and their pike-maker, Brian Furey, to gaol with no proof that they had been involved in the August uprising that had lasted less than an hour. They had had to witness the flogging of others, and Niall was still woken by nightmares.

"We have been betrayed before," said Fitzgerald. "How can we know there's not a traitor here tonight?"

Brannon's eyes narrowed. "We are Irishmen and loyal to the cause. Every man here wants to go home to continue the fight against the British. If we are betrayed, the punishment will be death."

302

The meeting broke up and they slipped under the canvas to vanish into the darkness. Niall and Paddy waited for the guard to pass, then crouched low and ran for their tent.

Niall crawled on to the lumpy mattress and pulled the frayed blanket over him. The nights were bitter, the summer still a couple of months away. His clothes were too ragged to offer even meagre warmth, and his skinny frame was convulsed with tremors.

"Do you think we can do it this time?" whispered Paddy, from the mattress beside him.

"With God's blessing and the luck of the Irish, I hope so," Niall replied, through chattering teeth.

"There's enough pikes hidden for everyone." Paddy was sixteen now, and experienced at sedition. "I made sure of that."

"Good. Let's hope we put them to good use."

Silence fell as exhaustion took its toll and others fell asleep. Niall curled into a ball in an attempt to get warm. Yet the thought of freedom kept him awake.

Two days later Brannon came into the forge where Niall and Paddy were working. "We've been discovered," he said softly.

"How?" demanded Paddy.

"Not a spy this time, just bad luck."

"What happened?" asked Niall.

"The man we sent to stir up support was captured and tortured into telling them everything. By all accounts, Macarthur of the New South Wales Regiment was planning to ambush us once we'd made our move."

With heavy hearts they returned to work. "There will be reprisals." Paddy dipped the glowing horseshoe into a bucket of water.

"But we haven't done anything," protested Niall.

"Since when has that been an excuse?"

Within hours Macarthur and his troops had arrested Brannon, Fitzgerald and the other ringleaders of the failed rebellion. Marsden, in his role as magistrate, zealously set about trying to discover the whereabouts of the hidden pikes he knew existed but which had so far eluded him.

Niall and the others cringed at the sound of the whip and the shouts of the soldiers as work was disrupted and the camp turned upside-down. He was asleep when the soldiers stormed into the tent.

"Right, bog-trotter," snapped one as he grabbed Paddy.

Dazed with sleep, Paddy was yanked to his feet.

A boot caught Niall's hip and he cowered into the blanket.

"Move yer arse, Galvin," barked the soldier.

Niall shivered with fear as his friend was hauled, protesting, out of the tent. The canvas flap slid back into place and he stared into the darkness. Paddy and he had made the extra pikes secretly when their convict overseer was out of the forge. His friend knew where they were — but would he have the courage to remain silent? If not, might he himself be the next to be dragged into the night?

For the next two days Niall lived in terror as tension grew and there was no sign of Paddy. When the order came to assemble in the clearing used for public floggings, he had hardly slept and was so frightened he could barely stand. He looked for Paddy, hoping against hope that he was among the chained men who had been released from the cells and made to stand apart from the rest.

Hope died as two men were dragged into the clearing. Paddy and Fitzgerald were barely recognisable after their beating and had to be held upright by the guards.

Marsden stood beside them, face red with rage. "I charge these men with making and hiding pikes and refusing to reveal their whereabouts. Fitzgerald will receive five hundred strokes, Galvin three hundred."

Paddy's head sagged and his knees buckled. There was a bitter taste in Niall's mouth as he watched Fitzgerald being tied to the flogging tree. The man's arms were pulled round the massive trunk until his chest was so hard pressed against it that he had no chance to evade the lash.

The two floggers prepared to begin and, with a shudder, Niall recognised them as the notorious man-killers all convicts feared. John Johnson, the hangman from Sydney Town, was right-handed, and Richard Rice was left-handed. They stood to either side of Fitzgerald, waiting for Marsden's signal.

Niall wanted to look away for he knew what was to come — but to do so would insult Fitzgerald. To witness the man's agony was to share it.

Marsden nodded. The floggers timed their strokes to perfection, lashing on the right, then the left with sickening accuracy and synchronicity. Spatters of Fitzerald's skin and blood flew from the ends of the whips and landed on Niall's face.

"Flog me fair," yelled Fitzgerald, as the leather split his flesh. "Don't strike my neck." They were the only words he uttered throughout the ordeal.

Marsden called a halt after three hundred lashes and ordered the government doctor to examine the prisoner. Dr Mason took his pulse and smiled at the floggers. "This man will tire you before he fails. Carry on."

Niall and the others stood in mutinous silence as the punishment was concluded and the silent Fitzgerald was untied. The man's legs gave way and he would have crumpled but for the two constables who grabbed him by the arms to lift him in to the cart that would take him to the infirmary.

"Let me go," Fitzgerald growled, using his elbows to wind them. As they gasped and bent double, he let loose a lethal left and right hook that sent them sprawling. Then he stepped unaided into the cart, defiance and pride in every bloodied inch of his ravaged body.

"That man should have had at least two hundred more strokes," muttered Dr Mason. "Damned Irish. Too thick-skinned and mule-headed to know when they're bested."

Niall's moment of jubilation was dashed when Paddy was tied to the same tree. His stomach clenched and he thought he might faint as the first hundred strokes opened his friend's back to reveal the gleam of his spine

— yet Paddy didn't protest, and showed no sign that he was in agony, so Niall watched the torture grimly and prayed to the Virgin to give Paddy strength to see it through.

Marsden signalled the floggers to halt. "Will you now tell me where the pikes are?"

"I don't know, and if I did I wouldn't tell you," Paddy gasped. "You may as well hang me now, for you'll get no music from me."

"Flog his backside," ordered Marsden.

Niall vomited as Paddy's buttocks were reduced to a bloody jelly.

"Aim the last hundred at his legs," shouted Marsden.

Paddy remained silent, and when it was over, he had to be carried to the cart.

Niall never saw his friend again, and never discovered what had happened to him, but it was soon common knowledge that the other main conspirators had received a thousand lashes and were sentenced to hard labour on the hulk *Supply*, which wallowed in Sydney Harbour.

Despite what he'd witnessed, and the terrifying punishment for sedition, Niall knew the fight for justice must continue. It was just a matter of waiting, watching and planning for the right time to rise again.

Kernow House, Watsons Bay, September 1800

Despite her best intentions, and the joy she took in Charles and Harry, her new baby, Eloise was unhappy. Her determination to make the best of her marriage had withered in the heartache of losing George and the reality of life with Edward.

His return that day in April 1798 had heralded a change in him that she had hoped would ease their life together. His lovemaking had been tender, his manner softer, and she had been lulled into hoping for the future. Yet it had lasted only a few weeks: he had become ever more troubled by his dreams and some indefinable worry that he would not discuss. From snippets of conversation she had overheard, she'd gathered it concerned a gambling debt, but knew better than to ask, and could only pray that it would be resolved.

The months leading up to Harry's birth saw him revert to the coldness and revulsion he'd shown before Charles was born. His long absences were more frequent, but rarely explained, and although she was easier with him out of the house, she felt abandoned.

Now Eloise sat in the drawing room, her book discarded on the couch beside her. Edward had invited his fellow officers for the evening, and she had left them to their cards and their rum and gone into the drawing room to read, but she found it impossible to concentrate with the noise that floated in to her from across the hall.

Her life was frozen in a circle of pain from which there was no escape. George had left Australia and hadn't been seen for more than two years, so she'd clung to the hope that something could be salvaged from the wreckage of her marriage. Yet the birth of a second son had changed nothing. A log shifted in the grate and sparks flew up the chimney. George was never far from her thoughts, and she conjured him up now, remembering all they had shared, the deep and abiding sense that they belonged to one another, and the knowledge that their love would live for as long as they both drew breath. She was distracted from her memories by raucous shouts from the other room. They were drunk and would wake the children if they didn't quieten, she thought. It would be hard for her to sleep, too, but it was time for bed. She rang for the housemaid and ordered her to dampen the fire, then went into the hall and past the dining-room door.

The voice was loud and slurred, but the words were clear enough and they chilled her to the core.

"You have the luck of the devil, Edward. Not many men can get away with what you have, then come back from exile, get promotion and make a fortune. Why, you even managed to bamboozle old Wickens into virtually giving his farm away so you could pay off your debts to Carlton."

This pronouncement was greeted with hearty cheers.

"That's nothing," said Edward, boastfully. "I've got Albert Rogers over a barrel, and his nice little business is within my grasp."

"How did you persuade him to sell?"

"Sell?" roared Edward. "He's giving it to me."

A chorus of disbelief greeted this announcement.

"I discovered he has a native mistress, and a couple of picaninnies, so I mentioned it in passing and hinted that the price of my silence was the bakery. I've given him until tomorrow to decide." He waited for the buzz to die down. "Still, it might be amusing to tell his wife anyway, once the place is mine. Poor Albert is no match for her sharp tongue, and I should enjoy watching him squirm."

Eloise could bear it no longer and fled to the sanctuary of her bedroom. Yet the words reverberated in her head as she lay there, unable to sleep. The shouts of laughter and the loud talk drifted up to her as she digested what she had learnt.

She stared at the ornate plastered ceiling as she fretted. Edward's business affairs had always worried her, and she'd suspected long ago that he wasn't entirely honest in his dealings. But blackmail?

She couldn't confide in anyone what she'd heard — especially not her father, who would storm in and make things worse. Jonathan Cadwallader was still in England, out of reach — surely he couldn't have known his son was a blackmailing cheat. He was a principled man and would have found it impossible to remain silent.

And what had Edward got away with? The man had alluded to an incident from the past that involved Edward's time upriver. It couldn't relate to the trial . . . could it? Doubt and suspicion flooded in. Snippets of conversation and gossip suddenly began to make sense and she saw, with sickening clarity, how Edward had manipulated the truth. "Dear God," she breathed, "that was what George was trying to tell me." She felt sick with dread. "What if he did violate that girl and was exiled for it?" She had to know the truth: everything concerning Edward and their life together seemed founded on lies. The wealth she had taken for granted had been built, like this house, through convict sweat and his dishonesty. From the beautiful gardens to the exquisite plaster mouldings, she could sense the fingerprints of hands that had been forced to toil on them, and the stench of corruption hung in the air.

When Edward came to bed it was almost dawn. Eloise feigned sleep. She couldn't bear the thought of him touching her.

Aboard the Atlantica, *November 1800*

George staggered along the deck as the ship heaved and rolled beneath his feet. The spume from the giant waves was needle sharp, the wind a battering-ram, making it almost impossible to walk. He battled his way on to the bridge and, in the lee of the tiny wheelhouse, stood for a moment to catch his breath.

Samuel's strong, callused hands were firm on the wheel as he fought to keep the ship on a steady course. "Bad weather for whales," he shouted, above the moan of the wind.

"Not so good for men either," George yelled back.

Samuel grinned, but kept his gaze fixed on the crashing seas. "Better than pining in Sydney."

George acknowledged that he was right. They had been away for more than two years now, during which George had refused all shore leave, preferring to be at sea rather than risk an encounter with Eloise and Edward. In the past two years he had sailed on every one of Samuel's five ships.

"You can't avoid her for ever," roared Samuel. "Sydney's your home, and your family need you."

"I'll visit them when we get back this time," he yelled. He thought of the letters he'd tucked away in his cabin, picked up from other whaling ships, or when the rest of the crew had been ashore. The news of the fire at Moonrakers and its awful toll had chilled him, and he had been saddened to hear final proof that his sister Florence would never return home. The knowledge that he'd not been there to offer comfort at such a tragic time gnawed at him even now, for Billy and Jack had been his boyhood heroes.

Samuel adjusted the rudder to the swell. "Family is important, son," he bellowed. "I might not have any of my own, but you and your parents have allowed me to become part of yours, and at times like these we must stick together. It's the same for my people back in Nantucket."

George took over at the wheel while Samuel lit his pipe and rested. The fire at the try-works had set Samuel back financially, but his main concern had been for the men and their families who relied upon his patronage. He had seen them right, had rebuilt and improved the try-works, the warehouses and the little cottages before he'd set sail again. George felt ashamed as he tried to read the ocean: he had ignored his family's needs. It was time to go home.

Night fell and still the seas raged. Samuel took back the wheel and remained at it, determined to see the *Atlantica* safely into a sheltering harbour.

312

George stayed with him and tried to take over as they headed for the coast of Van Diemen's Land.

"She's my ship," Samuel growled. "I'll see her safely in."

"You're tired," said George, noting the exhaustion in the older man's face and the tremor in his usually steady hands. "Let me have her for an hour so you can rest."

"Leave me be, boy! I'm captain of this ship and I'll stay here for as long as I please."

"Captain or not, I'm stronger and fitter and you need rest."

Samuel snorted. "I'm not in my dotage yet," he retorted, "but I'm glad of your company on this wild night."

The spray lashed against the window as the *Atlantica* rolled in the swell. She leant dangerously to port, righted herself, then plunged into an abyss of water between two mountainous waves.

Samuel's face paled as the bow rose high and the ship tried to climb the wall of water. He clung to the wheel, yelling obscenities at the ocean, the weather and the *Atlantica* as he urged her on.

George was flung to the floor and everything that wasn't bolted down slid there to meet him. He lay stunned and unable to move as the ship stood almost on her stern and battled to crest the leviathan wave. "I'm losing her," yelled Samuel. "She's not gonna make it."

George crawled up the floor and grabbed the sturdy iron that was fixed beneath the wheel. He dragged himself to his feet and tried to put his own weight behind Samuel's to keep the ship on a steady course.

The *Atlantica* began to lose purchase on the oily slide of the giant wave's back.

"She's turning turtle!" yelled George.

"I know that," snapped Samuel. His usually ruddy complexion had greyed and he grimaced as he tried to maintain his grip on the wheel. "Let go, Sam. For God's sake, let me take over."

"Hell, boy," he snarled, through gritted teeth, "I ain't finished yet. Just lend your weight to the wheel."

The *Atlantica* slid further back. The wall of water advancing on their stern was now so high they couldn't see the top.

Both men felt a shudder run through the ship and could only stare in mute horror as they were dragged back into the boiling maelstrom while the wall grew in strength and size behind them.

"Our only chance is to let her run before it," shouted Samuel. "Keep her on course."

George used all his strength to help Samuel keep the wheel steady, but the ship was being sucked in by the gathering force, sails flapping uselessly, keel lifting out of the water. He risked a glance over his shoulder and stared death in the face.

The mountain of water was towering above them, its angry head laced with white.

George felt the *Atlantica* shiver as she tried to remain upright. Her timbers creaked as her bow dug into the black water and she yawed as the sails snapped and finally caught the wind. With a sickening lurch she was

314

lifted on to the back of another wave and hurtled into the night.

Now they were running before the giant that was still threatening to sink them. It was like a Nantucket sleigh-ride, faster and more furious than either man had ever experienced — but it was a race for survival.

"We've done it, Sam," shouted George.

The older man clutched his arm and sank to the floor.

"Sam! What is it?" George tried to reach for his friend, but needed both hands on the wheel to keep the ship steady. "Sam!"

Samuel lay curled on the floor, his arms folded round his torso. "Nothing," he managed. "Keep her steady, son. You're doing a fine job."

George glanced over his shoulder, frustration and fear as tangible as the weight of water pushing at the stern. His battle with the ocean was far from over, but Samuel was fighting a battle of his own, and there was nothing he could do about it.

"See the ship safe," said Samuel.

George adjusted the tiller, keeping faith in the crew to see to the sails, and let her run. She was a sturdy craft, had survived waters as dangerous as these before, but would his lack of experience at the helm be their undoing? He could only wait and see.

"Always knew I'd make a sailor of you." Samuel had dragged himself into a corner. "Keep her steady, son."

George had no choice but to remain at the wheel as they were pitched and tossed between the peaks and troughs of the enormous seas. By now Samuel's face was livid and his eyes had sunk into his skull. Suddenly he looked very old.

As a grey dawn broke over the horizon, and the seas calmed, land was sighted to starboard. George breathed a sigh of relief as another crewman came in. "Take the wheel," he ordered, as the man bent to look at Samuel. "Steer us into the nearest harbour and drop anchor."

He rushed to Samuel's side and tried to coax him to sit up and drink the tot of rum the man had brought with him. "Leave me," Samuel gasped. "I can't breathe, and the pain . . ." He groaned.

George laid a finger on his neck to feel for the pulse: it was thready, and so weak he could barely distinguish it beneath the clammy skin.

"Don't you die on me, Sam." His voice was harsh with love. "We've sighted land, and as far as I can make out it's Norfolk Island, so I can get you to the garrison doctor."

Gnarled hands clutched at his thick coat. "It's time, son," Samuel muttered. "Let me go."

George cradled him in his arms. "Never. Just hold on. Don't give in when we're so close to land."

The blue eyes looked up at him. "The land holds nothing for me, m'boy. Let me die on my ship and feed me to the fish."

George was almost weeping with frustration and distress. "You need help, that's all, and we're almost there, old friend."

"You've been a good son to me," whispered Samuel. "Take care of the old girl. She's a fine ship with a brave heart."

George looked into the faded blue eyes and saw they were already focused on some distant horizon. Samuel was leaving him, and suddenly there were so many things he needed to tell him, so many questions he hadn't yet asked — but all he could do now was reassure him. "Of course I will," he murmured, on a sob.

A shudder ran through Samuel and he slumped in George's arms, the blue eyes closing for the last time.

George sat on the deck of the wheelhouse. "Goodbye, old friend," he whispered, into the thick white hair. "I'll never forget you, and what you meant to me."

Sydney Town, November 1800

Eloise had thought long and hard about what to do, and had finally come to the conclusion that she could trust only one person to tell her the truth. She waited until Edward was out of Sydney Town, then ordered a covered carriage so that she could sit outside the barracks without being recognised.

As Thomas Morely emerged through the gate, she tapped the roof with her parasol and the driver called him over.

"Eloise," he said, as she lifted her veil. "What are you doing here?"

"I must speak with you urgently, Thomas."

He raised an eyebrow but didn't comment as he climbed in. Eloise tapped the roof again and the horse set a good pace as they left the barracks.

"This is most mysterious," he said finally. "One would almost suspect I had been kidnapped."

She looked down at her hands, tightly clasped in her lap. "I'm sorry," she said, "but it was the only way I could have you to myself." She saw that she had startled him and smiled. "Thomas, I'm not about to seduce you."

He blushed to the roots of his hair. "Your sister will be relieved to hear it," he replied, with a hesitant laugh.

"My sister is not to know of this meeting, Thomas. You must give me your word of that."

"But she's my wife," he stammered.

"There are things I want to ask you — things that don't concern Anastasia — and I must know you will keep this meeting secret."

He thought for a moment. "Very well. You have my word."

The covered carriage drew to a halt on the brow of a hill that overlooked the town. Eloise ordered the driver to hobble the horse and go for a walk. When he had wandered far enough away, she said, "I have made enquiries over the past weeks and have learnt that Edward has been consistently cheating people out of their businesses to pay off his gambling debts to Mr Carlton. Now I want to know everything about Edward's trial and his time up-river."

She held up her hand to silence the platitudes she knew he was about to voice. "I have no illusions as to Edward's character, and I want the truth, Thomas, however ugly."

"What has he told you?" He was hedging.

318

"That the girl lied so he and the others were acquitted."

Thomas took her hands. "Eloise, are you sure it wouldn't be better to let things lie? What can you gain by bringing up what is past?"

She withdrew her hands and regarded him squarely. "You do not leap to his defence, which tells me I was right to come to you. Tell me all you know."

He licked his lips and turned towards the sprawl of Sydney Town that lay far beneath them. "Millicent Parker arrived here on the Second Fleet," he began. "She was barely alive, and George Collinson's mother, Susan, nursed her back to health, then took her in as one of the family. When she got her ticket-of-leave, she and Ernest Collinson became engaged."

Eloise sat very still, but her heart was pounding as Thomas's voice filled the confined space in the carriage. She hadn't known George's family were so involved, and she burnt with shame that she hadn't listened when he'd tried to warn her about Edward.

"Millicent was a quiet little thing, according to George, frightened of her own shadow. But on that particular night she'd gone to deliver a message for Susan and had got lost in the Rocks."

Dread crept over Eloise like a malevolent shadow.

"She identified every one of the men who had attacked her." He took her hands again. "Forgive me, Eloise, but Edward was one. In fact, it seems he was the ringleader." She remained silent. "I've read the court papers and there was no doubt that she had been brutally attacked."

Eloise closed her eyes, but the images in her head were too awful to contemplate. She opened them and asked, "How did they escape justice?"

"They lied," he said flatly. "Their bribe was large enough to ensure that the landlord of the tavern would swear they were all playing cards there until the early hours." He paused to light a cheroot. "Then the Earl of Kernow appeared and defended his son by revealing that Millicent had accused him of fathering her child, which had since died, and he blackened Susan Collinson's reputation by revealing that they had once had a liaison. He accused her of using the charges as revenge. The judge had little choice but to dismiss the case."

Eloise sagged against the leather seat, her blood roaring in her ears. The truth was far uglier than she had imagined, and the knowledge that Jonathan Cadwallader had played a major part in the deceit was a blow from which she would not recover.

"Poor little Millicent hanged herself. She couldn't face life any longer."

Hot tears coursed down Eloise's cheeks. "So Edward *was* exiled?" she whispered.

"The army couldn't cashier any of the men because the charges had been dropped and they were innocent in the eyes of the law, but neither did it want them in Sydney. The Earl of Kernow and the commanding officer put their heads together and had them exiled up-river under the guise of setting up a barracks and clearing the way for future settlers. It was the perfect excuse, and if the rumours are to be believed, Edward and the others took to their orders with relish."

Eloise saw disgust curl his lip and knew there was more — much more. "You may as well tell me everything," she said softly.

"The army have orders to clear the land of natives, but the remit from London expressly forbids the use of violence. Edward abides by his own rules." His lips were a thin line. "He and his coterie of men are responsible for wiping out entire clans — even the children."

Eloise fought to control herself. "If the army knows this, why doesn't it stop them?"

"With new settlers arriving on every ship and farming land increasingly vital, it turns a blind eye to what is happening." His expression was sombre. "But Edward and his cronies are sailing close to the wind," he added. "There was a raid on an encampment at Banks Town and this time two white missionaries were caught up in the slaughter."

Eloise listened as he told her about George's sister Florence. "Dear God," she exclaimed. "As if that family hasn't suffered enough." Silence fell between them, and she stared out of the window, seeing nothing but the ugliness of the monster she had married.

"Forgive me, Eloise," he said again.

She put her gloved hand over his. "Thank you for your honesty, Thomas. I know how difficult this must have been for you," she said shakily. "I wish you'd had the courage to tell me this before I married him."

"I didn't know all of it then."

"But you knew enough."

He hung his head. "What will you do now?"

"I shall leave him."

His eyes were dark with anxiety. "Think carefully, Eloise, I beg you."

Eloise was trembling at the audacity of what she planned, but now she knew the depths of her husband's depravity, she had little choice.

Kernow House, Watsons Bay, the same day

Eloise felt as if she was living on a knife edge as she packed her bags and hid them in readiness for her flight. Edward would return at any minute, and she would have to wait until tonight before she dared leave the house for her father's hotel. To run now would endanger them all if Edward caught them before they reached the town, but the waiting was agony. It had been hard to remain calm with the children, and harder still not to confide in Meg who had become her closest friend.

The convict nurserymaid stood beside three-year-old Charles, who was drawing a picture at a low table. "Something's wrong," she said, as she grabbed Harry, who was almost two and yelling with delight as he ran round the room. "I can always tell."

Eloise looked nervously out of the window. "It's better you don't know," she said, then took charge of her younger son and tried to tempt him with a picture book.

"I been with you a long time," said Meg. "If you're plannin' what I think you are, will you take me with you?"

Startled, Eloise looked up. "Of course. But how . . .?"

"I seen the bags in the nursery cupboard," she whispered, aware that others might be listening behind the door. The other servants were known for spying and she and Eloise were always careful of what they said, suspecting that Edward would be informed.

Eloise held tightly to the wriggling Harry and glanced at Charles. "We can't talk now," she said, as the elder boy gazed at her with solemn eyes. "But if you could begin to make preparations after tea?"

Meg paled and bright spots of colour appeared on her cheeks. "Tonight?"

Eloise straightened. "Tonight."

The horse galloped into the yard and was yanked to a slithering standstill. Yelling for the stable-boy, Edward leapt from the saddle and strode up the steps to the house. "Eloise, where are you?" he shouted, as he thrust his way through the front door.

In the drawing room Eloise was as tense as a violin string. "Papa's home," she said to the children. She picked up the picture Charles had taken most of the afternoon to finish. "And don't forget to give him this," she said softly. "It's very good and I'm sure Papa will be most pleased."

She waited, heart thudding as she heard his footsteps on the hall floor. He came into the room, his face still pink from the ride. It was clear that he was edgy with the excitement of his latest trip into the bush, and Eloise forced herself to remain cool and aloof as he kissed her cheek.

"I drew this for you, Papa," said Charles, timorously, "to welcome you home."

Edward took the picture and, with barely a glance, threw it on to a chair. "How's my big boy?" he said, grabbed Harry, who was hanging on to his leg, and swung him in the air until he shrieked with delight. "Not sitting about painting pictures, I'll be bound."

Eloise saw Charles's face register hurt and disappointment. "Charles took all day to draw that," she said stiffly, as she drew the child to her side. "You could at least have looked at it."

Edward dropped Harry on to the chair so that he landed on the picture and tore it. "When he does something sensible, I will give it my attention. Harry, on the other hand, is in need of a good rough-house." He grabbed the child and began to tickle him.

"Please don't do that," she said. "Meg has enough trouble getting him to sleep as it is."

Edward stopped, and smoothed back his hair. "It seems you disapprove when I ignore my sons, and disapprove when I don't. I cannot win with you, Eloise." He reached for the decanter. "Get them out of here. It's past their bedtime and I need a drink to wash away the dust."

"Dinner is about to be served," she said coldly and shepherded the boys out of the room, shutting the door firmly behind her. She gathered Charles into her arms,

324

took Harry's hand and climbed the stairs to the nursery. It would take a while to soothe them, but with Meg's help and a small tot of rum they wouldn't wake when they were taken from their beds later on.

She paused at the top of the stairs and met Meg's eye. The fear was almost tangible, but as the time to run drew nearer, Eloise discovered that her hatred for her husband had given her a strength of purpose that made her feel invincible.

Over dinner Edward was in expansive mood, but her frostiness had not gone unnoticed. "I don't expect to come home to a sour face," he sneered. "If you are unable to conduct yourself pleasantly, you may leave the table."

Eloise's loathing and resentment rose to the surface. She threw down her napkin and looked at him for the first time that evening. "I am not a servant to be ordered about," she said, "and if we are to discuss civility, I suggest you look to your own behaviour."

"My manners, civil or otherwise, are not for discussion."

"They were at a certain trial in 1793." The words had slipped out unbidden and could not be unsaid. She maintained a steady gaze as she saw him redden, but her heart was pounding and her hands were clasped tightly on her lap.

"Then you will know that the case was dismissed," he said, after a long silence, his tone dangerously calm.

Eloise ignored the warning signs, unable to remain silent any longer. "Dismissed, yes, but you and your friends were guilty none the less. In fact, you were exiled because of it. Only Millicent Parker paid the true price for what you did by hanging herself the night you were set free."

"I can hardly be blamed for some unfortunate girl's state of mind," he drawled.

"Oh, but you can," she said, with a steadiness that astounded her. "The evidence was clear, and you only escaped prison because her character was blackened by your father. You and the others lied under oath."

"Is there a point to this conversation, Eloise? It is tedious to be going over such old ground."

"The point, Edward, is that you have consistently deceived me."

"I have done no such thing."

"You lied even when I asked for the truth — but I know you now for what you are."

"And what am I?" His voice was low, his gaze almost feral in the candlelight.

She swallowed. She was terrified now, but had gone too far to stop. "You cannot deny my charges for I have unimpeachable proof. You are a liar, a cheat, a murderer and a thief."

His jaw stiffened and his eyes were slits. "Be careful, Eloise. Men have died for such slanderous talk."

"I have no doubt of it," she retorted, rage making her defiant. "But my accusations are not slanderous. You kill innocent women and children, use blackmail to take other men's businesses, and cheat at cards. Although you aren't so successful at that for your debt to Mr Carlton grows every day."

"How *dare* you?"

"I dare because I know who you are and what you've been about all these years," she quavered. She wanted to stand and leave the room, but she was trembling so much she lacked the strength to do so. She felt as trapped as a rabbit in a snare.

Edward stood, his face a mask of fury. "I expect my wife to run my home efficiently, entertain my guests and never question me on anything," he said. "I need not remind you that you have failed miserably. You will *never* speak to me in that way again, Eloise. I forbid it."

"You can forbid many things, Edward, but the knowledge that you murder native children and violate innocent girls will never leave me." She managed to stand, but clung to the edge of the table for support. "Our marriage is at an end."

"And what do you propose to do, Eloise? Return to your father?"

She nodded, mute with terror.

He moved with lightning speed round the table. "You will never leave me," he hissed, as he grabbed her arm.

Eloise cowered from the expected blow.

His fingers curled round her neck and pressed into the soft flesh as he forced her to look into his face. "You belong to me. And you will learn not to cross me." He released her roughly, strode to the door and locked it.

Eloise could still feel the pressure of his fingers on her neck, and was trying to catch her breath when he advanced towards her.

She backed away.

Edward's eyes glittered as he drew nearer. His hand encircled her throat once more. "It's time I taught you a lesson, wife." He ripped her dress from bodice to waist. "It's time you learnt that I am your master and I can do as I like, when I like and with whom. You will *never* leave me — *never* — and if you try to I will track you down and make you watch as I kill the whining Charles before I slit your throat."

Eloise stared up at him, stunned.

Edward's face was so close she could feel his breath on her cheek. "I've killed many brats. One more won't make any difference."

A keening sound rose in Eloise's throat. He couldn't mean it — could he?

"You think that was an idle threat? Would you care to put it to the test?"

Eloise was ensnared by his eyes and his grip on her neck, frozen in the knowledge that, if pushed, he might indeed kill their child. "No."

"Strip," he ordered.

She tried to shake her head.

"Do it! Or I'll do it for you."

Sobbing, Eloise wriggled out of the torn bodice and chemise, and fumbled with the ties at the waist of her skirt until the soft material fell to the floor.

Edward tugged at her petticoats. "All of it — and hurry."

Naked but for her satin slippers, she stood trembling in his grasp as he ran his free hand roughly over her breasts and stomach. His colour was high with excitement, and she shrivelled as he stabbed his fingers between her legs.

Dragging her to the table, Edward swept aside the china and crystal and thrust her back against the polished oak.

"No!" she begged.

"Keep struggling, wife. It's the way I like it."

She went limp as he took her swiftly and violently, and tried not to cry out when he hurt her — she could bear any agony to protect her sons.

When it was over he fastened his trouser buttons, strolled over to the tantalus and poured rum into a glass.

Eloise slid from the table and fell into a huddle on the floor among the broken crockery and shattered glass. There could be no escape. Not tonight. Not ever.

CHAPTER
FOURTEEN

Sydney Town, April 1801

"Thank you for coming today," said the lawyer. "Did you not receive our letters over the past weeks?"

George nodded. "I couldn't bring myself to deal with Sam's will," he muttered.

"It's never easy when a close friend dies," said the other man, "but the matter before us is straightforward. You are the sole heir but for a few minor legacies." He took off his monocle and polished it. "You are to be congratulated, Mr Collinson. Captain Varney has made you a wealthy young man."

George had lost a friend and mentor. No amount of money could compensate for that.

"He left this with me," said the lawyer, after they had gone through Samuel's bequests. "I am to give it to you now he is dead."

George took the sealed letter, shook the other's hand and left the office. Emerging into the sunlight, he paused for his eyes to adjust to the glare, then walked along the riverbank until he found a secluded, shady spot to sit and read the letter.

He broke the seal. The paper was expensive, the writing looped and flowing with the energy of the man who'd penned it. George felt the weight of his sadness as he read Samuel's last words:

My dear boy,
You have given me the chance to know the love of a father for a son, and I take great pride in all you have achieved.

You will know by now that I have left you the ships, my share in the warehouse, the house in the hills, and the money deposited both in Nantucket and Sydney banks. I leave it all to you in the knowledge that you will use it wisely.

But be warned, my boy. The sea is a hard task-mistress. She demands a man's full attention, if not his life. Don't be trapped like me, for although I have always loved the sea and professed no liking for shore duties, I have always yearned secretly for the solace of a wife and the pleasure of seeing children grow. Sadly it was not to be, but you are still young with many years ahead of you. Don't make the same mistakes, son. If your heart is true it will never lead you astray.

I wish you Godspeed, and hope I will live on in your heart as you do in mine.

With great affection,
Samuel Varney

George blinked away a tear as he folded the letter and slipped it into his pocket. Samuel's death had left him rudderless; his kind words and generous bequest had served to make the loss of him more profound. He stared out over the water to the ships anchored there. They were a pretty sight, bobbing on the crystal water that sparkled with diamond studs of light, but he couldn't dismiss the dark memory of an angry sea, and the soft splash as Samuel's body had been committed to the deep.

He determinedly shook off the gloomy thoughts, stood up to brush the pollen and grass-seeds off his coat and wandered back towards town. The *Atlantica* had taken a battering after her mad clash with the southern ocean, and had been hauled in for repairs that would take some months. The other four ships in the fleet were at sea, not expected to return until late summer. Thomas was away with his platoon, and although George had already visited his parents and been out to Moonrakers, he had promised to go back for a longer stay. With time on his hands and no particular purpose, he felt adrift from reality.

Across the bay Sydney Town shimmered in the heat. Despite his reluctance to return, he felt a stirring of something akin to love for the ramshackle place; an unidentified excitement for the promises it held. Eloise was close, he could feel it — could so easily remember their time together at Balmain. Could he persuade her to leave Edward — or had she found contentment with him? Was she still pining for him as he did for her — or had she forgotten their love?

Standing in the sunshine his thoughts whirled on the conundrum that had foxed him over the past years.

"Faint heart never won fair maiden," he said aloud. "You must try, George." For the first time in weeks he smiled, stuck his hands into his pockets and began to whistle.

He was collecting the mail from the store when he saw her through the grimy window. His heart skipped a beat, and he was on the point of rushing outside to greet her when he caught sight of her companions. The other woman was obviously a maid, and Charles was with them. It was the smaller child in the baron's arms who captured his attention — and the unmistakable fact that Eloise was expecting another. He stood to one side of the window and used the sacks of potatoes as a shield while he watched them approach along the boardwalk, his anguish increasing.

"Come along, Harry," boomed the baron, as he struggled to divert the small boy from his wriggling to be free. "Let us go and look at the ships."

"Can I come too, Grandpapa?" piped up Charles.

"Of course. But only if your mother promises to sit and rest."

George watched as Eloise smiled at her father. He saw her speak, but was too far away to hear what she was saying. He drank in the sight of her as Harry was set on his feet and she took his hand. Her face was full of love, glowing and bright-eyed, as she hugged her sons. George's heart broke when Charles touched her face and nuzzled her neck. There was no doubt that Eloise was happy — she was positively radiant.

"George? Are you not well?"

He turned to his store manager and tried to reply, but the words stuck in his throat.

"You're very pale," the man said, with concern. "Shall I call my wife?"

"No," he managed. He glanced out to the street, saw that Eloise was coming towards him and knew he must avoid her. "I have to go," he muttered. "I'll say goodbye to your wife and leave by the back door."

George roamed through the winding streets until darkness fell. He thought at first to drown his sorrows in a tavern, but he didn't want company — not today, not now his future yawned before him, and all hope had died.

As the moon rose and the stars twinkled, he sought the sanctuary of Samuel's cottage. Nestled among the hills, it was sheltered by trees and, in daylight, afforded a panoramic view of the town and its harbour. He turned the key and went in. His heart was heavy as he lit the lamp and wandered through the rooms, which were still redolent of Samuel's tobacco.

The main room was a clutter of books, papers and souvenirs from his friend's travels. Maps and model boats jostled for position on the shelves and tables with carved whalebone and pieces of coral. Samuel's chair was placed beside the empty grate, the imprint of his body still evident in the dented cushions. George touched the worn fabric, remembering the times he'd been here, the meandering conversations that had often gone on through the night as they drank rum and made plans for their next voyage.

George was determined not to give way to tears, for although Samuel was gone, his spirit remained. He could feel it in every timber and the air he breathed. He finally made his way upstairs. Samuel's room was uncluttered, blankets folded at the end of the iron bedstead as if awaiting his return. A telescope stood on its tripod at the window, a chair placed beside it so that the old seaman could watch the activities of the harbour in comfort.

George pushed open the double doors that led on to the balcony and stood there for a moment, inhaling the night scents. The moon was waning, but its clear white light gleamed on the water, and shone silver on the tin roofs. He gazed towards Watsons Bay, searching for — he didn't know what.

He closed the doors behind him, then went into the second bedroom and sank on to the stiff mattress. The room was impersonal, furnished only with the bed, chair and a washstand, on which stood a vast jug and bowl. In here there was no sense of Samuel but suddenly the loss of his friend and of Eloise overcame him. He gave in to despair.

Waymbuurr (Cooktown), July 1801

Mandawuy was eleven and, like the other youngsters of his tribe, his initiation into adulthood had begun several seasons before.

The Elders were wise: they knew a child's mind was more ready to accept their teaching than that of an adult. Each evening, from as far back as he could

335

remember, Mandawuy had sat with the other children as an Elder had told tales of animals, birds, reptiles or insects that were examples of the good and evil in man.

At the same time as he had learnt the traditions and legends of his people, Mandawuy had acquired the skills he needed for hunting and survival, and was familiar with the anatomy, haunts and habits of every animal in the bush. He knew all the birds, and even their mating calls, could tell from the position of the stars that a different season approached, and in the fruit of a tree that the great barramundi were heading upriver to spawn.

The seasons numbered six. *Gunumeleng* is the end of the hot, dry time, with storms and the first rain. *Gudjewg* is the season of flooding, when it is easy to catch the animals fleeing into the trees. *Bangerreng* follows when the floods subside, plants bear fruit and animals produce young. *Yegge* brings morning mists and drying winds; it is the time to fire-stick the grasslands and stimulate new growth. *Wurrgeng* is cooler, with less rain, drying the *billabongs*, making the flocks of birds easy to catch as they congregate on the shrinking waterholes. *Gurrung* brings dry, hot, windless days when all life seems drowsy before stormclouds gather and lightning announces the return of *Gunumeleng* and the rains.

Mandawuy could identify the track of every member of the tribe, for each footprint was individual; a stranger in their sacred land would be known immediately. Despite all he had learnt, Mandawuy knew his knowledge would broaden for the rest of his life.

They were camped far from the ocean, deep in heavily timbered grasslands where the hunting was good. A special place was found at some distance from the encampment so that the ceremonies could be held away from prying eyes. The initiation rites were a mystery to those who had not yet gone through them so a degree of tension and curiosity kept everyone on edge.

Mandawuy sat with the others and listened as the Elder spoke the wise words of Nurunderi — the sacred teacher who'd been chosen as the Great Spirit Creator's representative on earth during Dreamtime.

"Children, there is a Great Spirit in the sky, and you are a part of Him. He is your provider and protector, and although your life is like a day, He has willed that you fulfil His great plan during your short time on earth. You must nurture the land, take only what you need. You must control your appetites and never become slaves to desire, or let your minds suffer pain or fear — for that will make you selfish, causing misery to you and all around you."

Mandawuy understood that the lessons of the Elder and the forthcoming test would develop him so he would become acceptable to the Great Spirit Creator when it was his time to take the final journey in the sky canoe. But it was a heady realisation, and he felt the weight of responsibility press on him. To be a man and walk in the shadow of the Creator would not be easy — but he was aware that his grandmothers, Anabarru and Lowitja, were looking down from the sky, watching his progress to manhood with keen eyes. He could not disappoint them.

"It is time for your first real test," intoned the Elder, as he stood tall and leant on his spear. He eyed each of them sternly. "You will walk for two days. You will walk alone. You will hunt — but not eat. Do not return until the Elders find you and give permission."

Mandawuy shared a glance with the boy beside him. Kapirigi was his best friend, and they usually hunted together. It would feel strange to be out in the never-never alone, but his own excitement was reflected in Kapirigi's eyes. They stood with the others, clutching *nullas*, spears and *boomerangs* eagerly as they waited for the signal to move off.

Mandawuy had chosen to walk towards the black western mountains called Kalcajagga. The trek to this place of death and evil spirits would prepare him for the test of overcoming fear. It had taken him two days at a steady pace to reach it, and he had stopped only to spear a small goanna, which dangled from his hair belt. Now, as he stood and rested, trying to ignore the rumbling of his empty belly, he regarded the mountains he'd heard of in the stories of the Elders.

Kalcajagga reared out of the surrounding empty plains in twin jumbles of enormous black boulders that glittered eerily in the sun. There was no vegetation, and the sides of the mountains were honeycombed with caves, but even so, Mandawuy could see the black rock-wallabies hopping about, and knew that deep in those caves lived giant pythons that could swallow a man whole. It was said that many people had come here never to be seen again — and he meant to keep his distance.

He squatted in the meagre shade of a gum tree and listened to the eerie sounds that came from the caves. He shivered as he heard the moans and rustling whispers, and was tempted to run away. It was as if the fluttering spirits of the lost were seeking a way to escape. Yet he didn't run. To be a man was to show no fear. To be a man was to respect the ancient ways and learn from the legends that surrounded this place.

Mandawuy dug into the earth for the roots that held precious water, and when his thirst was quenched he turned his attention back to Kalcajagga. The Elders had told him the story many moons ago, and as he regarded the ominous dark peaks, he began to sing the tale, his voice a soft drone in the silence.

"When the land was young there were two brothers of the wallaby totem. Ka-iruji and Taja-iruji were mighty hunters in this land of shiny black rocks. One day they saw a girl of the rock-python totem digging for yams, and she was beautiful, and both brothers desired her. They could not fight for her with their hunting weapons, for that was taboo. They would have to find some other way."

Mandawuy resisted the yearning to eat the roots that lay at his feet, and battled to control the gnawing hunger as he unhitched the goanna from the belt and put it to one side. He closed his eyes, took a deep breath and continued.

"Ka-iruji and Taja-iruji saw the boulders and realised that if they piled them high enough, the victor could throw one down on his rival and smash him to pieces. Day after day they toiled and the mountains began to grow, but neither brother could get higher than the other. They worked so hard they didn't see Kahahinka, the cyclone, approach. Neither did the watching girl. Kahahinka's winds fell upon them, shrieking, tearing, smashing them to a pulp."

Mandawuy opened his eyes and regarded the mountains that had been built so many thousands of moons ago. He could hear the rustling of the girl of the rock-python totem in the deep caves, and could see the ever-waiting rock-wallabies foraging outside. He shivered at the thought of sleeping out there — but knew that if he was to prove himself to the Elders he had no choice.

He scooped out a hollow in the soft earth and, with his cheek resting in the palm of his hand, his spear at his side, settled down to sleep.

The Elder came to him silently and without warning, four risings of the sun later. Mandawuy stirred from his sleep, and started as he saw the old man squatting nearby. Bleary-eyed and dizzy with hunger, he stood to face him.

"I have been watching you, Mandawuy. You sleep soundly in this land of evil spirits. Are your dreams not troubled?"

He shook his head. "The python and wallaby are not my enemy. I have not intruded on their sacred land."

"That is good," murmured the old man.

Mandawuy's gaze fell hungrily on the goanna that now lay at the Elder's feet. His mouth watered.

"Your eyes speak for your belly, Mandawuy. But first you must build a fire."

He set off to search for anything that might burn, but this was a desolate place and the makings of a fire were difficult to find. Some time later he returned with dry grass and sun-bleached wood. He rubbed stick against stick and soon had wisps of smoke rising into the still air. Adding more grass, he blew on the sparks then sat on his haunches and watched the flames, the promise of the goanna making his mouth water.

The old man waited until he was satisfied that the fire was hot enough. Then he threw the carcass into it.

Mandawuy almost fainted at the delicious smell and his belly squirmed.

"It is necessary to control hunger," said the Elder, a little later, "for when the *wanjina* — the water-spirit — does not come, Mother Earth cannot provide." He took a stone tool from his own hair belt and sliced off a hefty chunk of charred meat.

Mandawuy licked his lips, his gaze fixed on the food.

The old man ate with relish.

Mandawuy knew it was part of the test — but it was torture.

Soon only a tiny piece of the goanna remained. The Elder held it out. "You have done well, Mandawuy. Eat now."

He took the meat, and although he knew he should savour it and make it last, he gobbled it. His belly grumbled, wanting more, but all he could do was lick his fingers and wipe the grease from his chin.

The Elder stood. "You have passed two of the most important tests, Mandawuy, those of hunger and fear. But there are more to come. You will leave this place and wander for another three risings of the moon, but you will not eat again until you return to our camp on the day of the fourth."

Mandawuy looked at the remains of the goanna, blackening in the fire. There were still remnants of meat on the bones. The old man was watching him closely. "Until the day of the fourth moon," he said, then turned away and went north.

He wandered the land of his people, remembering the legends of Garnday and Djanay, the events that had taken them to the homes of the south wind and the north wind. He climbed the red outcrops and studied the cave paintings of the Ancient Ones, and the sacred Dreaming Places they had left in his care.

The hunger ebbed and a strange lightness flooded him as at last he understood the reason for the stories and the tests. He was part of this land. It was where he belonged — his inheritance. His life was nothing if he could not defend it.

Mandawuy pondered on these things during the long walk back to the camp. His grandmother's uncle, Pemulwuy, had fought bravely against the white invaders for many seasons. Now he was dead, shot by the white man's gun. Pemulwuy's son Tedbury continued the raids on the white farms; he had come to the *corroboree* and spoken of his battle to free the

342

southern lands. Mandawuy had listened to the rousing speech and wished with all his might that he was old enough to join him, for only a handful of warriors had been willing to help in the fight.

His feet made little sound as he padded across the dark red earth towards the green haze of bush on the horizon, but the images in his head and the memory of what had happened when he was a child were as vivid as ever. The knowledge that the white men were slowly moving north, and spreading south and west across the sacred song-lines of Dreamtime meant that danger was closing in.

Mandawuy stopped when he reached the last of the hills. He could see smoke from the campfires through the trees and the glitter of the ocean stretching to the end of the earth. These were his people, and this was his land to protect for those who would come after him. He squatted in the noonday sun. The tests of fear, hunger and isolation had brought him to this moment, and it was important that he should think clearly — for to go against the Spirits of the Ancient Ones was to be banished for ever.

The sun had long since slipped behind the mountains when he rose to his feet and walked towards camp. His step was light as he hurried down the hill to the campfire for he had come to a decision.

Kernow House, Watsons Bay, August 1801

The baby gave an angry howl as it slid into the world, and Eloise collapsed on to the pillows. It had been an exhausting labour: this latest child had seemed reluctant to be born. "What is it, Meg?"

"A boy," the newly emancipated Meg replied, as she cleaned and wrapped the baby in a blanket. "Will you hold him or shall I take him straight to the nursery?"

In reply, Eloise opened her arms for the squalling bundle. "It's not his fault that he was conceived in violence."

The baby was dark-haired and red-faced, his little fists waving in fury as he blindly sought her nipple. Eloise felt love wash over her as his mouth captured her breast and tugged. "I never thought I could love him, but how can I not, when he's so perfect?"

"He'll always be a reminder," said Meg, with a frown.

Meg had come to Eloise's rescue the minute Edward had left the house that awful night nine months before. She had been hovering on the landing and had heard everything. Regardless of the other servants, who were watching with avid interest, she had covered Eloise with the tattered remnants of her clothes and helped her up the stairs to the bedroom. She had bathed her, then soothed her with balm and wrapped her in warm towels, holding her close and rocking her into an exhausted sleep.

"Everything in this house is a reminder," Eloise said, "but this little one is a gift from God — the only good thing to have come of that night. We shall not speak of it again."

344

Meg took the child and smiled. "He's red and plump with shouting — just like the baron," she said. She coloured. "I shouldn't have said that."

Eloise patted her arm. "You may speak freely, Meg, and all new-born babies resemble my father — it's in the plump cheeks and furious frown."

Much relieved, Meg put the baby into the cradle that stood beside the bed. "What will you call him?"

Eloise laid her fingers lightly on the little one's soft cheek. "Oliver," she said. She saw Meg's look of surprise. "Edward insisted," she explained. "But it's ironic he should choose that name for one conceived in violence, for it means 'peace'." She laughed. "Actually," she confessed, "I think it suits him."

Meg's silent disgust for Edward was far more eloquent than words.

"Bring Charles and Harry in to meet their new brother, then go to bed and rest," said Eloise. "You've been up all night and must be exhausted."

Meg shook her head. "I'll put a mattress in here. You might need me in the night if *he* comes home and disturbs you."

Eloise looked at her with affection. "I doubt he will now he's moved into the other room. But thank you, Meg."

She closed her eyes. There was little chance of Edward coming home to see his new son — in fact, she had been blessed with his absence for weeks on end after that terrible night. She had no interest in what he was doing or who he was with. As long as he kept his distance and left her in peace with her children she could cope with anything.

Waymbuurr (Cooktown), October 1802

Mandawuy walked beside his friend, Kapirigi. They had been hunting together and were returning to the secret encampment that had been set up for the last of the initiation ceremonies. "Do you think it will hurt?"

Kapirigi nodded. "But my brothers and my father will be shamed if I cry out."

Mandawuy tried to smile, but he was very nervous and couldn't quite manage it. "I have heard there is special smoke to help turn the mind from the pain," he said. "We must be strong, Kapirigi."

"Come." The Elder emerged from the trees and stood in their path. "It is time."

The boys handed over their kill, two wallabies and a snake, and followed him deep into the bush to where a fire was smoking in a ring of stones that had been placed in the centre of an open grass *gunyah*.

"You will enter," intoned the Elder, "and take your place on the reed mat."

Mandawuy clenched his teeth. He must not cry out — no matter how painful it became — for that would shame him and his grandmothers. He closed his eyes as he heard the Elders enter the *gunyah*, and listened as they chanted. The smoke was heavily laden with eucalyptus, making his eyes water and burning his throat.

The lightness in his head increased and the chanting seemed to take him over, thrumming through him like the music of a didgeridoo as the sharp stone cut welts into his flesh. The tribal markings would remain with him for ever — a badge of pride — an acceptance of who he was and the part he would play in the future of his clan.

The final ordeal was to have his nose pierced by a sharpened bone, and it took all of his depleted strength to resist the scream of pain. Yet resist he must, for to fail this final test was to be banished from the tribe. He would be unable to marry, or to sit at the fire and share food with the others.

When it was done and the Elders had left, Mandawuy heard the chants from outside, which were accompanied by the regular beating of sticks on the ground. It was the sound of a great, marching army, and he knew it would continue until sunset. He closed his eyes, drifting into the music, losing himself in the smoke that drifted over him in ghostly plumes.

"Come. It is time."

Mandawuy opened his eyes, smiled at Kapirigi, and they moved out of the *gunyah* to cries of congratulation. The feast was ready and their pain was almost forgotten in their hunger. He and the other newly initiated boys and girls fell upon the food and stuffed themselves until their bellies bulged.

The rituals for their initiation into adulthood took two seasons. During that time there was much rejoicing and feasting. Bull-roarers — flat pieces of wood of varying lengths, tapered at each end and decorated with tribal markings — were spun from hair cords. Their soft, vibrating hum increased at times like a mighty wind, and at others diminished to a moan. The earthy, pulsating rhythm of the *yidaki* — the didgeridoo — accompanied the clap of sticks and the thud of feet as the celebrations continued night and day.

On the final day, Mandawuy and his friends followed the Elders into the centre of the encampment. The newly initiated girls emerged from their ceremonial grounds and stood with them.

The chief Elder raised his hand for silence among the watching clan. "I declare these young people to be men and women of the Ngandyandyi people. Welcome them."

The watching women bowed their heads as their men rose to their feet. Each man raised his spear and *nulla* — the wooden club used to stun or kill — and pointed to the setting sun. "Boys and girls," they shouted, "you have fought the battle of life and won. Manhood and womanhood are perfected in you. The Great Spirit is pleased and waits for you in the Home of the Spirits."

Mandawuy felt the power of his Ancestors surge through him and knew that the decision he'd made on the hill over-looking the camp was about to be fulfilled. He looked at the familiar faces and knew he would never forget them, even though he would probably never see them again. After the celebrations tonight he would leave Waymbuurr and head south to

348

be with Tedbury and his small band of warriors. The smell of the white man's blood was in his nostrils, and he wouldn't be content until he was rid of it.

CHAPTER
FIFTEEN

Castle Hill Government Farm, 2 March 1804

Niall had been moved with the other Irish prisoners in July 1801 to the government farm that had been set up in the Castle Hill Reserve to help feed the ever-growing colony. They had slept in tents for the first two years and then, in 1803, they had moved into the rough cottages they had built round the two-storey stone barracks. Life continued to be hard, but rebellion still stirred the blood, and at fifteen, Niall had been involved in many thwarted plans for escape.

Niall smiled as he thought of the fear those plans had roused in Governor King and the settlers around Sydney Town. There had been many attempts to seize a ship, and he'd heard that the governor had ordered several American clippers out of Sydney Harbour for fear their seamen would sympathise with the Irish rebels.

"What are you grinning about, fellow-me-lad?"

Niall turned to John Cavenah, who was working beside him in the forge. "I was thinking how good it is to poke a finger in the eye of the governor and make him sweat."

"And to think he imagined we'd roll over and play dead because England and Ireland have formed a union." He hawked phlegm and spat into the furnace. "We've been fighting the bastard English for years — as if a piece of paper could change that."

"At least we now have a priest," said Niall, hammering the molten metal into shape.

John nodded. "Father Dixon is a good man," he said. "He'll always turn a blind eye to our meetings after Mass, and will never betray us."

Niall plunged the door-hinge into the bucket of water, stood back from the cloud of steam and mopped his brow. The heat in the forge was overpowering, sweat stung his eyes and his thirst was never quenched. John was one of the rebel leaders and a close friend of Phillip Cunningham, a veteran of the 1798 battle of Vinegar Hill in Wexford, Ireland, and the leader of a short-lived mutiny on the convict ship *Anne*. "Is something afoot, John?"

"Isn't there always?"

"I've seen you talking with Cunningham and Johnston, and I can tell you're plotting."

"Better you know little about it, me lad." He took a drink from the leather pouch at his waist and began to hammer again. "Cunningham understands that secrecy and untraceable lines of communication are vital to a successful rebellion."

"I want to fight," said Niall, as he threw the hinge on to a pile. "I'm not a boy any more, John. I want to be among the leaders the next time we rise up."

"Your time will come," the older man said, "but for now it is better you remain in ignorance. As our main pike-maker, you will do us no good in irons."

"But I want to do more," he protested.

"Then keep your mouth shut and make more pikes."

Niall was silent, his thoughts on the pikes he'd buried behind the cottages. "It's happening soon, isn't it?"

"Let's just say this might be one of the last days you forge an Englishman's iron."

Hawkesbury River, 3 March 1804

Mandawuy crouched in the long grass and, through the clouds of dust, watched the activity in the penned-off area of the clearing. The white men were chasing the calves, throwing ropes round their necks, then flinging them to the ground. The man on the horse held the rope tight, and another knelt on a calf's side and pressed hot metal into its rump.

"Why do they do that?" he asked Tedbury.

The older man shrugged. "Perhaps the white man makes his mark on his beasts so he can keep them to himself." He chewed a plug of tobacco, his eyes narrowed to keep out the dust sifting over them from the trampling hoofs. "They take everything," he muttered.

Mandawuy grimaced as two black men prepared the hot iron in the fire. "They dress like the whites," he hissed.

"Many of our people live and work with them and take on their customs. It is what I have been fighting against." His expression was grim. "We will strike when the sun is at its highest. That is when the white men eat, and sit in the shade like old women."

Mandawuy had been on many raids with his hero Tedbury, and had listened in awe as the older man had told him of his previous exploits and bravery in fighting to keep their tribal lands. He had made the right decision in coming so far south.

He followed his hero into the deeper shadows of the bush until they found the others, busy sharpening their spears as they ate the last of the fish they'd caught that morning. Pride swelled in Mandawuy as he joined the small but fearless group of warriors. They had lost many to the white man's sabre and bullet in their fight for the right to live on their tribal lands, but those who remained had never faltered.

Mandawuy ate, his thoughts on the coming raid and the black men who had betrayed their people by living and working with the enemy. Others had been persuaded to join them after such raids. Perhaps today these men would see the truth: that this was Aboriginal land and the white men had no business there.

Tedbury led them back to their vantage-point as the sun reached its zenith. The click of insects was accompanied by the occasional caw of a crow, but beyond the trees there was silence.

Mandawuy crept through the grass using the woodland as camouflage to draw nearer to the homestead. He could see two women on the veranda, and one was holding a child in her arms. He tasted the bitterness as he remembered how his grandmother had carried him from danger all those years ago — and the trampled bodies at the Place of the Honeybee Dreaming. Now it was his turn to seek vengeance. His heart was pounding as he waited for Tedbury's signal and raised his spear in readiness.

With a scream of defiance Tedbury let loose his war-spear.

Mandawuy rose from the grass and, in one fluid movement, sent his own straight at the man sitting on the step. He screamed as it sank into his thigh and Mandawuy fixed another spear in his *woomera* and flung it after the first.

He hissed with frustration as it missed its mark. He'd thrown too soon, and his hand had been unsteady because of his excitement. Peering through the grass he saw the women grab the children and run into the house, heard their screams as their men reached for rifles.

The blast from the guns was deafening as the bullets spat round him, and Mandawuy crawled through the grass to find another vantage-point. He'd been fired at before, but his grandmothers had watched over him and he'd not been hit. He kept an eye on the men with rifles, waited until they were aiming away from him, stood and threw his spear.

The blast came from the shadows. The thud of the bullet knocked him to his knees, and as he slowly collapsed into the grass, he tried to understand what had happened.

354

Mandawuy heard Tedbury shout encouragement to his men. He saw the flash of spears, the dark shadows of his friends as they ran for cover, and smelt the unmistakable odour of blood. He tried to move, but his legs wouldn't work and he stared at them in consternation. He saw the meat and bone of his thigh, ripped apart by the bullet. Saw the blood and finally felt the agony. Darkness was filling his head, and he could hear his heart hammering in his chest. "Don't leave me," he whispered, as he heard his friends run into the bush.

He felt the coolness of something on his forehead, heard the soft croon of a woman's voice, and in the moment before he opened his eyes he thought Anabarru had come to fetch him. But as his eyelids fluttered open he saw the white face of the woman who leant over him and froze.

"It's all right," she said. "My name is Susan Collinson and I'm going to make you well again."

He flinched as she touched him. He hadn't understood her words, and although her hand was gentle and her voice was soothing, she was white, and therefore not to be trusted.

"I have taken out the bullet and sewn you up," she said softly, as she pointed to his thigh. "Those pieces of wood are splints to keep the bone still while it mends."

Mandawuy eyed the white cloth and the sticks and although the white woman's medicine seemed to have lessened the pain, he had no intention of remaining here. With a swipe of his hand he pushed her away and struggled to sit up, but his head was swimming and he found he couldn't move. As he slumped on to his back he saw the man who had come to stand behind the woman, and felt a fear so great he thought his heart would stop.

"My name is Ezra," said the man in the black coat. "What is yours?"

Mandawuy stared at him. The man had spoken in his own tongue. Was this yet another trick of the whites — or was it magic? Either way, he decided, he would not give his name.

"You are a brave warrior for one so young," said the man. "But your friends have deserted you, and your wound is such that you would not survive in the bush on your own. We do not mean any harm to you. We want only to make you well again."

Mandawuy saw that his smile was kind and that his voice held no threat. If he had been black he would have revered him as an Elder — but he was white, and therefore the enemy. He closed his eyes and turned away his head, as he tried furiously to work out how he could escape.

Kernow House, Watsons Bay, 4 March 1804

Eloise was sitting by the open windows of the drawing room, reading the *Sydney Gazette*. Oliver would wake soon from his morning nap, and demand noisily to be fed. At two and a half, he was already showing signs of his grandfather's impatience.

She glanced out of the window, saw that Charles and Harry were occupied with their ponies and Edward was in conversation with the groom. Revelling in the quiet, she returned to the newspaper.

The convict, George Howe, had been given permission a year ago to print the weekly news-sheet from a shed behind Government House. Its tone was moral to the point of priggishness, servile in its patriotism and unbearably pompous, but it carried shipping news, auction results, crime and agricultural reports. Religious advice and government edicts for settlers and convicts alike took up most of the four pages, and the news from abroad, which came in on the clipper ships, was usually ten to fourteen weeks out of date. Eloise devoured it every week, for it was the only newspaper in the colony, and it kept her in touch with what was happening beyond these four walls.

She froze when she heard Edward's raised voice, then stood up and hurried to the window.

"You stupid boy!" he yelled. "How many more times must I tell you to sit up straight? No wonder you keep falling off." He hauled Charles to his feet and almost threw him back into the saddle. "You're nearly seven, for God's sake. Stop that snivelling."

Eloise clutched the curtain as she watched Harry come to his brother's defence. "It's not his fault," he said sharply. "The pony's not had enough exercise, and keeps throwing him off."

Eloise saw Edward smile up at Harry and felt a mixture of relief and despair. Harry had just turned five, but he had learnt to distract his father when he was berating Charles — her husband favoured him over his brother. But how unfair that Harry should feel he must take it upon himself to do so.

She knew that any interference would be met with scathing disdain from Edward, and was glad when the groom stepped forward to help Charles compose himself and settle into the saddle.

It seemed the storm was over, for Charles nudged his pony into a trot as Harry rode alongside him. Edward had stopped shouting and was leaning on the corral railing, smoking a cigar, while the groom encouraged the boys as they rode round the corral. She resumed her seat and picked up the paper again.

She was smiling at the pomposity of a particular article when she heard the slam of the front door. Her stomach clenched as footsteps approached.

Edward entered the room and threw his hat on to a chair. "I've had a message from the barracks. There's been trouble on the Hawkesbury River. Tedbury and his renegades attacked the Collinsons' place."

Eloise kept her head low so that Edward didn't see her reaction, but her thoughts were haywire. "Was anyone hurt?"

"One of the convicts got a spear in his leg, and the Collinsons lost several bullocks in the raid. Ezra Collinson is tending the only wounded black — but he's a fool. The others got away as usual." He grunted. "We should follow the example of Lieutenant Moore at Risdon Cove in Van Diemen's Land and shoot the bastards before they get the chance to attack."

Eloise did not rise to this inflammatory speech. Edward needed no excuse to do such a thing — they both knew that.

"There will also be trouble at Castle Hill soon," he added.

Eloise felt much calmer now that she knew George and his family were safe, so she put down the newspaper. But her husband's face was flushed with excitement, and she tensed again. The promise of bloodshed always heralded trouble. "It is always suspected there," she reminded him, with her customary coolness, "but it comes to nothing."

He gave an exasperated sigh, reached for the decanter and poured some rum.

Eloise clasped her hands on her lap to stop them trembling. Over the years it had become his habit to drink early in the day, and she wondered if this had anything to do with the recurring nightmares and the failure of several recent business ventures but right now she suspected it had more to do with his recent demotion to captain. "I know nothing of Irish uprisings," she said, "except they are always dashed."

"As this one will be." He drained the glass. "An Irish overseer turned informant last night, and this morning two rebels were discovered. One, John Griffen, had been relaying a message to Furey that the rebellion is on for tonight. He was supposed to send word to the convicts of Parramatta, Windsor and Sydney, but the message was not delivered. Castle Hill will be isolated and the rebellion easily quashed."

Eloise knew better than to comment, but she felt sorry for the Irishmen. They appeared desperate for freedom, more so than any other convict.

"The Corps has been put on alert, and so have the two companies of the Loyal Association Militia. We leave as soon as we have the order from Governor King." Edward poured more rum and shouted for his manservant to draw him a bath. "Damned Irish. We send their rebel leaders to Norfolk Island, and separate the trouble-makers, but they can always produce more."

He began to pace, voicing his thoughts. "There are four hundred and seventy-four convicts on the farm, and with each convict ship we have more Catholics. These seditionists are veterans of the Wexford battles, mostly leaders of the United Irishmen and other such groups. Any hint of trouble must be put down immediately."

Eloise glanced at the newspaper, wishing he would leave her in peace to read it. "Governor King has tried to make things easier for them," she said. "But with men like Samuel Marsden in charge, one cannot help but feel sympathy for their plight."

Edward stopped pacing. "*Sympathy?* They're a superstitious, seditious rabble. Letting Father Dixon preach to them was the worst thing King could have done. Give a Catholic a priest and you give him sanctuary for his plotting."

Eloise refused for once to be brow-beaten. "Marsden is too free with the lash. No wonder he's called the Flogging Parson. One cannot beat obedience into a man — it merely makes him more rebellious." It was a barely concealed barb.

"You should spend less time reading newspapers," he rasped. "A little knowledge is dangerous, Eloise, and it is not your place to have opinions on how we deal with insurrection."

Eloise bit back a sharp retort. It was pointless to argue. Edward's condemnation of her views was just one of the weapons he used to cow her. "I will ask the cook to bring you some food," she said, rising from her chair.

"I'll eat at the barracks."

"Very well," she said. "But please see Charles before you leave. You upset him earlier."

"There is little point," he replied. "I can hardly have an intelligent conversation with a child who cringes whenever I come near him."

"That is unfortunate, but perhaps if you did not shout at him quite so loudly, and if you were to temper your impatience, things might improve."

"I doubt it," he snapped. "You've made him a milk-sop."

"He's frightened of you, Edward, and one can hardly blame him."

"Harry isn't," he said, and puffed out his chest. "Neither is Oliver. Both boys are true Cadwalladers, tough and sturdy."

Eloise forced herself to look at him. "They are different characters, I agree," she said, "but you should give Charles time to get to know you. He'll soon be racing about on that pony — you'll see."

Edward curled his lip. "He bawled when he saw it, bawled when I put him on it, and carried on bawling when I tied him into the saddle." His face lit with pride. "Not like Harry, who was riding on his own before he was three, and would have slept in the stables if I'd let him. He's a born horseman — an asset to the Cadwallader name."

Eloise's heart twisted and she didn't dare look at him. Her sons were her joy, the only good to come from her disastrous marriage. If only Edward could be more patient with Charles, life would be easier for all of them. "Charles will learn to appreciate his pony, as Harry does, if he's treated gently."

"I have no time to discuss Charles's failings. Major Johnston has ordered us back to barracks within the hour." He left the room, slamming the door.

Eloise listened to his footsteps clattering on the stairs and heard the thump of his boots as he walked across the floor of his room. With a sigh she reached for the paper and tried to concentrate on some of the poetry that had been submitted, but gave up when she realised she hadn't taken in a word. She set it aside and walked through the open doors on to the veranda.

The smooth lawns ran down to where the sea sparkled as it lapped the sandy shore. Gulls and curlews wheeled above the beach, their cries sharp on the wind. She breathed in the salty air and caught the scent of the roses but it didn't bring the usual solace for her heart was heavy.

She watched the boys kicking a ball about with the convict gardener and his young apprentice, Harry taking the lead as usual. Charles was laughing, his fair hair glinting in the sun as he ran back and forth, his face alight with fun — so different from the wan little boy who quaked in his father's presence.

They seemed content for the moment, but she couldn't help wondering if the boys' closeness had been brought about by the atmosphere in the house. She had tried to keep up a happy façade for their sake, but it was hard when Edward seemed determined to make life difficult.

Eloise wandered down to the beach and, heedless of the damage to her dress, settled down on the sand and burst into tears. She was a prisoner in a web expertly woven by Edward, and his continued fault-finding with their eldest son was more than she could bear.

Castle Hill, 4 March 1804, nine p.m.

The flames rose into the night sky as Cunningham's sleeping quarters burnt. Shouts of "Death or liberty," rang out. It was the signal they had been waiting for and Niall joined in the stampede to overcome the policemen and ransack the government buildings. "Help me break this door in," he yelled, as he reached the armoury. It splintered against the weight of six shoulders and they scrambled in, grabbing guns, ammunition and swords. Hands snatched them as they emerged, and they went back for more.

Niall left the crush and unearthed the pikes he'd hidden behind Cunningham's burning hut. Handing them out, he kept tight hold of the last and forced his way through the pandemonium in search of Cunningham.

Two English convicts had dragged the flogger, Robert Duggan, from his bed and were beating him to a pulp. Muskets were firing, while shouts, smoke and milling men added to the confusion as constables were knocked to the ground and overseers thrashed.

"Call to order," yelled Cunningham, as he leapt on to a barrel and fired his musket into the air. "Discipline will win the day," he shouted, as the men surged round him. "We cannot hope to win our freedom by brawling."

The men stilled, and Niall felt a glow of pride for the man who led them.

"Now we have overcome our gaolers, we will torch Macarthur's farm to draw the Parramatta garrison out of town. Once that is done the rebels there will rise up and set fire to it as a signal they are ready to join us. We will gather at Constitution Hill, then join the Hawkesbury rebels before we march on Sydney."

Niall pushed his way to the front as Cunningham led them away. It would take most of the night to get to Constitution Hill, for they would ransack the farms they passed on the way. But the promised success of the rebellion was heady, and at last he could taste freedom.

Parramatta, ten p.m.

Word of the uprising had reached the garrison within an hour of Cunningham firing his musket. Samuel Marsden, an obvious target of hatred, fled with

Macarthur's family by boat. The air was filled with the roll of drums and muskets shots as the military and private militias were called to duty and convicts were locked in the prison. Governor King arrived shortly after and declared martial law.

Moonrakers, ten thirty p.m.

As the door burst open, the two women dropped their sewing and leapt from their chairs in alarm. "What do you want?" demanded Nell.

"Your guns and ammunition, food and rum," was the reply.

"Food we've got, but you ain't takin' the gun." Nell stood with her back to the door that led to the children's bedrooms.

"You ain't in no position to deny us anything," the drunken man replied. "Search the place, boys."

Nell and Alice watched in growing fury as the kitchen was ransacked, and the rifles were carried off — but as the men advanced further into the house they stood firm. "There's only my children back there," said Nell, "and you ain't goin' anywhere near 'em."

The youngest man nodded. "We have what we came for," he told the others. "There's no pride in frightening women and children."

"They've probably got an arsenal back there — all these farms have at least a dozen rifles. I'm for searchin' proper."

"Where are your men?" asked the Irish youth.

"Due back any minute," lied Nell. "They've gone to shepherd the ewes."

"And your convicts?"

"Asleep out back," she replied.

"Go and rouse them," he ordered the others. "I'll search the rest of the house and join you in a moment." He waited until they had left, then turned again to the women. "My apologies, ladies," he said, with an Irish lilt. "Our revolution is not about frightening women, but I will have to check the other rooms."

Nell eyed him suspiciously. She saw a youth of about fifteen, whose clothes hung from his wiry frame like a scarecrow's. His hair was black, his eyes blue, and the set of his jaw was determined — but at least he was sober and polite. "Keep yer noise down, then," she said. "The children are asleep."

Nell led him down the short corridor, but before she could reach for the latch, the door was flung open.

Amy stood in her nightshift, silhouetted by the lamplight, russet hair tumbling about her shoulders, eyes very blue as they regarded the intruder. "Who are you and what do you want? You've woken everybody up."

"I'm sorry," he blustered, face reddening, "but I need to search for arms."

"If I had a musket I would have used it on you," she retorted.

Nell watched the exchange with some amusement now she knew the boy meant no harm. At thirteen, Amy was growing into a beauty, but she had her mother's fiery temperament and stood no nonsense from anyone. The youth was filled with admiration and trying hard not to show it. If the situation had been less fraught, she might have found it funny.

"Well?" Amy folded her arms. "Are you leaving?"

"I'll wish you all a good night," the boy muttered. Then, as if in defiance, he raised his arm and shouted, "Death or glory. Up the revolution!"

They stood frozen to the spot. The silence was deafening.

He turned a deep puce and ran from the house.

Nell caught Alice's eye and they collapsed with laughter. Amy giggled. "That told us," she spluttered. "God help the revolution if he's in charge."

Constitution Hill, 5 March

Niall and his fellow convicts arrived at Constitution Hill as the sun was breaking over the horizon. Their ransacking of the farms had provided them with muskets, ammunition, food and rum, and most were far from steady on their feet.

Cunningham and his co-conspirator, William Johnston, were still waiting for news from Parramatta. "We will practise drill until we have the signal," shouted Cunningham.

Niall joined the others as more straggled in. "It should have come hours ago," he said to Cavenah. "Do you think we've been betrayed again?" he asked, as they presented arms, marched back and forth in rough formation and loaded their muskets in readiness.

367

The older man shrugged. "Who knows? But at this rate none of us will be fit to fight. I'm exhausted."

Niall was weary too, but the thrill of what they had achieved so far, and the memory of a red-haired girl in a diaphanous nightshift, kept him going.

An hour later Cunningham brought the drill to a halt. "The message couldn't have got through," he told them. "Without the rebels from Parramatta, we are too few so, rather than face the garrison head on, we will march to Greenhills and meet the Hawkesbury rebels there."

The track to Parramatta, six a.m.

Edward's enthusiasm for a good fight had been dampened: Major George Johnston had ordered the twenty-nine members of the Corps and fifty militiamen to march through the night. Impatient, and in the worst of tempers, he kept his horse at a walk along the track and swore vengeance on the Irish bastards who were always causing trouble — and on the major who seemed determined to take the longest time possible to quell them.

As he rode to the sound of tramping feet and jingling harness, his thoughts turned to his own troubles. He'd been demoted because of some nonsense over the rout at Banks Town, and although he had tried to buy his way up through the ranks again his efforts had come to nothing. Not that he could afford to buy a higher rank, he thought bitterly. Money was tight, and he'd had to sell even more of his land. Several business ventures had failed because someone else had got in first, and his gambling debts had once again reached an almost obscene amount. He dreaded Henry Carlton calling them in: he would have to sell the bakery and the dry-goods store to raise capital — and doubted that would be enough. Precious few options were open to him. The family fortune had taken a hefty blow following Napoleon's blasted wars, so he couldn't even rely on tapping his father. The baron had made it clear he wouldn't lend him a penny, and Eloise's dowry was long gone.

His hand tightened on the reins. Eloise's coldness was his fault. He should never have lost his temper that night and taken her by force, but her threat to leave him had made him lose all reason. After it was done he had known things could never be the same between them.

Yet his wife constantly surprised him, and he couldn't help but admire her tenacity and strong will. She was tougher than he'd expected, less malleable, but he didn't like the way she seemed able to make him aware of his faults without a word. Her expression showed her contempt, and the chill in the eyes he had once so admired made him uncomfortable.

His thoughts were interrupted by the trooper returning from his reconnaissance.

The rebels had been sighted at Toongabbie. At last. A chance for action. Edward forgot his troubles and spurred his horse into a gallop. As he raced along the track with the other officers, he raised his sword in readiness.

★　★　★

The Irish rebels melted into the darkness, hiding in the bush, running swiftly out of reach. There were too many, and they were too fleet, and as Edward charged back and forth and tried to cut them down, they vanished. He looked for the troopers who should be routing them out, but the foot-soldiers were already exhausted after their enforced march, and their pursuit was half-hearted.

Edward raged at the futility. If Major Johnston had had any sense he'd have had everyone mounted and they could have made short work of killing the bastards. Instead they were thrashing about in the bush, and he was getting filthy and more ill-tempered by the minute.

Major Johnston encouraged his men to pursue the Irish through Toongabbie and Sugar Loaf Hill, but although shots were fired, only one rebel was killed. As they disappeared into the bush, the soldiers gave up and Johnston came to a decision. "The rebels seem to be gathering in the distant hills. I'll despatch the priest to talk to them," he said to Edward. "We must convince them to surrender."

"I doubt they will," replied Edward.

"So do I," sighed the major. "But the priest might slow them down enough for our troops to catch up."

The priest was given a horse and sent on his way. A short while later, he returned, his mission a failure. The rebels had taken up their position on the highest hill in the area, and refused to surrender.

"Come, Cadwallader," said the major. "We will negotiate with them."

370

The thick scrub gave way to a broad clearing at the foot of a steep rise. Edward was startled by the number of rebels gathered there, and that they were armed and orderly. Whoever was in charge of this uprising had certainly picked an advantageous spot: the British troops would be forced to take the hill from the valley floor — and against two hundred armed men stoked with sedition, the odds on success were against them.

"I bring you the governor's offer of clemency if you will surrender," Major Johnston called across the clearing. He waited for the murmur of defiance to quieten. "I challenge your leaders to make themselves known so that we may negotiate."

Two men stepped forward.

"Your names?" barked the major.

"Cunningham and Johnston," was the surly reply.

The major was struck by the coincidence: one bore the same name as himself. "Will you surrender and take this offer of clemency?"

"We will not negotiate with the English army," said Cunningham, "but if you send Father Dixon back to us, we will talk to him."

The major wheeled his horse away. "I will fetch the priest," he said to Edward, "but only because the delay will give our troops more time to assemble."

When they returned with the priest, Edward knew the troopers and militia weren't far behind.

The rebel leaders, Cunningham and Johnston, walked down the hill to meet them in the centre of the glade, the Irish convicts forming ranks behind them.

"I have brought you your priest," said the major. "You have fifteen minutes to talk with him."

Edward sat on his restless horse and watched the black-frocked cleric cross the valley to negotiate a solution to this stand-off that wouldn't end in bloodshed. If he'd had his way, he'd have ordered the troops to circle the hill and advance to the rebels' rear, firing into them and killing as many as possible before they had a chance to regroup. But he wasn't in charge — and the enmity between him and the major meant that his advice would be ignored.

Time was up and the rebel leaders, Cunningham and Johnston, once again approached the major, who had now dismounted and was striding impatiently back and forth. "We will not surrender," said Cunningham.

"Then what *do* you want?" The major's face showed his fury.

"Death or liberty!" Johnston shouted, raising his arm to a roar of approval from his followers. "And a ship to take us home to Ireland."

The major drew his pistol swiftly and held it to the Irishman's head.

Edward did the same to Cunningham as the redcoats appeared in the valley.

"Charge and fire!" ordered the major.

Niall fired his musket and fumbled to reload as the troopers advanced across the clearing. He knew the rebels outnumbered the militia, but the redcoats were capable of firing their prepared rounds swiftly and efficiently. He stumbled back and fired again.

372

With the precision and economy of movement that comes with military training, the redcoats formed rank upon rank, interchanging, loading and firing as they advanced on the untrained and frightened convicts.

Niall felt the sting as a bullet traced heat across his cheek. Then his musket jammed. Leaderless and unprepared for the onslaught, the men around him were throwing down their pikes, staves and spent muskets and running for cover. Niall glanced towards their leaders who still had pistols to their heads and knew it was over. He ran with the others.

Edward was forced to watch the rout from a distance, his pistol still jammed against Cunningham's temple. His anger made his finger twitch on the trigger.

"Pull that, Captain Cadwallader, and I'll hang you for murder," snarled the major.

Edward swallowed. Johnston's eyes missed nothing, and his loathing was almost tangible. Edward had little doubt the threat would be carried out if he disobeyed.

The redcoats ceased firing. The battle had taken a quarter of an hour and the rebels had fled. Only a few of their wounded and dead remained.

"Round up all you can find and take them prisoner, the wounded as well." The major released the Irish leaders into the custody of the sergeant-at-arms.

Edward dug his spurs into his horse and galloped to where the wounded and dying lay. He heard a moan of anguish, and ran the man through with his sword.

Others followed suit, but they were spotted by the major who rode towards them, firing his pistol over their heads. "I'll shoot any man guilty of murder," he yelled. "Take the prisoners alive."

Edward spurred his horse into the bush in search of any rebels who might be hiding there. He would finish them off out of sight of Johnston.

Niall ran until his chest ached and his legs refused to carry him any further. He had seen Cavenah fall, cut down as he limped from the scene of battle by the soldier on horseback. Now the man was after him, drawing closer by the minute.

He looked wildly for cover, dived beneath the fronds of a spreading fern and clawed his way into the shadows until he was hidden by the bushes. He lay there, trying not to breathe too heavily, for he knew he would be heard.

The horse thundered past. Niall heard the soldier swear, the return of the hoofs, slower now, the swish of blade through grass.

Niall's heart hammered as he continued to crawl through the tangle of ferns and lantana, and found a hollow at the heart of his hiding-place where death by snake or venomous spider might come at any moment.

The horse walked towards him. It paused, and there was silence. He heard a sword hack at the grass and overhanging ferns.

Niall pressed himself into the earth and prayed to the Virgin.

"I know you're there, you little bastard," muttered the soldier. The sword slashed at branches and shrubs.

374

Niall squeezed his eyes shut as the sword hacked at a branch just above his hip.

The soldier swore. After another slash at the grass, he moved on. The sound of hoofs faded.

Niall released his breath, but remained hidden in the dark, dank hole beneath the ferns. The soldier was clever, and might be waiting to ambush him.

He huddled in the darkness, flinching at every rustle in the surrounding cover. The whole enterprise had been a disaster, despite careful planning. Good men had been killed or captured and the reprisals would be swift and cruel. Would he ever be free? Deliberately he turned his thoughts to the girl with the red hair. She reminded him of his sister, for they shared the same fiery spirit. Would he see either of them again?

As night fell and the moon rose, he judged it safe to make his escape. He crept out into the stillness of the bush, glanced over his shoulder and ran full tilt into the arms of two troopers.

New South Wales, 6 March

Governor King's retribution was swift. Phillip Cunningham was hanged from the outside staircase of the public store at Greenhills that afternoon. The other leaders were tried before a judicial panel that took less than fifteen minutes to find them guilty. Six were hanged immediately.

William Johnston was hanged from the tree that stood in a small hollow on the road between Prospect and Parramatta, his body left in chains in the centre of town as a reminder to all of what happened to seditionists. Yet the story of the uprising would live on, and the site of the short-lived battle became known as Rouse Hill, or Vinegar Hill in honour of the Irish battle at Wexford.

Kernow House, Watsons Bay, 7 March 1804

Edward returned home and regaled Eloise with the lurid details. "I would have preferred Governor King to wipe out all of them," he said, as he finished dinner.

Eloise didn't reply, and he looked at her sharply. She was pale and had hardly touched her food, but as she had always accused him of keeping her ill-informed, she could hardly complain now when his exploits upset her.

"King was wise to punish the leaders heavily, but he made a mistake in flogging the others and sending them to the coal-fields at Newcastle, or to Norfolk Island where they will only incite more rebellion."

"What of the men who followed Cunningham and the others? I have heard there were Englishmen, and even free men, such as Charles Hill, among their number."

Edward threw his linen napkin on the table and, without asking Eloise's permission, lit a cigar. "King was being pragmatic, letting most of them of with a hundred lashes. After all, more than two hundred were involved in the uprising — almost half the work-force at the government farm — and he couldn't afford to lose such a number when the colony needs feeding."

"And the priest?" Eloise's eyes were shadowed with distress.

"Father Dixon was made to put his hands on the raw backs of the flogged men to remind him never to take part in a rebellion again."

Eloise blanched, and Edward felt a glow of satisfaction. She wouldn't question him about his work again.

Castle Hill, 10 March 1804

Niall almost bit through his lip as the lash flayed his back. He had long since lost count of the strokes. He closed his eyes as the chains kept him pressed to the flogging tree and tried to find escape deep inside himself. None of the others had cried out, and although he was among the youngest, he would not allow his age to excuse any sign of weakness.

At last Marsden ordered him untied, and although he wanted to walk proudly from the tree, his legs wouldn't hold him. Rough hands threw him into the cart, and as it trundled over the rough ground he felt it jar every inch of his battered body.

The surgeon smeared something on the cuts that stung like a thousand bees, and roughly wound a bandage round his torso before he was given another shirt and ordered back to work.

The overseer showed him no quarter as he struggled to lift the heavy tools in the forge, but Niall remained silent despite the agony. The so-called justice that had been meted out to the rebels had forced him to take stock of his position in this land of torture and starvation. The cruellest irony was that the bite of the lash had taught him an invaluable lesson, which would probably save his life. Although he still burnt with hatred for the government, he had come to realise that his enemy could never be beaten. He would keep the desire for revenge in his heart, serve his time and ignore future plots. He would be more of a challenge to the English if he was alive and free.

PART FOUR

Revelations

CHAPTER
SIXTEEN

Van Diemen's Land, July 1804

"I wish we'd discovered this place," said George. "Ebor Bunker had the devil's luck to be asked to join the settlement expedition at the end of last year. To think we've missed out on all those whales."

Herbert Finlayson, his second in command, stood beside him and looked towards the huddle of shacks that lined the Derwent estuary. "I heard he caught three, but the *Albion's* a speedy vessel and Bunker always had an eye for opportunity."

"I still don't understand why Governor King didn't ask me," said George. "The *Atlantica* is just as fast, and it would have been an adventure."

Herbert laughed. "Still hungry for adventure after all this time, George? Samuel certainly picked the right man to inherit his ships."

George felt the familiar twist of sadness. "He would have been as disappointed as I am to lose the chance to escort the expedition and enter the history books. He and Ebor were old rivals."

"Doesn't look much of a place," said Herbert, as he scanned the ramshackle settlement. "I feel sorry for the few hardy souls that were sent here. It's even more isolated than New South Wales."

"That's probably why they decided to build a fort here. No convict could ever escape in these waters. They'd freeze to death."

Herbert put down the telescope to take a pinch of snuff. "When do you imagine we'll return to Sydney Town?"

George kept his gaze on the estuary. The thought of Sydney and Eloise was never far from his mind, and he still dreaded arriving at the harbour. "In about two months," he said quietly. Then he smiled. Herbert had met a girl on his last shore leave and was impatient to return to her. "She'll be waiting for you," he said.

"We've been away for a long time," Herbert reminded him. "She might have found someone else and be married by now."

George stared at the shoreline. "It happens," he said, the pain of his loss as sharp today as ever it had been. "But if she truly loves you she'll wait."

Herbert nodded, but George could see the man was suffering. He tugged his collar up to his chin for the wind was bitter. "Go below and see to the docking," he said. "Then rustle up some warm drinks before we disembark. I doubt there will be much on the island. The settlement's too newly founded."

As Herbert left the wheelhouse, George concentrated on steering the *Atlantica* safely into harbour. That done, he watched as the men swarmed over the deck and tied her up. A small welcoming party had arrived on the quay, and he decided to let Herbert do the honours — he had little desire to be sociable today.

He leant against the wheel and contemplated the mountain that soared above the fledgling town, its peak lost in the clouds. The latest letter from Thomas Morely had been handed over by the crew of the *Porpoise*, another of his whaling ships, and its contents had worried him.

Thomas was now the proud father of three small girls. His dislike of Edward Cadwallader hadn't diminished, and he saw no reason to keep to himself his concern for Eloise's well-being. According to Thomas, the marriage was a sham. Edward was away most of the time, and Eloise was a shadow of her former self. She rarely came into the town, saw her sisters only when her husband was absent, and stayed with her children in the house by the shore. Edward's debts were mounting, his reputation in danger of being ruined along with his fortune because of the rumours surrounding a certain rout at Banks Town and his dubious business dealings. It was well known in the mess that his temper was erratic, and even his coterie of loyal followers were deserting him.

George dug into his pocket for his pipe. All attempts by his family to see Edward brought to justice over Florence's untimely death had failed. The army looked after its own — but it wouldn't turn a completely blind eye especially since Edward had been demoted.

As for Eloise, she was the love of George's life, and he hated to think she was unhappy. But he could do nothing about it, for it had to be her decision to leave

Edward. Eloise knew she could always contact him, that a passing ship would relay her message and he would be back for her immediately. But there had been no word from her since that day in the glade by the beach — and he had to accept that her unhappiness, real or imagined by Thomas, could not be strong enough for her to run away from her marriage.

He read the letter again, and frowned. He had the feeling that a deeper message lay between the lines — there was urgency and true concern in the hastily penned words.

He puffed at the pipe as the men went ashore and tried to make sense of it. The *Atlantica* would be here for just long enough to build a try-works in the nearby cove so they could boil the blubber more efficiently than they could on board. Then they would return to New South Wales.

George came to a decision. He couldn't avoid her any longer, and for his own peace of mind he had to see her. On his return to Sydney Town he would take a horse along the beach at Watsons Bay. Eloise had once told him she liked to ride there in the early mornings. It would be the perfect place to catch her alone and discover the truth for himself.

Hawks Head Farm, August 1804

Mandaway leant on his crutch and roared with laughter as the boys tried to catch the piglets and return them to the pens. They were such a funny sight, grabbing the air as the piglets shot between their legs.

"It's good to hear you laugh, Mandawuy," said Ezra, as he joined him by the fence. "You'll soon be well enough to join in the fun, but that leg must heal properly first."

Mandawuy stopped smiling. He could now understand what the old man was saying, for he'd stayed many moons at Hawks Head — but he rarely replied in the same language. "I must return to my people," he said, in his own tongue. "Your ways are not mine."

"Can we not persuade you to change your mind?" Ezra's voice was soft. "Here you will have food, shelter and work, and our natives will welcome you if you wish to join them."

Mandawuy watched the naked boys racing about the yard. Ezra spoke the truth, which was strange, because he hadn't expected to make friends with these blacks who lived in harmony with whites. They had made a point of offering friendship, and had spoken well of the whites who protected them. It was all very confusing. Mandawuy's experience of the white man had come from the massacre at the Place of the Honeybee Dreaming, and the raids on the farms where they had been met with bullets and whips.

Ezra seemed able to read his thoughts. "Not all white men are cruel to your people, Mandawuy. Susan heals the sick and teaches the children, and I, in my small way, try to bring them into the Church of God. We are all His children, Mandawuy, black and white, and therefore it is our duty to lead them on the right path to His Kingdom."

Mandawuy had discovered that Ezra was a special man — a white Elder with great wisdom — so he had listened politely as Ezra told his stories. However, they made little sense to him, and seemed strange compared to those he'd learnt as a child — which made him restless to return to his people. "I will hunt for food, and the earth is my shelter," he replied. "I have no need of your God."

"Susan will be sad," said Ezra, as his wife came to join them. "She has grown fond of you."

Mandawuy looked shyly at the woman who had treated him so kindly. He would miss her, for he had come to like her even though she smelt different from the woman of his tribe and wore such strange clothes.

"It's time we got you out of this sun," she said. "Let me help you."

He was angry with himself for feeling affection for a white woman — furious that he'd been weakened by her kindness and soft voice. He shifted the crutches and tried to put his weight on the damaged leg. He was growing stronger every day, and the pain had dulled to an ache that was bearable until he tried to walk unaided. He hissed with annoyance.

"Come," coaxed Susan. "Lean on me."

Mandawuy shrugged off her hand and made his way across the clearing to the shade of a pepper tree. He threw down the crutches, sagged to the ground and glared as she followed him. "Woman alonga boss," he shouted. "Mandawuy warrior. No want woman like piccaninny."

386

"Suit yourself," she replied, and smiled. "Food will be on the table in ten minutes, so if you're determined to fend for yourself, you can come and fetch it."

Mandawuy stared moodily into the distance. The sooner he left the better it would be, for he was growing soft in this place — just like the other natives who lived here. He wondered what had happened to Tedbury and the others, for it seemed they had abandoned him. He'd heard Susan and Ezra discussing a raid at another farm further up the river, but he hadn't understood all they had said, and had been too proud to ask them to explain. Now, it seemed, Tedbury had disappeared into the bush and didn't care what had become of him. It was hard to accept he hadn't mattered enough for his hero to come and find him — and even harder to accept that he liked living here with these white people.

The smell of meat cooking made his mouth water and he looked longingly at the table where the others were gathering. He reached for the hated crutches and hauled himself upright. All this thinking had given him an appetite.

George was standing on the quay at Port Jackson, shouting orders to his men as they hauled the heavy barrels of whale oil from the hold, wrestling with the ropes and pulleys so that they landed without splitting. There were twenty more to come, but the men were eager to be ashore and becoming careless as time dragged by.

"Mind what you're doing, you fools!" he yelled, as a barrel swung over his head and crashed against the mast. "Get it steady before you try to swing 'er or we'll drown in blubber."

He heard a polite cough behind him — knew who it was — and let rip with the foulest of language to prove he wouldn't be intimidated.

"It seems I have chosen an inappropriate moment to approach you, Mr Collinson."

George glared at Jonathan Cadwallader. "It's always inappropriate where you and your family are concerned," he snapped. "Leave me to my work."

"I will stay here until you have the decency to give me a moment of your attention."

"What do you want?" Another barrel swung out over the side of the *Atlantica*. "Pull the bloody rope, you idiot," he bellowed. "Don't let it hang loose like that."

Jonathan moved round him until he was between George and the ship. "I want your undivided attention for one moment."

"Stand there and you're likely to get the undivided attention of the barrel that's swinging over your head," retorted George.

Jonathan seemed unfazed. "Is your mother still at Hawks Head Farm?"

"What's it to you?"

"I have a letter for her from England."

"Give it to me." George stuck out his hand. "I'm going there tomorrow, and will pass it on."

"I think not," said Jonathan, his expression unreadable. "Despite your incivility you have given me the answer to my question. I bid you good day."

388

George watched him walk down the quay, and was tempted to follow him. His mother would not appreciate a visit from that man, regardless of the letter's content. He hesitated as Cadwallader marched into the livery stable and was about to chase after him when there was a warning yell from the deck.

"Look out!"

George side-stepped, but wasn't quick enough.

The barrel plummeted, to hit the cobbles within inches of his boots. A geyser of whale oil shot into the air and covered him from head to foot. He stood there as his men roared with laughter and didn't see the joke at all, for now he couldn't possibly stop Cadwallader.

Eloise had spent the morning with her father, and at his suggestion they had left the hotel and were now bowling along in his carriage for a breath of fresh air after luncheon. Charles and Harry were sitting beside the driver, and Oliver was in his grandfather's arms.

"This young man has too much energy," the baron puffed, as he struggled to stop the child falling over the side. "I wish now we'd brought your girl to look after him. I shall be exhausted by the end of this outing."

Eloise took Oliver, sat him on her lap and gave him a biscuit. "Meg's courting, Papa — and, anyway, you wouldn't miss having the boys for an afternoon."

He studied her thoughtfully. "You need a rest, Eloise," he rumbled. "You don't look yourself — far too thin."

She forced a smile and tried to ignore the pain in her side where Edward had punched her the night before.

It had been a swift blow, delivered in a fit of temper as he'd pushed past her to reach the decanter. "It's all the running around I do to keep this one out of mischief," she said lightly.

"Hmph." His brows knitted as he leant towards her, his gaze penetrating. "You might think you can fool me, Eloise, but I know you too well. Something is wrong."

"Papa . . . please don't spoil our afternoon."

He folded his hands over his belly. "There's always a home for you and the boys with me. You need not remain with him."

Her eyes widened. She had thought to keep her misery hidden from him. "Thank you, Papa," she said quietly, aware that Charles and Harry were within earshot, "but I'm just tired."

Oliver was squirming in her lap and she bent to place him on the floor of the carriage, giving herself time to quell the urge to tell him everything.

"By Gad, Eloise, it's Jonathan Cadwallader," boomed her father.

Startled, Eloise turned to look at the rider who was galloping up behind them.

"Jonathan!" he shouted. He tapped the driver's shoulder with his cane. "Stop the carriage."

Eloise felt a chill as the earl pulled up his horse beside them. She couldn't bear to look at him — not now that she knew he had deceived her over Edward's true character.

"Jonathan," bellowed the baron, as he lurched to his feet. The carriage-springs protested. "I didn't know you'd returned from England. How are you, my friend?"

Jonathan raised his hat to Eloise, who made the barest acknowledgement.

The baron grabbed his hand and pumped it so enthusiastically that the carriage bounced and the two older boys were almost thrown off their perch beside the driver. "When can you come to dinner? Tonight? Tomorrow?"

"It is good to see you again, old friend, but I cannot accept for a while yet. I have a matter of some urgency to deal with, which might take a few days."

"Intrigue, eh?" The baron's ruddy face grew rosier as he winked and grinned. "Tell me, who is she?"

Eloise saw that Jonathan's smile was tight and unnatural, his manner less relaxed than she remembered. It was clear that he was in a hurry.

"I'm afraid I must disappoint you, Oskar," he said, gathering the reins to leave. "I need to see an old, dear friend for I have discovered something on my travels that cannot be ignored." He glanced at Eloise and frowned as she maintained a frosty silence.

"That sounds most mysterious," muttered the baron. Then he realised that Eloise had not spoken. "Come, my dear. Will you not welcome Jonathan home?"

She was saved from having to speak by Harry, who was talking very loudly and at great speed to the grandfather he'd never met before. Charles and he were vying for Jonathan's attention. Eloise gathered up Oliver and plumped him on her knee.

Jonathan's gaze rested on her. "You are to be congratulated, Eloise. You have three fine boys."

Eloise nodded, but wouldn't look him in the eye.

"So, tell us, Jonathan. What is it you discovered that can't wait another moment?"

"I'm afraid I'm not at liberty to tell you, Oskar. But I will say that my search in England led me on a journey of discovery — and now I must tell the one person to whom it will matter most."

Eloise looked at him, curiosity overcoming reluctance.

"I will bid you all good day," said Jonathan, and tipped his hat to Eloise. He ruffled the elder boys' hair, and grinned. "I will come to see you scallywags in a day or two," he promised. Then he galloped away, leaving a cloud of dust in his wake.

Mandawuy could walk without crutches now, but he tired easily and his leg still ached if he went far. He stood alone in the yard, staring out at the bush. Susan and Ezra didn't keep him prisoner, and the frustration of not knowing what had happened to Tedbury — and why they hadn't come for him — was wearing him down. Yet he was torn. To leave or not? It was a question he'd asked himself every day, and time had weakened his resolve.

He limped out of the yard and walked slowly along the riverbank, trawling the fast-running water for fish. They grew fat in this water, and it was a good time of day to catch them, for the sun was in the west and the reeds cast long shadows. He eased out his leg as he squatted in the grass, his attention on the flash of silver he'd spotted in the shallows. His hunting spear was light in his hand as he raised it, balanced perfectly for the short flight.

"Mandawuy, who's that?"

The fish darted away and he spat with fury. Susan had approached quietly enough, but her voice had lost him his catch. "Why you talk when Mandawuy alonga fish? Fish alonga rivva — no catch 'im now."

"It doesn't matter," she said, as she shielded her eyes and looked into the distance. "Can you make out who that is, Mandawuy? Your eyes are better than mine."

He followed her pointing finger, saw the horseman and shook his head. "Man alonga you, big hurry."

"Yes." Susan frowned. "He's riding that poor horse as if the devil were after him." She sighed. "I hope he isn't bringing bad news."

They stood together by the river, the white woman and the black youth, and watched the rider approach. Mandawuy fingered his hunting spear, ready to protect her should their visitor prove unfriendly.

The man was shouting something, and waving his hand, but he was still too far away for them to make out what he was saying. Mandawuy tightened his grip on the spear, for Susan had turned pale.

"Susan!" The rider's voice drifted to them over the sound of the hoof-beats.

"Jonathan." Her hand flew to cover her mouth. "What on earth . . ."

Mandawuy had thought she was fearful, but he'd been wrong. Something deeper and stronger drew her towards the man on the horse, and her face glowed. His grip on the spear loosened.

The horse was foamed with sweat as it raced towards them and the man on its back stood in the stirrups, waving his hat and calling her name. Then, as if in slow motion, the mare's delicate foreleg sank into the ground.

The horse gave a shriek of pain and pitched on to its neck.

The man, already unbalanced, was tossed into the air over the animal's head. He hit the ground and was still.

"Jonathan!" Susan began to run.

Mandawuy hobbled after her, amazed that such an old white woman could move so fast, and annoyed that he couldn't keep up with her. The horse had got to its feet, but its front leg hung awkwardly, and it was obviously in pain.

Susan threw herself on to the ground, her hands fluttering above the prone figure as though she was afraid to touch him. "Jonathan?" she whispered. "Jonathan, can you hear me?"

Mandawuy stood and watched, unsure what to do. The man was pale, and his eyes were closed. Was he dead?

"Jonathan?" Susan touched his face and the eyes opened. "Thank God," she breathed. She took his hand and kissed it, then held it to her heart.

Jonathan was looking at her. "Susan," he said, "my dearest love."

"Don't talk," she pleaded. "Rest while Mandawuy goes for help."

394

Mandawuy knew he should fetch someone, but curiosity held him there.

"Why did you lie to me?" Jonathan's fingers brushed her cheek.

"I don't know what you mean," she sobbed. She looked up at Mandawuy, her eyes brimming with tears. "Get help! Go!"

Mandawuy took a step back, but he had no intention of leaving just yet. This was far too interesting.

Jonathan's hand dropped from her face and he fought for breath. "It was only one lie," he panted. "But it was the cruellest." His breath rattled in his chest.

Susan's face was leached of colour as she bent over him. "It wasn't meant to be cruel, my love," she murmured. "I didn't want to, but I was afraid that if you knew the truth it would destroy any love you had for me."

His gaze held her as he struggled to breathe. "Never," he panted. "It was too strong for that." He tried to touch her again, but didn't seem to have the energy. "I found her, Susan. I found our daughter . . ."

"She's alive?" Susan grasped his hand.

Jonathan remained silent, his breath coming in jagged gasps.

"Tell me about her," she said urgently. "Jonathan, please. Speak to me."

"She looks like you," he murmured, and was still.

"No," cried Susan, and flung herself across him. "You can't leave me — not now," she raged. "Jonathan — you must tell me where she is. Please, my love.

Please! I've already lost one daughter. Don't condemn me to losing another."

Mandawuy took a step back as Susan stormed and pummelled the dead man's chest. It was as if the Spirits had filled her head, and he didn't like this different Susan.

"Susan, whatever is the matter?" Ezra was hurrying towards them through the grass. He reached Mandawuy and his face paled. Susan didn't notice him, for she had gathered the dead man into her arms and was rocking him as if he were a baby. "What happened here, Mandawuy?"

"Man alonga horse fast, fast. Horse fall, man alonga crash ground."

"He was coming to see me," said Susan, as she raised her tear-streaked face.

"Why? What possible reason could that man have to come here?"

"He had news from Ann, your sister-in-law," she said, as she tried to stem her tears, "but he died before he could tell me what it was."

Mandawuy frowned. He must have misunderstood the scene he'd witnessed, for Susan's telling of it wasn't how he would have described it. He looked from Susan to Ezra in confusion. He would never understand these white people.

Ezra had been followed swiftly by others. The horse was shot to put it out of its misery, and Jonathan's body was lifted into the back of a wagon. Susan walked behind it, a solitary figure weighed down with grief.

396

Mandawuy watched them until they turned into the yard and were lost to sight. He had learnt a great many things from these good people — things he would carry with him always. It had been proved to him that black and white could live together, that they shared the same fears and joys — but not all whites were like Ezra and Susan, and his people must be wary.

With one final glance towards the homestead, Mandawuy took the first step in his long journey north. It was time to go home.

CHAPTER
SEVENTEEN

Kernow House, Watsons Bay, September 1804

Edward sat in the drawing room, deep in thought. A good fire was blazing in the hearth to chase away the chill of winter, the curtains were closed and the boom of the sea was muffled in the distance. Eloise and the boys were visiting her father and the house was quiet.

He frowned as he eyed the stack of letters the servant had brought in. He would read them later. Leaning back in the chair he gazed into the fire and thought about his father. His death had come as a terrible shock, the news broken by a rider who'd been sent from Hawks Head — though what Jonathan had been doing there remained a mystery. Edward had had barely enough time to gather his wits before his father's body was brought to town on the back of a wagon. The funeral had been held the same night.

With a deep sigh, Edward thought back on that strange day. The Collinsons had not stayed for the service, and Eloise had refused to attend. He had stood with the baron beside the hole in the ground as the minister droned through the service, unable to take in what had happened. He wished he could mourn. But the years of hurt his father had caused him by ignoring him in childhood and bringing about his exile were too firmly entrenched. Yet now he was gone he felt a great sense of loss. He pondered on the irony that perhaps his hatred had been a form of love — for love and hate were close allies.

He turned his attention to the letter with the all-too-familiar seal. It was time to read his father's will.

"Papa is not faring well," said Eloise, as she came into the room some time later, bringing the scent of salt air with her. "Charles and Harry tried to cheer him, but he is deeply saddened by your father's passing."

Edward looked up from the will. He had barely registered a word she'd said for he was numb with shock. "He's betrayed me."

Eloise eyed him warily. "Who has betrayed you?"

"Father," he said hoarsely.

"How?" she asked. "He's dead."

"In his will."

"I don't understand," she whispered. She was trembling with fear as she took a step back from him.

Edward's rage made him almost incoherent. He snatched up the letter that had accompanied the will and waved it in her face. "The two merchant ships were sunk off Cairo by Napoleon's invading fleet and all cargo was lost. His neglect of the estates has meant they're in ruins, and the farms haven't been profitable in years."

He gritted his teeth. "There is some money tied up in the London property and, of course, the land and villages in Cornwall will always provide some income — but it won't be much."

"Perhaps you could use the fortune you've made here to return the estates to their full potential?"

"Don't be stupid, woman!" he snapped. "What I have wouldn't begin to repair the damage my father has done." He flung the papers at her. "And that's not the half of it. Read the will and see for yourself."

He strode to the table and poured himself a large quantity of brandy, knocked it back and poured more.

When she finally looked up from the papers, her face was pale, her eyes huge with anxiety. "There must be some way round this," she said nervously. "Perhaps if you went to London . . ."

"And do what? Go cap in hand to the lawyer and beg him to let me have the last few guineas he's holding in trust for the boys? Get him to ignore the deeds and covenants with which he's so neatly tied up everything for the rest of my damned life?" He emptied his glass and poured still more. "My father was always a devious bastard, and his will proves he was determined to best me even in death," he ground out. "He has put everything of worth into trust for the boys so all I inherit is a ruin in Cornwall and a worthless title."

"But it says that there is an income for life from the trust," she said, "and we live comfortably here. With your other interests it should be enough."

Edward flung the glass into the grate where it exploded into fragments. "Damn you, Eloise! Haven't you been listening to me?" He stood over her, gripping her arms. "I was counting on my inheritance. How the

400

hell was I to know my father would bypass me for my sons and leave me with little less than pocket change?" He pushed her away.

"What have you done, Edward?"

"I've borrowed against my inheritance," he said. He turned his back to lean on the mantelpiece. "The promise of a title and estates in England are always good for a loan." He clenched his fists and took a deep breath. "I never suspected he'd leave me a pittance."

"How could you rely on your inheritance when your father might have lived for many more years?" she asked.

He moved away from the fireplace and dug his hands into his pockets to stop himself hitting her. "I'm going out."

"Edward, wait." She reached out to him in entreaty.

"I've told you enough." He left the room, strode out of the house to the stables and yelled at the convict to ready his horse.

Then he swung into the saddle, dug in the spurs and galloped for the beach. He had to find some way out of this disastrous mess before his meeting with Carlton at the end of the week. A fast ride along the sands would clear his head — he would need all his wits about him if he was to avoid ruin.

Sydney Barracks, six days later, September 1804

"I don't know what to do," he said, as he paced the private apartment at the barracks. "There's nothing in the pot and I'm to meet Carlton in a few hours."

"I tried to warn you," muttered Willy Baines, "but, as usual my advice went unheeded."

Edward didn't like the smugness in the other man's tone, yet he had to accept the accusation as correct. The need to beat Carlton at cards had become an obsession and, as the debts had grown and his business ventures had failed, its grip had tightened.

He licked his lips, hating what he was about to do but knowing he had no choice.

"I don't suppose you could lend me fifty guineas? I've dug you out of trouble often enough and you must have a fair amount hidden away." He was aware of how desperate he sounded, but he had to do something to stall Carlton's demands for payment.

The harsh laughter held little humour. "Where would I get that sort of money? I have no estate or private income — unlike some. You'll have to sell some of your fancy horses — or that house at Watsons Bay."

"Never."

Willy shrugged. "Pride won't pay your debts," he said, with the carelessness of a man who had little sympathy and nothing to lose. "Carlton would take the house off your hands in return for your letters of debt, and the sale of the horses would leave you enough to start again." His smile was a barely veiled sneer. "It wouldn't hurt you to experience how the rest of us have to survive on army pay."

Edward's fury rose. "How *dare* you speak to me like that? Your insolence is intolerable."

"It ain't me on me uppers, Captain and I'll remind you that I know too much for you to do anything about my 'insolence', as you call it." He put on his cap. "Carlton was always gunna get you one day — we both knew it but you was too cocksure to admit it." He headed for the door.

"You have *not* been dismissed!" roared Edward.

Willy turned. "I've asked for a transfer to Van Diemen's Land," he said. "As from today, you ain't my commandin' officer."

Edward sank into the chair, his head in his hands. During the past couple of years his close-knit troop had disintegrated and with Willy's departure the rest would follow. "Let them all rot in Port Phillip or Van Diemen's Land, or whatever hell-hole they've gone to — I'll survive without them."

He listened to the distant sounds outside, feeling the chill of isolation. He could no longer trust anyone. His thoughts meandered, turning repeatedly to his father and the devastating blow he'd delivered by leaving everything to the boys.

The chime of his pocket-watch stirred him. Carlton would be on his way to the meeting-place, and he had nothing to offer him. All he could do was hope — but he had a nasty feeling time had run out.

The French Jew, James Larra, had been picked up in London for trading in stolen goods but, like Oskar von Eisen, he'd seen the opportunities to be had in Australia and, on his emancipation, had taken up his land grant and built an inn at Parramatta. The sale of drink was profitable, and he had fast gained a reputation for the fine food he served. Edward wasn't surprised to see that Henry Carlton had ordered dinner while he waited.

"You look like a man with a great deal on his mind," he said, as Edward threw himself into the chair opposite. "Would you care for some food?"

The thought of eating made Edward nauseous. "I'll just have some wine," he said, taking the bottle and pouring himself a generous measure.

Henry Carlton finished the perfectly grilled fish, set aside his cutlery and dabbed his lips with a linen napkin. "Let's get our business out of the way quickly so that we can relax." He leant back in his chair, his posture that of a man perfectly at ease. Only the steeliness in his eyes told Edward that he was running out of patience. "Have you my money?"

Edward found that his hand was shaking as he took a sip of wine, and quickly placed the glass back on the table. "I am in mourning for my father," he said, his face set in suitable solemnity. "Discussing money at such a time borders on vulgarity."

Something shifted in Carlton's eyes. "Vulgar or not, sir, you owe me more than five hundred guineas."

"I need more time."

"You've had plenty."

"But it will take weeks to settle my father's affairs. Once that is done you will be paid."

"I think not," said Carlton. "Your sons are his main beneficiaries." His gaze was steady and impersonal.

Edward stared at him. "How did you know that?"

"My contacts are many and varied. Lawyer's clerks are not well paid. So, where is my money?"

"I don't have it."

The grey eyes regarded him coldly. "I suspected as much. How do you propose to settle your debt?"

"I have horses, good bloodstock. They must be worth close to a hundred guineas."

"I have my own horses."

"I own a bakery and two grog-shops in the town. They aren't worth much as property, but they make a good profit."

"I have no wish to go into trade."

A trickle of sweat ran down Edward's spine. "There's my house."

The smile didn't reach the grey eyes. "Ah, yes. I hear it's very fine. Quite grand for these parts."

Hope kindled. "It is indeed," Edward said hurriedly. "Built of the finest materials, with three acres of grounds and a stable-yard. It's sturdy and strong and has a magnificent view of the ocean."

"I'm sure," Carlton murmured. "I hear also that the plaster mouldings are exquisite, and the chandeliers were imported from Italy."

"The cast-iron fire-grates came from England," Edward said eagerly.

Carlton seemed unmoved, and unhurriedly poured more wine as the Frenchman cut a fresh cigar and lit it for him. Having savoured both wine and cigar, he returned to Edward. "It would be a shame to deprive your wife and children of their home," he said.

Edward was now sweating profusely, despite the sharp wind that whistled through every notch in the ship-lap walls. "I will provide another," he said quickly. "It might not be as grand, but it will have to do until I can afford better."

Carlton's expression was unreadable. "You have made a great deal of money from your business enterprises over the years. The monopoly you and other officers hold over the sale of rum must provide a healthy income," he said. "Why do you persist in lying about your capacity to pay your debts?"

"I have expenses," Edward admitted. "The income barely covers them, and although the trade is brisk, it is spread among many." He hated the humiliation of laying himself bare before this man — hated to admit that he'd failed in everything he'd touched. "So, you see," he said, with as much calm as he could muster, "I haven't lied."

Silence fell, and as it stretched, Edward fidgeted. Carlton was toying with him. "The house, the horses and the shops are all I have to offer. Take one or all of them, and the debt will be cleared."

"I have no need of a house," Carlton said, as he finished the cigar and crushed it in a glass dish. "My lodgings are adequate, and I plan to leave for my farm in Cape Town by the end of next year."

"Then what *do* you want?" Edward balled his fists, tempted to drag the man from his chair and pummel him until he was pulp. Yet he knew he must control himself. This was not Eloise, who could be beaten into submission, and to use his fists would serve little purpose: the debt would remain.

"Everything," Carlton said quietly.

"But you said . . ."

406

"I didn't refuse your offers, merely pointed out that I have no need of shops, horses or a house — but they are assets that can be sold. Your debt has been mounting over the past year, and although it was initially five hundred guineas, by my reckoning the interest on that will bring it to seven." The gaze was level, the expression stony. "Do you have seven hundred guineas, Cadwallader?"

Edward shook his head. "But if you take everything how will I live?"

"You seem to have forgotten you have a wife and sons, Cadwallader. You appear unconcerned as to their welfare."

"Then at least leave me with enough to build another house for them," he pleaded.

"Another monument to your vanity?" he sneered.

Edward's thoughts whirled. "Vanity or not, I must provide a home for my family."

"You should have thought of that before," said Carlton. "How do you think those poor souls managed when you blackmailed and cheated them out of their farms and businesses? Did you give a moment's thought to their children? Your greed is as great as your vanity, and I take pleasure in being the architect of your downfall."

"How do you know so much about my affairs?" Edward felt his skin crawl.

"I have discovered much about you and your dealings, Cadwallader. I have made it my business to do so." He held up his hand to silence Edward's protest.

"You are unscrupulous, unprincipled, a liar and a cheat."

Edward had nothing to say in defence.

"My skills do not rest with cards alone," Carlton said. "The Americans have a saying, that if you don't know who the fool is at the card table it is yourself. Have you suffered any unexplained business losses recently? Or found that someone else has got in before you when you were about to sign a deal? Perhaps the man you thought was keen to do business with you suddenly sold up and moved on."

The words rang in Edward's head. "That was you?"

Carlton smiled. "It was indeed."

"But how?"

"That is for me to know," he replied. "Suffice it to say, I have always been one step ahead of you, and it's been gratifying to see you squirm."

"Why me?" demanded Edward. "What have I done to you to deserve this?"

There was a long silence as Carlton regarded him with undisguised loathing. "Cast your mind back to your schooldays. Do you remember an Arthur Wilmott?"

Edward felt chilled. He did indeed remember the rather sickly boy with fair hair and blue eyes who had spent most nights weeping for his mother. Edward and his tightly knit group of friends had seen him as fair game, and had found great sport in making his life miserable. "What of it?" he blustered.

"I'm sure you will recall how cruel you were to him," said Carlton. "The poor boy was grieving at the loss of

408

his mother when you and the others locked him into that cellar."

"We were all harried at that age," he retorted. "Wilmott needed toughening up."

"You refuse to admit culpability for his death?"

"We didn't kill him," snapped Edward.

"You left him there for more than twenty-four hours."

"We meant to go back for him, but the headmaster gave us extra work to complete in our studies, then the doors were locked for the night."

"That is no excuse," barked Henry. "You could have sent someone to let him out. It was mid-winter, and you left him naked in that damp, rat-infested cellar. When he was rescued he was half out of his mind with fear and dead of pneumonia within two weeks."

"We were boys," Edward muttered. "We didn't realise the consequences of what we were doing."

"You were *fourteen*," snapped Carlton, "old enough to know exactly what you were doing." He leant forward and rested his arms on the table. "You are still that cruel schoolboy, with little regard for anyone, and a careless approach to anything that doesn't directly affect you or your comforts. I'd heard you'd come to Australia, and when I saw you standing on the quay that morning, I knew I had my chance to teach you a lesson you would never forget."

Edward was silent.

"It was easy to stoke your vanity, easy to play you at your own game — for you don't have my skill with the cards, and you're too arrogant to listen to the warnings of your erstwhile friend Baines."

"He was your informant?" Edward was profoundly shocked.

"You have made many enemies, Cadwallader, and enemies talk. Piece by piece, I took everything from under your nose. It was like stealing sweetmeats from a baby."

"Who are you?" whispered Edward.

"Arthur Wilmott was my beloved nephew, my only heir — and I have waited many years to avenge his death."

"Why me?" Edward heard the whine in his voice and reddened. "I wasn't the only one who put him there."

"They have been dealt with," said Carlton, his tone flat. "Two are in debtors' prison and one hanged himself."

Edward digested this news. Carlton was a dangerous man — far more deadly than he could ever have imagined. "So you would see my wife and children on the streets for your revenge, and my career in tatters with no hope of providing for them?"

Henry Carlton shook his head. "I seek no revenge on your family. They are innocents caught up in your deceit. As for your career, it has been on the wane after your actions in Banks Town."

Edward's pulse jumped. Willy Baines had talked too much, and if he caught up with him he would cut out his tongue. He forced his thoughts into order. "So, you will leave me the house?"

"No."

Edward froze. "What, then?"

"Your horses must be delivered to my lodgings before nine tomorrow morning. Your wife's mare and the boy's ponies need not be included. I will take receipt of the deeds for the shops and the house tomorrow morning at eleven. Meet me at the offices of White and Marshall."

"But you said —"

"Listen, Cadwallader, and do not interrupt." Henry Carlton glared at him from across the table. "Your father was a wise man, and his final testament has given me the idea of what to do about the house." His smile was feral. "Oh, yes. That clerk was most accommodating. I know every clause of your father's will." He drank some wine. "And there would be no point in trying to find the man. He has since moved on."

Edward gritted his teeth.

"The deeds of the house will be made over to your sons, with the proviso that your wife may live there until her death — or her departure, whichever comes first." His grey eyes were like flint. "It is up to her whether or not you share the accommodation, but should she leave you, or die before you, you will vacate the property immediately."

Edward shoved back the chair and stood up. "You cannot do that," he snarled.

"I can, and I will." Carlton stood and took his hat and cloak from the Frenchman. "Remember, Cadwallader, I hold the cards — and should you consider sticking a knife between my ribs, you should know that I have people who watch my back at all times."

Edward followed his gaze and saw a tough-looking man in the doorway.

Carlton put on his hat. "I will see you at eleven tomorrow."

At Carlton's departure, Edward sank back in the chair. He was about to call for a bottle of whisky when he realised, with a jolt, that he lacked money in his pocket to pay for it. He stared at the remains of the wine, then poured it. It tasted bitter — like blood.

Watsons Bay, October 1804

Eloise dismissed her anxieties over her husband's strange behaviour since that day two weeks before, and kept her mare at a walk as the three boys nudged their ponies into a trot. She had few fears for Harry and Oliver — they had taken to riding as if born to it — but Charles bounced on his mount's shaggy back, and she hoped he would remain seated this time. The sand was soft and his falls had been cushioned, but Harry was leading him closer to the water where it was less forgiving.

She coaxed the mare into a trot and followed them. Charles had just celebrated his birthday and was relaxed enough in the saddle to laugh as his pony's hoofs splashed up the water, soaking his legs. If only he could be as carefree with his father, she thought.

They had come to the beach this morning to revel in the crisp coolness of the early hour and the freedom that only an empty shore could offer. The house was out of sight, Edward sleeping off the night's excesses, and the world seemed bright and fresh after the gloom that had hung over them these past weeks.

Edward's moods had grown darker by the day, the nightmares returning with greater frequency, making him ill-tempered to the point at which she feared for his sanity. She had tried to discover what had happened to make him so disagreeable, but Edward had blocked every question. The sudden removal of the horses hadn't been explained, and she had noticed that several fine pieces of porcelain were missing from the cabinets, and that her diamond necklace and earrings were no longer in her drawer. All she could conclude was that Edward's debt to Carlton must have been called in.

She supposed she should be grateful that he hadn't sold the ponies and her mare — but she resented the loss of her diamonds, which had been a gift from her father. If only he would learn from this experience, she thought. His gambling and wanton spending must end before they lost the house and everything else — yet Edward was determined to keep her in the dark.

It was too fine a day for such dour thoughts. She urged the mare into a gallop and, with the wind tugging at her hair and skirts, let the joy of the moment surge through her as they raced along the sand. "See you at the end of the bay," she called to the boys, as she galloped past them.

She leant forward in the saddle, exhilarated by her horse's speed. Then she saw a rider in the distance and felt a jolt of disappointment that her solitude was at an end.

His horse was standing in the shallow ripples at the water's edge, and she could tell, even from this distance, that he was watching her approach. She slowed the mare, suddenly wary — but as she drew nearer she saw that this was no stranger, and her heart leapt as the much-loved face came into focus.

She kept the mare at a walk, taking in the sturdy, vital figure that lived in her dreams. "George," she murmured, as she halted beside him. Their eyes held, the longing clear but unspoken.

"I'm so glad you've come at last," he said. "I've been here every day for the past week, and I wondered if you had ceased your rides on the beach."

"I've been taking the boys across the fields and into the bush." She glanced over her shoulder. The three small figures were still in the distance. "My children are with me," she said urgently. "They must not see you."

There were questions in his eyes as he looked into hers. "I see you now have three sons," he observed.

"They are my joy."

"But are you happy, Eloise?"

She saw love and concern in his face. She couldn't tell him the truth, for it would serve little purpose and bring him sorrow. "I am content," she replied.

"I have heard otherwise. Tell me the truth, Eloise, I beg you."

The need to pour out her unhappiness was so great that she almost lost control. Yet loving him as she did, and knowing how swiftly one word from her could bring the wrath of Edward upon them all, she chose to make light of her situation. "You should know better

414

than to listen to gossip," she chided. "A marriage is private. Only those bound by it can know the truth. My boys give me joy, and that is enough."

"Come with me, Eloise," he begged. "Leave Edward and bring the boys. We will make a home far from here where he cannot reach you." He clasped her gloved hand. "I have money," he said urgently. "We can go anywhere."

She looked down at the sun-browned fingers gripping her. Their touch brought back the memories. "It's too late — impossible."

His grasp tightened. "It's never too late, my love. Nothing is ever impossible if you want it enough."

She drew back her hand and blinked away tears. "I may want a great many things," she said, "but to pursue them would destroy my children — and that I will never do." She saw that the boys were fast approaching. "Edward is now the earl and I am his countess, which means little — but Charles is his heir, and he would carry through life any scandal attached to me."

"Will you return to Cornwall?" The pain was clear in his eyes, defeat in his tone.

"There is nothing to go back to," she said. "The boys will be here in a minute. You must go."

George's gaze remained steady on her face. "I wish you well, Eloise," he said. "Know that I love you — will always love you with the same deep, abiding passion I felt from the moment I saw you."

Eloise wanted to throw caution to the wind. To fling herself into his arms, to have him hold her again, to revel in the love that only he could offer. Yet the voices of her sons, and Edward's threats, kept her frozen in the saddle.

He took her hand and kissed it, his lips lingering. "If you ever need me, send word and I will come for you. Goodbye, my beloved."

"Goodbye," she whispered.

"Who was that, Mummy?" said Charles as he drew the pony to a halt.

Eloise wiped away her tears before she turned to her sons. Their faces were pink from the fresh air and salt winds. "Someone who likes to ride on the beach as we do," she replied. She gathered up her reins. "Race you to the house," she challenged.

As her mare galloped back along the sand, tears mingled with sea-spray to fall down her face. "I love you, George, and I had to lie to you — but it was for the best."

Hawks Head Farm, November 1804

"Something troubles you, George," said Susan, as she sat beside him on the veranda. "Perhaps if you talked to me about it, it would lose its magnitude."

George smiled, but could tell that she wasn't fooled. "Forgive me, Mother," he said, on a sigh, "but no amount of talking will solve my dilemma."

She rested her careworn hand on his arm. "An affair of the heart is never an easy burden," she said softly, "but I have found that time lightens it."

He was surprised. "How did you know?"

She smiled, but he could see the sadness in her lined face. "I was young once," she said, "and have had close acquaintance with heartache. I am familiar with the symptoms."

George took her hand. His mother suddenly appeared frail, the toll of life's experience etched in her face and in the silver hair that was coming loose beneath her bonnet. It was difficult to imagine her as a young girl in love — but her youthful romance with Jonathan Cadwallader had almost brought the family to destruction. Yet he was beginning to understand the torture she must have endured when forced to choose between love and her family. He had been unfair to Eloise — how thoughtless in expecting her to give up everything for him — yet his need of her overrode reason and, selfish or not, he would have asked any sacrifice of her to have her at his side.

"Is she married?" asked Susan.

George nodded.

"I suspected as much." She sighed. "No wonder you are so troubled for there can be no resolution." She squeezed his fingers. "Are there children?"

"Three. But I know she doesn't love him," he blurted out, "and that's what makes it so hard." His eyes brimmed. "She is my life, Mother, my heart and soul, the very breath I take. How can I live without her?"

"My dearest son," she said, "if there are three children there must be some substance to her marriage, regardless of what she may tell you. You must let her go."

George was fighting for control, but his mother's words echoed the doubt he had felt when he'd seen the third child.

"I wish I knew how to console you," she went on, "but words are meaningless when the heart aches so sorely — take it from one who knows."

George heard the catch in her voice, she was remembering her own pain. "You loved him, didn't you?"

Susan nodded. "But it was a destructive love," she said, "one that could be fulfilled only by tearing two families apart. It had to end." She turned to him. "She has made her choice, George, as I did all those years ago. You must accept it."

"If only we'd met before she was entangled with Cadwallader," he said bitterly.

"Edward Cadwallader?"

He saw the anguish in her face as other memories crowded in — of Edward's part in Florence's downfall. "It seems our two families are destined to lock horns, and now that Edward has inherited his father's title it is impossible for her to leave him."

She nodded, but her gaze was focused on some distant point beyond the clearing, and a pulse throbbed in her neck.

George felt a pang of guilt. Jonathan's death had been a terrible shock to her, and she was still mourning him. He shouldn't have let his tongue run away with him.

Susan stood up and tucked the stray wisps of grey hair back beneath the bonnet. "I love your father," she

418

said. "Have no doubt of that, George. He is my rock, my best friend, and I count myself fortunate that he understands my need to grieve for Jonathan. He forgave me the liaison a long time ago and I have been blessed in so many ways."

George could see that she was trying not to cry, determination clear in the set of her jaw and the rigid spine. "I know, Mother," he said. "I never doubted it."

She turned back once more to the vista that spread before them. "But Jonathan held a special place in my heart. He was my childhood friend, my first love — the man with whom I thought I would spend my life until Fate intervened." She lifted her chin and squared her shoulders. "Destiny can be cruel, George. Don't make the mistakes I made. Let her go."

He tried to speak, but could find no words to console her.

"I need a little time alone," she said.

George rose from the bench and watched her dignified progress across the clearing. His mother's pain was visible in every curve of her too-slender body and as his heart went out to her he admitted that she was right. It was time to let Eloise go — to accept her decision and walk away before their love destroyed them and the next generation.

CHAPTER
EIGHTEEN

Parramatta, January 1805

Niall's thirst for revenge had been slaked by the whip. The experiences of those terrible few days after the uprising had made him take stock of his situation. His longing to return to Ireland was a dream — and he would hold on to it until his dying day — but he had accepted that he would be freed only if he obeyed the rules and learnt as much as he could from his English persecutors. Then his dream might become reality. It was a bitter acceptance of how far he'd been cowed — but in a strange way it gave him strength, for now he had a goal.

Niall was released on the day after his sixteenth birthday and, with his ticket-of-leave in his pocket and the tools of his trade on his back, set out for Parramatta. He had heard there were many farms in the area, and with the skills he'd honed in the prison forge he could make an honest living and hold up his head with pride. But there was a far deeper reason for his choosing Parramatta, and it lay in his vision of a girl with red hair.

It hadn't taken him long to find what he'd been hoping for. The owner of the forge had died some months before and the place was falling apart. Yet Niall had seen potential in the rat-infested, tumbledown smithy, and with a hefty chunk of the money he'd raised through selling his emancipation land grant, he had bartered a fair price with the farrier's widow. Despite his youth there was an instant demand for his services, and he'd worked into the night for many weeks to repair the roof, strengthen the wooden supports and sort through the heaps of rubbish the previous owner had collected. Now, ten months later, it was clean and orderly, the rats banished, and customers were clamouring. It was time to go courting.

That morning he had risen earlier than usual, and as the sky lightened, he washed and prepared carefully for the day. His clothes were patched and faded, but clean, and although his boots were past their best, he'd spent some time the previous night giving them a good scrub. First impressions were always important so he had to be presentable.

Gathering up the leather apron and the canvas bag of tools, he carried them outside and placed them in the wagon with the horseshoes, nails, hinges and latches. He'd realised within days of setting up the forge that farmers often needed such things, and he always made sure he had a good supply to hand.

His excitement was tempered by nerves: his last visit to Moonrakers had been on the night of the insurrection, and he wondered if they would remember that and send him on his way. Yet the urge to see the girl was irresistible, and he knew he must try.

As he climbed into the wagon and took up the reins, he looked at the little wooden shack he'd built next to the forge. The walls were slabs of bark, the roof a sheet of corrugated iron. With sacking over the door and windows and the ugly stove-pipe jutting out at the side where the rain-butt stood it wasn't the most attractive of dwellings, but it was home. The single room was warm in winter, the truckle bed reasonably comfortable, and the old armchair he'd been given by a homesteader was perfect after a long day.

Pride rushed through him as he viewed his tiny kingdom. "It might not be everyone's idea of heaven," he murmured, "but 'tis surely me own." Warm with pleasure, he slapped the reins on the cob's broad back and they trundled down the dusty road towards Moonrakers.

As he crossed the bridge and entered the yard he drew up by the homestead steps and saw that he was being watched. With a tug on his hat, he climbed down and approached the woman who stood, arms akimbo, on the veranda. This was Mrs Nell Penhalligan, he knew, for he'd asked questions about the family in Parramatta.

"Niall Logan," he said, by way of introduction as he shook her hand. "I own the forge in Parramatta."

The blue eyes flashed with humour. "I remember you," she said. "Still fighting the revolution?"

He reddened as the girl appeared in the doorway. "It's a foolish man who fights a lost cause when he's been given the freedom to prove he's worth more than he's credited, missus," he said. He took in the tumble of red curls he'd remembered, the blue eyes and freckles.

"Well, I'm glad to hear it," said Nell. She spun round as the door slammed behind her, then turned back to Niall. "I believe you two have already met," she said, with a knowing grin. "This is my daughter, Amy."

The colour rose in his face as he nodded to the girl. He felt a right eejit.

"Can you shoe horses?" Nell asked.

"Yes, missus." He was unable to tear his gaze from Amy.

"Then, if your price is right, we can do business. We haven't seen a farrier in months, and although most of the men 'ere can replace a cast shoe, they haven't the skill to do more."

Niall listed his prices. "I've also got iron in the wagon should you need latches or nails, and fire-irons and buckets, should you be wanting them," he added, remembering his sales patter.

Nell smiled. "I think he'll do, don't you?" she asked Amy.

Amy eyed him from boot to hat, and when her eyes met his she smiled. "He's still a bit skinny," she murmured, "but, yes, he'll do. Shall I show him to the stables, Mother?"

"Why not? We can't stand 'ere all day makin' sheep's eyes and blushin'." Nell laughed. "We'll never get any work done."

Niall was about to protest when Amy grabbed his arm and steered him down the steps. "Take no notice of Mother. She's teasing." She looked into his face and grinned. "Up the revolution, eh?"

Niall grinned back, relief flooding through him. Amy was making it clear she had forgiven him, and perhaps even liked him a little.

Moonrakers, November 1805

Alice and Nell drew their horses to a halt before the flock of sheep grazing the lush grass. "The numbers are still down," said Alice.

"Five years of drought 'asn't helped," replied Nell. "Thank Gawd the rains started six months ago so we could make up some of our losses with the spring lambs."

"It's a pity John Macarthur wouldn't lend us stock from the government flocks to tide us over. It seems two women and three children aren't to be trusted to pay their debts."

"He's greedy," Nell muttered. "He's got the biggest flock in New South Wales, and is only keeping the numbers down so he can profit from the rising price in mutton."

Alice swung down from the saddle and took the cold damper bread and meat out of the saddlebag. "Let's forget about Macarthur for now," she suggested.

They sat in the grass to eat their simple meal, which they washed down with the cold tea Nell had brought in a stone bottle. Alice had been out there for a week, checking the livestock, birthing lambs and monitoring the waterholes. She hadn't felt lonely, but she appreciated Nell's company today.

"It's so peaceful out here." Nell propped herself on her elbows and raised her face to the sun. "I suppose it's the silence."

Alice nodded. "Its beauty brings solace," she said. Despite her words, the pain had never left her, and she still couldn't quite accept that she would never see Jack again.

"I still get angry, you know," said Nell. "It flares up now and again when I think of how they was snatched away without us even having the chance to say goodbye. We should be growing old together — not left . . ."

Alice took her hand. "I know," she said. "But here we are, and this is their legacy. What better way to remember them?"

Nell dashed away her tears. "Dear sweet Alice. However would I have coped without you?" She flung her arms round her friend.

Alice blinked away her own tears. "We had each other. We did it together."

They drew apart. "You taught me a lot," said Nell. "Who'd've thought I'd learn about shearing, dipping and all the rest that goes with sheep?"

Alice laughed. "You weren't the easiest pupil. Remember how you argued about everything and nearly fainted when you first had to castrate the lambs?"

Nell pulled a face. "It were 'orrible." She giggled. "I even 'ad to give up me pretty frocks for a man's trousers."

"They're more comfortable, though."

"But they ain't pretty."

"The sheep aren't bothered."

"Bloody sheep," muttered Nell. "What do they know?"

Alice hugged her knees. She and Nell still argued over everything, but they never got too heated; over the years, they had discussed the stock, the supplies, the work that needed doing and found they shared the same determination to keep the place going, however hard it might be.

The convicts were a blessing: certain tasks needed a man's strength — and although their rum consumption had to be carefully supervised, they had rallied well and proved their loyalty. Two had even settled on land grants close by after they were emancipated, and the workload was shared in the busy lambing and shearing seasons.

Nell's friendship had seen her through, Alice thought. To grieve alone was to dwell on the pain, but to know that others relied on her had helped. The children's simple, unquestioning love had been a balm to her soul.

"What's so funny?"

"I was thinking about Amy and Niall," she said. "They're always arguing, but I suspect that young man has ideas about the future."

426

"Amy's only fourteen," replied Nell, fiercely. "'E'd better keep 'is 'ands to 'isself."

Alice laughed. "With you as a future mother-in-law, he wouldn't dare step out of line." She got to her feet, brushed the grass from her trousers and tightened the string at her ankles and knees. The bow-yangs kept spiders and creepy-crawlies from getting up the legs, but they were forever coming loose, and chafing her skin. She pulled her hat low on her brow, climbed back into the saddle and waited for Nell. "Let's go home, cook a meal and spend some time with the children."

Three weeks later, Nell had finished feeding the chickens and the pigs and was sweeping the stable-yard. The sun was sinking, but there was still work to be done, and because she dreaded the loneliness of her empty bed, she would carry on until she was so tired she could barely move.

With the yard swept she took the washing off the line, rested the basket on her hip and made her way through the long grass to the homestead. In the first months of grieving the house had lost its atmosphere of permanence, security and warmth, and had become a prison filled with memories and sorrow. Yet as time had gone on, she and Alice had grown closer, and the feeling had crept back. Now it was the refuge it had always been.

She went inside and dropped the basket on the table. "What are you cooking?" she asked Amy.

"Roast mutton with vegetables from the garden," she said, basting the meat. "There's enough here to feed an army, so may Niall come for supper?"

Nell shared a grin with Sarah, who was peeling potatoes, and began to fold the laundry. "You'd better leave that to your sister and ask him," she replied.

"I sent Walter with a message," said Amy, the red cheeks not entirely due to the heat of the range. "He had nothing else to do and was under my feet."

Nell remained silent, the smile still softening her lips. Niall had become a regular visitor. Her daughters were on the brink of womanhood, she saw, with a pang, yet they still had the naïvety and enthusiasm of childhood that she'd lost before she was eight. Their upbringing had been so different from hers. If only Billy could see them now, she thought wistfully. He'd have been so proud.

She returned to folding sheets. Amy was still very young — too young to be thinking of romance — and the boy's experiences had made him old beyond his years. Yet that maturity brought with it the understanding that he must wait until Amy was old enough to commit herself to him, and she admired him for that. She also admired the reputation he was fast gaining for reliability and hard work. His business was flourishing, and he'd even added another room to his little bark hut.

Nell had few qualms over his heritage and religion, and he had already proved his worth. Also, it had been clear from the start that he adored Amy. If, in a few

428

years' time, they were married, she would have no anxiety about her daughter's future.

The sound of horses coming into the yard made Amy race for her bedroom. Nell put aside the laundry basket to help Sarah set the table. Soon Niall and Walter came in, laughing. Nell saw how Niall's gaze swept the room for Amy, and his disappointment when she wasn't there.

"She'll be out in a minute," said Sarah, with a giggle. "She's primping for you."

"Hush," said Nell. "Don't mind Sarah," she said. "She's only teasing." Walter, as usual, looked as if he'd been dragged through a hedge backwards. "Go and get washed," she said. "You're not sitting at my table looking like that."

"You sound like Aunt Alice." He dodged the hand aimed to clip his ear.

Instead Nell sent him on his way with a flick of the dishcloth. "Good," she retorted. "Perhaps you'll wash behind your ears as well, then." She set about rescuing the forgotten mutton.

"I'm starving," said Alice, as she came into the kitchen. "What's for dinner?"

"Burnt mutton, soggy vegetables and thin gravy. Amy's 'ad her mind on other things," she said, jerking her head at Niall.

Alice set about writing a long list of things she had to buy when she went into town the next day. They were running low on flour, salt and syrup, and Walter needed new boots. The rum would come from the government stocks, as would tobacco and new trousers for the convicts.

"I'd like a length of cloth for a dress," said Nell. "Me old one's fallen to bits."

"I'll see how much I have left when I've bought the rest," said Alice. "A new dress isn't essential."

"I know." Nell sighed. "But I'd love to feel like a woman again."

"Why don't you go into town this time, then? I've plenty enough to do here, and the trip will cheer you."

"Perhaps your mystery man will ask me to take tea at that hotel on the quay," she teased.

"He's not my mystery man," Alice retorted. "I've told you before, Nell, that Mr Carlton is simply an acquaintance I see now and again when I'm in town. You shouldn't make any more of it."

"If you say so," said Nell.

"I wish I'd never mentioned him."

"But you did. Wouldn't mind meetin' 'im meself — give 'im the once-over, see if I approve."

"Oh, for goodness' sake!" Alice was exasperated.

Nell's eyebrow rose, but she knew she'd teased Alice enough. She turned her attention to the meal and made no further comment.

The talk was lively as they ate, and a cool draught came through the open door, which went some way to diffuse the heat of the range on this summer night.

Nell watched Niall and Amy exchange small-talk, their eyes saying more than their words. She knew that Alice, too, felt the ache of loss, for the youngsters reminded them of how it had been before the fire. She saw again the expression on Billy's face when he'd come to the weaving shed and asked her to marry him, her wedding day when he'd been so handsome in Ezra's old suit, and the warmth of his kiss as they had set off with Jack for their new life at Moonrakers.

A horse clopping over the bridge into the yard brought her to her feet. A visitor at this time of night could only mean trouble. She stood in the doorway and peered out into the darkness. "Who's there?" she called.

"I apologise, Mrs Penhalligan, for calling at such a late hour." The tall, handsome man climbed off his horse and approached the veranda steps.

Nell saw grey at the temples, kindly eyes and a warm smile. The cloth and cut of his clothes were expensive, and the horse he'd tied to the veranda post was a thoroughbred. "You have the advantage, sir," she said, "but you're welcome."

"Henry Carlton at your service, ma'am," he said, as he took her hand. "I see I have disturbed your dinner. I do apologise."

Nell was aware that conversation in the kitchen had stopped, and that every eye was turned on her and the newcomer. So this was Carlton. No wonder Alice had blushed when she'd mentioned him. "Would you care to join us?" she asked politely, hoping the boys had left something.

"Thank you, no. I have come merely to enquire after Mrs Quince."

Alice had finished her meal, and as the conversation floated to her through the open door, she rose from the table and went to rescue Henry Carlton from Nell, who was bombarding him with questions. "We meet again," she said, with a smile, "although I'm surprised to see you so far from town."

"I hope I do not inconvenience you," he said, "but it has been so long since your last visit to Sydney Town that I came to see how you are faring." His handsome face lit up in a smile. "I am delighted to see you."

Alice curtsied awkwardly, all too aware that her old trousers were tied up with string, that Jack's shirt was faded and patched, and her boots were worn. Hardly the appropriate clothing to entertain a gentleman. "Will you come in, Mr Carlton?"

He glanced at Nell. "If you don't mind, Mrs Quince, I would appreciate a private word with you. I will not keep you long."

Alice and Nell exchanged a puzzled glance. "We can walk by the river," said Alice. "It's cooler there."

Henry offered his arm and she placed her hand on it as he led her down the steps. She couldn't understand why he was there, or what could be so important that it had to be said in private. Yet she was curious, and walked beside him knowing that everyone in the house was speculating.

He finally stopped. His face was strongly carved, the pale moonlight throwing shadows on his cheekbones and brow. "Mrs Quince, I must commend you for your labours. I understand the farm is flourishing and your flock is almost back to its original size. You and Mrs Penhalligan are much admired in Sydney Town for your tenacity and strength of character. Lesser men would have given in before now."

"The farm is all we have," she replied. "The work is hard, the land demanding, but it has helped us pull through."

He smiled. "I always knew you were a gem," he said, "that nothing would beat you after that night at sea when the rain was lashing down and you were almost blown off your feet as you went to tend your sheep."

"You seemed to make a habit of rescuing me," she said, through laughter. "Why, you even had to haul me out of the street when you bumped into me that morning in Sydney."

"I remember it well, and would deem it an honour to save you again, Mrs Quince."

"What can you mean? I don't need rescuing. I'm quite safe here."

"Perhaps I have used the wrong word," he said quickly. He hesitated, then rushed on: "Mrs Quince, you have fascinated me from the moment we met on board the *Empress*, and as the years have passed and we have shared brief moments during your visits to Sydney, I have come to think of you as a friend. A much respected and admired friend. I have made a point of following your fortunes and, although you might see this as an intrusion, I had to speak to you before I left for the Cape."

Alice was so taken aback she didn't know what to say.

"Mrs Quince," he said urgently, "my regard for you is greater than ever. Your strength and pride in who and what you are shine from your eyes."

"Please, Mr Carlton, you go too far."

"I know," he said. "But I am to leave soon for Cape Town, and I had to speak to you, regardless of the impropriety." He reached out as if to take her hands but then, perhaps realising he was too forward, dropped his own to his sides. "Will you at least do me the honour of hearing me out?"

She could hear the sincerity in his voice and see the determination in his eyes, and although the conversation was taking on an air of fantasy, she couldn't resist learning what he had to say. She nodded.

"I am a wealthy man," he began, "with estates in England, South Africa and America. I have prospered since I found gold on my property in South Africa, but I have no one with whom to share my good fortune." His eyes were downcast, his voice deep and musical. "My wife died many years ago, and there were no children."

Alice's heart went out to him for she understood his sadness. Yet she was beginning to suspect where this might be leading, and didn't know how to put a stop to it.

"My property at the Cape has several thousand acres, mostly given up to cattle." He smiled. "I'm not a farmer. My strengths lie in running my businesses with a keen eye and steady hand."

Alice felt as if she was on firmer ground. "Farming is a business like any other."

"You see? We are of like mind. I knew I was right to talk to you." He glanced back at the homestead where their audience was now seated on the veranda, making no pretence of their curiosity. "My house in the Cape is large, with stables and servants' quarters. The cotton plantation in America is equally comfortable, and then, of course, I have my estates in Wiltshire. I have a good life, Mrs Quince — but a lonely one."

Alice was bewildered. "What is your point, Mr Carlton?"

He suddenly lost his poise and, for the first time since she'd known him, appeared unsure of himself. "I am asking you to marry me, Mrs Quince," he said.

The words hung between them. "I'm — I'm honoured, Mr Carlton," stammered Alice.

"We are already friends — good friends, who find much to talk about when we meet all too infrequently. But we could become closer," he pressed. He smiled, and she could see he was making an effort to rein in his enthusiasm. "You stole my heart that night on board the *Empress*, and each time we meet I have become ever more certain that you are the woman for me."

Alice was speechless with astonishment.

"I'm not so foolish as to believe you will give me an answer tonight. I'm willing to wait, Mrs Quince — Alice — as long as it takes."

"Mr Carlton, I don't know what to say."

"Then say nothing. Think over what I have asked, and when you are ready to reply, send a message to me in Sydney Town."

Alice studied the man before her. He was not only handsome, but intelligent, kindly and wealthy — the sort of suitor most women would have willingly accepted. Yet his friendship was all she'd wanted — all she'd expected — and his proposal had changed things between them. It was flattering, but disconcerting.

"I'm deeply honoured you have approached me," she began, "and although I am still startled, I can tell you are sincere." She smiled up at him. "But I'm the daughter of Sussex farmers, raised in a hamlet, educated at a village school, the widow of a convict. We're from different worlds, Mr Carlton —"

"Superficially, perhaps," he interrupted. "But we share the same love of the land, the same desire to make the best of opportunities that open to us. Your education may have been poor, your background very different from mine — but our friendship has proved we are well suited. This is a new world, Alice, and it is ours for the taking."

"It's a new world, certainly," Alice agreed, "but my corner of it lies here on the land I helped my husband to clear. I'm a farmer, Mr Carlton. I wouldn't know where to begin at anything else."

"Then let me show you," he pleaded. "You once had a sense of adventure or you would never have come to New South Wales. Find that adventurous spirit again, Alice. Come to the Cape and see for yourself how good life can be there."

She stepped back from him. "Please stop, Mr Carlton. I have no wish to leave Moonrakers." She held up her hand to silence his protest. "Jack was the only reason I found the courage to come all this way," she said quietly. "Now that he's gone, there will be no other."

436

"But you are still in the prime of life," he remonstrated. "You cannot dedicate the rest of your years to the memory of a dead man."

She stiffened. "Jack may be dead, Mr Carlton, but he lives on in every corner of Moonrakers, for it was here that he regained his freedom and his pride, here that he taught me the importance of remaining true to what matters. I will never leave."

Henry Carlton's fingers plucked at the strips of leather round the crown of his hat as he twisted it back and forth. "He was a lucky man to have the love of a woman such as you, Mrs Quince," he said. "My judgement was right, though somewhat misplaced, for I sensed in you the strength and courage of your convictions, and had hoped — foolishly — that you might share them with me. My most sincere apologies for speaking out of turn." He smiled. "It seems that, for once, I do not hold all the trump cards."

Alice didn't understand what he meant. "Thank you for your kind words," she said, into the silence that had fallen between them. "I do appreciate them, although I must decline your most generous offer."

He placed the hat carefully on his head and tipped the brim so it shadowed his eyes. "You are a very lovely woman, Mrs Quince. It is an honour to call you my friend. I hope my having spoken to you will not destroy that."

Alice was about to reply when an outrageous idea struck her. Without pausing to give it full consideration, she said, "Mr Carlton, do you know anything about merino sheep?"

"Only that their wool is the finest in the world," he replied, clearly taken aback by this diversion from their previous discussion.

"It is indeed," she said, her thoughts shifting and taking shape with almost alarming clarity. "You're a man who evidently enjoys a challenge, and I have a proposition for you."

He laughed. "You're a surprising woman, Mrs Quince. Tell me what you have in mind."

"We need investment in our stock if we are to compete against the larger landowners like Mr Macarthur, but as he holds the government purse-strings and the biggest flocks, we struggle." She took a deep breath, shocked by her audacity, yet determined to see it through. "Would you consider investing in Moonrakers until we are on our feet?"

His expression was thoughtful. "A short-term investment?"

Alice nodded. "I would have to talk to Mrs Penhalligan, my partner, but yes. A short-term investment for a maximum of five years — not of money but of sheep, which you could send from the Cape. We can split any profits four ways during that term."

"Why the four-way split? I thought only you and Mrs Penhalligan held the deeds to this place."

"We have to give a proportion of our profits to the government, but it's not great. We would split the rest between the three of us."

Henry Carlton threw back his head and laughed, the sound ricocheting across the river and into the trees.

"Oh, Mrs Quince," he said, "I come a-courting and instead of a wife I find a business partner."

She grinned. "So you agree to it, then?"

"I do indeed," he replied, shaking her hand. "I will have my lawyer draw up the papers. He will probably advise me to hold the deeds of Moonrakers until the end of the five-year term but, rest assured, I will not do that. Moonrakers belongs to you, and if all I can be to you is a friend and business partner, I am more than satisfied."

"Then you'd better come indoors to meet the others. They're in danger of catching cold if they sit out on the veranda eavesdropping for much longer, and we have much to discuss."

"Are you sure you know what yer doin'?" said Nell, as she lit her evening pipe. Henry Carlton had left, Niall and Amy were down by the barn saying goodnight, the twins were in the stables, and the two women were drinking tea on the veranda.

"It's the only way to bring in new stock and keep the quality of the wool and meat up to standard."

"I ain't talkin' about the bloody sheep, woman," retorted Nell. "I meant Mr Carlton. 'E's 'andsome and rich and wants to marry you — but you turned 'im down."

"I don't love him," protested Alice.

"Then yer need yer bloody 'ead testin'. Most women would cut off their right arm to 'ave 'im chase after 'em."

"I know," Alice admitted. "But you wouldn't have accepted his proposal either — and don't you dare pretend otherwise. Not even a man like Mr Carlton could replace either Jack or Billy."

"Yeah, you're right — as usual." Nell sighed. She looked through the pipesmoke at Alice. "It looks like me and you are stuck with each other, then."

"Indeed we are," replied Alice. She reached across the table for Nell's hand. "I'm glad we're friends at last."

"So am I," she said, round the stem of the pipe. She laughed. "I used to reckon you thought yerself too good for us — but Billy was right. You and me will be the makin' of this place 'cos together we're a good team."

Alice lifted her teacup. "Here's to Moonrakers, Alice and Nell."

"Nell and Alice," she corrected, with mock ferocity. "Don't forget, I was 'ere first."

PART FIVE
Mutiny

CHAPTER
NINETEEN

Hawks Head Farm, January 1808

George and Ernest were herding the cattle towards the lush pastures by the river as they discussed the disturbing turn of events in the colony. The new governor, William Bligh, was at odds with the New South Wales Corps and the powerful Macarthur, and people were taking sides in the feud.

"Bligh should never have been made governor in the first place," said George, heatedly. "He was causing trouble even before he landed here. Mark my words, Ernie, this feud between him and Macarthur will lead to a mutiny that rivals the one on the *Bounty*."

"He's a difficult man, I grant you," replied Ernest, as they rode side by side. The cattle were strung out in front of them, the dust of many hoofs rising in a choking cloud. "But he forced Macarthur to loosen the strings on the government purse when we had that flood last year. We couldn't have survived without replenishing the stock from the government herds."

"I'm not saying he hasn't done some good in the colony," said George, "but he seems determined to rid Macarthur of any power. He's even banned him from importing brewing stills and distributing cheap wine to the Corps. He's making a powerful enemy there, and the traders as well as the Corps are seething."

"The barter system worked well enough, but it was only the Corps and the traders who made any money during last year's flood when everything was at a premium because of the shortages. William Bligh is cutting a swathe through all those who've grown fat on our labours. I commend him."

George snorted. "You wouldn't say that if you were in my position," he said. "Bligh has begun to forfeit traders' shipping bonds since an escaped convict stowed away on one of Macarthur's vessels. We're all at risk now that a precedent has been set, and I have to make sure our ships are searched from bow to stern before we leave port. Losing the right to trade here will finish me."

"I doubt that." Ernest pulled the neckerchief more firmly over his nose to keep out the dust. "You trade between here and the Americas, and your new try-works in Van Diemen's Land gives you greater freedom than most."

"I still say the man's trouble," insisted George. "This new city plan of his is causing problems for those of us with leases on government land. He's made several leaseholders remove their houses and offered no compensation."

"Your warehouse and shop are safe, though, aren't they?"

George grunted. "At the moment — but who's to say what the man will do next?"

"He's our governor," said Ernest. "He has the power to do as he likes."

"He abuses it," growled George. "His language is foul, his manner bullish to the point where he's earned the nickname Caligula. I wouldn't be surprised if Macarthur and Johnston don't mount a coup to oust him."

They rode in silence as the cattle bellowed on their way to the more verdant pastures by the river. George knew his brother wouldn't be shifted from his opinion, and as it was pointless to argue he gave up trying. Bligh had obviously been chosen as governor by the British government because of his reputation as a hard man — and that was what was needed to rein in the Corps. But he was going about it in the wrong way, and would get his comeuppance: the New South Wales Corps was a powerful body, and with Macarthur stirring them up, trouble could not be far away. He was glad he would be at sea by the end of the month.

He tipped his hat-brim over his eyes to keep the dust at bay. The floods brought by the heavy rain the previous year had long since disappeared and now the earth was rock-hard, the grass wilting — and although the Hawkesbury River still raced through the valley, it was lower than usual. Australia did nothing by half, he thought gloomily. Flood or drought, feast or famine, with nothing between except fire, marauding natives, and the occasional escaped convict to keep life interesting. The old restlessness returned and he counted the days until he would feel the salt spray on his face and the icy winds blowing from the Antarctic.

"So, George," said Ernest, a little later, "you have finally brought a young lady to meet Mother. I can't tell you how relieved we are that you've come to your senses. Mother had despaired of another woman joining the family, and Miss Hawthorne seems delightful."

George kept his gaze on the cattle as the dogs nipped and chivvied them onwards. He ached after so many unaccustomed hours in the saddle. "She's a friend, Ernie," he said gruffly.

"You're thirty-three, and it's time you settled. Miss Hawthorne is smitten, and I doubt you would have invited her if your intentions weren't honourable."

It had been a mistake to bring her, thought George. He'd known it the minute they'd set off from Sydney Town in his gig and within an hour her presence had irritated him. It wasn't her fault — he should have known from past experience that no other woman could match up to Eloise, yet Miss Hawthorne had expressed a wish to visit Hawks Head, and he'd been fool enough to invite her. Now his family had scented romance.

"I have no intentions, honourable or otherwise, towards Miss Hawthorne," he said. "She merely expressed an interest in the farm so she could relate to the children she teaches. I shall be taking her back to Sydney tomorrow morning."

"If you say so," responded Ernest, as they herded the cattle into the fenced-off pasture and the convict shut the gate. He took off his hat and left a smear of dirt on his brow as he wiped away the sweat. "But I believe the lady has other ideas."

George climbed down from the saddle and stretched. "Then she must think again. I'm not ready to marry, and have already made clear to her that I offer only friendship." He glanced at his brother. "I was foolish to bring her. I should have known she would read more into it. Poor Agatha. It seems she's doomed to remain a spinster schoolmistress."

Ernest eyed him thoughtfully. "You certainly haven't been fair to the poor woman. She seems a pleasant little body."

George yawned. "She is, Ernie, but she's not the one for me." He slapped his brother's shoulder. "I'll introduce her to a couple of my friends — find her someone more suitable."

Ernest wasn't fooled by his brother's cheerfulness. "I remember using false jollity to cover my heartache over Millie," he said quietly. "Perhaps you're doing the same. Does your determination to remain unmarried relate to rejection? If so, understand that life moves on, and even the deepest love becomes a distant memory. There is little point in wasting one's life in regret." His slow smile lit up his face. "Miss Hawthorne is very pretty," he coaxed, "and Mother is taken with her. Will you not reconsider?"

George balled his dusty handkerchief and stuffed it into his pocket. "I'm old enough to choose my own wife — and when I do, you and Mother will be the first to meet her."

"Who is she, George?" Ernest's voice was quiet. "Who has you spellbound to the point at which you prefer this solitary existence to that of a wife and family? Why is she not at your side?"

George was disconcerted by Ernest's astuteness. He'd thought to hide his heartache. "Dinner will be getting cold by the time we get back," he muttered. "We mustn't keep the others waiting." Before Ernest could comment, he had turned away, his heels lifting the dust as he strode across the clearing.

Sydney Barracks, January 1808

Edward and the other officers had risen early and were now waiting to leave for court. Tension was high, the air filled with pipe smoke.

Bligh had forced the judge-advocate, Richard Atkins, to issue an order for Macarthur to appear on the matter of the shipping bond he'd refused to pay the previous December. Macarthur had disobeyed the order and had been arrested, then bailed to appear for trial at the next sitting of the Sydney Criminal Court, which would take place later that morning.

"It's time we got rid of Bligh," muttered one of the men. "He's ruined the rum trade by prohibiting the use of spirits as payment for commodities. My income is sorely affected."

"The enforcement of penalties is crippling me," said another. "Sales of spirits are permitted only at Bligh's discretion, and our monopoly on the trade is all but gone. Can't the fool see he's making enemies of the most powerful people in the colony?"

"Bligh and Macarthur don't see eye to eye," said the first. "Bligh's determined to make him a scapegoat and, of course, the judge-advocate is playing into his hands. He and Macarthur have been enemies for years."

Edward was sweating, the lack of a drink making him impatient and edgy, but he remained silent as the others grumbled. The loss of the rum trade and barter system had been a deep blow after he had had to hand over almost everything he owned to Carlton, and he was hoping that, after today, Macarthur would call for Bligh's dismissal so the colony could once more be in the hands of the military and monopolists.

Yet he could see beyond the petty rivalry and bickering. It was a struggle for power — something he understood all too well — not merely the ousting of an unpopular governor by a rich landowner who had too much to lose.

He tamped down on the driving thirst he could never slake, and listened as the arguments went back and forth. Previous governors had wanted to keep New South Wales as an open prison with a primitive barter economy, but Bligh had far grander ideas, and therein lay the rub. Despite his intelligence, the man was a hothead with an acerbic tongue and a manner that set all against him. He'd ceased handing out land grants to Macarthur and men like him, but had awarded himself and his sister over four thousand acres. He had dismissed the assistant surgeon and the magistrate without explanation, and had sentenced three merchants to a month's imprisonment for writing him a letter of complaint he considered offensive.

But it wasn't only the powerful in the colony he had upset: six Irish convicts had been tried and acquitted of revolt, but he'd imprisoned them anyway, and some of the poorer lease-holders had been forced to tear down their hovels to make way for Bligh's grand town plan. The whole colony was up in arms. It was a powder-keg, about to explode at any moment.

Kernow House, Watsons Bay

"It was a farce." Edward threw himself into a chair.

Eloise put down the newspaper she'd been reading to Charles and Oliver. From what she had gleaned in the press, she'd expected as much — but knew better than to voice her opinion. The Corps was playing a dangerous game, and Macarthur should be brought to trial for treason.

"The court assembly was made up of Atkins, the judge-advocate and six of us officers from the Corps. As you're aware, Macarthur and Atkins have been enemies for years, and Atkins owes him money. Macarthur objected that Atkins was unfit to sit in judgement. Atkins rejected his protest, but had to stand down because we officers supported the protest. Without the judge, the trial couldn't take place."

"But I thought that was the whole idea?"

"It backfired," he muttered. "Macarthur is still under arrest, and Bligh has accused me and the other officers of mutiny."

"*Mutiny?* But that's a hanging offence."

"It won't go that far. Major Johnston refused to deal with the matter, citing ill-health. But he wouldn't dare accuse us of such a crime."

"Let us hope not." She looked at her husband, noting the lines in his bloated face, the bleary, bloodshot eyes and jowls at his chin. Nightmares and drink had taken their toll, and there was little now to remind her of the handsome young man who had charmed her into marrying him. These were worrying times, and it seemed he was at the heart of them.

"What are you boys doing indoors on such a good day?" Edward's question broke into her troubled thoughts.

"They've been out all morning," she said, in defence.

"I wasn't talking to you," he snarled. "Charles, why aren't you out riding?"

Charles paled at finding himself the focus of his father's attention. "I . . . w-w-went riding this morning, sir," he stuttered.

"Hmph. You should be out making mischief at your age, not sitting with your mother like a little girl."

"I . . . I —"

"If you can't talk properly, hold your tongue." Edward's face brightened as Harry come in. "That's more like it. A boy with dirt on his face and sweat on his shirt. What have you been up to?"

"I've been helping Ned in the stables. The mare has sprained a leg."

"Good boy." His face glowed with pride as he stood up to pour a drink. "Thought I might take you shooting at the weekend," he said. "You're already a fine shot, Harry, but your namby-pamby brother Charles needs backbone."

"Charles *is* a good shot," said Harry.

Edward grimaced. "Oliver," he said sternly, "it's time you did some real shooting instead of taking pot-shots at targets."

Oliver's face lit up. "Really, Papa?"

Eloise shuddered at the thought of her youngest boy being exposed to the gore of a hunt. "Harry and Charles find little pleasure in killing things," she said, "and Oliver is too excitable to be trusted with a rifle."

"Mama," protested Oliver, "I'm nearly seven."

"Indeed you are," she replied, "but the hunt is no place for little boys." She turned back to Edward. "Why not take them for a ride instead?"

His bleary gaze raked over her. "I said I would take them hunting, and that is what I'll do. If you molly-coddle them they'll never grow into men."

Eloise remained silent. If it took pleasure in killing birds and small animals and getting drunk to make a so-called man, her sons would be better off ignoring their father's example. "Perhaps we should await the outcome of all this to-do with Macarthur and Bligh," she said instead. "There is still the charge of mutiny against you, and until it is cleared it's impossible to plan anything."

"Mutiny or not, I'll take them hunting! They are my sons, and I'll do with them as I damn well please."

Eloise shooed the boys out of the room and left him to his rum. Wearily, she climbed the stairs. She fell on to the bed and shut her eyes. Why couldn't Edward see that his constant belittling of Charles was as destructive as his perceived abandonment by his own father? A child needed to be nurtured, not harassed into submission, and Charles lived in constant fear when his father was at home.

She opened her eyes and stared at the ceiling, her heart heavy. Edward's pride in Harry was all-consuming. He deliberately set him apart from his older brother in the belief that the younger boy loved and admired him. How wrong he was, she thought. Harry was merely in awe of Edward's wrath, and had learnt early on that he was expected to show no fear — to be a little man, a smaller version of his father. Yet he feared Edward's disapproval, and had confided in her that he hated the way their father treated Charles.

Despite Edward's efforts, Charles and Harry were as close as brothers could be, for Harry was protective of Charles and often took the blame when something had angered their father. Even Oliver, young as he was, understood that the alliance of brothers was protection against their father's heavy-handed ways.

She shivered as she thought of the threat that hung over Edward. Even if he escaped the noose, the future seemed bleak. While the children were small she could devote herself to them, but in a few short years they would be men, leaving home to make their own way in the world. Once they were gone, what would become of her?

She saw the years stretching ahead, cold and lonely, herself trapped in a loveless marriage with a man she despised. If only she'd had the courage to leave with George all those years ago. But it was too late for regrets — too late to snatch the happiness he'd offered for she had spurned his love and sent him away. She buried her face in the pillow as a tear splashed on to the starched linen.

Edward and the other officers of the Corps had been summoned to appear at Government House early the following morning.

"Your officers' actions are treasonable," ranted Governor Bligh to Major Johnston. "I demand the return of the court papers that the Corps is holding."

Edward stood with his fellow officers and tried not to show how nervous he was. Bligh was furious enough to hang them all, and he could only pray that Johnston kept his nerve.

"I demand a new judge-advocate, and Macarthur's release on bail," said Johnston, as he stood to attention. "My officers will not be brought to trial, and you have no jurisdiction over army affairs."

"You're in no position to demand anything," roared Bligh. "I am the governor, sanctioned by the Crown, and therefore at liberty to see you all charged with treason."

Johnston glared at his adversary, the ensuing silence heavy with menace. Without replying, he turned on his heel and left the room, followed by his men. "I'm going straight to the gaol to release Macarthur," he muttered, when they reached the garden.

"Is that wise, sir?" Edward was decidedly edgy. All this talk of treason and hanging made his need of a drink ever more urgent.

"If you haven't the stomach for it, Captain, you may step down," snapped the major, in disgust, "but I warn you, Cadwallader, it will not look good on your already less than honourable record."

Edward looked at him with loathing. Johnston had been trying to get rid of him for years, and he was damned if he would give him the opportunity to do so now. "Then I will, of course, support you all the way, sir," he replied.

"All of you will return to barracks and wait. I will bring fresh orders once I've released Macarthur."

The morning was almost over when he returned. "I have a petition drafted by Macarthur that has already been signed by several of our most prominent citizens. I have also drawn up a charge that I will hand to Bligh on his arrest. I expect you all to sign it."

Edward scanned the wording, then added his signature, but his hand was trembling so violently it was barely legible. There was little doubt that they were committing treason for the charge against Bligh was that he was unfit to exercise supreme authority in the colony. Johnston and all officers under his command demanded his resignation and submission to arrest so that they could take over. He just prayed Johnston knew what he was doing — he could already feel the noose tightening round his neck.

At six o'clock that evening the Corps was assembled and, with colours flying and a band to send them on their way, marched to Government House to arrest Bligh.

Edward watched as Bligh's sister wielded her parasol to great effect. She was the governor's only defender, but was making life most uncomfortable for those she was jabbing with it. As she was bundled unceremoniously into a cupboard and shut in, Edward and the others were ordered to search the house.

Bligh was discovered in full dress uniform under his bed.

"You're nothing but a coward," sneered Johnston, "hiding behind your sister's skirts, and crawling about on the floor."

"I was trying to find important papers I'd stowed there," Bligh declared, as he was dragged to his feet. "I am no coward."

Johnston read out the charge. "You will be placed under house arrest until you agree to resign your position and return to England."

"I was appointed by the British government," retorted Bligh. "I will remain here as governor until I am lawfully relieved of my duty." He was breathing heavily, his rage clear in his high colour. "I'll see every one of you buggering bastards hanged for this."

Edward was sweating as they rode away. The deed had been done and there was no turning back — but the consequences promised to be dire.

None of those who had taken part in the arrest and confinement of their governor knew that there would be two more long years of wrangling before Bligh was officially relieved of his duty.

Waymbuurr (Cooktown), March 1810

Mandawuy's long trek back to his tribal lands had taken many seasons, for he had visited other clans along the way, hunting, fishing and accepting their hospitality. Their Elders had listened as he'd told them of his time with Tedbury, and how the good people who lived by the great river had healed his wounds and treated him with respect and kindness.

In return, he had heeded the wise old men who counselled him, for the white man was spreading ever further northward, and he knew that, soon, his own tribe would come into contact with them. He would use the knowledge he had gained from his travels and experiences to guide his people in how to prepare for the invasion.

Now he was among his own people, willing them to understand the message he brought. "The white man *will* come," he said, to the circle of Elders who had gathered on the shore. "It may not be for many seasons — but it *will* happen, and we must be ready."

"We will fight them with our spears and *nullas*," shouted one of the men. "This is our sacred earth. They will be squashed like insects."

Mandawuy shook his head. "If we break open an anthill there are too many ants to squash them all. And that is good, for we rely on insects to show us the seasons and to lead us to honey, water and the leaves

457

our women use for healing." He softened his tone, aware that his frustration was causing the senior Elder to frown at his disrespect. "Black and white can live together, as we live with the insects," he said. "They have different ways from ours, believe in many strange things — but they can heal us, feed us, shelter our women and children in times of hunger, and teach us many things."

"We have lived as our ancestors did when they walked this earth. There is no need for the white man's medicine or shelter." The old man glared at Mandawuy. "You left your people to go with Tedbury. The lust for fighting made you take up your war spear — why are you now against war with the white man when you have spilled his blood?"

"Their skin is white, their eyes pale, but they walk as we do and believe in the Spirits. We can learn from them, and they from us."

The old man nodded. "I will consider what you say, for your grandmother Lowitja was a wise woman and spoke of such things before she was sung to the stars."

"The Elder Watpipa, husband of Anabarru, also spoke of the white man who came many moons ago. Perhaps Mandawuy's words should be heeded and discussed."

The old man frowned at the interruption. He fixed his beetling gaze on Mandawuy. "Go now," he barked, "and wait until I am ready to speak with you again."

Mandawuy rose to his feet and made for the campfire and the woman who would become his wife at the next full moon. The knowledge he had gained over the past seasons would be talked and argued over, but he had faith in the Elders to reach the right decision. His people would be prepared for the coming of the white men — and in welcoming them they would avoid the bloodshed that had decimated the southern tribes.

Sydney Town, March 1810

"It's grand to see you after so long, George," said Thomas Morely, as they shook hands.

"It's good to be back," said George, as he settled into a chair and signalled to the barman for whisky. "I understand things have been lively since my last visit."

Thomas grunted. "That isn't the word I'd have used," he said. " 'Unsettling' may be more appropriate."

They waited for their drinks to arrive, and after he had taken a sip, George unbuttoned his coat and relaxed. "I understand there was a military coup, and Macarthur and Johnston set themselves up as governor and judge-advocate?"

Thomas nodded. "But for all their wiles, Bligh refused to be ousted. It was the talk of the colony, but thinking back, it had its lighter moments."

George loved a good story. "Do tell," he said gleefully.

Thomas settled more comfortably into his chair. He was becoming portly now he'd left the army and, at forty-one, his belly bore testament to his wife's cooking and the comforts of his large home at Balmain. "They put Bligh under arrest in Government House, but he refused to resign. Johnston notified his superior officer,

Colonel Paterson, of events, but he was in Port Dalrymple in Van Diemen's Land and was reluctant to become involved until clear orders came from London. When he heard that Fovcaux was returning to Sydney as lieutenant-governor, he left him to it."

"What happened to Macarthur?"

Thomas grinned. "He had to step down when Foveaux took over. He'd been handling most of the colony's business after Bligh was arrested, and I suspect he thought he'd be given the governorship, so he wasn't best pleased."

"He's always had a high opinion of himself," muttered George. "I can't say I'm sorry to hear he's been taken down a peg or two."

"Foveaux left Bligh under house arrest and got down to improving the roads, bridges and buildings that had been neglected. When there was still no word from England about Bligh, he sent an order to Paterson to come immediately."

"And did he? Or did he wash his hands of the affair again?"

"He sent Johnston and Macarthur to England on charges of treason, confined Bligh to barracks until he had signed a contract agreeing to return to England, then retired to Government House and left Foveaux to run the colony."

"The man has to be admired for his nerve." George guffawed.

"In fact, it's Bligh who should be admired," laughed Thomas. "Back in January last year he was given captaincy of HMS *Porpoise* on condition he returned

460

to England. As soon as he was out of sight of shore, he made straight for Hobart and sought support from David Collins, the lieutenant-governor of Van Diemen's Land."

"The man has the cheek of the devil," George spluttered.

Thomas nodded. "Collins might have helped if Bligh had held his tongue but, as usual, he insulted the man by haranguing him in public and Collins took umbrage. Bligh was stranded aboard the *Porpoise* for almost a year. Word finally came from London, and Lachlan Macquarie was appointed governor this January."

"And Bligh? Is he still in Van Diemen's Land?"

Thomas finished the whisky. "He's in Sydney now to collect evidence for George Johnston's court-martial in London. He's expected to leave soon, because the hearing is set for October."

George smiled. "There's clearly no way to keep a good man down. It strikes me that the only one to come out of this with any glory is Bligh. It wouldn't surprise me if the Admiralty didn't give him promotion and his own fleet."

"Stranger things have happened." Thomas ordered another round of drinks. "At least the colony is more ordered now Macquarie's in charge. He's a clever man."

"How so?"

"He's reinstated all the officials Johnston and Macarthur dismissed and cancelled all land and stock grants made during their period of governing, but to keep things calm he made some appropriate grants to prevent acts of revenge. He seems impressed with what Foveaux achieved during his administration, and has put him forward as Collins's successor."

"Foveaux's achievement in taking over as he did should certainly be recognised," George mused. He sipped his whisky. "I see you've put on a bit of winter condition there, Thomas."

His friend patted his belly with a rueful smile. "Army life kept me trim," he admitted, "but I find I can't resist my wife's German pastries." He gestured at George's trim physique. "You're as fit as ever," he said, "with the figure of a boy."

George grinned at the compliment. "Why did you leave the Corps, Thomas? I thought you were set to remain until you retired."

"I was," he said, through a vast yawn, "but the Colonial Office recalled the regiment to London, and replaced it with the Seventy-third Regiment of Foot. It was their commanding officer, Colonel Nightingall, who was supposed to be our next governor but he fell ill so Macquarie was commissioned in his stead." He plaited his fingers over his belly. "I had no wish to return to England so I resigned. I'm very happy, and my family is thriving. I have no regrets."

George thought of the plump little Anastasia, and wanted to talk about Eloise. "How many children have you now?" he asked instead.

"Six at the last count," he replied proudly. "Three of each, which the baron spoils at every opportunity."

"He is well, I take it? What of his other daughters?"

462

"The baron is not as hale as he was. He had an episode of ill-health last year but he keeps a close eye on his hotel. Irma is married to a young naval officer and has two daughters, while Eloise has the three boys." He sat forward in his chair and lowered his voice. "Things haven't been easy in that quarter," he confided. "Edward was tried for treason with the other officers who signed Johnston's charge against Bligh."

"About time he was charged with something," muttered George. "I hope he's rotting in prison?"

Thomas shook his head. "Unfortunately he was acquitted. But it didn't end there," he said, with a grin. "Johnston was determined to be rid of him, and eventually gathered enough evidence against him to have him cashiered."

George felt the rapid beat of his pulse. "Where is he now?"

Thomas hesitated. "He and Eloise still live in that house at Watsons Bay. We don't see much of them, and on our occasional visits we find the atmosphere most uncomfortable."

"How so?" George made an effort to hide his concern.

"Edward feels the world has cheated him, so he is trying to drink the colony dry," Thomas said dismissively. "He is prone to rages and dark moods, and there have been whispers of nightmares and fits of madness."

"Then Eloise must leave him," said George.

Thomas frowned. "She will never do that," he said flatly.

"You sound very sure of yourself," said George. "What are you not telling me, Thomas?"

"I made a promise a long time ago, and will not break it now." He looked hard at George. "She had the opportunity to leave once before and didn't take it — I can only assume she stayed out of loyalty."

"I find that hard to believe. He must have cowed her into staying with him."

"I knew you'd had a soft spot for Eloise, but not that you were still enamoured." He tweaked his moustache thoughtfully. "It would explain why you've never married. Is she aware of your feelings?"

George was trapped. To deny it was to deny Eloise, but to admit it would condemn her. "My feelings are private, and have always remained so," he hedged.

"I'd keep it that way, if I were you," advised Thomas, as he stood up. "Eloise has enough to contend with without you declaring yourself. That would only make things worse for her." He tugged at his jacket in an effort to reduce the strain on the buttons. "Enough gossip! We sound like a couple of matrons. Will you come to Balmain for dinner? Anastasia is looking forward to seeing you again."

George accepted his friend's invitation, but he knew the evening would be difficult: Thomas's house overlooked the tiny bay where he and Eloise had consummated their love — the bay where they had kissed for the last time. He fetched his hat and followed the other man into the street, his thoughts confused. Eloise had once had the chance to leave Edward but had not taken it. Why? And, more to the point, how did Thomas know so much?

Parramatta Garrison, March 1810

Mandarg stood in the graveyard by the weathered board that now leant against the white slab of marble. The girl's burial place was almost flat, but the grass was bright with flowers, the words on the old marker partially obliterated by the elements. But Mandarg could feel her spirit, trapped beneath the earth, clawing for freedom to sail to the stars — and knew he had to release it if he was to find his own peace of mind.

He hitched up the cumbersome trousers, squatted in the grass and closed his eyes, letting the warmth of the sun take the chill from his ageing bones. John, the preacher, was a good man, and as Mandarg had learnt to trust him, he had explained the guilt he felt at leaving her there so obviously touched by the mind-wandering Spirits — and of how his own spirit was troubled by what he'd done in leading the white men to the settlement.

John had told him he would be forgiven if he truly repented, and Mandarg had listened attentively to his stories of a loving, forgiving God. He came to like the idea of belonging to a family again — the family of the unseen God who lived in the sky with the Ancestor Spirits, which would take the place of the family he had lost since the coming of the white man.

He had learnt that not all the invaders were cruel, that it was possible for white and black to live side by side as he'd followed John on his missionary work. He had even gone so far as to let the minister pour water over him and make the sign of the Holy Cross on his forehead, but there were certain things in John's preaching that troubled him.

Vengeance, warned John, was for God — but that was not Mandarg's way, and not the way of the Spirit Ancestors. He pondered on this as he kicked off the restrictive boots and felt the earth warm his feet. It was difficult to follow the white man's God and forget his childhood lessons. The initiation rites and ceremonies that had followed throughout his life were as much a part of him as the earth on which he sat. How could it be that this white God expected him to turn his back on the customs and beliefs that had been so deeply ingrained in him from birth? Was it so very wrong to seek revenge against a man who had led him down such a dark path, who had filled his nights with terrible dreams and sent the whispers of the dead to haunt him?

He opened his eyes and stared once more at the marker. He couldn't read the words, but John had told him what they meant. His gaze drifted from the graveyard to the surrounding bush and he saw again the carnage of that night, and remembered how, as a younger man, Lowitja had told him what the stones had foreseen.

He thought of her now, and knew the white man could never be defeated. She had been wise, and had told of the disintegration of the life they had known. Now the southern tribes were all but gone. Black was fighting black, tribe against tribe, the warriors and their women losing their pride without the guidance and spirituality of their Elders, following only the white man's ways and their need for his rum. They lived as outcasts in the land their Ancestors had willed to them — with little sign of John's forgiving and gentle God to give them solace.

Mandarg grew drowsy in the sun, and as the hum and chatter of insects overlaid the throb of the heat, he thought of the old ways. The Spirits were around him, and as he felt them draw nearer, he began to chant a song that had been handed down since Dreamtime. As he communed with the Ancient Ones he felt the pulse of their energy fill him. "Show me a sign," he muttered, "and I will do your bidding."

Time lost meaning as he sat there, but he was drawn back to the present by a soft, deep screech and the rustle of feathers. Mandarg opened his eyes and stared in wonder at what the Spirits had sent him.

The grass owl stared at him with small black eyes that seemed marked by the tracks of tears. Her breast was snowy, her wings glinting brown and orange, and her heart-shaped mask of a face was edged with ochre.

"You are welcome, beautiful one of the Spirits," he whispered. "Lowitja said you would come. What message do you bring?"

Her unblinking gaze was penetrating and hypnotic. Then she spread her wings, and flew silently in circles above his head.

Mandarg rose to his feet. The white owl was his totem, given to him at the moment he'd quickened in his mother's belly. She was a creature of the night, a bird that lived in the land of Kakadu, but she had been sent far south on this bright day to guide him.

He suddenly felt the need to be cleansed of the white man's influence in her presence: he kicked away the boots and stripped off the uncomfortable clothes. Naked and proud, he followed the owl's flight as she rose higher and higher in ever-widening circles.

She flew on the hot wind, her beady eyes searching for prey. Then she swooped, long, yellow legs stretched out, talons bared.

Mandarg held his breath. He understood what she was trying to tell him: if she caught the prey he was to seek revenge; if she did not, he must return to the nomadic life and forget all that had happened.

The owl plunged like an arrow from the sky, eyes fixed on quarry he couldn't see in the long grass. Then, with a screech of triumph, she rose once more, a lizard held fast in her talons.

Mandarg followed her progress as, once again, she circled overhead, then settled on the fallen branch before him. He looked into her eyes as she dropped her catch at his feet, and knew what he must do.

As she rose once more into the air, he picked up the lizard, tucked it into the hair belt that had never left his waist and followed her into the welcoming shelter of the bush. The Spirits had spoken, as Lowitja had foretold. Now he would walk alone, recapture the spirituality and pride he had once possessed and learn once again of the ancient ways as he awaited their next command.

PART SIX

The Bitter Cup

CHAPTER
TWENTY

In the bush, August 1810

It was a crisp, bright morning, the bars of sunlight reaching through the remnants of the night mist to pool on the bush floor. The air was filled with birdsong as the riders made their way through the trees.

Edward saw the lack of zeal in his two elder sons and felt the familiar shaft of impatience. "Stop dawdling," he shouted. "Our prey will be gone at this rate."

Harry and Charles exchanged a glance and nudged their ponies into a trot. "Can't we just watch the kangaroos, Papa?" said Charles, as they drew alongside him. "I don't like killing them when they have young in their pouches."

Edward snorted. "They're vermin." He reached for the ever-present flask at his hip and drank. "Culling them is the only answer." He saw the distaste on Charles's face and, despite his best intentions not to show it today, irritation got the better of him. "The pelts bring in the money that provides you with food and comfort — and I haven't seen you turn up your nose at either."

Colour suffused the boy's face. Harry's eyes flashed with something akin to anger, but he held his tongue — perhaps knowing that any retort would merely fuel his father's ill-temper.

Edward's head was pounding with a hangover, the brightness of the sunlight hurting his eyes. Charles was almost thirteen, his lanky figure filling out, the first hint of golden fuzz already showing above his lip. He was a handsome boy, he acknowledged, and wished he could feel a modicum of affection for him — but his delicate bone structure and long-lashed blue eyes were too like his mother's while his liking for schoolbooks and his squeamishness set Edward's teeth on edge.

He felt a swell of pride at how fearless and strong Harry was, compared to his brother. At eleven, Harry was everything he'd wanted in a son, and he could already see glimpses of the man he would become; the boy reminded Edward of himself at that age. Like Oliver, he didn't bear the birthmark of the Cadwalladers — only one in every generation did — but he was a true scion of that noble family, from his dark hair and eyes to the tip of his aristocratic nose. Edward was dismayed that he wouldn't inherit the title and follow in his footsteps.

He took another sip from the silver flask, hoping to ease the vicious headache. He'd been looking forward to this trip, had planned it for days in the hope that it would bring him closer to his eldest son, for although he didn't often listen to Eloise, she had slowly made him see that his relationship with Charles bore all the hallmarks of that which he'd had with his own father.

Yet it seemed that, no matter how hard he tried, he would always fail.

He felt a pang of regret that Oliver hadn't come with them this morning. The nine-year-old was confined to the house with measles, and Eloise had refused to allow him outside until the spots had cleared. It was a damned nuisance — the boy's presence would have gone some way towards making the expedition more satisfying; for he was a good shot and his enthusiasm for the hunt might have instilled a little more eagerness in the others.

Unhappiness surged through him as he reviewed his life, and he gripped the pommel as his vision blurred. His eldest son was a disappointment, his career had ended in disgrace, the nightmares still haunted him, he had little income, and there was no comfort to be had from his wife. Maudlin with drink and bitter disappointment, he almost fell from the saddle.

"Are you unwell, Papa?" Harry helped him regain his balance. "Perhaps we should return home so you can rest."

Edward made a concerted effort to sit upright. "The fresh air will soon clear my head." He could barely focus, he realised, but he'd hunted like this before and saw no reason to abandon his plan. "Come, you two. I'll race you to the clearing."

The boar peered short-sightedly into the undergrowth, his short, sturdy legs planted firmly in the mud of the waterhole. He had drunk his fill and was preparing to forage when he heard the noise and stilled, alert for danger. His snout twitched, the coarse bristles of his dark coat rising as he scented the unmistakable presence of man and horse.

With the innate sense of self-preservation that had come from being caged by man, he lumbered angrily out of the mud and shoved himself among the ferns and scrub. His irritability was heightened because he could see little and he was hungry — the hunt for food had been interrupted by the intruders. His small black eyes glared into the darkness, and his tail twitched as the scent grew stronger.

George had finally persuaded Thomas to tell him the truth, and he'd come to the beach every morning since. Yet there was still no sign of Eloise. He was worried as he sat on his horse, surveying the empty shore. The tide was out, the sea already taking on the deep turquoise hue of the clear sky, the waves sighing on the sand. It was a perfect morning for a ride, so why hadn't she come?

Unable to dispel the feeling that something was wrong, and unwilling to leave without seeing her, he urged the horse down on to the hardened sand above the high-water mark. It tossed its head and danced about as if aware of its rider's unease.

"Steady, boy," said George. "I'm as nervous as you, but I must see for myself."

As he rode along the beach he heard distant rifle shots, and wondered if a hunting party was out on Edward's land. If so, he must be careful — Eloise might be entertaining the wives, and he could think of no reason to appear uninvited.

He slowed the horse to a walk as the house came into view. It stood on a gentle rise beyond the beach, and although a wisp of smoke rose from the chimney, the shutters were closed, and there was no sign of life in the garden and stables.

George frowned, the sense of foreboding growing stronger. Thomas had assured him the occupants were at home — that Eloise rarely left the house — and yet the place looked abandoned.

He nudged the horse into a walk and approached the gate, noting that the paint was peeling and the wood weathered. As he let it slam behind him he saw that the lawns needed cutting and the flowerbeds were overgrown. When he approached the front door, neglect was evident in the poor state of the veranda.

He slid from the saddle and tied the reins to the rotting balustrade. His mouth was dry, his pulse racing, but his feet took him up the sagging steps. Before he could ponder the wisdom of such an action, he rapped on the front door.

After his solitary time in the bush Mandarg felt invincible. It was as if he'd been reborn, had revisited the painful initiation ceremony that had bound him to his tribe and the beliefs of his people, and returned him to the spiritual heart of his Ancestors.

He had hunted alone, chanted the songs of the Ancient Ones as the moon rose, and reacquainted himself with the cave paintings that told the stories of

Dreamtime, and with the earth that had nourished him and given him life. Now his body was lean, the muscles honed, his senses as keen as they had been in youth.

His steady lope had brought him to the white devil's land before the sun had risen. In the grey of first light he had smeared his face and body with the red clay that surrounded the waterhole, and knew he was perfectly camouflaged in the shifting shadows of the trees. With his spears held loosely at his side, he'd melted into the trees and watched the man and the two boys ride past. There were rifles slung from the saddles, and the man had a pistol at his hip.

This did not worry Mandarg for he could bring death without warning on the silent swiftness of his Ancestors' weapon. The war spears he carried were longer than the ones he used for hunting, and he had spent many hours grinding the flint heads until they were lethally sharp. They had then been plunged into the squirming innards of a rotting carcass so that they were liberally smeared with poison. A single graze from this deadly weapon was enough to fell the most powerful beast.

Mandarg heard the rustle of wings. There, on a branch, was the Spirit Owl, her white chest feathers gleaming in the halflight. He nodded to her and she blinked. As he moved stealthily in and out of the shadows, following the riders deeper into the bush, she flew beside him. She would judge when the time was right. Then he would strike.

476

Edward reached into the pouch, dragged out the tiny joey and slit its throat, then tossed it away. He held the bloodied knife out to Charles as he squatted beside the mother. "Slit her belly and peel off the hide," he ordered. "But mind how you do it. A torn pelt is worthless."

Charles backed away, eyes wide with horror, face blanched. "I can't," he muttered.

"You'll do as I say," shouted Edward, making a grab for the boy and pressing the knife into his hand. He gave him a shove and sent him to his knees beside the stricken kangaroo. "Get on with it," he snarled.

"I'll do it," said Harry, and reached for the knife. "You know Charles hates the sight of blood."

"Then it's time he learnt to be a man." Edward snatched the knife and returned it to Charles, who had turned a ghastly green. "The boy's spineless. I'm ashamed to have such a weakling for a son."

"He's not weak," shouted Harry. "He has a gentle heart — and that is no reason to be ashamed of him."

Edward raised an eyebrow. "My, my." He swigged from his flask. "You'd better curb your temper, boy, or you'll feel the weight of my belt on your back."

"It's all right, Harry," said Charles. "Father's right. It is time I learnt to do this." He began tentatively to cut into the soft underbelly.

"Ha!" scorned Edward. "Look at him, pale and trembling, weeping like a girl." He snatched away the knife. "Damn you! You're as much use as a wet sack of flour."

He knelt unsteadily over the carcass, the knife slippery in his hand as he tried to concentrate on the delicate process. The pelt seemed reluctant to leave the carcass and the knife felt blunt, but he hacked until it was free. He was sweating as he rolled it up and stuffed it with the others into the bundle on the back of his saddle. As he mounted, he hoped the two boys hadn't noticed his clumsiness, but Charles and Harry seemed diverted by the white cockatoos that were swooping in and out of the trees.

Edward shook his flask and drained the final drops. His thirst was raging, his head bursting and his temper barely contained. He had hoped this would be a chance to teach Charles some bushcraft, to show him how skilful he was and try to instil some interest in the boy — but his fear was well founded: Charles was indeed a whimpering fool. It was all very well for Eloise to praise his ability at his books and admire his extraordinary talent for drawing, but neither would make him a man — and Edward's frustration made him thirstier than ever.

He gathered up the reins as the surrounding trees seemed to whirl round him. As he peered into the shadows he thought he saw a black face and a pair of staring eyes. They looked familiar — like the eyes that haunted him nightly.

He was determined not to be rattled, and put the vision down to an over-heightened imagination. "Come, Harry," he said gruffly. "Let's see if we can track down that escaped boar we've heard so much about."

Mandarg's expression was grim as he met the white devil's gaze. He had seen the fear in those eyes and welcomed it; drunk as he was, the man had recognised him. He stood in the shadows and watched them ride away, suddenly troubled. The need to avenge the deaths of his black brothers and sisters and to release the white woman's spirit was greater than ever, but he hadn't bargained on the presence of the two boys.

The owl ruffled her feathers, and her low screech made him look up.

He stared into her unblinking eyes, hearing the Spirit voices of those who'd brought her. When silence fell once more he gripped the spears and followed the tracks, certain now that the Spirits would show him their plan.

The sound of George's rap on the door echoed back to him, speaking of empty, silent rooms. Emboldened by fear for Eloise, he knocked again, louder this time, his urgency making the door shudder. The hollow echo was followed by the sound of hurrying footsteps. He took a step back as a key was turned and a pair of suspicious brown eyes were pinned on him through the narrow opening. "The master isn't here," she said, poised to close the door on him.

George planted his boot in the gap. "It is your mistress I wish to see," he said. "Is she at home?"

"She is not."

George didn't believe her. "Where is she?"

"That ain't none of your business. Get your boot out'a the door and be on your way."

479

He kept the boot where it was. "I know she's here and I wish to see her," he persisted. "Please tell her it's George. She'll speak to me."

"She's not here." The brown eyes were belligerent.

"Eloise!" he called. "Eloise, it is George."

The eyes held a glint of triumph as no reply was forthcoming. "You can yell all you like," she muttered. "There's no one to hear you but me and Ned — and I wouldn't wait about if I were you. Ned's only in the yard, and he's got a gun."

George knew he couldn't knock the woman off her feet, no matter how much he might want to. "Eloise," he called again. "Eloise, please let me in. I have to know that you're safe." At that moment he heard the sound of a rifle being cocked.

George turned sharply, and as he did so, the door slammed behind him. "You must be Ned," he said, somewhat shakily, as he looked down the gun barrel.

"Don't matter who I be, sir. You's trespassin'."

The grim face and steady eyes told George he was beaten. Ned would have little compunction in shooting visitors on the doorstep, and was presumably under his master's orders. He untied his horse and swung into the saddle. "I hope you don't treat every caller so," he said, trying to make light of the situation.

"Only them what's not invited," Ned replied dourly, as he lifted the rifle to underline his threat.

George kicked the horse into a gallop. He jumped the picket fence and was soon racing down the beach. Yet he knew that could not be the end of it. He had to see Eloise. The only problem was finding a way to do so.

"Has he gone, Meg?" Eloise sat in the shadows of the drawing room.

"Yes, m'lady. My Ned's seen 'im off."

"Thank you, Meg. I would appreciate it if the gentleman's visit wasn't mentioned in my husband's presence."

Meg folded her arms. "You can trust me and Ned." She cocked her head, boot-button eyes filled with concern. "You should rest, m'lady. You look peaky."

"Thank you, Meg. I will rest in here until dinner. If Oliver should wake, please let me know."

"You'll 'ear 'im soon enough," she replied, with an affectionate grin. "The only time we get any peace in this 'ouse is when 'e's asleep."

Eloise leant into the cushions as Meg closed the door quietly. Meg knew nothing of her love affair with George, but she was fiercely protective. It was strange that her closest friend and ally should be an emancipated convict — but these were strange times and her circumstances were unusual.

George's unexpected arrival had thrown her into confusion. It was imperative he didn't see her — that he left before Edward returned — because she couldn't trust herself not to fall into his arms and beg him to take her away. Just the sound of his voice, so sharp with urgency, had touched her heart. How much more difficult it would have been to face him.

Eloise rose from the sofa and approached the mirror above the fireplace. Her face was a pale glimmer in the soft light that pierced the broken shutters, and she traced her fingers across the ugly bruise that swelled on her cheekbone. It was the latest in a countless number, and she'd learnt long ago to detect the signs of Edward's ill-temper and stay out of his way. But he'd caught her unprepared this morning, the blow almost knocking her off her feet when she'd refused to allow Oliver to join the hunting trip. "At least he doesn't hit the boys," she whispered. "I can bear anything if he leaves them alone."

She looked into the reflection of her troubled eyes. Slowly but surely Edward had reduced her to a meek, trembling shadow who had lost the will to fight back. The ghost of the woman she'd once been still echoed somewhere, but she no longer had the strength to find her. She sank back into the sofa, defeated by the knowledge that she didn't have the courage to leave.

The boar snuffled in the undergrowth. He had scented the juicy fungus that grew at the base of the tree, and hunger made him reckless. He buried his nose in the soft earth, digging with his curved incisors in a frenzy of excitement as the scent grew stronger and all thought of danger evaporated.

Edward checked that they were downwind and reined in his horse. "Look," he muttered. "See the ferns swaying? Something large is in there, and I would wager it's the boar." He fumbled as he drew his rifle from the saddle holster and almost dropped it.

Charles and Harry had never hunted boar before, and knew it could be dangerous. They cocked their own rifles, aware that even the soft click was enough to alert it to their presence.

"I'm going to flush him out," murmured Edward. "Charles, go over there and, Harry, stay here. Shoot the minute you see him and don't miss. An injured boar is highly unpredictable."

Satisfied that the boys were placed where he wanted them, Edward followed the creature's passage through the undergrowth. He would have given a king's ransom for a drink, but the flask was empty, it was too far from home, and the boar wouldn't wait. He made a Herculean effort to control the trembling in his limbs.

The horse was reluctant to enter the bush once it had scented the boar, and Edward dug in his spurs to make it move, but the animal was making so much noise that the beast was sure to hear them.

The boar lifted his snout, black eyes peering myopically through the undergrowth. He could smell man and horse, could feel the vibrations in the earth beneath his trotters and knew danger was close. With a grunt of unease, he sought deeper refuge.

Edward realised there was no point in trying to make a stealthy approach, the horse was too jittery — so he kicked his mount on and began to shout as they hurtled towards their prey.

Now the boar was bewildered and frightened. The noise was all around him and there seemed no escape. He couldn't see beyond the end of his snout, and his short, sturdy legs were getting sucked into the mud as he twisted back and forth in a desperate attempt to find a way through the scrub. As the crashing hoofs and loud bellows drew nearer he plunged full-tilt through a gap in the ferns.

"He's yours," yelled Edward, as the boar hurtled out. "Quick! Before he gets away!"

The boar felt the first bullet scorch his flank. He screeched as the second bit deep into his snout. Maddened with pain and fear, he raced blindly across the clearing.

"You've only grazed it!" yelled Edward. "Fire again!" He fumbled with his rifle, trying to maintain his balance as his horse threatened to bolt. Sweat stung his eyes, and fear made his heart race — Harry was in the boar's direct line, but his rifle was jammed, and his pony was shying.

Then Charles's pony reared.

The boar hesitated as the vibrations beneath his trotters grew stronger. The pain in his snout was excruciating, his rage at his predicament overwhelming. He saw dancing hoofs and spun in search of another target. His ears twitched as he saw the human fall and, with furious intent, hurtled towards him, curved incisors primed to rip and tear at his enemy.

"Charlie!" screamed Harry, as his brother hit the ground. "Charlie, get the rifle. Shoot! Shoot!"

Charles reached for the rifle — but it was too far away. He screamed as the boar raced towards him, and tried desperately to scrabble out of its way.

The boar had scented the enemy and was closing fast. He dipped his head for the charge that would deliver his fangs deep into the body.

Edward was sweating with fear as he tried to clear the fog from his brain, steady his hand and get the boar in his sights. He pulled the trigger.

Mandarg threw the spear as the shot rang out.

The boar's fangs were inches from the boy's chest when the spear felled it.

A shocked silence filled the clearing as the three froze.

"It's a miracle!" shouted Harry, as he almost fell from his horse in his haste to reach his brother. "Charlie, Charlie. It's all right, the black man saved you." He flung himself to the ground, dragged the still-twitching boar off the boy's legs and reached for his brother.

Edward clambered from the saddle, his gaze fixed on the warrior who stood at the other side of the clearing. Befuddled with drink, his heart was still pounding with fear.

"Charlie!" screamed Harry. "Charlie, no!"

Edward tore his gaze from the black man and stumbled across the clearing, confused as to why the warrior had appeared and why Harry was shrieking. Yet as his shadow fell across his sons his confusion was swept away in the realisation that the nightmare had only just begun.

Charles lay still in Harry's arms, his chest torn open by the bullet.

"You've killed him," shouted Harry. "You've murdered my brother."

Edward looked into his son's hate-filled face and stumbled back. "No," he whispered in disbelief. "I was aiming for the boar," he stuttered. "I never miss."

Harry was sobbing as he laid his brother on the ground. "You do when you're drunk," he snarled. He leapt to his feet, rage spurring him to pummel his father's chest. "Drunken murderer!" he howled.

Edward stood like a rock and tried to absorb his son's painful punches. Suddenly he was more sober than he had been for years, and as he withstood the battering he looked beyond Charles's still body and met the black man's eye. They stared at one another for what seemed an age until the warrior disappeared into the bush.

Harry's blows were lessening in intensity now, the rage that had given them strength ebbing into heart-rending sobs. Edward shook off the feeling that the black man had been trying to tell him something and grasped the boy's arms, holding them fast until the child was in control of himself. He didn't know what to say or do to ease his son's pain but he understood that there would be no absolution for the crime he'd committed today.

Eloise was reading to Oliver when Meg rushed into the bedroom. The sight of her maid's ashen face made her leap from the chair. "What is it?"

"There's been an accident," she sobbed. "A terrible accident."

"Look after Oliver." Eloise pushed past her and flew down the stairs. The front door was open and she raced on to the veranda, stumbling to a halt as she saw the riders reach the yard. Her gaze darted from Harry and the pony he was leading to the still figure in Edward's arms. "No," she breathed. "Dear God, please, no."

She ran down the rickety steps to where Edward waited for her. Her darling boy's face was bloodless, his chest torn apart — and as she reached to touch him, she knew he was gone.

The scream of anguish was trapped deep inside her as the tears rolled down her cheeks. "How did it happen?" she whispered.

Edward, mute in his suffering, made no move to climb from his horse or relinquish his tragic burden.

Harry put his arm round her waist, and as she stood trembling in the yard's deepening shadows, she learnt how her son had died.

Eloise stared at her husband with overpowering hatred. Yet when she spoke, only a quaver in her voice betrayed her inner turmoil. "Ned, give me your gun," she ordered. It felt heavy and unwieldy, but reassuring in her hands. "Now take my son and carry him into the house." She put her hand on Harry's shoulder. "Go to Oliver."

Harry's protest was silenced by the look on her face, and as Edward silently gave up his son, she followed their progress across the yard and into the house.

After the door had closed on them, she cocked the rifle and faced her husband. "It would give me the greatest pleasure to shoot you," she said, "but I am no murderer and my sons need me to care for them."

His relief was visible as he shifted in the saddle and prepared to dismount.

"Stay where you are," she rapped. "I will shoot if I have to."

"Come, Eloise —"

"You will leave now," she stated, "and you will never return."

"You have no right to send me away."

"Unless you go I will have you arrested for murder," she said.

"It was an accident. I didn't mean to kill him."

She held the rifle steady, the barrel aimed at his chest.

"Be reasonable, Eloise," he pleaded. "Harry and Oliver are still my sons and this is my house. You cannot deny me access to either."

"You lost your right to them and to your home when you murdered Charles." Her voice broke but she steeled herself to remain calm.

Edward gathered up his reins. "I will see you tomorrow at the funeral," he said. "Perhaps by then you will have come to your senses."

"You will not be welcome at the funeral, and you will never approach me, Harry or Oliver again. Now go, before my finger grows heavier on the trigger."

"You will not get away with this," he snarled. "I'll see you on the streets before I let you take the house." He dug in his spurs and galloped out of the yard.

The house was silent, the candles guttering and the lamps turned down. Harry and Oliver had fallen into fitful sleep, the loyal Meg sitting with them through the night as her husband, Ned, patrolled outside.

Eloise rose from her chair as the first rays of light pierced the shutters. Her lonely vigil was over, but the day stretched before her and she wondered how she would survive it. Yet survive it she must. Having rediscovered her strength in facing Edward, she would use it now to help her boys through not only today but the weeks and months to come.

She looked towards the light as it grew brighter, and as she felt its timorous warmth, renewed vigour flooded her. She would never again be brow-beaten or punched. She would stand tall and proud — and would defend her right to be the Eloise she was meant to be, regardless of what was to come.

Her thoughts turned fleetingly to George, and the ghost of a smile touched her lips. If he still loved her, perhaps there was even the chance of a new life — but this was not the time to ponder such things. George had waited many years. If his love was true he would wait a while longer.

★ ★ ★

The news had come to George earlier that morning and he had wanted to fly to her side. Yet common sense told him he must bide his time, be patient until Eloise called him.

He had followed at a distance as the black-plumed horses pulled the gun-carriage across the straw-strewn cobbles in the narrow streets of Sydney Town to the convict-built church. Now the funeral was over and he had returned to his home on the hill where he could sit on the balcony in the stillness of the starlit night and mull over the events of the day.

He couldn't dispel the image of Eloise, her bearing showing renewed steel even though her face was hidden behind the black veil. She had held her sons' hands as they stood at the graveside, and had not succumbed to noisy tears as her sisters had.

George had learnt from Thomas that she and the boys would move into the hotel tonight, to be with her father, and he doubted she would ever return to that house by the beach.

Edward's absence from the funeral had been remarked upon by the crowds that filled the cemetery and spilled into the lane. For once in his life Thomas had been cagey when questioned about the rumours that were circulating, which had made George even more uneasy about the truth behind the hunting accident. "Perhaps the rumours are true," he murmured. "I pray to God, for all their sakes, that they are not."

Edward crashed through the back door of Kernow House and stumbled across the kitchen into the hallway. He had been drinking steadily ever since his confrontation with Eloise, and although he had intended to be at the funeral, he had passed out in a back room at the Parramatta tavern and the day was gone.

"Eloise!" he roared. "Show yourself, woman!"

The echoes resounded in the empty rooms and filled his head. He staggered across the hall and into the parlour. As he poured himself a generous measure he frowned. The furniture was covered with dust-sheets, the shutters were closed, the curtains drawn and all sign of Eloise and the boys had gone.

His disbelief was laced with a fear he refused to countenance as he lurched from one room to the next and found they, too, were empty. On his return to the parlour he picked up the decanter, tore the sheet from his chair and slumped into it. "So you finally left me," he muttered. "I thought you'd never find the courage."

He had never felt so low, or so alone, and he closed his eyes on the treacherous tears of self-pity. He had no money, no career and no family. His eldest son was dead, his beloved Harry hated him and, no doubt, Oliver did too. Eloise had shown more spirit than he'd ever thought possible, and the authorities were probably on their way to arrest him for Charles's murder. As for this house . . . He shuddered. It would never be his, for Carlton's threat would become reality now that Eloise had gone.

The darkness was profound when he opened his eyes, and the chill had crept into his bones. He struggled to light the fire Meg must have laid earlier, and as the flames licked the wood, he put out his trembling hands to warm them.

Staring into the flames, he saw broken bodies, burning *gunyahs*, bloody swords and men on horseback. He tried to look away but found he couldn't, and as he watched he heard the cries of the dying and the rattle of war shields.

He spun round to peer into the darkness, the terror a creeping thing that seemed determined to consume him. "Go away," he rasped. "I've been punished enough."

A soft snicker broke the silence.

Someone was playing tricks on him. He lit the lamps, but the shadows remained, closing in on him as they did in his dreams. "I lost my son," he shouted at the demons. "Is that not enough for you?"

Dancing shadows were his only answer.

Edward tripped over the dust-sheet and knocked into the delicate table. The decanters and bottles crashed to the floor where they shattered into glittering shards. He stared at them stupidly, saw the fire reflected in the crystal and raced for the door. He had to get out — had to escape the voices and images that were driving him insane with fear.

Mandarg sat close to where the boy had been killed two days before. He didn't know why he'd chosen to remain there, but he seemed to be fulfilling some purpose the Spirit Owl had not yet revealed. He had built a fire and was cooking a goanna he'd caught earlier. The wild pig still lay in the clearing, and he knew its meat was far sweeter than that of the lizard — but the pig had been poisoned by the spear. To eat it would mean death.

He stared beyond the flames as he ate his meal, at one with the night and the star-filled sky, content to have returned to the ancient ways. When he left this place, he would travel across the mountains into the lush hunting grounds where the remnants of his tribe had gathered, far from the white man's influence.

His thoughts were broken by the sound of trampling feet. The lizard forgotten, he reached for his spears and stood, the clay markings on his body gleaming in the firelight.

The Spirit Owl swooped down and landed softly on his spear arm. It was an unmistakable command to wait.

Edward had no idea where he was as he stumbled over tree roots and became entangled in creepers. He'd been trying to escape the voices but they were following him, and with every step he took he sank deeper into despair. A branch caught him a glancing blow to the cheek, but it was nothing compared with the agony he was already suffering, and he lumbered on.

As if guided by an unseen hand to an unknown destination, he staggered through the bush until he saw a glow through the trees. He paused, wondering what it meant. It seemed to draw him, and he stumbled towards it.

The naked warrior stood by the fire, his lean body gleaming with the grey of his war markings. The eyes in the dark face stared back at him, and on his arm a white owl shimmered in the firelight.

Edward knew this was his tormentor, the warrior who had haunted his dreams and watched him from the shadows. The energy to run ebbed away. There could be no hiding-place from the demons that tormented him.

As he reached for the pistol at his hip he saw the owl's eyes, unblinking and accusing. He raised the pistol to his temple and, mesmerised, pulled the trigger.

EPILOGUE

Hawks Head, October 1812

The mission chapel was a rough wooden shack perched on stilts away from the riverbank. It had had a fresh coat of whitewash for the occasion, and a new cross had been erected at the gable end so there could be no doubt as to its purpose. That morning Ezra's congregation filled every seat, and the Hawks Head natives jostled for position outside.

"I can see that my girl is happy at last," murmured the baron, as he handed Eloise down from the carriage. "You are radiant."

Eloise felt a flutter of excitement as she smiled at him. "I'm about to marry the man I've loved for years," she said. "I'm the luckiest of women to be given another chance of happiness."

"He's a good man," the baron concurred, as she took his arm.

Eloise nodded, her joy so great she couldn't find words to express it. George had never stopped loving her. He'd given her time and comfort when she'd needed it after Charles's death, had loved her quietly

495

and deeply, waiting until she was able to see beyond the pain and look to the future. Now, at last, their dreams could be fulfilled. "Come, Papa," she said. "We are keeping him waiting."

As they exchanged their marriage vows Eloise looked into George's eyes, and when he kissed her and proclaimed her his wife she felt an overwhelming sense of rightness.

"At last you're mine," he whispered. "I love you, Mrs Collinson."

Eloise touched his face and the new wedding ring flashed in the sunlight that poured through the window.

The moment was broken by the clash of chords as Susan began to play the old piano. It hadn't been tuned for years and was badly chewed by termites.

"That is our cue," said George. "Mother's enthusiasm is all very well, but that piano won't last much longer."

Eloise took his arm and they faced the congregation. When she saw Harry and Oliver beaming with delight, her joy was complete. At thirteen, Harry was so grown-up in the short waistcoat and cutaway coat, and although Oliver was trying manfully to maintain a serious bearing, exuberance was clear in his face. She kissed them both, then they followed her and George out of the chapel into the blinding sunshine.

Nell dabbed her eyes with a handkerchief and sniffed back the tears. "I love a weddin'." She sighed. "Nothin' like a good cry to set you up for the day."

496

Alice gave her a swift hug, managing to avoid having her eye poked out by Nell's preposterous hat, which was over-laden with silk flowers, feathers and ribbons. Nell had lost none of her flamboyance, but Alice had come to accept and admire it — without it, her friend simply wouldn't have been Nell. Her own hat was a sensible straw with a pink ribbon tied under the chin as befitted a woman of fifty-one, and her simple dress looked plain beside the brilliant green of Nell's.

"My compliments to you both," said Henry Carlton, as he handed them each a glass of the champagne he'd imported. "You look lovely, Alice. And, Nell, what a magnificent hat."

"You don't look so bad yerself," replied Nell, taking a gulp of the champagne. She winked at him over the glass. "For an old bloke, you scrub up 'andsome."

"Sixty-one isn't old, Nell," he retorted, grey eyes twinkling. "I'm in my prime."

Alice watched as they teased one another, and warmth flooded through her. Henry Carlton still proposed to her whenever he came to Australia, but they both knew it would never come to anything. Their friendship had deepened, certainly, and although his short-term partnership in Moonrakers had ended long ago, he was a regular and welcome visitor. She and Nell respected his advice and guidance.

"Henry!" The baron had lost none of his bombast, and his voice could probably have been heard in the next homestead. "Good to see you, my friend. Now, tell me, where did you find such excellent champagne?"

Alice and Nell watched the two men stroll towards the tables that had been set up beneath the trees. "Blimey," breathed Nell. "The old fellow's still got a voice like a cannon."

The baron had become quite a personality in Sydney Town, and was often to be found in the bar of his hotel, regaling his guests with outrageous anecdotes. Yet, despite his age and bonhomie, he never lost sight of his business, and his staff were often pushed to the limit of their patience.

"There's Amy," said Nell. "I should go and tend the baby."

"He's quite happy," murmured Alice. "Look, he's with Niall over there in the shade."

"They make a pretty picture, don't they?" said Nell, as Amy went to sit beside her husband, who was cradling their son tenderly. "Who'd have thought my Amy would settle to marriage and motherhood so calmly?"

"I don't know about calm," said Alice, with a wry smile. "They're always fighting over something."

Nell grinned. "But they only do it so's they can enjoy the making up. That's the best part of marriage."

A momentary silence fell between them as they remembered how it had once been with Jack and Billy. The ache was still there, but softer now that the balm of time had healed the wounds.

Alice put her arm through Nell's. "Come, we'll find the twins. There's nothing like a wedding for romance to blossom, and I want to know if Sarah's beau has plucked up the courage to propose."

★ ★ ★

George was helping Harry and Oliver to pack the last of the cases into the back of the wagon. The trunks had already been stowed aboard the *Georgeana* in readiness for their departure the following evening, and the boys were planning what they would do during the long sea voyage to England.

He stepped back, delighting in their excitement for the coming adventure. He knew how they felt for he'd experienced the same thrill when he'd boarded the *Golden Grove* all those years before. He smiled as he remembered leaning eagerly over the side of the ship so he could watch the rest of the First Fleet sail from Portsmouth. When Eloise's sons returned to Australia in two years' time, they would bring the memories with them, and perhaps yearn to see more of this exciting new world.

"George?"

He turned at his mother's voice. "I was thinking about the *Golden Grove*," he said, as he put his arm round her. "Were we brave or foolhardy to make such a journey into the unknown?"

Her face was suddenly youthful. "It was a mixture of both," she replied. "It was terrifying and exciting, and I often feared for our lives, but look what we've achieved in these twenty-four years."

He followed the sweep of her arm, which seemed to encompass the growing family. Ernest and Bess were talking to Nell and Alice. Meg and Ned had come from their smallholding with their daughter, and Henry Carlton was in deep conversation with the baron, who had been accompanied to the wedding by Eloise's sisters. Thomas had been joined by Irma's husband and they were sleeping off the champagne in the shade of the pepper tree while a clutch of children, black and white, raced about. Nell's twins were sitting with their sweethearts on a blanket by the river, and Amy and Niall were engrossed in their baby.

George tipped his hat and grinned as the Aboriginal stockmen sauntered past with the convicts on their way to the laden table. Stoked with rum, their shouts of congratulation were a little slurred. There would be sore heads in the morning.

"I'm glad your papa has taken to Eloise," said Susan, as they watched them stroll by the river. "She's a sweet girl and innocent of any blame for what happened."

George hugged his mother and kissed her brow. His heart was too full for words.

Then Susan looked up at him. "George . . ."

He frowned. "What is it, Mother?"

"There is something I wish to give you before you leave for England." She rummaged in her pocket and pulled out two letters. "You will see that the first is addressed to my sister-in-law, Ann." She looked towards Ezra as if to confirm that he was out of earshot. "Give it to her when your uncle Gilbert is otherwise occupied," she said.

George had a sharp memory of his father's brother, a bluff, good-hearted man who had used his position as Australia's first judge-advocate to see fair play in the courts. "It sounds a bit cloak-and-dagger, Mother," he joked. "Are you sure I can be entrusted with such a secret document?"

"Don't try me, George." Susan rapped him on the arm with her fan. "Just give me your word that you will deliver it safely."

He took the letter, his curiosity piqued as he noticed her high colour and the urgency in her tone. "I will do as you ask," he replied, "but it's not like you to keep secrets."

"Isn't it?" she replied tartly. "I might be your mother, George, but you don't know everything about me." She shoved the second letter into his hand. "This is for you. It is not to be opened until after my death."

"Mother, really," he protested. "We'll only be gone for two years, and there's plenty of life in you yet." He thrust it back at her. "I refuse to take it."

"Do as you're told for once, George." She glanced once more at Ezra as she pressed the letter into George's hand. "Your father knows most of what this contains, and approves. Neither of us is getting any younger, and it's only right that we put our affairs in order."

George held the letter as if it burnt his fingers. The last thing he wanted today was to be reminded of his parents' mortality, and his mother was behaving so strangely that he was beginning to fear for her well-being. "You say he knows most of what you've written, what of the rest?"

"It will all be explained when the time comes," she said, as Ezra and Eloise came towards them. "Now put it away and forget that we've had this conversation. Your bride is ready to leave."

Cornwall, July 1813

They had been in England for six months, and had approached Mousehole in the carriage he'd hired in Bath. George had gazed out at the familiar blue of the sea and the towering cliffs that sheltered the tiny fishing villages along the coast. There were white sails on the water, gulls overhead, the smell of the moors in the air, and, as the carriage had slowed to negotiate the steep hill down into Mousehole, he had seen the house by the church. It had changed little since his childhood. The huddle of cottages, far below, came into view, exactly as he'd remembered them. It was almost as if he'd never left.

It was the homecoming he had envisaged, and although his heart had sung with recognition at every turn of the steep hill, he had felt an uneasiness he couldn't dispel. As the horse had plodded towards the stone quay and the squabble of gulls that fought over the remains of that day's catch followed them, his thoughts had turned once more to his mother's letter.

He had given it to his aunt, watching her closely as she read it. Her sharp intake of breath and her sudden pallor showed how deeply she'd been affected by it, yet she had refused to answer his questions and had thrown the letter into the fire. It was a mystery, and George didn't like it. Yet he was relieved he'd lodged the second letter with his solicitor in Sydney before they left for England: the temptation to open it after his aunt's reaction would have been too strong to resist.

502

A week had passed since their arrival in Mousehole and, having settled into a nearby inn, George had taken Eloise and the boys to his childhood haunts. They had visited the old house, sat with the new incumbent over tea, and even attended a long and tedious morning service in the church where his father had once preached. Their welcome home had been warm and generous, and although the older generation of Collinsons was gone now, his parents were still talked about fondly even by those who had never met them.

The day had dawned brightly, but with a chill wind blowing off the sea — a chill that touched his heart, for today he was taking Eloise and the boys to see Harry's inheritance. The atmosphere in the carriage was heavy, for Eloise was tense, Harry had made it obvious he had little interest in the proceedings and Oliver was unusually silent. He tried to lighten the mood by whistling, but stopped when Eloise rather crossly told him to be quiet.

George frowned as he steered the horse and carriage along the cliff-top track and finally between the crumbling gate pillars and up the weed-infested drive. He had expected Eloise to be reluctant to visit this place, but he hadn't foreseen how strongly she would resent being here.

Trying to make light of the situation, he forced a smile. "There it is, Harry," he said, as he pulled the horse to a halt. "Treleaven House, the country seat of the Earl of Kernow."

Eloise stiffened beside him. George knew he shouldn't have brought her: her face had paled and her eyes were shadowed — perhaps with memories of Edward and Charles.

"Why do so many places start with 'Tre'?" Oliver was looking at the letters carved above the once magnificent door.

George dragged his attention back to the younger boy. "It's the Cornish for 'farm'. Treleavean means 'Leaven Farm'," he explained. "Like 'Kernow' is the old Cornish for 'Corn-wall'."

Harry eyed the ruined house and the unkempt parklands that swept towards the sea. "It's a good thing I don't want to set foot in it," he said, with a grimace. "The place looks as if it's about to fall down — and as far as I'm concerned it can rot."

"It's not that bad," protested Oliver. "Mind, it would need a lot of money to put it right — but I can see how it must have been. It would be fun to bring it back to its former glory."

"You seem to share Grandpapa's ability for looking beyond the obvious, Oliver," said Eloise, stirring from her thoughts. "Perhaps . . ." She fell silent. Then she looked at Harry. "Are you sure you don't want to explore?"

He folded his arms, his expression mutinous. "I shall never go into that house. I want nothing to do with anything that man left me."

George saw the pain in Eloise's eyes and clasped her hand. Harry hated his father and all he had stood for — but who could blame him after what he'd witnessed?

"You won't be able to avoid the title, Harry," said Oliver. "It's your birthright."

504

Harry grunted. "Be quiet, Ollie."

"Well, I think you're being short-sighted," said Oliver. "I wish I was the earl. I'd soon have this place in fine fettle."

"There might be a way," murmured Eloise.

George frowned. "How? Harry's the heir, and nothing can change that."

"Of course you're right," she said hastily. "It was just wishful thinking."

George regarded her thoughtfully before he took up the reins, steered the horse round the lichen-covered fountain and headed for the gates. Harry had obviously made up his mind to reject anything to do with Edward, and Eloise was clearly disturbed — it had definitely been a mistake to come here.

As they bowled along the cliff-top path his thoughts were legion. Despite Harry's wish to be rid of the title, and Eloise's aversion to anything of the Cadwalladers', the boy would have to take his place in the House of Lords on his majority. All he and Eloise could hope was that he would see sense in maturity, grasp the responsibility and bring a new, honourable order to the house of Cadwallader.

It was a week after their visit to Treleaven House, and they had only four more days in Cornwall before they left for London. In the spring, they would sail for South Africa and stay with George's sister Emma, whom he hadn't seen since he was a boy, then head for Australia and home.

They had dinner, then made themselves comfortable beside the roaring fire that took up most of one wall of the tavern. Soon, though, the boys were racing outside to go beachcombing, almost knocking over the maid as she came to clear the dishes.

George leapt from his chair. "Forgive them," he said, as he steadied her.

The girl bent to retrieve her tray, dark hair veiling her face. "I'm fine, sir," she said. "No harm done."

She straightened and smiled at him. George was struck by her likeness to his mother.

The blue-green eyes lost their sparkle, and the dimple at the side of her mouth disappeared. "You've gone ever so pale, sir," she said.

George tried to pull his thoughts into order. "You remind me of someone," he blurted, "but you're not from Cornwall, so I must be mistaken."

She raised a dark brow. "You are, sir," she replied. "Somerset born am I."

"You aren't related to the Penhalligans?"

She shook her head. "Never 'eard of them," she muttered, her hair once again hiding her face.

George frowned. "But you are so much like my mother. I could have sworn you were a Penhalligan." He had a flash of inspiration. "You're not related to my sister Emma, are you? She married an army officer and went to live in South Africa. You might be her daughter."

The maid left the dishes and faced him, hands on her hips, the lovely eyes flashing with anger. "I'm flattered you think I might be related to you, sir, but I ain't never

506

been to no South Africa. Somerset born and proud of it. I'd be obliged if you wouldn't keep on." She tucked her hair behind an ear, picked up the tray and bustled out.

George plumped into the chair beside Eloise. "Did you see what I saw?"

Eloise took his hand. "Lots of people have birthmarks," she said. "It doesn't mean anything."

George wasn't convinced. The teardrop-shaped birthmark on the girl's temple was too reminiscent of the Cadwalladers — and combined with her likeness to his mother and sister . . . His thoughts whirled. "You don't think my mother and Jonathan had a child, do you?"

Eloise patted his arm. "You're letting your imagination run away with you, George. Your mother was *not* that kind of woman — and if the maid *was* one of Jonathan's by-blows, she's probably best off not knowing it. Besides," she added, "the girl is very dark, almost swarthy, and your mother is fair. I wouldn't mind betting there's Spanish or Italian blood somewhere."

"You're right," he said, determined to banish the ridiculous idea. "They say that everyone has a double, and if she really was related to the Penhalligans the family would have swooped on her and taken her in."

"I'm glad that's settled." Eloise leant across to kiss him. "Now, Mr Collinson, the boys will be out for at least an hour," she murmured, "how do you think we could occupy our time?"

507

He smiled and all thoughts fled but for his need of his lovely wife. "I'm sure I can think of something." He lifted her into his arms, then carried her out of the room and up the stairs.

It was their last day in Cornwall, and George and Eloise were tramping along the shingle beach that lay beneath towering granite cliffs.

"I'm so glad we decided to make this trip," panted Eloise, as she battled against the wind. "The boys needed new horizons to help their recovery from all that's happened, and our return to Australia will be a contented homecoming after such an adventure."

"What do you think of my Cornwall?"

"It's very beautiful," she replied, as she tried to keep up with him, "but so cold for summer."

George tucked her hand into his arm and pulled the thick scarf more tightly round her neck. "It's a good thing we'll be in London for the winter." He laughed. "It's even colder here then."

"Like Bavaria?" she asked.

He smiled down at her. "We rarely have snow so far west, but the cold is much damper than it is in Europe, and the wind is ferocious. It's what we Cornish call bracing."

"I suspect that is an understatement." She tugged at his arm and they came to a standstill. "Look at those boys," she said, with fond exasperation. "They must be soaked."

George watched as they scrambled in and around the rock pools and remembered that as a boy he'd done the same. It was almost like watching himself at that age, and as he stood there he realised how much he'd come to love them. They had given him such joy, and now that the shadows of the past were being chased away, they had begun to look upon him as a father.

He would be a good father, he vowed silently. A loving and encouraging father, who took time to listen and advise when asked — and the wisdom to remain silent when they had to fight their own battles.

"George? You're day-dreaming again."

"I was counting my blessings," he said. She shivered and he realised they'd been out in the wind for more than two hours. "Let's go back to the inn. I feel the need of scones, jam and thick yellow cream."

She poked his belly. "Not too much cream. I don't want you out of condition."

He pulled her to him. "You're a fine one to talk. I used to be able to get my hands round your waist — and now look."

"At least I have good reason to thicken a little." She giggled.

"Since when have scones and cream been . . ." His eyes widened and as she smiled up at him his face lit with joy. "A baby? Our very own baby?" At her nod he folded her into his embrace. "Oh, Eloise," he sighed, "have I told you recently how very much I love you?"

Eloise nestled against him as they were buffeted by the wind and serenaded by seagulls and terns. "Not since this morning," she murmured.

Also available in ISIS Large Print:

Lands Beyond the Sea

Tamara McKinley

By the 1700s, the Aborigine had lived in harmony with the land in Australia for 60,000 years. But now ghost-ships are arriving, and their very existence is threatened by a terrifying white invasion.

When Jonathan Cadwallader leaves Cornwall to sail on the Endeavour, he is forced to abandon his sweetheart, Susan Penhalligan. But an act of brutality will reunite them in the raw and unforgiving penal colony of New South Wales.

Billy Penhalligan has survived transportation and clings to the promise of a new beginning. But there will be more suffering before he or his fellow convicts can regard Australia as home . . .

ISBN 978-0-7531-8038-9 (hb)
ISBN 978-0-7531-8039-6 (pb)

Dreamscapes

Tamara McKinley

Catriona Summers' debut in show business came early. When she was barely minutes old, her father, the leader of a travelling music hall troupe that toured the small towns of the Outback, carried her on stage in order to introduce her to her first audience.

From such humble beginnings Catriona had grown up to emerge as a rare talent, her voice garnering her praise from the public and critics alike. But her journey from performing popular songs for a few pennies to becoming an accliamed opera diva on the Sydney stage, was fraught with hardship and tragedy. And now some old scandalous secrets from her teenage years are threatening her present, her family and all she has achieved . . .

(from A1)

ISBN 978-0-7531-7529-3 (hb)
ISBN 978-0-7531-7530-9 (pb)

Undercurrents

Tamara McKinley

In 1894 the SS Arcadia sets sail from Liverpool. On board are Eva Hamilton and her husband Frederick, a newly married couple setting off for a new life. Only, a few miles from the western shores of Australia the Arcadia is hit by an unexpected storm . . .

Years later, Olivia Hamilton makes the same journey. Still dealing with her mother's death and her experiences of war torn London, she has returned to her homeland to discover the truth behind the secret cache of documents among her late mother's effects.

Olivia had grown up in the secure knowledge that her mother loved her. This had more than compensated for her older sister's dislike. Olivia believes that the documents could tell her why, but she needs Irene's help. But the years have not mellowed her sister's hatred. And while Olivia is determined to pursue her quest, like Eva Hamilton all those years before, she has no idea where this journey will take her . . .

ISBN 978-0-7531-7281-0 (hb)
ISBN 978-0-7531-7282-7 (pb)

Summer Lightning

Tamara McKinley

A new saga from the author of Mathilda's Last Waltz

"... saga that will keep you reading happily all day. Relax and enjoy." Woman's Weekly

Miriam Strong had been looking forward to her family arriving at Bellbird Station to help her celebrate her seventy-fifth birthday. Yet, with the discovery of the first tangible clue to her stolen inheritance, has come the time to face the painful memories of a time long past — and an old enemy. Like a Summer Lightning, Miriam's quest for truth is set to change things forever. Especially for Miriam's grand-daughters, Fiona and Louise. One will find love, ant the other will find the courage to acknowledge her true worth and become the woman she was meant to be.

ISBN 978-0-7531-7099-1 (hb)
ISBN 978-0-7531-7100-4 (pb)